The Man Who Cared Too Much

The Man Who Cared Too Much

Darryl Kennedy

To order additional copies of this book, contact:
Xlibris Corporation
1-800-618-969
www.Xlibris.com.au
Orders@Xlibris.com.au
503643

Contents

By the same author:

The Wednesday Arrangement.
Love Is The Disease (most worth having)
The Last Act.

Cover Design by Marie Bliss

Who will go drive with Fergus now,
And pierce the deep wood's woven shade,
And dance upon the level shore?

W. B. Yeats.

'Be disloyal. It's your duty to the human race. The human race needs to survive
and it's the loyal man who dies first from anxiety or a bullet or overwork. If you
have to earn a living . . . and the price they make you pay is loyalty, be a double
agent—and never let either of the two sides know your real name . . .'

—"Under the Garden," *A Sense of Reality*. Graham Greene.

Teresa, aged fifteen:
Getting the Spitballs Out

Teresa Mahone sat on the family sofa in her crumpled up convent uniform as if waiting to be called into the Headmaster's office. She fiddled distractedly with her long dark hair, pulled it across her face making a moustache of it. She had made a tasty Italian dish for everyone that evening. Try as she might, it wasn't going to do her any favors. It was Monday night. Her parents were now at a Parent-Teacher meeting. She was not looking forward to having to face the music with her mother in the morning for yet another bad school report. Her head was on the block. Same old, same old: 'Teresa is vague(read dopey), dreamy(read slow), and oblivious(?)'

Teresa didn't even know what 'oblivious' meant, but she did like the sound of the word. 'O'Blivious' would make a much better Irish surname than Mahone. Moan, moan, moan. That's what the other kids called her, and for no reason at all. She was not one to complain, yet wasn't going to beat herself up over some dumb school report. Teenagers have problems greater than that. Issues to be dealt with.

She glanced up quickly at the wall clock. It was nearing 7 o'clock. She pouted her bee sting lips, despondently school miserable, waiting for the telephone to ring. Like the final bell after last class, she didn't like the sound of it much, had mixed feelings, relief and concern, for that was when her real troubles started.

Her attention was suddenly drawn to a ladder in one of her dark school stockings, blaming her cat for that. Teresa hated wearing them in winter. They looked hideous. She lived in the Tropics, for heaven's sake, where temperatures only varied a few degrees each year. Yet another example of nuns' prudishness, she mused. Teresa didn't like the nuns much. They were always on her case. They said life was all about making choices. Their choices. So-o-o narrow. "What choices do you want to make, then?" her mother had asked. "I want to leave school," Teresa replied abruptly. "Just forget it, young lady, and buck up your ideas."

She absent mindedly picked at threads above the hemline of her blue, Tartan tunic. It was like taking stubborn legs off a bug. She wanted to go to bed yet couldn't, knowing she had to face the music on the hour, and at breakfast next morning over the report card—'Teresa could try much harder,' her report had said, yet once again. Although addressed to her parents, Teresa had opened the envelope herself, read it through, then penciled in boldly at the bottom 'We have BOTH failed but at least I have TRIED!'

She got a good telling off for that. She saw her teachers as the slackers. Her mother said that she was just 'passing the buck.'

It wasn't as if she was brain dead. Quite the opposite. But she did think about things far too much.

Hot stockings. Tepid report. Teresa suddenly felt her legs strangely lassoed like a calf. Nowhere to go. She began fidgeting, moving her hands behind her head, picking at the back of her violet black hair.

Uncle would sort it out. Uncle sorted everything. For everyone. Always had.

Her uncle was no corruptor of youth or seducer of innocence, one who would make her catapults to go out and kill the birds; he would just . . . well, somehow MISLEAD her, slingshot her out of trouble. He was as tough as teak. He didn't pass the buck. He never washed his hands of anything. Well, of blood, maybe. And he had lots of trophies to prove it.

Usually, he stayed weekends only. Tonight he sat alongside her at her mother's work desk near a corner of the family room. The TV was off, the silence overwhelming, broken only by the sudden chugging grind of his fax machine. He was preparing sales for the next day.

"Uncle?'

"Yes."

"I've got a problem." Her voice was weak and tentative.

"Are you coming down with something?"

"No-O!" Her voice was defiant, final o soaring to the air.

"School head lice again?" He joked, looking up from his paper work, only further upsetting her unease. He'd noticed that she was picking at her hair.

"Don't be smart. Only ever had them once. I was seven. I'm getting the paper spitballs out."

"Don't sit at the front of the class, then."

"I've always sat at front of class. Then I don't have to talk or look at anyone, do I?"

"That's not good, Tess." He turned to her and frowned.

He knew that the boys picked on her, not because she was weak but pretty. She was shy, didn't know or think that she was particularly pretty, which only served further to whet their appetites. Her hair was lustrously dark. She had taken her bunches out. Hair spread round her shoulders like the opening of a raven's wing. Her eyes, so black and protuberant, and often full of mischief, were not so tonight. They were faraway. Dreamy. Just like her school report had said.

Girls at school envied her figure. Boys figured her with a kind of envy. Teenage lust. She had a great physique for her young years, yet she gave everyone the cold shoulder. The brush off. Hence, the spitballs.

Teresa was not that popular, or particularly confident, or any kind of rebel at school. She did not wear those heavy thrash metal concert T-shirts at weekends like the other girls in class. Nor wear a backpack covered in questionable slogans. Most thought of her as 'that religious chick.' There was a natural coyness about her, distinct lack of posturing. She'd disliked school from day one. Yet it wasn't school but the getting home which terrified her, getting along Hope Street, not to spook the herd, start a stampede. She constantly felt like she had to duck for cover. Old clunker cars would backfire their engines as they passed her on the street. That scared the crap out of her. She literally thought of each day's journey home in religious terms. To Teresa, Hope Street was the path to ruin. A no-go area of lost redemption. Road to perdition. Honest to God, Hope Street was where you prayed to St. Anthony for things lost; St. Jude, patron of lost causes. Hope Street tested her faith and charity.

It wasn't quite a ghetto up there. You didn't have to dodge gasoline bottles with wicks and rags. It was more like a childish game of throwing pebbles, then running away. What made it so insidious was all the dumb stuff, stupid behavior, silly as boys chasing pigeons; those endless pests and truants bored out of their brains looking for kicks and cheap thrills. Her suspicions were now habitual.

There were no gangs up there. No rumbles. It was far too hot for much activity, or any jubilation. Everyone just stood round jobless in groups like in a holding pen, listless on day release, wearing their dark hoodies, cool shades. Activity was no more than breaking things, bouncing a ball against a wall. Teresa reckoned most of them were too tired to get of the way of their own shadows. To her, it was like an odyssey each day—get along Hope, turn into Edward, into some kind of hate-free zone. Her mouth would feel so dry by the time she got to Edward that there'd be no spittle left. She'd twirl the leather straps of her school bag slung crossways to her side. It was like twisting the chamber of a revolver in a game of Russian roulette. Games of hit and miss. Giving them the slip. One boy had attacked another on the sidewalk two days before, hit him over the head with a watermelon. The sugary smell on the street was still fresh in her nostrils.

Her parents would politely ask at evening meal 'How was your day, dear?' They got an un-sugary mouthful in return.

But uncle was different.

"Is the problem school?"

"No . . . yes . . . sort of."

"'Sort of' doesn't mean anything."

"Boy at school."

"Why's that a problem?"

"He's ringing me here tonight. He knows Ma and Pa are at the PT meeting. He thinks I'm . . . home alone." She sarcastically intoned her final vowels.

"So? Why the problem? Does he want to come over and see you? He can. I'll stay downstairs. I've got plenty of paperwork to do."

"NO! I don't even want to speak to him."

"Why not? Is he a bad boy?"

"No."

"Well?'

"He's in my class."

"Then you must handle it yourself."

"Will you do it for me?"

"Affairs of the heart are not really my bag, Tess. You must do it."

"But he's a pest. I can't get rid of him. He drives me crazy."

"Love can do that to people. Especially puppy love."

"You've got to be kidding me! He's awful."

"Tell him straight, then."

"Yeah, right. Talk straight, just like you do. That's a joke if ever I heard one."

"Why's he a pest?"

"He won't leave us alone. He picked on Jennifer, then it was Marcia, now it's me."

"Is he lonely?"

"Yes, I guess. He's from the country, lives here with his aunt and uncle to go to school. He wants my company. The boys don't like him because he's such a sap, so he picks on all of us."

"I'm sure he's got good reason to like you. One better than that."

"Well he hasn't."

"What's his name?"

"Paulie. Paulie Potato-head. Paulie the Pest. I don't remember his surname. All I know is he won't get it. He's impossible. He follows me round like a bad smell. He's a dropkick, looking for a sidekick. I wouldn't even want to be seen with him on a see-saw. He's fat. Ugly."

"That's not a very nice thing to say, Tess. Do you only like handsome boys?"

"No. Don't like boys at all. Don't like Paulie because he's obnoxious."

"Have you told your mother about it?"

"No. What's the point? I hoped you'd handle him. Give him the short shift."

"You have to be careful with hearts, Teresa."

"But he just goes one to another. I don't want his company anyway. He's immature, calls me 'Kitten' because he knows I own a cat. How creepy is that! I feel like reaching out, scratching his face."

"All the more reason to be careful. The sooner you handle this sort of thing once, better for the future."

"You just said 'sort of' doesn't mean anything."

"Did I!"

"I can't handle it. I've had enough. Best way to handle bullies is to give in. I just hold my ground, try and take it as it comes. Or make a run for it."

"You don't mean that."

"Yes I do."

"Report him to your teachers, then."

"What! Like, raising my hand in class? Like. Please, Sister Fish-face, I want to leave the room?"

Her uncle remained silent. He knew she had to handle far worse than that.

"I have to put up with all the creeps and their name-calling every afternoon up on Hope. I probably look sad and pathetic to them but I don't care, they're the ones who are pathetic. I walk home each day like a sleepwalker. Why answer back a bunch of louts? Boy's filth? They think they're just 'funning' with you. All boys are filthy."

"'All' is a bit on the high end."

"But it's true. They all are."

"What are they calling you up there now?"

"Latest?"

"The latest."

"Monica Lewinsky. Because of my . . . lips."

"Do you know who she is?"

"Of course. I read stuff. Find things out. What she did with that American President. I know what Roman Polanski did, too. That film director. Years ago. That girl was only thirteen."

He didn't respond.

"Anyway. I took your book 'Lolita.' I've read it with Sharn up in the fig tree." Teresa looked at her uncle with that superior look of O, how grown up I am.

"I wondered if you'd taken it."

"Did you notice it missing? Sorry. Sharn wanted to read it."

"Did your mother know?"

"Yes. I told her. And told Sharn to look after it."

"Did you like it?"

"What do you think of that Humbolt? What he did to Lolita? She was only fourteen. He was her step father, for heaven's sake."

"Humbert," he corrected. "Yes. He was a monster."

"I'm glad he died in the end. Why did Nabokov make her die, too?"

"Because that's life, Tess. It's only fiction. Just a story. It was tragic she died so young. Medical reasons. Childbirth." He looked away. For reasons of his own, he didn't like to think or talk about young girls dying.

"Did you discuss it with your mother?"

"Yes. We discussed some."

"Good." Her uncle did not correct her, say that she shouldn't be reading adult fiction at her age, pinching books from his downstairs library. There was little he could say. She liked to hang around the adults. Their things. She avoided the magic of teenage books, even though she had read her Harry Potters. No magic up on Hope Street. Just grim reality. She often wished that her uncle was her teacher. He'd have them all outside reading his books up in the school trees. Maybe not Lolita. Just interesting stuff. School bored her. Constantly.

"All his la de la talk, but he was an evil man underneath. He picked on Lolita." Teresa ruffled up the back of her hair with her hand. Another spitball was unsettling her mind.

"Uncle?"

"Yes."

"Can I have a happy ending then when this dickhead rings me tonight? Will you put him off for me? Just be yourself. A bit mad. Please, Uncle. It's far too hard. I don't like being hurtful. I won't even answer girls back at school any longer. Answering back is mean. I feel badly about it for days after doing it. I've tried my best to get rid of him. He won't budge. He makes my skin crawl. After a bout with him in the library I feel like taking a bath. And he's mean."

"How's he mean?"

"There's one girl in a lower class. Her name's Debbie. She has braces on her teeth so he calls her Metal Mouth. But what really gets my goat is there's this boy, Ian. I sometimes sit with him in the library at lunchtime. He has Down's Syndrome. We pull faces at one another. He's nice. It's easy to make him laugh. Every time I see him we give each other a high five. So Paulie picks on him, calls him Chubby Fingers and Frog, mocks the way he eats. Ma says Ian has a narrow palate, can't help the way he speaks, or the way he shovels food round in his mouth. He gets tongue-tied sometimes because of it. He needs patience. One day Paulie pinned a note to Ian's back. 'I suck real good.' I tore it off. I felt like hitting him. I hate feeling like that. I told Paulie just to lay off him."

"Does he?"

"He won't. He wants my attention. He thinks it's funny acting like a retard. Ian isn't a retard. I teach him things on computer. He picks them up easily. And he knows when someone's being cruel. Ma told me there are people with Down's Syndrome who have university degrees." Teresa then added as an afterthought, with a sly grin. "What I like best about Ian is he calls the nuns 'Dude.' That's totally fun. He coos the word at them like a lovesick pigeon—DO-O-O-O-DE."

Teresa puckered her lips with the word, then sat back giggling to herself.

Her comment was ignored.

"Yes, he is mean. All right. When he rings I'll put him on speaker phone." Her uncle shut his work diary at his desk, swiveled slightly on the castors of his chair to give his niece his full attention. He knew school was a disaster for her, even at best of times. She was always pinching his books, mostly novels from his study downstairs, reading them up the fig tree. He judiciously hid a few from sight, not wanting her to turn up to geography with his copy of Henry Miller's 'Tropic of Capricorn'(in which they lived), she thinking it might help her understanding the terrain. Her uncle had been an A grade student. She preferred learning from him than from school.

That in itself was a problem. School reports were always the same: 'Teresa has a far too vivid imagination.'

He had to take some of the blame for that.

It had been the same for years now. While other girls would be out raking the streets in their small town at weekends, hanging round the Mall, getting up to no good, or just down the skate park flirting with the boys, Teresa stayed at home.

Uncle came to stay at weekends.

He'd helped her out with her spelling, vocabulary, composition, reading comprehension for years now—how boring is that at weekends! Yet it wasn't boring. Not to her. He filled her head with foreign songs, faraway places, fantastical stories to make your hair stand on end. Uncle had been right round the block, up many a Hope Street in his day. And come out of it unscathed.

He never told her to shut up, leave him alone, go away, always finding time for her. He threw parties for the adults at weekends. For the kids too. He acted like the leader of the band, a kind of Pied Piper, even if leading everyone a little astray.

If only he could pipe the rats up on Hope Street over the nearest cliff.

"Seven o'clock. It's just . . . I won't talk to him, Uncle. I won't even look at him. He traps me. He wants me to go over his place. God only knows why. I DON'T LIKE HIM. And he will not take NO for an answer. He's HORRRIBBLE."

"Have you told Sharney?"

"Yes. But you know what my Twisted Sister next door is like. I said he probably wants to play Leggo. Sharn said 'more like Leg-gover.' Fat use she is to me. No help. Like that book, she thought it was going to be dirty. It wasn't. She says I've got to be more bold. Be upfront and confident. Don't be a 'freaking dormouse, Tessie,' she always says. Tell him to 'you know what.' Why should I use that word, Uncle? I'd be using it every afternoon up on Hope. Be as bad as them."

There was a long pause. Her uncle could only agree.

Yet he was a past master of skinning a cat. There were a hundred ways of doing it, a metaphor he could not use in front of her (she loved her cat). He was full of cunning. Often his instructions were deceptively simple. He was the type the man to give his niece an expensive penknife for her birthday, then tell her to go off and gouge her initials in her school desk. Metaphorically speaking. Only thing was, those initials were to be carved perfectly.

"Give him your usual, Uncle. PLEASE, put him off for me."

Teresa slumped back on the sofa. She put a schoolbook up over her eyes. She was glad that her parents were out. She was frustrated, perturbed, glancing up with a sense of inevitability at the wall clock.

Her uncle sat back idly fumbling his paper work next to the telephone. Whatever he said would probably only compound the problem. She wasn't too sure. She'd take the risk. She hoped a mouthful from him would put the boy off . . . FOREVER.

His fax machine had been chugging for hours now, e-mails sounding. Uncle was no filing clerk; he was loaded. He lived south in the city, sold liquor, and franchises to sell it, came north weekends to do business and stayed with them. Sometimes he would have to stay on a few extra days. He and his sister Caitlin, Teresa's mother, had always been very close. He had bought Caitlin and Maddox the house in which they lived, and that of next door for his sister's best friend, Colleen and Declan, Sharney's mother and father. It was an odd situation. Then again, he was not a very typical man. He had a secret past that not even his sister knew much about. Many speculated that it was criminal.

"Thanks, Uncle, it will take a load off my shoulders."

"You mean a lot of spitballs from the back of your hair," he grumbled.

Her uncle sat back in his dark suit trousers, suit jacket over the backrest of the chair. He wore a spotlessly white shirt, silk blue tie, expensive Spanish leather shoes. Uncle was cool. He wore Armani suits, looked a little like Charles Bronson, chiseled as stone, did not wear those crumpled button down shirts and cheap gray trousers like the lay teachers did at school. He was a businessman, had slicked back hair, broad shouldered, muscular arms, yet he was not the kind of person ever to come on tough. He didn't need to. Unlike Teresa, he was confident, never lost for words, had lots of friends, and had always been a bit of a renegade. And family was important to him, the little of it he had left.

"When I was your age, Tess, there was this girl who kept ringing me on Saturdays for a date. I kept putting her off."

"How?"

"I kept finding excuses. I didn't want to be hurtful."

"Like what?"

"I said I'd be ironing clothes all Saturday morning, folding the rest of the washing, washing my hair that afternoon. I'd be too tired to go out in the evening." He grinned across at his niece.

"Liar. Liar." Teresa smirked back. "More like going out and belting some opponent into the middle of next week."

Teresa went quiet. She pondered the lie he'd just told her. He was not the kind of liar to try and convince you that oranges had a skin, apples had a rind. Like many of his lies, there was an element of truth in them. He'd brought up his younger sister, Teresa's mother, for much of her teenage years. He refused to allow her to be fostered. Maybe he had spent his Saturdays that way.

Yet she knew that he'd stick up for her. He always did. Well. 'Sort of.' In his own peculiar way.

He was also a very generous man. Ask him for a glass of water and he'd give you a gallon. What you then had to watch out for was he was just as likely to follow up by hurling the kitchen sink at you.

Imaginatively speaking.

They sat quietly together. Like two old pals. Yes. He would fix it. Soothe her discontent. Uncle the Rainmaker, Uncle the Hitman. Uncle didn't miss a beat; he had his eyes wide and ears open. He'd throw mud in Paulie's. Teresa just hoped that he wouldn't go so far as knocking Paulie's lights out.

Ring–Ring

At 7:15 the telephone rang. Her uncle noticed it had startled Teresa like a thrown rock. He made light of it.

"Lo Lee Ta!" he mocked the Nabokov book then chuckled to himself.

"Stop it." Teresa began putting on airs and graces. "At last. My 7 o'clock . . . just—get—rid—of—him!"

"Fifteen minutes late, Tess. Not a very good start for romance. Not very dependable, is he?" He picked up the receiver, turned it to speaker phone.

"Hello."

"Is Trees Moan there?"

He looked to Teresa. She scrunched up her face, poked out her tongue, shook her head angrily at the telephone, her black hair sweeping the air, then pretended to mock vomit with disgust like Miss Piggy before slumping back in despair, putting the schoolbook back over her face again.

"Trees? T-R-E-E-S M-O-A-N! This isn't the Forestry Department. If it were then I'd have to go out and dig her up, wouldn't I? To whom do you wish to speak, young man? People only talk to TREES, that is trees which MOAN, in 'Lord Of The Rings.'"

"Can I speak to Terese Mahone, then?"

"That's better. And it's Teresa Mahone. You may speak to Little Odd Sox, but you can't. She was feeling poor-ly.(Fergus purposely drawled the word) so I made her go upstairs, take a bath. She's suffering from prickly heat."

"Can you take the phone up to the bathroom, then?"

"Dear Lord, no! She's far too self-conscious for that. I wouldn't be allowed up the stairs. She'd rather drown herself like a sack of kittens than be seen taking a bath, even though she bathes in pure white milk. One thing she hates about baths is getting naked. Anyway, I won't kid with you, kid, I don't see what you see in her. She's certainly nothing to write home about."

Her uncle's mouth was soon running away from him, picking up on bits and pieces already mentioned.

He took the receiver away from his ear, placed it down on his desk, sat open mouthed looking across at Teresa, awaiting response. Teresa chuckled, this time covering her face in her hands. Teresa knew that her uncle used words with the same fury he once used his fists in the boxing ring, peppering, pulling punches, feinting, bringing opponents to a stand-still. Or just having some fun. Like a song and dance man at center ring.

"Are you her father?"

"No. I am her uncle. My name's Fergus. And yours? You should always introduce yourself before asking to speak to anyone. Even if to the trees. Trees are living things."

"Paulie. What you doin' there?"

"Doin' there? Doin' here! I'm here *in loco parentis.*" Fergus only used the Latin term because he knew Teresa understood it. "In place of parents." The expression was used in a recent school newsletter.

"What's that mean?"

"You must know what 'loco' means. Crazy. I'm a 'sort of' mad parent." Fergus looked to Teresa, who peered back through her fingers. He grinned across at her, wrapping the 'sort of' in inverted commas with his fingers in the air.

"Yeah, I've heard you're a bit crazy."

There was a short silence. Teresa took her hands away, looked to her uncle. Nobody ever spoke to Fergus like that. A look from Fergus could kill. Fergus immediately altered the tone of his voice. He spoke softly with cold deliberateness. Unlike some of the boys up on Hope Street, marbles did not run loose in his head. They gathered, formed an impenetrable defense. He could also use words like a headlock, tighter and tighter as he went on, tying you up in knots. Teresa knew this kid was in way over his head.

"You should learn to be a bit crazy yourself, young man. Girls like to laugh. It's just that most of them like to be left alone, as well. Not to be laughed at or ridiculed. Do you think Teresa wants to be left alone?"

"Yeah. She's real uptight at school."

"Well, you must find ways to make her laugh then. I don't mean laugh AT her. Or AT anyone else, for that matter."

"I want her to come across my place."

"Now that'd make her real uptight. I don't think she's the kind of girl to come across just yet to anyone's place. Anyway, we'd insist she have a chaperone. We're a respectable family here."

"What's that?"

"A chaperone? Somebody to accompany her. Strange house. People we don't know. Then, of course, she'd have to want to come, wouldn't she?"

"She could bring her kitten with her."

"Wouldn't work. The kitten would be even worse than we would. Tear your furniture apart. The cat's fiercely protective of her."

"I heard you're a real strange lot. Like that mad Addams family."

Fergus looked to Teresa. He didn't know who the 'Addams family' was.

"Have you, now? And you're quite right. We are. We're all Adam's family, aren't we, Paulie—Jennifer, Marcia, Teresa. All put here on earth to learn not to be clumsy beasts as males. Young girls aren't gifts. They're not given freely. They don't fall off the back of trucks. You must learn to talk to them properly. With good cheer. Respect. Only then will they answer your calls. To win a young girl's heart you must first learn to wait at her gate. Wait and wait and wait. Wait with a dozen red roses. Don't ever expect her to come across to yours."

"She's real strange. Religious. I bet she's up there right now praying in the bath."

Teresa threw the schoolbook beside her away in anger.

"Do you, now? Are you a betting man, Paulie? I doubt it. Since the Middle Ages the church's forbidden women to pray naked. Father Kevin will confirm it for you at school. Check it out with him."

"Yeah. I heard you two are friends. You used to be a national boxing champion, right?"

No response. Fergus had suddenly had enough of this.

"My father said you were real good. And that you're a cranky Communist."

"ENOUGH! Goodbye, Paulie. Don't you ever ring here again."

Fergus hung up abruptly then turned silently back to his paperwork on the table. He wasn't the least angry or upset. Teresa had never seen him at fever pitch, anything other than cool headed. Just another call. Matter to be dealt with. Business. Sometimes she wondered if he ever got sad, or cried. She knew, deep down, that he had a sadness which would not go away. It was as heavy and painful as living under a lid of ice. It was a matter never discussed at home.

Remember back when

"Thanks, Uncle. Whew! That was a real mouthful. We are a bit of a mad family, aren't we!"

"No. Only me. But you've got to learn to play the game, Tess. Bamboozle them with words. Make up the rules as you go."

Teresa reflected silently. "I don't want anyone waiting at my gate."

"Dominic does. Every morning."

"That's different. He's my brother. Sharney's my sister. He lives next door. We are the only two school kids in the area. You try getting up and down Hope Street by yourself each day and see how much you like it by yourself. No other kids have to walk it."

"Does he walk with you?"

"No. He walks behind me. Way behind. Breathing in the same dope as me. What do you think happens? That we walk along hand in hand together like Donny and Marie?"

"But he's there for you? Everyday?"

"Everyday. There's school signs on lamp-posts on Hope which say 'Travel In Pairs,' but we only walk together up Edward to home. We are the only two kids in it. You know that. There's even a school ban on entering Hope Street."

"But he's still there for you."

"Yeah. Every horrible day."

"Is it really that bad on Hope?"

"Sure is. It almost came to scuffles the other day."

"What happened?"

"You don't want to know."

"Yes I do. Tell me."

"You know where those bollards are by the ATM to stop the ram raiders?"

"Yes."

"Boys lean on them. They won't let me pass. Or they push me, trying to cop a feel. That's why I wear my Lycra bike shorts underneath, and they're easier for climbing trees when I get home."

"And?"

"These creeps started calling me names."

"What kids?"

"White kids. They're all white kids. They run the street."

"What names?"

"Usual stuff. Slag, hoe, skank, slut, mole. You name it. I've been called it. I just keep moving, like my cat does. That's why I like cats. They don't answer to anyone's call. And I don't even like boys. I do nothing to provoke them, but no one is going to take their fun away. That's why they all left school so young."

"So you've said before." Fergus paused. "Names don't hurt, Tess."

"They have called me names at school ever since I was seven."

"And what did they call you back then?"

"They called me 'Trees' instead of 'Teresa,' just like that little creep did before on the phone."

"Why was that?"

"Because they're lazy. Far easier for them to say."

"I don't believe you."

"All right. If you really want the truth. I was made to give a talk in front of the class. I hate public speaking. I had to say what I liked doing most, so I told them the truth—climbing trees."

"I know you hate public speaking."

"Hate it? It's an achievement for me to get through a day at school without talking to anyone."

"That's not good, Tess."

"So they then started calling me Trees. Putting mock telephones up to their ears. Is that you, Trees? Sorry, must have the wrong branch. Stuff like that."

Some might have thought that witty. Fergus was not amused. One's name is important, especially aged seven. "Sticks and stones won't break your bones, Tess."

"That's what Dominic says. He just gets mad when they say they'll do filthy things to me. They did the other day. They said convent school girls are the dirtiest bitches of all. Do filthy things, instead. Saving themselves for marriage. Dominic got angry at that. I thought he was going to take three of them on. They think I'm an uppity bitch because I won't talk to them. You tell me—why should I say 'Yo, bro, guiss us a high five,' to some bored creep who has just scraped his door key across a bunch of cars? Why speak? Most of them don't even have a door key. Anyway, most of them have mouths the size of dustbin lids. What comes out, just rubbish. Give them a high five? They'd miss, end up slapping your face. Ian doesn't do that, he's got Down's and is still more coordinated than those creeps."

Fergus looked at her sadly, ignoring her questions. "What came of it?"

"Nothing much. They're frightened of Dominic. He told them they weren't worth the skin off his knuckles. And that Declan says he'll give him a hiding himself if Dominic ever fights at school or in the street. Dominic told them that, but if they didn't lay off me he'd give them a real good hiding for the belting he'd get at home."

Teresa's voice began to get angry. She'd had enough of the street. It was always hot getting home at three o'clock each day. By the time she made it home she felt about as ratty as a roach.

All students were required to wear a floppy hat to and from school for the UV rays. It was often 30 degrees centigrade by nine o'clock in the morning(double it then add 30 for the Fahrenheit). Teresa had given up on hats in Hope, years ago. They would flick it off her head as she passed. Unemployed boys, many of them truants, stood round in groups, all wanting to be the man.

Boys stank. Like the garbage they spoke. Bunch of grubs. You just couldn't win with any of them, Teresa would often say. It was all Ho, Yo, Bro, Joe, Moe, says who? Says who? Who are you? All a big stutter and stammer. And staring. Giving her the evil eye. Smell of dope, spilled beer, greasy takeaway food. Most days she would clutch at her St. Christopher medal, keep moving, pushing her way through the panic.

Even their dogs had sly eyes. She'd never want to pat one. Just barge your way through. Get home.

She told Fergus this.

Fergus shuffled his paper work around distractedly on his desk. He didn't look up once, then began responding as if talking to the table top.

"I'll show you and Dominic how to fight properly next door one weekend, Tess. Don't worry, I'll tell Declan first."

"What? Pistols at fifteen paces up on Hope? Against a bunch of creeps? You got to be kidding me? We wouldn't stand a chance."

"No Tess, I'll teach you how to fight as dirty as the way they talk to you. The both of you could take on six. More. All you need is a bit of imagination."

"Does 'a bit of' mean about the same as 'sort of'? Nothing at all?"

"No, you can do anything you like, but only if you're cunning enough."

"What? Like that fox that got in our yard and killed my goose and gander?"

"Well, I told you we would get a guard dog at the house for protection after school until your parents come home."

"I didn't want a dog. It would torment my cat. So you went out and got me a goose and gander to create a din if anyone came near."

It was a sore point, one which Teresa had trouble getting over. She liked her goose and gander. The eggs had been great for baking cakes.

"I'll buy you a truckload of hogs, if you like. Think of the noise they'd make. No one would ever get in. And they'd give that fox a good run for his money."

"Ha, ha, ha!"

"I will, if you want. Don't worry about it, we're all Catholics here. Catholics are right into swine." Fergus smirked while desperately trying to rid the memory of it.

"Very funny. They'd EAT my cat. And they're unclean." Tess paused for a moment, then stared at Fergus with a grin in order to get in the last word. "Just like you are."

Fergus grinned back at her inanely. He was a master at teasing his niece. "That's true. That's why 'uncle' and 'unclean' are right next to one another in the dictionary."

"Is that so, Uncle! You're impossible. I'm going upstairs. I will have a bath, after all."

"Remember, no praying. Are you sure there's enough milk?"

Teresa slapped him on the arm as she walked passed to the kitchen. "That was real funny when you said that. I'll make you a coffee before I go."

Teresa clattered about within the cupboards for some crockery. The microwave sounded. She returned soon after with a coffee mug, a heated up pancake for herself.

Fergus shut down his computer, turned to give her his full attention.

She sat grinning, threatening to sling shot the syrup in her spoon across at him.

"You remember back to my seventh birthday? Me? Taking a bath?"

It was Fergus' turn now. He put his hands up over his face.

"You locked me in the bathroom. You rat."

"Did I!"

"You and Declan together are such big teases. Pa's not much better, either. You egg them on. They always side with you. So I wouldn't come down. You came up the stairs. Knocked on the door. Asked me what I was doing in there."

"What you doin'? Have you drowned, or what?" Teresa imitated his voice with the mock lyricism of his Irish brogue.

"I said I was 'thinking.' You said only philosophers think in the bath, so you locked me in, threw the key on the floor outside, said I could 'darn well stay in there.'"

"Surely not!" Fergus gave her a crestfallen look of remorse. "O, dear," he muttered, as if by way of apology.

"Yes you did, you rat! That was the birthday you bought me a soap on a rope. I thought I'd fix you lot. I got out, dried myself, got dressed, cleaned the bathroom, jumped up on the toilet cistern, got out the frosted window, ran along the roof, shinned down the drain pipe, came in by the front door. Everyone stood up and clapped me. Even Father Kevin. He's sometimes as bad as the rest of you. It was so-o-o embarrassing."

"I knew you'd do it."

"How did you know?"

"Because you climb trees all the time, don't you! I knew you'd find a way out of there. That's what I mean. Use your imagination."

"Imagination is my downfall. That's what they write on my school reports. Dreamy. Always looking out the window at the trees." There was a long pause. "You know what Sharn said to me that night?"

"No."

"She said don't worry about it, Tessie, he'll be gone soon."

"And I did go, my dear. But I taught you to use your imagination, didn't I?"

School, via Hope Street

Teresa's school, St. Ignatius', despite lots of pep talks from the nuns, wasn't that big on academic achievement. This was Hicksville. Parents didn't save hard for any future or college funds. It was a small school with a red brick façade, poorly funded, housing four nuns in an adjoining convent, two lay teachers assisting in middle school. They were extending it. Teresa and Dominic would go on into upper school there. Sharney, who had walked home with Teresa, had now left to work with her mother in a hair salon. O, how she missed her. No one messed with Sharn. She gave no one the peace sign. She gave them a piece of her mind.

Religious instruction, although much encouraged, was not compulsory, for many of the fee paying students were not Catholic. Fees were often slow in coming. Many couldn't afford them. It looked like a brick jail with few windows from the street, had darkened corridors reeking of floor polish, smelling overwhelmingly of paper, ink toner, sweaty shoes, chalk dust from blackboards. To Teresa, her trees smelled like baby breath by comparison.

It had a small church incorporated into the building. Few carried on with education once they'd left. Boys wore a hideous-looking full grey uniform, suitable only for prisons. The girls looked less dull. White blouses with school insignia. Blue tartan skirts. Blue dresses in the hottest months. If boys stayed on after the age of fifteen, it was usually only for sports. Teachers gave up on them. The gymnasium took over from the museum. Coaches from outside would come in, give their services voluntarily. Girls with potential often changed to another school at that age. State or Protestant. Teresa envied them their choice.

Teresa just hid out friendless in the library. She carried all her books in a leather bag, fearful of bullying at the lockers. She left her locker unlocked and empty. Boys used to stuff dirty notes in the crevices. She observed a self imposed vow of silence. Like a Carmelite nun. That kept everyone at arm's length. Sit up the front, nose to a schoolbook, passing the time. There was an art in passing the time, avoiding trouble. Why sit with the dickheads tilting their chairs at the back, throwing paper darts, spitting jets of paper spitballs through empty biro pens. She'd dream her life away up front. Teresa found most classes boring, the teachers uninteresting, classrooms without valuable resources. She liked the electives of sport and dancing, only because those classes were single sex, where she would stomp out her frustrations on the gymnasium floor. Then again, she also liked going to chapel, simply because it was quiet. There she prayed for safety, not guidance.

She could see her school clearly through her spyglass from her fig tree at home, yet seldom bothered to look at it. Somehow it just didn't seem right, like looking through people's windows. School, to Teresa, could sometimes be as harebrained as the street.

The Road to Jericho

Sometimes on Friday afternoons, if uncle arrived home early, he'd walk her from school along Hope Street to home. He'd just driven long distances, yet never collected her by car. Fergus enjoyed walking. Fergus believed in walking. Philosophically. Walking, to Fergus, was a form of salvation. Literally, a saving health. When younger, he had walked thousands of miles under a heavy backpack.

Teresa liked being seen with him. People here knew him by reputation, even though she was never quite sure how that reputation stood in the community. And he always looked so swishy compared with the usual Hope rank and file. Boys wore beanies on the street, even in this heat, belt-less shorts falling off their butts. Lots of young pram pushers were out in full Friday afternoon, sly drug pushers, face pullers, a bunch of drones looking for a queen bee. No queen bees up there. Just stingers. Sometimes the misery of the street overwhelmed her.

The other side of the street, the so-called shady side, was even worse than the side Teresa traveled. That was a no-go area. Her mother forbade her ever to walk that side: street girls, legs skinny as tooth picks beside darkened alleys, and their hangers on. Teresa would rather put up with the twisted shit on the sunny side than ever take her chances over there.

Teresa and Fergus had always been close. They enjoyed one another's company. Through circumstance, Teresa's mother, Caitlin, was closely bonded to her brother too. Similarly, Colleen, next door. Teresa never quite understood why, yet knew Fergus had to rear her mother after the death of their parents and other sister. Caitlin and Colleen had been best friends while growing up.

Teresa also knew that there was an ulterior motive at work here, almost a family conspiracy—Teresa hardly ever said a word all week at school; her uncle provoked her to match him in a feinting game of words, thereby picking up the slack.

Teresa hated Hope. She reckoned you almost needed a first aid kit to walk it. Her mother worked at the hospital nearby. First aid kits just patch things up. Sometimes Teresa wondered if she or Dominic would one day end up in Casualty themselves.

Fergus would hold her hand, take her into a Luncheonette for something to eat and drink, then call in to speak with Spiro, the Greek, in his corner store on Hope and Edward on the way home. Everyone called him Spiro the Greek. His surname was unpronounceable. Spiro and Fergus were friends. Spiro was a big man, had a loud booming voice, a man who constantly ordered his family around in his shop. Teresa knew that it was only a guise to make rough customers on Hope fear him. She envied his children. They went to a non denominational school.

Dominic was always asked to join them. He refused.

"You remember that Friday you came for me after school? I asked you what those white rubber things were over drains in the gutter. I was ten. You said they were called dead rubbers." Teresa grinned at her uncle seated opposite. "I asked what they were used for. You said a dead rubber is a kind of sport's game played when the results had already been decided. Played now just for the fun of it. For your information, they're called condoms. Good one, Uncle. Do you always tell fibs? No wonder the nuns say I should control my imagination."

Fergus sat back languidly in his chair at the table. He showed not a glimmer of emotion. There was still not a fleck of gray in his darkly trimmed beard as he sat back passively in his black clothes. His eyes were as dark as Teresa's, always as alert. He had the eyes of a hunter. He could strike out like a mongoose in the boxing ring, dislocate an opponent's shoulder with a single punch, yet Teresa had never seen him angry, anything other than kind. Sharn always hit him up for a few bucks at weekends to pay off shoes or cosmetics. Fergus was a real soft touch. He always gave freely, never asking what the money was for. Teresa would never do that.

He shifted his short black coffee cup round and round in the saucer. His hands were unusually large, knuckles white with calcifications from years in the boxing ring. The place was grimy. His cup chipped. The place sold tinned soup. Served tepid. Tinned corn beef, sodden with fat. Served cold. There was a reek of urine from the toilet behind, beside a cracked wall mirror. The sign read 'Out Of Orda,' uncertain whether it was mirror or toilet. A wino had gone to sleep, or passed out, at one of the back tables. His trousers were visibly undone. Maybe he'd urinated on the floor. Surrounding walls were conspicuously brown as though there'd recently been a stove fire there. Nobody had bothered cleaning the smudge away.

Teresa would have been far too scared ever to come here by herself. She took it all in through the disguise of her dark hair round her face. Her hair was as lustrous as a silky mane with her bunches out; her olive skin clear as a typical day in the Tropics. Yet her neck felt strangely pinned to the table, as if by a boot. All color had left her face.

The pool hall was next door. By the time Teresa got to it each afternoon Dominic was right behind her. Crazy-ass boys would sometimes jump out the windows with their pool cues. Crazy as loons.

But Fergus felt quite at home around here, not batting an eyelid at the squalor. He'd lived in places in South America far lower and more dangerous than this. Fergus was part of Teresa's problem—he insisted one should cope in one's surroundings.

"What else could I say, Tess? You were ten. Better you saw them than a lot of hypodermic needles in the drain. Some things you have to find out for yourself. One's allowed to tell fibs to old people. And the young. The ship's Captain tells fibs when he says everything's all right. Just before putting all passengers on the life boats. There is no need to get alarmed."

"Well, Captain Pugwash, no amount of fibs will put this street right. Don't see any life boats out here. It's like a bad joke. Ma cleans bedpans cleaner at the hospital than this street is. At least hospitals smell better. This street smells worse than a zoo. And please don't tell me life's just one big rewarding journey we must make. Like they tell us at school. All those nuns stuck up in their cloister. Sister Shuffle-Bum. Old Fish-Face. They live in another world. This street's like walking through the Reserve next to the house."

Teresa hanged her head, purposely slurping her banana drink, almost slumping to the table.

"Ever walked through the Reserve, Tess? I'll take you through it one day, if you want. You can then tell the nuns you've walked through God's garden."

She didn't answer, wrinkling her nose up at the thought, as though far too arduous. Like school. Yes, she'd been through the Reserve. Once. And recently. Chased through it. It had only frightened her pursuers. Not her. They were only trees, trees with venomous snakes maybe, dangerous spiders, lots of crawlers and critters. Trees didn't frighten her. She was an expert climber.

"Is it really that bad on the street?" Fergus inquired softly.

"Sure is. They now call me Troll, as if I live under a bridge. That's the latest. Other words I'm not even going to repeat. There's even one creep out there who calls me 'Mucker Mahone.' How he knows my surname, I don't know."

"Does he! That's surprising. You know what a 'mucker' is?"

"Who cares! Can only guess. He probably likes the sound of it. All means the same to me—shite."

"That's exactly what it is. You say you learn 'stuff,' know about American presidents. They used to call President Kennedy and his elder brother 'muckers' at school. It is a Protestant insult for Irish Catholics. Hands always in the Irish dung. The word 'manure' means to handle dung by hand. Shoveling crap. Sheep. Cattle. Goats. Horses. Hands in the Irish peat. It's a good word. Sticks and stones, Tess. Good expression for your mother, too. As you say, she's always cleaning out bedpans at the hospital."

"But President Kennedy must have gone to a Catholic school, too."

"He didn't. His father made the elder boys go to a Protestant one. More ambitious there. More acceptable. More likely to get on in the world."

"I want to go to a Protestant school, too."

"Your mother won't let you. You know that. It doesn't really matter in the end anyway, does it! You don't want to get on in the world, do you!"

"Yes I do. I just want to do it in my way, that's all. I'm more than happy to shovel shite. I just don't want to be made to eat it, too." She then lowered her voice and added. "By a bunch of scumbags proud of being stupid."

Teresa was not annoyed with her uncle. She knew what he said was true. She didn't like tests or exams, that feeling of being pushed along on some human conveyer belt. She was a slacker, easily given over to distraction, partially her uncle's fault because he had always made learning more interesting. He'd traveled widely before settling back in the city, coming here weekends to her parents.

Her face suddenly lit up.

"Do you remember the fibs you told me about the places you'd been?"

"When was that, then? What fib this time?" Fergus grinned. He was an artist. A B.S. artist. Underneath his fibs there was usually a deeper seriousness.

"When I was eight."

"No. Remind me." Fergus smiled. He remembered. He was a dreadful liar, even when it came to remembering his lies.

"You said you'd swum with the fish in the coral reef in the Dead Sea."

"Did I really?" He sounded alarmed.

"Don't you try backing out on me now. There are no fish in the Dead Sea. Too much salt. No fish could live in it."

"I meant the Red Sea."

"Yeah, right. So you said when I tripped you up."

"I was only testing. Your Ma said you'd just done a study on Israel."

"Bet you haven't even been there."

"I have."

"Doing what?"

Fergus muttered quietly. "Wandering about." He was never too specific as to where he had been or what he'd done. Bad things, she guessed.

"Tell me about it. Is Israel as dangerous as Hope Street on a Friday afternoon?"

"Anywhere can be dangerous, Tess." Fergus sipped his coffee. It was cold by now. He ordered himself another. "You want anything else?"

"No. Just for you to answer my question. No fibbing this time."

Fergus seemed suddenly to change faces by taking on another guise, answering her honestly. An astute liar, he knew the only subject at school that interested her much was religious instruction, and that was partly because Fergus' friend, Father Kevin, took her for it a couple of times a week. She was never too sure where her uncle stood on things, being a Communist and all that, yet knew Fergus knew what he was talking about, even if he 'lied' along the way. Fergus' lies were planted fairly and squarely to keep her on her nettle.

"There's a road there. I traveled it a few times. Jerusalem to Jericho, and back again. That's dangerous, as dangerous today as it was two thousand years ago."

"Why?"

"Because it winds about, meanders, making it very easy for ambushes."

"Did Jesus travel it?"

"Yes. So did the Good Samaritan. It was on that road the parable was set. Very dangerous there to pick up a passenger, as the Samaritan did. Robbers, or people acting they are hurt, laid in wait so they could lure travelers in and seize them. That's why the Priest and the Levite in the parable are not condemned for not helping the man, because that sick and beaten man could have been fooling them."

"But the Good Samaritan had more compassion than they did."

"Not really, Tess. I think the point of the story is he had more courage than them."

"I wouldn't have the courage to help anyone on this street. They're all faking it. Like at those bollards the other day. Lying in wait. Ambush. As for the other side of the street, it's full of street girls and prostitutes. No way would I ever go over there."

"Yes, you're probably right, but one day you may have to. I'm sure you'll help them when the time comes."

"Yeah, right. Just hope I live to tell the tale."

Shop and Dine

Wednesday night was Mall night for Teresa and her mother. While Caitlin went into the pharmacists and butcher's Teresa got the groceries from the supermarket, scrupulously keeping to the written list she and her mother had worked out together. It was a weekly ritual. Teresa would trolley them out to the pick-up, lock them in, then herself inside the cab. Teresa reluctantly returned this night to her mother in a junior clothes boutique to give back the grocery bankcard.

Teresa hated the Mall—the artificial atrium, the water feature, the perfect shrubbery, which never died, even the predictable key changes of the piped music. She disliked the long rows of beige curtains of paint, the brandishing of brands, the sickly candy stall and the silly sushi train, the over expensive food court, the lack of children playing, the hundred eyes watching them from the closed circuit TVs, the fact that everyone was just there for—'stuff.' (Going up, Tupperware and Trinkets. Going down, Tracksuits and Toilets, she mocked). Even though free of the goo of Hope Street, the artificial scents of the Mall made her want to hurl.

Everything seemed so plastic. If not plastic, then bubble wrapped.

She'd much rather listen to Fergus' music on her compact disc up in the fig tree, see all the natural greens round her, the world from a distance through her spyglass, which Fergus had bought her years ago. She preferred the roughness of her house and yard. They didn't have automatic sprinklers and neat edges, not like those gated communities by the ocean. It was 'hi' only to school acquaintances as she purposely busied herself along the aisles and shelves. Some of them referred to her, behind her back, as 'that God bother-er.' That was hardly the case. She bothered no one. God didn't pull faces, talk behind hands, play tricks on you out in the street.

They all knew her by now, knew she was short on conversation, even worse than that, her mouth clamped shut, a timid girl who never took any risks. Not socially savvy. They did not see her as having her nose in the air, not quite a Miss Goodie Two Shoes, even though top of the class in Christian Instruction.

Just plain weird.

She'd never invited any kids round to her house. Nobody invited her to parties in return. That was the reason, they thought, that she always seemed to have the glooms at school, that look of 'Give us a break, why don't you.' Nobody liked, or disliked her. The girls, somewhat begrudgingly, admitted that she was pretty. All knew her as that rather crazy kid who climbed trees. Word had got out that her Morton Bay fig tree at home was nearly a hundred feet high.

The Mall gave her a headache. Literally. The atrium looked like a giant chessboard. It screamed out at her. A duty manager had said 'good evening' in a fruity voice as she passed. She turned, looked at him, put her hand over her mouth, yawned in a kind of stupor, then felt rude for being so stand-offish. At least he'd been polite. And quickly moved on. She hated being stared at. Silence was the answer to everything. Except with her family, and with those next door. With them, she talked nonstop.

"Come on. I'm going to buy you some new clothes." Caitlin had said. "Then we're going to have some Mexican at the food court. You like Mexican."

"Yes, Ma, but . . . but it's so-o-o expensive."

"The world's expensive, Tess. Come on, dear, get used to the fact it's also full of Malls," Caitlin said nonchalantly while examining a rack of garments.

"Ma. Stop it. You're being naughty. They'll cost you a fortune! I don't need any new clothes. I'm ok."

"You need some new clothes for your Sunday best. Come on, you always say no to me when out shopping. I know you like buying at Good Will places. There's no call for you to dress in hand-me-downs. Like a bag lady."

"I like wearing my old jeans. Grungy stuff. It's more comfortable." Teresa hanged her head. "They cover my various veins."

She didn't like even being SEEN at The Mall. She'd only ever go there with Sharn. And that was only once in the bluest of moons. Sharn loved the Mall. It was a wonderland to her. Sharn wouldn't be seen dead buying at Teresa's Thrift shops.

"They're called 'varicose' veins, Teresa. And teenage girls don't get them. You can wear these to the Blue-light disco. I saw Mrs. Harrison today. She commented on how pretty you look. Come on, make an effort. You have to go out sometimes, be with other people. You can't stay at home all the time."

"I don't want to go to a Blue-light disco, Ma. What? Look like some flossed up fairy. Girls at discos look like they should be out on Pa's fishing boat—fishnets, cheap jewelry heavy as sinkers, dressed up like lures, fiddling with their designer eyewear—it looks so-o-o dumb. They're fifteen, for goodness sake, and wear garter belts, G-strings shaped like red hearts, pay the earth for that stuff off eBay, and then they go and jump up and down like a bunch of spastics. Spastics can't help it. They can. Arms going out in all directions. That's not dancing."

"They're still having fun, dear. And it really doesn't matter in the end."

Caitlin might have agreed in fact, yet there was also a deep Puritanism within Teresa which sometimes bothered her mother.

"I don't know if they're having fun. Most girls just like to leave the sad stuff at home. Only cheerful when they're out. Me, I'm opposite. Weird. Like uncle is."

Caitlin ignored that.

"You must let go. Have something, Teresa. Wear something light so your skin can breathe. Jeans are not healthy in this tropical heat."

"What? Like that crop top? That skirt! They look like someone's boiled them up in a copper. I like my jeans. Kicking about in them. Kicking them round my bedroom. If you want me to wear some light clothes buy me some pajamas, then."

"No they don't, Tess. Feel the texture of these tops. They're good quality, so you have to pay more."

"They all look pretty beige to me."

"No they're not. The colors are pretty. They'd suit you. What's wrong? You don't have to have the crop top. Just a nice round neck then. Not too plunging. Where's your sense of adventure? Do you think they'll make you feel like you've a heaving bosom?"

"What's a heaving bosom?"

"It's a . . . just an expression they use in the classics. Don't worry about it. They'll make you look nice. Don't you think? You need some new garb."

"What's garb mean?"

"Clothes."

"What, is that like-as-in-garb-age?" Teresa strung the word out, turning her nose up in disgust.

"Don't be silly. What are the girls at school wearing when they go out?"

"Usually not enough. Or those horrible Goth frocks with white faces and black fingernails. They look creepy, or just look like a bunch of bims. Or X-rated stuff. I like X-rated, too. XXL. I like big, floppy tops." She grinned at her mother with a kind of comic disgust.

Teresa reflected a moment. "Girls at school see me buying stuff at the Thrift Shop on Saturdays. They call me 'retro chick,' stuff I wear looks 'so-o yesterday,' they giggle together, whispering behind their hands, leaning into one another like a bunch of stuffed toys. Ma, I mean it, I don't care what they think."

Caitlin looked at her sadly. "Come on. You are slim and pretty. You don't need to wear those. It's not as if you're fat or look like someone addicted to . . . chocolate."

"Girls at school are addicted to chocolate. Then to a bunch of diet pills. Ritalin with their muesli-bars. Some are on anti-depressants. They hide out in the disabled toilet popping pills, bawling to their friends on their phones. How dumb's that! Expensive clothes won't put it right. Marcia's always away sick because she's trying to pump her stomach. Or taking those appetite depressants."

"Suppressants." Her mother corrected.

Teresa began to grin. "Her absent note to Sister Susan the other day read. "Marcia could not come to school on Monday. She had the shits." Her mother couldn't spell diarrhea. She gave up in the end."

"And you can spell it?"

"Yes. I looked it up. With and without the O. Needed to. Never a truer word written. Every day school gives me waves in the stomach. Not much better here."

"Well then, you are lucky you're not like them, aren't you! Marcia may have a problem with her thyroid. You don't know."

"Marcia and her mother compete in dressing up. Her mother likes to look real young. Mutton dressed up as ham."

"It's 'as lamb.' I don't do that, do I!"

"No."

"Good. All the more reason for you to have some nice teenage clothes. I'm going to buy you some, whether you like it or not."

"I don't know, Ma." Teresa looked away vaguely, then briefly to the clothes her mother was holding up to the light.

Caitlin had been doing the same here three weeks previously. She'd stepped outside for a moment for a better light to shine on the garment. The electronic tag set off. Security came running. It was an inadvertent mistake, and was accepted by Security, but it had really freaked Teresa. Her mother was not a thief. How dare they! Prices here were highway robbery, anyway!

Teresa continued.

"Last time I came in here was with Sharn. She told me off. She knows I hate the place. She said 'Watch it, Little Sister, otherwise you'll grow up to be a whiney little bitch.' Do you think I'm a whiney little bitch, Ma? Is she right?"

"No. But you'll never make the cut with a sack on your head. Sharn's right, though. You have to learn to accept the things of the world."

"Is it a sin to wear clothes that cost too much? Seriously, Ma? Jesus dressed like a real geek. He kicked round in Roman scandals with a bunch of smelly fishermen. He didn't care much about having clothes for Sunday best."

"No, it isn't a sin. If you want 'seriously,' then what about that New Testament story of the wedding guest being thrown out of the banquet because he wasn't properly attired? Uncle buys things for you from the city, then he throws the receipts away so you can't return them. People are sometimes required, expected to dress properly. That's the way of the world."

"Uncle doesn't buy me clothes. Just floppy T-shirts." Teresa smirked. "Uncle says they make me look like Jesus. Like a Jew. Because I like to wear things inside out. He showed me some pictures of Orthodox Jews. I like the way they look. They don't care what we think of them."

Caitlin ignored that. "But he buys other things you like. He always dresses nicely himself."

"O.k., then. Just this once. I like that skirt, this top. They'll fit me. I'm not changing in the cubicle. The assistant always stares like I'm about to steal something. I'll put them on hangers in my wardrobe. I won't kick them round my room. Let's pay for them. Get out of here. And you're being real naughty, Ma. But thank you, anyway."

"And then we'll go and have some Mexican? Come on, Tess, you deserve it. I wouldn't manage that easily without you. You're a great help to us at home. You never complain about helping out."

"Only if it's steamed, organic, germ free," Teresa smiled at her mother, then rested her head on her shoulder.

"Just like the Mall?" Caitlin retorted.

"Yes, Ma. Just like the Mall."

Fleecing Fergus

They paid for the clothes then went and ordered two plates with enchiladas, loads of potato bake and hot sauce. This was their guilty pleasure. They both knew it was fattening. Teresa felt guilty about it. Guilty about being at the Mall. Mother and daughter stood together in the short queue.

"What's Pa having for his dinner?"

"Colleen's cooking for him. He's over watching TV with Declan."

"Do you want to hear something REALLY funny?" Teresa grinned up at her mother, feeling better about that, after having tapped her mother's shoulder in the queue.

"Yes. Tell me. I know you want to."

"Sharn and Fergus. Saturday night."

"Oh, no. What disaster this time? What did that little brat do to him?"

"She hit him up for money. Again."

"That's not unusual."

"It was so-o funny. She blackmailed him. It was for hush money."

"She WHAT!"

"Fergus was manning the barbeque. She went and stood right in front of him, hands on her hips, like the little drama queen she is, said that Father Kevin had just been dirty dancing with her, had touched her, here, here, and here." Teresa touched her own cheek, then her breast, then jumped round on the spot in a full 180, like in playing hop scotch, pointing her finger up and down to her butt with the words "Da-DAR!"

Teresa then stood still, tittering with laughter.

"Disgusting little brat. She needs that bottom smacked."

"Fergus didn't say anything. He just reached in for his wallet. How much? Sharn said 'TEN BUCKS.' I could see in her eyes she wanted more. Fergus gave her an extra five, told her to keep quiet about it, not to go and ring Child Line."

"She's a little horror head. I should tell Colleen."

"Fat use that would be. She then got all indignant, told Fergus 'I'm not a child, I'm NINETEEN.'"

Caitlin threw her hands in the air in despair. "She wants to watch what comes out of that mouth of hers. Father Kevin would no sooner do that than fly to the sun. He's a lovely man. I love having him at the house. Fergus and he have been friends since before they went to school."

"I know that. Nobody else heard her. She was just clowning round."

"What did she want fifteen dollars for, anyway?"

"We went and got some take-out." Teresa tittered guiltily.

"You little brats! A fine buddy system you've got going for yourselves, haven't you!"

"She is naughty, Ma. She is always saying can I borrow, which means spend, never give it back, off me, too. But Uncle doesn't care. I don't care much about money, either. Only Dominic makes her pay it back."

"Don't ever underestimate your uncle, Teresa. I've never known a man to care as much as he does." Caitlin stared seriously at her daughter.

"Yes. I think I've learned that by now."

They ate silently a while. They could not be mistaken for anything other than mother and daughter. Two peas in a pod. Slim, tall and willowy. Caitlin always wore her jet black hair tied back away from her face. It did not make her look severe; it was a kind face; she had dark but gentle eyes, which sometimes seemed sad, just like Teresa's.

"The other weekend Sharn also hit Fergus up for money. Money for drugs this time." Teresa chuckled in her chair. "He never asks what it's for anymore. He used to." Teresa then began imitating the both of them. "What you want ten bucks for? Another late fee on 'Bambi?'" "Fergus, I'm EIGHTEEN. I hate Bambi. Far too sad for me." She doesn't even say 'thank you.' "If I need some more then I'll have my people call you." She is so cheeky."

"Oh, no. Were you with her?"

"Sure was." Teresa imitated Sharn again. She said 'Fergus, me and Tess wanna go out and buy some drugs.' He just reached in for his wallet, corrected her grammar, 'Teresa and I,' then said 'How much?' 'TEN BUCKS.' He gave her the ten. Sharn then said 'Me and Tess, sorry, Teresa and I, wanna buy ourselves two joints, two ecstasy tablets, two lines of cocaine.' Guess what Fergus did?"

"Gave her some more, didn't he?"

"Sure did. He always stops at fifteen."

"You two brats ought to be ashamed of yourselves."

Yet there was no real tone of reprimand in Caitlin's voice. It was just a game. Fergus actually liked Sharn, for she had his measure. And asking Fergus for money was like asking for an extra sausage from the barbeque. He just shoved it with lots of extra on your plate, without moment's hesitation.

"He is so funny, Ma. Uncle's a bit like the Devil, isn't he—if he knew the truth he'd only lie about it."

"Devil or not, you won't pull the wool over his eyes. He's always ten steps ahead. He's like that electric hare at the greyhound races—you're never going to catch him, no matter how hard you try."

"He just refuses to get hung up over things, doesn't he?" Teresa mused.

Caitlin did not answer her. Teresa suddenly got the feeling that her mother was holding out on her. She didn't probe any further.

Boys just like to Watch

Teresa was idyllically happy at home. She loved the madness of weekends. Uncle Fergus was always up to something. Usually no good. Her parents had always got on well. Her father doted on her mother. She never heard arguments. Colleen and Declan from next door treated Teresa as if their own. It was like one big extended family. Bunch of Communists. Amish people. A big Roman holiday. Yet there was often also lots of confusion in Teresa's mind. She was never sure what her uncle thought. He now drove a flash Mercedes Benz. And he sold liquor. Fergus, a Communist, who may, or may not, have believed in God, said God gave liquor to the world to keep mankind happy. He could give every biblical reference, chapter and verse for the importance of it. He blessed their house with food and gifts from the city, alcohol and cigars. Fergus would become more instructive, in both religion and language, with every drink. Teresa knew that family dinner was not quite sitting round the table of knowledge when Fergus was present, yet she didn't know quite what to think. He once said to Teresa at dinner:

"Teresa, the word 'infant' means 'being unable to speak.' The reason infants are unable to speak is, just having been born, they are much closer to God. At this point they know everything. They can't speak, or won't speak, because if they did—the whole world would appear stupid to them."

He then whispered to her as an aside. "Sharn was never an infant."

Caitlin rolled her eyes, walked away. Teresa knew that Sharn was right into crystals, still wore her fluffy pink animal slippers, had porcelain flying ducks on her bedroom wall. Teresa got the impression that her uncle expected better than that.

Yet Teresa also knew that Fergus, for reasons of his own, and a mystery to her, seemed determined to keep their two families happily together.

He also once said that the word 'believe' has a 'lie' in it.

He would carry on like that, everyone of his words untrustworthy, then just as likely to suddenly turn to seriousness like some gravitational pull back to earth.

Often Teresa didn't know what to believe. It was all a big game. Like up on Hope Street. Fergus created confusion. It kept Teresa on her toes. At least she felt safe around him.

*   *   *

Teresa put her knife and fork down from her Mexican dish in the Mall and started to grim.

"Jennifer has had a stud put in her tongue."

"Don't even ask. You're not allowed. It's forbidden at school."

"Guess how her mother found out?"

"How."

"She suspected something was wrong. Jennifer hadn't spoken for a week. Her mother made her go and take it out. The hole closed over in a day."

"Good."

"It would take them a year to find out at school if I had one."

"Just forget it, young lady."

Teresa grinned at her mother. "How would they know? I don't talk to anyone."

Caitlin reached across the table and clutched Teresa's hand. "That's no good. You always talk at home. We can't shut you up. Not that we want to. Anyway, how are they treating you up on Hope, Tess?"

Teresa picked up her knife and fork again. "Same old, same old. Boys are all the same. They just like to watch, don't they! Watch, watch, watch. They look at you like they want to snap shots of you sitting on a toilet seat. Bunch of creeps."

"But so do you. You watch everything from up in your fig tree with your spyglass, that's the only difference."

"Maybe. At least I don't put hurt on people, create a stink like those bozos do. That's all the rage up on Hope. One of them asked me the other day 'Hey ma-a-n-you-gotta-name?' I felt like saying 'Yeah, sure have, but I left it at home.' Sometimes I do wish I could wear a sack over my head."

"Why didn't you tell him, then?"

"Because then I'd have to talk back to them, wouldn't I! That would only start an argument."

"Does Dominic stop and talk to them?"

"Sometimes. He knows most of them. He reckons half of them are on day release. He doesn't have any time for them, either. But he's a boy, isn't he. All boys are the same. I'm not Whitney. He's no Kevin Costner. I can look after myself."

"Not all boys are the same, Teresa."

"Yes they are. Boys only like big boobs . . . and big burgers. Bigger the better. That's what they mean by 'with the lot.' Sharn's no better. I love Sharn. She's my big sister. She is so-o funny at times. But she can be just as disgusting. She reckons it's tits what get you into the night-clubs. If that's true, then I don't even want to know about sex."

"Well, you have nice breasts, Teresa. And a lovely figure." Caitlin did not know what else to say. She clutched her daughter's hand. Caitlin loved Sharn, too.

"Wish I hadn't."

"Well, it's all your own fault. Climbing trees all your life. No wonder you're so strong and agile."

Teresa didn't answer. She sat pensively reflecting on what her mother said before starting again. "Maybe you're right. I do like to watch things from up in my tree. Maybe I should get out more. But other girls like to watch, too. They all go down to the skate park, stand round like a pack of flat bottles of beer watching the boys making all their moves. Why don't girls just bone up, go out and get some roller skates of their own, do things for themselves? I would. I'm going to save up, buy me some."

Caitlin said yes, that that was a good idea, why don't you.

Caitlin must have mentioned this to Fergus when he was home. The following weekend he brought back three pairs of skates to the house, one pair for Teresa, one pair for Sharney, one pair for Dominic. So typical of Fergus. On birthdays, Teresa only got the dumbest of presents from him, free coupons and samples of cosmetics, only then to be spoilt by him for most weeks throughout the year.

They could now all skate to their hearts' content, honking and hollering along the safety of their vacant Edward Street.

I'm running away

Sometimes Fergus would casually ask the forbidden question at dinner on a Friday night after he arrived back from the city.

"How's school, Tess?" He knew how and when to press all the wrong buttons.

It took the heat off Caitlin and Maddox asking. Caitlin knew that Fergus, as an ex boxer, would come in at her from all angles.

Teresa put down her knife and fork, glowering across at him. All it did was excite her, get her heart rate up.

"Attendance, perfect. The rest? Heifer dust! Heifer dust!(no one was allowed to swear at the dinner table). I'm sick of hearing how life's supposed to be so FAIR, everyone gets their TURN, it's all about taking PART, you only get out of life what you put IN. One big cheese after another. That we're all so SPECIAL, can do anything if only we TRY, says Sister Susan. Sister Sue. Sister Emu. Burying her head in the sand. I guess it stops the cuckoos sounding off in her brain. I feel like saying 'go watch television news at night. See what is happening in Sudan. Thousands have died in those drug wars in Mexico. Try walking down Hope street every morning and afternoon then you'll see how everyone gets a 'PRIZE." Every day's an 'ADVENTURE!' The silly old cow tried to give me a hug the other day. I pulled away. I don't want anyone touching me. As if hugs make it all BETTER."

"No guarantees in this life, Tess." Fergus replied softly.

"That's for sure. Auntie Teresa can tell you that." Teresa stopped, slumping back in her chair. She realized that she'd said the wrong thing.

"Are they picking on you in the street again? Is Dominic still walking with you?" Caitlin asked. For yet another time. She needed the reassurance. That walk home still rang alarm bells with Caitlin. Police sirens.

"No, as I said, he follows way back. He doesn't want to be seen with me. Don't worry, Ma. I look after myself. I'm happy just to get home. Up the tree. At least it's clean up there. I'd rather spend time with Ballou. She's micro-chipped, doesn't stray, and she's DE-SEXED. Like me. I'm a cat. Boys are dogs. As different as that."

There was a long silence. They let her sound off. Fergus said nothing. Caitlin wished that she would think less about things. She was safe enough out in the open, and they knew that they could rely on Dominic.

Teresa soon changed the subject.

"Ma, I want to get a stud in my tongue. And a nose ring. Like Sharn has. How 'bout a nut and bolt in the tongue? Like Jennifer had. I may as well. It will prevent me from talking. Talking about school, at nights, at dinner."

"It'll chip your teeth, dear. And it costs far too much for dental nowadays." Maddox said. She liked her dad. He never told her off. She playfully pushed him around. He worked hard with Declan next door. They let her alone. She often worked for them on a Saturday, they taught her how to screed the concrete driveways, get the right levels. They were fence builders and concrete workers. They spoilt her, paying her more than they should in wages. Sometimes Fergus would help out too on Saturdays, if the men were really busy. Teresa would come home covered in concrete slurry, laughing her head off, picked on, giving it back to them.

"Forget it, young lady. Body piercing is illegal until you're eighteen. And not tolerated at school." Caitlin knew the provocation was a hint to talk about something else.

"Nothing's tolerated at school. Sharn does them down the salon. She's been trained properly. No one would know if I got a belly or nipple ring. They'll look so good when I become a belly dancer. Five earrings? Each ear?" Teresa sat forward to spoon in a mouthful of food. Before she did she said "Or down in the other place."

"Where might that be, then?" Caitlin asked, trying not to be horrified. Teresa stood, turned, flicked her butt out from side to side. She had a nice butt. Her breasts had filled out. They looked like rounded peaches. She was now feeling her own sexuality, even though denying it.

Caitlin never minded her plying her moves. Anything to get her talking.

"Sit down or I'll reach across and smack it," Maddox said, feigning anger. He was working long hours out in the heat. He and Declan were concreting footpaths and driveways, pushing heavy concrete cutters where the glare and dust were unforgiving. He wasn't always in the mood for Teresa's carry on.

They'd never punished her. She was never naughty. She'd give her right arm to be put under curfew, grounded at weekends. She kept her room tidy, despite her own protestations that she didn't, kept the house orderly, never forgot her chores, prepared meals when asked, helped her mother bake, genuinely wanting to learn to house-keep properly. She never wrote instructions on her hand, needed magnetized notes on the refrigerator—told once, she remembered. Her memory was sound.

Fergus had given her a simple accounting disc so she could punch in all receipts on the PC for her fathers and Declan's concreting business. She did it without complaint.

And, in the middle of one of her cheeky outbursts, she'd suddenly stop, say "I'll go" to her mother, who'd be moving off to the kitchen for the coffee pot or something similar. In a strange way, they welcomed her cheek, despite Caitlin giving her a cold flick of the eyelashes, Maddox frowning with disappointment. It was becoming a kind of pent up evening practice after her disappointing day at school, the glooms after walking home.

After a long pause.

"Why do they call it Hope Street? Sister Shuffle-Bum, the Penguin, says it's named after the virtue of Hope. Is that right?"

Caitlin winced at the name calling. They often corrected her, admonished her lack of respect.

Fergus didn't. He wasn't standing for that. "She's wrong. It's named after a Captain, the Honorable Louis Hope. He's called the father of the sugarcane industry. One hundred and forty years ago they began planting sugarcane on the river flats for over two thousand kilometers. Sydney to Mossman. It refers to him. It says so down at the council office."

"Interesting. I should tell Sister Sea-cow that. But I won't. Maybe they might burn Hope Street down one day. Like the stubble after cane harvest They say human flesh has a real sweet smell. Burn the litter louts, that's what I say. Like sugar litter. We can only hope, can't we!"

"That's enough, Teresa. That's a mean thing to say. You can leave the table." Caitlin growled at her.

Teresa got up, picked up her cat next to her chair, then went to her room. She then thought better of it. At the foot of the stairs, she turned to her mother.

"I'm going up to my room now, packing a pillow slip of clothes, tying them up in a bundle on the end of a stick. I'm running away. Me and Ballou. Like Dick Whittington and his cat." She grinned to the wall.

"And where do you intend running? London? Like Whittington did. Earn your fortune, become the Mayor?" Caitlin smirked.

"No. I'm going over next door to live with Colleen and Sharn. Get high on hair spray."

"You'll be back. Declan is the worst tease of all." Caitlin said.

"No I won't. I won't be allowed to. I'll have my hair up like Lady Ga Ga's in a few days, lots of piercing. Tattoos. I promise."

"Yes you will." Maddox said knowingly. "You'll be back. No trees to climb over there."

To the South Seas

Teresa sat between her parents on the family sofa, feet up in her pajamas, wrapping her legs with her arms. The TV was on. She'd wait for her right moment in order to say the wrong thing. She was like the meat in the sandwich. Say the wrong thing and her parents would immediately close in on her, crushing her like two pieces of bread.

School. How she loathed the tedium, privation of it, which she had wittingly chosen for herself. School was becoming about as unlovely and uninviting as the suburb. And the walk home. There was little anyone could say or do. On Hope street, she moved along like a shadow dweller, no different from the musty corridors of St. Ignatius'. Senior boys joked to Dominic that they'd drive her home. If she was willing. They never quite understood his concern when he answered 'She's my sister. Leave her alone.'

"Ma. I'm in the doghouse at school again. But it's ok. I'm running away."

"What? School getting you down?"

"'Fraid so."

"What've you done now?"

Silence.

"Flirting with the boys under the stairwell when you should've been in class?" There wasn't much conviction in Caitlin's voice.

"Hardly. I'd rather go hide in the broom cupboard." Teresa looked at her mother with utter disgust. "You know I don't discuss my private life with anyone."

"Anyway. That's nice, dear. Where are you running off to this time? I thought you wanted to go to London."

"Pacific Islands. Samoa." Teresa pointed over and away to its approximate direction far out in the South Seas. She huffed the hair away which was clouding her eyes.

"Well you make sure that you ring your mother if there's anything you need. It really doesn't matter what time of day or night." Maddox reassured.

"And you're not taking Ballou. We'd miss her too much. The cat stays here." Caitlin rejoined.

"Where will you live over there?" Maddox wondered.

"In a tepee. Maybe a wigwam."

"Hardly. It would be blown away in their cyclones. Anyway, they all live in big long community houses with thatched roofs. Twenty to a room. You won't like that much. But I guess you'll soon learn to climb the palm trees." Caitlin said.

"Good. I like coconuts."

"Why Samoa? What's the attraction there? We're not trying to put you off, of course." Maddox was genuinely curious.

"Tattoos. It's a Samoan word. That's where tattooing started. I want to be covered with them. Head to foot. Forehead, chin, ears, toes." Teresa pointed to each in turn then put her hand on her heart. "My heart's so heavy. Leaving home will stop it. Then I'll come back. Then nobody would ever want to employ me. No school. No job. 'Just look at that girl,' they'll all say. 'More ink on her than in an octopus.' I'd then have to stay at home. FOREVER."

"Tattoos hurt, dear. They use a real bone chisel and hammer over there. And only men do it. That would mean someone would see your naked bottom. You don't like boys looking at your bottom, do you. You have to think these things through properly, Teresa."

Caitlin had sure thrown a chisel in the works. It shut her up. Momentarily.

"I don't care if boys see my butt," Teresa reassessed. "I'd also like to pose for Hustler or Playboy. Wear a wig, makeup for the tattoos. Nobody would ever recognize me. I'm going to be really famous one day. My picture will be all over the world. Who wants to be a pillar of the community just to die in the bosom of Mother Church!" She then readjusted her own, with a deliberate wiggle.

"Why don't you try Dolly magazine first?" Maddox offered.

"Too cheesy," Teresa turned up her nose.

"We'd get you new clothes for it. Or second hand." Maddox proposed.

"Don't need new clothes."

"Where have you seen these magazines, young lady?" Caitlin inquired. Part of Caitlin blamed Sharn for Teresa's carry-on. Part welcomed it. It brought her down to earth. Sharn had been well behaved at school, no scholar but certainly more industrious than Teresa ever was, as she was now hard working at the hair salon. Sharn was good at her job. She loved to be coarse, boasting to Teresa that her 'pubic triangle' was now a number one, soon to go Brazilian. Shame was, Teresa had far more potential academically, yet she didn't care.

"In the gutters up on Hope. Boys bring them to school. They shouldn't even be in Hope street. And you think I'm revolting! Why don't girls just bone up, see boys for what they really are?"

"We'd recognize you in Playboy. Instantly." Maddox chuckled to himself. "You wouldn't fool us for a moment. You'd be the naked model with her hands up over her face covering her eyes."

Teresa folded her arms, leaned forward, grunted, lowering her bottom lip in a huff.

Pushing the Boundaries.

Three nights later. Another night, this time of swinging legs, on the sofa. It was her time to mouth off. She certainly felt that she deserved it. After getting home from school she had put through three loads of washing, pegged it out, brought it in, for it had dried in an hour, folded it, put it away. She knew that her parents were tired. Helping out gave her the right to mouth off.

"The teachers say I've got to become more 'integrated' in class. What's that supposed to mean? Go through the mince machine? Sister Shuffle Bum asked me in the corridor 'Have things changed since last we spoke?' I felt like saying 'Nope. Change is real slow with me. How about on the first of NEVER.'"

"Tess, you're just making a rod for your own back." Caitlin said quietly.

"We have these signs up in our classroom. We must not make any sexual or sexist comments at school. We must not say anything racial or ethnically offensive. If I was at a State school then they'd have to add we must not make any religious comments, too."

"Don't think about things so much. And you're not changing schools, Teresa. Get that idea right out of your head. It just isn't feasible." Caitlin said.

"What's feasible mean?"

"That we can't manage it with the bus routes being what they are. It's too difficult."

She looked at her mother with a long stare. Teresa knew that it was a lost cause. Time to move on to something else.

"Anyway. I have to write another story called 'Hope and Celebration.' Want me to read it to you? It's good. Real radical stuff. Off the scale. Like uncle. I got a pasting for my last assignment because they said I liked Communists, so now they can get a load of this."

As if they had an option.

Teresa pulled a folded sheet out from her jacket pocket, carefully smoothing it out. It was a mass of corrections, White-Out. Ink smudges.

"I think I have lots of hidden artistic talent. Not too gay. Not too straight. A glass not too full. Not too empty. A frosted rim of sugar coat. Maybe some salt. A simple twist on the side. Twist of lemon. Olive on a skewer." She spoke just like her uncle would with his knowledge of liquor. Maddox looked sheepishly across at Caitlin. Somehow or other, they were not quite expecting Jane Austin. Tess didn't do Jane Austin.

"Just get on with it, will you," Caitlin prompted. She was not going to blame her uncle for her carry on. Fergus had worked feverishly hard at school. At everything. He had the discipline of a soldier.

"Hope And Celebration."

A dramatic pause. Her eyes scanned her parents either side of her for their full attention. Her eyes bulged like the boundaries she was just about to push.

"There were celebrations up on Hope Street this Saturday night. Like Halloween. Any excuse to run amok. Plenty of candy. Up the nose. Scuzzball was getting married. Strange really, because the only two things he hated were chicks and pussies. They'd hired out a big warehouse for the festivities, being way too rough to go clubbing. Too stupid ever to score the fake IDs. Anyway, Scuzzball always liked spitting on the floors. Grossing people out. No big deal to Scuzz."

Teresa paused. "New paragraph."

"He'd already belted two kids out of this chick. He'd been banging the bimbo for years now, mainly during visitation hours while in the slammer. He'd been a pickpocket at naptime ever since on the carpet at pre-school. Now free, older, dumber, they were finally tying the knot."

"That's interesting," Maddox interrupted. "I thought couples only communicated inside on the jailhouse phone. A big glass barrier between them. It's amazing what comes out of a pen."

(Caitlin glowered across at Maddox. He lowered his hand behind the sofa as though to say let it pass. Hear it out. For the moment.)

"Where was I?" Teresa continued sarcastically, as if rudely interrupted. "Here we are."

"But first they had to have a stag party. Porn. Other nasties. No broads allowed. The girls didn't mind. They knew it was a guy, not a chick thing. They were having their hen's down the road. All to meet up later. Everyone brought plenty of booze. Scuzzball had a packet of blow. Crystal meths. Needles to celebrate on Hope . . ."

"What's 'blow,' Caitlin?" Maddox interrupted, curious.

Teresa looked to her mother.

"She means 'Bo' Botox." Caitlin replied.

Teresa looked to her father.

"No it doesn't. No 'l' in Botox. Must be Collagen. Silicon. Something like that. It gives you those big bee-sting looking lips, just like Teresa's got. That's what the needles are for. Inject it into your face." Maddox puckered his lips grotesquely.

She was about to begin again.

"What's 'crystal meths?'" Maddox asked again in wonder.

Teresa looked to her mother.

"She means mentholated spirits. You know. You clean windows with it. Fergus drinks it. Not out of spray bottles, of course. Must be in crystal form. You chew them. It's nice. It just makes you a little unpredictable, that's all."

Teresa grinned. "So that's why you can never trust uncle."

Her parents ignored that.

"Right. Silly me. Sorry, Teresa. Do carry on." Maddox smiled apologetically.

"Anyway. 'They all got smashed, smoked lots of shit until someone wheeled in this enormous sponge cake on a trolley. It arrived unexpected, like a clap of thunder. It was enormous! Must of weighed a freaking TON.'"

"No, Tess. Watch the repetition of 'enormous.' And it's 'must HAVE weighed a ton.' And I think it should read 'arrived unexpectedly.' Watch your grammar." Caitlin corrected.

"But 'freaking's' quite o.k. Under the circumstances. So is 'festivities,' 'visitation.'" Maddox added casually. "I rather like it. Carry on."

"Scuzzball was now right out of it. His brains were fried. Then, suddenly, out of the blue, this Asian stripper from an Ashram in India appeared out the top of the cake. She wore next to nothing. Drop dead gorgeous. She had her nipples pierced, shaven downstairs, lots of tattoos, all covered in cream. Her tongue glided up her arm, licking it clean. Everyone wore UV sunglasses. She was that hot! She then began lap dancing for him. She sat on his legs, grinding his thighs. That did her no good. She tried sitting on his face but he was away with the fairies by then. That made her real cranky. She held out her fingers, pinged her sticky knickers on his face. Then walked, got her sorry, cream covered Bollywood shaking ass out of there. Disgusted.

"THE END."

There was a long silence. Caitlin then looked at her sternly.
"Wake up to yourself, girl. You'll get expelled if you submit that."
"Don't worry, Ma. I won't."
"Where did you draw your inspiration for this?" Maddox asked.
Teresa grinned. "Sharn heard the story down at the salon."
Silence.

Teresa stared, straight ahead with a thoughtful look. "All they ever want to hear at school is cheese. Cheese, cheese, and more cheese. They say we mustn't be judgmental. I thought I'd give them some real cheese. Blue cheese."

Teresa folded the scruffy piece of paper and moved off to bed, sad and angry. "Sister Susan would probably say it's sexist. It's not. It's just dumb. Filthy. Celebrations on Hope always are. Girls wearing those sawn cut-offs, flashing their titties on the other side of the street, taking money for sex. She also says we must live and let live. The nuns don't mean it. Words mean nothing anymore. Everything I say and think gets smacked down with a ruler. I'm running away. I'll recruit soldiers for the Revolution. Live and let live. Heifer dust! Heifer Dust. LONG LIVE GUEVARA!"

She punched a clenched fist into the air as she took to the stairs to her room.

To Get a Tattoo

After a sullen day at school, Teresa saved up her pent up ammunition for home. Another night of swinging her legs sandwiched between her parents on the sofa. It was as if a buzzer sounded in her head "You've got mail."

Mail was to be shared.

"I mustn't sit down. I have to use the computer for work." Caitlin was tired after long shifts at the hospital.

"No you don't. I've done it. I saw the papers there, typed them in for you." Teresa lent across bumping into her mother's shoulder.

"Did you! Thank you. I've still more to do."

"Leave them beside the computer. I'll do them tomorrow after school."

"Thanks, Tessie, you're so much quicker than I am."

Caitlin was genuinely grateful.

The Federal Police had recently been to the school instructing students about cyber-bullying and, just as importantly, the dangers of credit card fraud, the police hopeful that they, the students, would then instruct their parents.

Teresa did all the Internet banking, paid bills online, if unsure of anything on computer she would ask Fergus at weekends.

Teresa then lent across, bumping her father the other side of her. "Grab Declan's receipts from the timber yard each day. Tell him not to put his thermos on top of them. It leaks on the paper. They are too hard to read when I transfer them to computer. He's hopeless." Teresa grinned at her father.

She liked helping them out. She knew that their days were busy. Hers were not. She did as little as possible at school, her homework in library and free periods.

She resented the pat answers and easy familiarity of schoolwork in knowing that she would then always have to step out into the blind indifference and dangers of Hope street

"All right. Thank you, dear. But shouldn't you be doing your own homework?" Maddox asked.

"No. I do it in the library during lunchtime and break."

"Why, Tess?" Caitlin said with genuine concern. "Why aren't you relaxing with your friends outside in the sun?"

Teresa said nothing, as if they should know the answer to that by now. Days at school just seemed to congeal one into another for her. Best change the subject.

There was silence.

"Tess, don't you talk to other kids at school?" Her father asked.

"Nope. Moment I get to the school gates words shut off, slip down a black hole somewhere. I shut up like the closing of a door. My thoughts are too private to be shared with idiots. I only talk at home."

Silence again. If she was going to talk, she thought, then why not demand!

"Did you know the second most popular tattoo in the world is a cross symbol, plus two words? Guess what it is." Teresa looked to her mother.

"I know. The words are 'FORGET IT,' and I'm getting cross with you."

"Wrong. It's Harley Davidson and its cross symbol sign. Guess what is the most popular. One word only."

"I know that one, too. It's the word 'NO'." Caitlin wasn't interested.

"Wrong again. It's the word 'MUM.' But I don't want that. Yuk!"

"Thank goodness for that." Caitlin thought that the end of conversation.

Teresa brooded awhile. "I really want to get a tattoo. I have been praying for one for ages now. Every night. P-L-E-A-S-E, Ma. Declan has got tattoos. Sharn has a blue dolphin on her ankle, a butterfly square on the back of her neck. How cheesy is that! I don't want some Irish shamrock or loony looking leprechaun. They're so corny. Or those little red devils with pitchforks toasting away on my butt. Just something cool."

It was like asking for the impossible. It got little response.

"See if you can have your prayers transferred for Sharn next door," Caitlin offered.

"Fat chance of that. I want to have tattoos like Posh Beckham has. Or Popeye. Or those Hope Street warriors. It would look so cool. I could then talk posh, couldn't I? At least it would sound better than Popeye, wouldn't it, or the Hope Street boys."

"They look revolting," Caitlin barely bothered answering.

"I'm fifteen. I'm supposed to be revolting." It was a little whiny voice.

"Stop it." Maddox said.

Teresa spoke softly to her mother. "Piece of cheese, a mother daughter thing? You have the cheese, me a rat?"

"Enough," her mother said.

Teresa kept pushing it. "I heard of this guy with a fox's head and shoulders tattoo coming out of his pooper, a blood hound next to it holding its nose. I think that would be really nice, considering."

"Considering what?" Her mother inquired.

"Considering a fox got in our yard and killed my goose and gander two years ago. It would at least keep the fox in its proper place then, wouldn't it, up my butt."

She had never got over that day.

"The answer's still no." Her mother knew her sadness about that fox. "Tattoos are not transient things."

"What's 'not transient' mean?"

"It means that they last. Won't go away. You have lovely skin. Don't mess it up. Tattoos can shift over time."

"Interesting. That fox's head just might end up anywhere then, mightn't it!"

"Don't be cheeky."

"But I want to be a tattooed, baby faced, pill popping, pooper kicking ass wipe like the boys are on Hope street. P-L-E-A-S-E, Ma."

"No."

"Then just a spider web tattoo on my neck. I promise I would put dead flies in it."

"Is that a promise?"

"Yes, I promise."

"Still no." Caitlin lent across, kissed Teresa on the cheek. "Now go to bed."

"All right, if you insist. I'm now going to run upstairs and slam my bedroom door."

She picked up her cat, pretending to be angry. She went upstairs, and didn't.

Her Lady's Bureau

Some months before, Caitlin had sent Teresa over next door to help Colleen this particular Friday evening. There were dishes to prepare for Saturday. They always had a party Saturday. Fergus would bring home lots of party food and CDs from the city. He, Maddox and Declan, would hang out fairy lights, place stereo speakers round the yard, a small stage, often microphones. Spiro and his wife would come round, bring tapes of Greek music. Even Father Kevin called in. Often he stayed over. Sharney's friends stayed over too, sleeping in a tent.

It was fun. Teresa loved it. When younger, she and Sharn would dress up in their mothers' old clothes, act real stupid, clown about, egged on by Fergus. Often it turned into chaos. Fergus was always the one to blame. Sharn said it was because he was a Communist. Communists turn all revelry into riot.

On one Saturday night Maddox and Declan went across the road, cut the fence wires on the vacant properties opposite, then everyone tore round in a circuit in their pick ups and cars. A sort of roller derby. Teresa went in with Fergus. Not the Mercedes, of course. It was madness. Fergus had put the men up to it. They had all been drinking since mid afternoon, strong liquor, mostly that cloudy ouzo Greek stuff which Spiro brought round. "Blame the Greeks for bearing gifts," Fergus said.

Lo and behold, Father Kevin was the eventual winner, cutting Fergus off, most unfairly, just before the finishing post.

Fergus was furious with him. He got out of his car, ran across, wrestled Kevin to the ground then made Colleen and Sharn go sit on him, yelling 'Repent, Repent,' Kevin hitting the ground repeatedly with his hand, showing submission. Teresa almost wet herself with laughter.

Fergus never seemed to care about much. He stopped at nothing. These nights, like a nightmare or fairytale, always seemed to turn out all right at the end. And Maddox and Declan, being fence builders, strained up the fence wires again the next day. All was well.

There'd been far worse Saturday nights than that. On one such night Caitlin could easily have died. Maddox, not waiting for an ambulance, rushed her off to Mercy Hospital, three carving knives flapping on her upper torso. The Police immediately arrested him at the hospital doors, Caitlin's place of work, no less. He was taken away. Teresa screamed at the Police that it wasn't her father's fault.

Caitlin had slipped on the tile kitchen floor from water leaking from the dishwasher when she'd opened its door. She promptly fell forward into the cutlery tray. That was the truth of it.

Fortunately, Caitlin was all right. She did not severe any arteries or tendons. She was just so-o embarrassed it being her place of work.

The Police, who also happened to be Catholics, reluctantly went round to Fergus for a fuller explanation. They knew what he was like. He'd just heard that Caitlin was quite o.k.

Fergus told the Police that he'd been throwing knives at her. Why? they asked. Because she's always talking on the damned telephone! Getting no sense from him, they asked if Father Kevin had been there, surely a more reliable witness.

Fergus, still half drunk at the time, said yes, that he was, but he'd not be of any help—Fergus had confessed his sin to him, had received his forgiveness, and now the secrecy of confession forbad Kevin ever to tell them the truth.

The Police walked away, bewildered.

But Colleen had said this evening that she needed some help. Sharn was working late at the salon. Teresa stayed on for dinner, not suspecting any reason to keep her out of the house, then helped washing up, put dishes away, then moved off home to bed.

She often ate over at Colleen's. Colleen was like her second mum. They loved having her there. Sharn was her big sister. They had fun together. She and Sharn would hit the sink for the dishes, have soap sud fights, sound off, hoot and holler, the radio blaring; they'd even form a conga line down the hallway, their heads covered in soap suds.

Colleen never bothered correcting them. It was often a fight for survival at their house, but no real dramas. Declan came into his own teasing everybody. Dominic just ate, then disappeared out to his back shed. Sharn was too much for him to handle. He gave her the annual Raspberry rather than an Academy Award for her histrionics.

*   *   *

Fergus had arrived home. Teresa found the others talking over coffee.

"Have a drink with us before bed, Tess." Fergus said casually. "I've put a bottle for you in the refrigerator."

She looked everywhere for it. Teresa would sometimes indifferently sip a glass of wine but much preferred the pineapple and cranberry juices Fergus brought back from factories on his way home. Then, there next to her drink compartment, she noticed a small bottle of dark blue ink. There, right beside it, was a shining new golden fountain pen. It looked really expensive.

She whooped with elation at the sight of it, ran from kitchen to dining room, then punched her uncle's leg. "You big tease! I love it!"

"You mustn't hit your uncle, Teresa!" Caitlin growled sternly. "Take your cat, go to bed. Go on." But Caitlin then grinned, raising her eyebrows as if to suggest another surprise awaited her upstairs.

"O dear, Ballou. In the doghouse again." Teresa scooped up her cat, took to the stairs to see what was in store. When she opened her bedroom door she stood back mouth agape: there was a small antique writing desk with beautifully curved wooden legs, a daintily wrought chair beside it. The desk had an inlaid porcelain inkwell, an open roll top of horizontal slats, a non slip green felt cover top on which was a bundle of expensively stiffened stationery, large pieces of blotting paper as well. There were pigeon holes to slot envelopes, sets of drawers, troughs for pens and pencils, a pull out tray extension for writing.

Teresa could not believe her luck. She ran her fingers along the smooth mahogany, the soft green felt, the cold porcelain fount. It must have cost someone a fortune. She grinned from ear to ear, remembering how she'd seen one similar to this in an antique shop not long ago, while out shopping with her father and Fergus.

"Isn't it nice," she'd said to her father. "What's it called?"

"A bureau," he replied. "They sometimes call them a lady's writing desk."

Fergus said nothing.

She dreamily placed the ink bottle down, deciding not to fill the fount, then sat gazing at the fine golden pen nib.

"You mustn't take the pen to school, dear," said Caitlin later on. "It's 14ct. gold."

Her mouth opened. "They're the best things anybody ever gave me."

*   *   *

Next morning, Teresa wrote three separate letters of thanks in her very best hand, blotting the paper, sealing each in envelopes, hand delivering them downstairs. When she'd turned seven, Fergus was home. He'd asked her what she wanted for her birthday. Teach me to write, she'd asked, just like he did in his frequent letters overseas back to Caitlin. Caitlin would read them aloud at the dining table. Teresa would take each page one at a time, touch the fine fountain pen ink. His handwriting was perfect, the letters so balanced and clear.

Fergus had spent three weeks teaching Teresa to write. So much for his good turn. She got in trouble at school for writing her homework. The teachers didn't want her getting beyond herself, showing the other kids up. Teresa went back to printing.

She wasn't too sure who'd bought the desk, yet suspected it was Fergus.

"Uncle," she said soon after, "I've to do a term assignment on a famous person. Don't know who to choose. Can you help?"

Her parents were glad that she'd asked. Mention of schoolwork always made Teresa clam up. Fergus grunted, moved away.

"I'll think about it. First, get me the question from your assignment journal. 'Famous' is a word which can get you into tricky territory. If you insist upon using F words round the house then you'd better find out what they mean. Go on, get going, get me the journal."

Teresa skipped up the stairs not questioning her uncle doubted her. When she returned Fergus had a large dictionary beside him. She opened her journal. The question read: 'Write about a famous person in history' It then detailed length, use of pictures, graphs, time-lines, footnotes, even the inclusion of a bibliography.

"I don't even know what these terms mean," Teresa said quietly.

"It's o.k. We'll look them up. I don't even know what 'famous' means. Do you?"

Fergus looked at her seriously, pointed to the dictionary.

"Yes you do." Teresa grinned.

"Look it up."

Teresa carefully turned the fine tissues of the heavy tome. Words did not daunt her. Fergus had helped her before, as had her mother. Fergus would give her lists of Greek and Latin prefixes to learn, short cuts to understand language. Teresa enjoyed it.

She knew the word was an adjective. He suggested she start with the noun.

"Fame," Teresa pointed a finger to underline, "it says 'that which people say, common talk.'"

"Exactly." Fergus said. "Make sure you define the term at the beginning. It has a Latin root meaning 'rumor.' The word's been pumped up to mean something greater than originally was. Famous doesn't mean good or bad, just what the common talk is. Bring your ink, pen and paper downstairs at lunchtime. I'll suggest someone to work on."

Her School Assignment

They always sat outside at the long barbeque table for Saturday lunch. Caitlin and Teresa often made themselves a light soufflé because there'd be so much food to eat Saturday evening.

Not today. There were three plates of Colleen's pasta there when Teresa sat up with her pen, paper, ink beside her. She glanced at Fergus' place setting. It looked so scruffy in comparison—an old enamel camping mug filled with black coffee, an out of shape metal plate, in it stale, broken bread, fit only for birds; an opened tin of stone-cold red pinto beans. A camping spoon was stuck inside. Maybe her mother was playing a joke on him.

He deserved it.

Teresa tied back her hair with a rubber band to keep it from her eyes. She suddenly got the notion that she might be in for a shock.

When everyone was seated, Fergus strolled out from the house smoking a fat Cuban cigar, wearing a jacket and trousers of olive green battle fatigues, a black beret, a tiny gilt star at front. He stood dramatically beside the table, opened out his arms and palms. He spoke through the side of his mouth, which billowed smoke.

"Famous! I'm the most famous man of all time," Fergus drawled in a thick accent, slowing with deliberate pauses.

Teresa stared. Who was this one star soldier? Just another of Fergus' exaggerations. He looked some kind of Action Man out of comics. He stood so proud, puffing before speaking again.

"I never liked having my picture taken. I once made a living as a photographer in Mexico. One day a man came and asked me if he could take my photo. Yes, I said, but first you must cut sugar cane for a whole week. His name was Korda. He did. The photo he took became as famous as The Mona Lisa's a painting. And more sad. Posters of me hang from Tierra del Fuego to Cuba, Boston to Beijing, Vietnam to Paris to Prague. My face's plastered round the world—on posters, silk screens, by tattoo, even on watch faces. Young girls in Brazil even wear my picture on each cup of their bikini tops, and down the other place, front and back."

Fergus leaned across as if to punctuate his point.

Caitlin and Maddox carried on eating as though this was nothing unusual. His hand then came up, placing a book on the table from his chair. The man's face stared at Teresa. He looked like Fergus. More than just a faint resemblance. Fergus had imitated him with great skill.

"I can't spell the names of all those places, Uncle." Teresa said, frustrated, furiously trying to jot them. She looked to the face on the book. She'd only ever seen comic characters on bikinis. What had this man ever done to deserve it!

"Don't worry, Comrade," Fergus paused. "I've got books downstairs for you to work from."

Fergus spoke with such firm assurance. He swiveled left to right to show his profile, then sat placing his now extinguished cigar on the side of the bread plate. He would never do that, ordinarily. Teresa was quite shocked.

Suddenly he began to wheeze. Teresa put down her pen, picked up her knife and fork. Her eyes boggled. This was Uncle at his most fierce. He looked truly frightening dressed up as a soldier.

"Forgive my breathing, *por favor.* Asthma, Comrade Teresa. I was pronounced militarily unfit as a young man because of it. But I'm a doctor now. My name? Ernesto Guevara de la Serna. Born? Rosario, Argentina, 14 June, 1928. Died? Shot by soldiers, Bolivia, October, 1967. My father? Irish descent. Mother? Spanish. Free thinkers. I was born to be brave at sports and games. I am known to the world as 'El Che.'"

His sentence ended with a long hissing 'a.' It seemed to never end. Fergus purposely waited a few moments then pulled two volumes of poetry from his jacket pocket placing them on the table.

"I read poetry. The Frenchman, Charles Baudelaire, Spaniard, Pablo Neruda. Don't be deceived by my fancy books, Comrade. I've the soul of a fearless man."

His lips spread tightly. Fergus hanged his head muttering words in Spanish, then sat up pointing to the food.

"I've always been weighed down by hunger, weapons, misery of the world. I've sat on the sacrificial stone of Macchu Pichu, built rafts with lepers in jungles, led the triumphal march with Fidel Castro beside me into Santiago de Cuba. Nothing lasts. I've spent most of my life not scared but making myself scarce. I'm a phantom. I shall be free one day, or a martyr. I speak only of victory. Taking initiative. I like to have cheerful people with good humor round me. Like telling funny stories. I like long, serious talk. Life can be a cabaret of dance, if you allow it to be, without any evil. I'm a Doctor. Killer. Economist . . . Communist."

He leered at her before suddenly snapping out of his pose to normality again. "Have your lunch, Tess. We'll finish this afterwards."

Teresa had placed her knife and fork down to scribble.

Fergus drank his coffee down in a fierce gulp. It must have been stone cold. Caitlin picked up the coffee pot to refill it Fergus stopped her with a motion of his hand. He waved it up and down like a cow bell.

"No! We don't serve one another here. We serve ourselves." Fergus wheezed dramatically, then reached to his mouth for effect with a mock vital inhaler.

Teresa looked to the words she'd just written. "But Uncle, doctors are supposed to save people. Not kill them. Be without evil."

"Clever you picked that up so quickly. It's a point you must state in your assignment. Look up the word 'contradiction.' Here was a doctor of medicine who used to say to his soldiers "Aim well, you are about to kill a man." Che believed man should go straight to the source. What caused the disease. He wanted to remove human sickness. History's never made by cowards, Tess. We must all learn to function under fire."

Fergus continued silently on in his role. He broke dry bread, dipped it in his coffee, which he'd refilled himself, then ate the cold pinto beans with the spoon from the tin.

Teresa offered him some of her pasta. He motioned no. Teresa got the notion that he'd probably eaten this way many times before.

Caitlin and Maddox didn't speak.

They'd not heard this one from him before. Often he'd put on an act, just for the sake of it. They also knew that he was not really looking for converts to communism when he cunningly resumed.

"Schooling was important for Che. When his soldiers rested on their route march to Havana he made them sit, do their homework. Mathematics. The few who could read taught the others to read." Fergus looked at Teresa, raising his eyebrows.

"Why?" Teresa looked at him with disbelief.

"Why? Why not? We must all learn to read and write so as not to be deceived."

"Fight, as well?" Teresa asked seriously.

"Fight as well. But. That said, he was known to call his soldiers under him to attention, let those, who wanted, to leave their weapon on the ground, abandon them if they were not prepared to die for the cause, but they were never to be seen by him again. He gave them a choice. To fight, or not to fight."

He said no more.

Everyone ate silently.

For the first time, Fergus purposely let his manners slip by fingering the dry bread round the rim of the tin.

He took Teresa downstairs to his library that afternoon for books on Che.

There were a few of them on his many shelves. On the way he told her that he'd once been to Che's house in Cordoba where Guevara was raised, how that city is the second largest in Argentina. Called The City of Bells, it is filled with churches. The Jesuits were very strong there. Fergus said Che could not go to school because of his asthma. His family moved there for a drier climate. Fergus pointed to a map of Argentina on his wall.

What he did not tell her, and had often argued with Father Kevin, her Christian Instruction teacher at school, was that Cordoba was a city of many religious intrigues, that the Jesuits had gained much power there over the centuries, giving bribes to the nobility. Many Jesuits were kicked out. The Jesuits aligned themselves with the landowners, who in turn aligned themselves to those in power.

Fergus and Kevin had been close friends since boys. They often argued like Kilkenny cats together, especially some Saturday nights when he came to the house, but they were never angry arguments, just pitting their wits against one another, more for the exercise of it.

Teresa liked Father Kevin, perhaps because he was her uncle's friend. Teresa was not good at her other schoolwork, yet at this subject she'd topped the class each year.

"You are just having a go at the Jesuits again," Father Kevin would say.

"Too darn right I am," Fergus would reply.

Fergus bought Teresa a poster of Che that following week. The Poster itself. The most reproduced photo in history. The one which had gained him superstar status. He showed Teresa the smaller original; how they'd cropped the palm trees away to make a single image. He told her what the poster didn't show—that Che was weeping for his dead comrades at the time.

"Did Che and this Castro man ever tell fibs, like you do, Uncle?" Teresa asked. It was asked as a serious question.

"It was Castro's intention never to tell lies, not to be like other politicians."

"Did he?"

"After a time he built concentration camps for counter-revolutionaries against his government. For homosexuals, too. And for others."

"That's not freedom. That's not fair."

"No, Tess. It isn't. Che had moved on by then."

"So? So? What do I write, then?"

"Write it just as you see it. Don't you tell any fibs. Tell it with a cold eye."

Teresa took the books up to her room, wrestled with the difficulties, concentrated for the very first time with her new golden pen at her new desk, asked her Ma and Pa questions that she did not quite understand, even rang Fergus at work during the week. She wrote out a rough draft with her pen then typed it in on the family PC as a final copy.

Fergus didn't spare her. He explained such things as petroleum jelly of napalm, what it did to people, what dum-dum bullets were, shrapnel, the feudalism practiced in the 1950s, even directing her to grim pictures of living conditions of the time. But he also insisted that it was not to be a sad tale of a man furious with the world.

Fergus pointed to Che as both an adventurer and man of curiosity. His vocation was that of a drifter, continually moving on, not putting down roots.

Teresa wrote three times the length required, ending with large capitalized words "GUEVARA IS DEAD . . . LONG LIVE GUEVARA."

Her assignment had an index, pictures from the photocopier, a glossary of terms, a short bibliography, all in perfect alphabetical order. She even handed it in before time.

Fergus purposely didn't ask to check it. Caitlin did. Teresa wanted it word perfect. Sister Susan corrected everything in red ink, circling mistakes, exclamation marks for a lack of sense. Teresa hated that.

In the Doghouse Again

Teresa never expected to get any gold star, like that on Che's beret, to stick on the refrigerator, but she received a fail mark, 49 out of 100. Teresa was clearly disappointed. It read like a mark on a lavatory wall. She had once overheard her mother confide to Fergus that the marking of Teresa's assignments didn't always seem quite right. Fergus said nothing.

Sister Susan's comments on it were scathing.

Teresa read them to Fergus when he came home that following weekend.

"A poor choice of fame. And far too long. Too much praise for a man you obviously see as a kind of Christ. I did not ask for a folk hero. He was not a religious man. He was a Communist who believed hope can be found on earth without God's grace. Communists kill priests. And nuns. He did not believe in one woman, one family. But your work is very well written."

Teresa looked to Fergus. "O dear. In the doghouse again."

But Fergus clapped, and fiercely. No mocking slow-clap.

"Well done, Tess. It's all that you need. That your work's well written. The rest doesn't matter that much. Beliefs are always going to be questioned. Those last words read to me like a blast on a golden horn."

"But is Sister Susan right? What she says? Wrong to see him as a Christ?"

"I don't know. He too died surrounded by his enemies. So man could recover some hope in this life, not in the next. He was more interested in building schools, ovens for the poor to bake bread. Is that so wrong? He wanted poor people industrialized, educated, not praying in holes in the ground, living with their pigs in a sty while the rich exploited them. I think Che even wanted them to kick him out as well, along with all the Spaniards, let indigenous people have their lives back. You must decide these things for yourself. He didn't care too much about dying. He always put himself in great danger. They say Castro kept giving him more bodyguards to protect himself. The point is, it was his belief in courage that we should respect."

"You won't talk about this with Father Kevin, will you?"

"No, Tess. We argued these things over, years ago. He's my friend. We've been friends since boys. You like him. You must listen to him. He's ok. You do well in his Christian Instruction. Keep it up. You must know the arguments before you can counter them. We need him, now and again, for some divine intervention. Meantime, just concentrate on writing well."

Teresa seemed less dejected.

She smiled. "One boy in our class got 82 out of 100. He wrote on Andre The Giant. He likes wrestling. Sister Susan likes him, too. But I don't care. I'd rather stick with Che. Any day."

"Let me give you those army fatigues and beret. Let the hat remind you of the Crown of Thorns, if you like. I'll get Colleen to shorten them, have them taken in. You can be our soldier up the tree. Che put the gilt star on it when they made him a Major. Poke out your tongue at Declan whenever he teases you over the fence. Point up to your beret. You're our Major now. Everyone calls him DS. He's only the Drill Sergeant."

Teresa giggled. "I'd like that."

She paused to reflect. "Sister Susan asked me why I didn't choose a famous woman."

"Fair question. I thought of that, too. I was going to suggest Eva Peron. You liked the musical 'Evita.' Maybe Sister Susan would've liked her more."

"Why?"

Fergus smirked. "Because she died at thirty three, the same age as Christ, although the Vatican resisted all calls for her canonization. Lots of people in Argentina wanted her made a saint."

"How did she die?"

"Cancer."

"I remember the movie, but what made her so famous?"

"Because of her, women got the vote, a public health service was developed in Argentina. But I resisted it. Her life was a little too outrageous. She had sexual affaires when young, and she failed. As did

Che. If Sister Susan just sees famous as having more wins than losses then we'd all better stick with Andre The Giant, hadn't we?"

"I should have chosen Nancy, from Sid Vicious and Nancy." Teresa grinned.

"Yes. Stay with music and song. Little else beats them." Fergus said.

"It's all rather pukey-pukey, isn't it? School. Just different kinds of cheese." Teresa reflected. "Sometimes I get so frustrated I could strangle my teachers, especially the nuns," she said calmly while looking to Fergus for a reasoned response.

He leaned across, gently clutched at her hand. "Just make sure that you do it with a pair of rosary beads."

"Uncle, you're no help. I'd get better marks at a secular school."

Fergus said no more, stood calmly before moving away.

Unexpected Call

After sunset, on a very warm Wednesday evening, a lateral bower broke from the fig tree stretching out over next door's shed. Teresa fell thudding onto the tin roof. It just had to happen, sooner or later. Teresa was like the last straw breaking the camel's back, her extra weight finally too much. The bough had been starved of water for so long.

Oh, no, Teresa muttered as she fell with the tree-house planks down beside her. It had seemed safe. It wasn't. Something had to give.

Dominic was inside at the time, listening to music. Fergus had made him up a tape, mostly female country music artists. Teresa had gone out too far along the limb, craning to hear the voices. She'd heard Dominic playing it in there once before, only caught occasional words, particularly that of 'faces.' 'I would walk all the way from/Boulder to Birmingham/If I thought I could see, I could see your face.' Then, one track later, 'Just a face in a crowd/On a bus from St. Cloud.'

'Good ones, Uncle, killer tunes,' Teresa thought. Fergus always brought them music from the city. But, here between Emmy Lou Harris and Trisha Yearwood tracks, down came Teresa, tree house and all.

Too preoccupied to care, Dominic hadn't noticed the changing sky that evening. Summer rains would build up out at sea, move around from the south, then in, hitting the district hard. At first he thought it was a lightning bolt that had either hit a bower or struck the roof. He jumped up, ran outside.

There was Teresa sitting shame-faced on her backside, rubbing her ankle on the corrugated iron roof. He'd forgotten that Teresa was up in her fig tree in all weathers.

"So it's you, Bo Peep. 'Angel Flying Too Close To The Ground.' You o.k.?" That Willy Nelson song was also on the tape. Dominic put a hand up, scratching his head.

"It's me." Teresa sighed despairingly. The tree house was now no more than a broken heap of planks wedged under the bower. "I'm o.k."

"I'll go get you a ladder."

While he went back inside, Teresa immediately stood awkwardly on the roof pitch then jumped off to the ground. She was embarrassed. Caught, eaves-dropping. She'd wanted to jump from roof over fence back into her own yard, then thought better of it. She'd hit her head. She put her hand up feeling for blood.

Teresa had been shopping with her mother, not changed since coming home before taking to her tree. She was wearing a short skirt, a kind of pleated cheerleader number, which she only bought for its greens to camouflage herself up the tree. She didn't want him to see her up there. Nor beneath her either, holding a ladder.

"Humpty Dumpty altogether again? Thought I'd been hit by a meteorite." Dominic stood idly by holding a stepladder.

Teresa never knew quite how to take him. He wasn't the kind of boy to say 'love your earrings' 'cool skirt.' Sharn was all cuddly and lovable. She'd have got up ON the roof, had she been there, lay down with her waiting for the stars to appear. It was only a tree house. Go build yourself another one.

Dominic, two years older than Teresa, had always been private and aloof. A tough kid, he'd always treated Teresa remotely like some kind of weird, freakish Jane living up a tree(even Fergus would call Teresa down for dinner at weekends with a Tarzan yell from the front porch). They seldom spoke to one another. He followed her home each day, as asked to do. He was, to her, just part of the wake of Hope Street's disappointment.

"Want come inside?" he asked, indifferent to her diffidence, as though saying 'you may as well now that you're here.' He was taller than she, his chest flat and wide, upper arms strong from exercise and weight training. Sharn had always teased his straightness. He was a boxer. Teresa hated boxing. She usually found some excuse not to go to see his fights. The sets of parents always watched him box, as did Fergus, if at home. Dominic had now won ten bouts with no defeats. Declan recognized his son's potential. Fergus sometimes offered the boy advice yet always recoiled from suggesting that he make a future of it.

Teresa sidled in, leaned up against the corrugated iron wall beside the door. There were no insulating walls or floor coverings. It seemed, to Teresa, as basic as her tree huts. It was essentially a tool-shed. She moved across, perched herself cautiously on a sawhorse. She'd never really been in there before, except to stand at the door, call her father away to the telephone, and always treated it as Dominic's inner sanctum.

That was the way he liked it. He'd stay in his hut. She up in hers. Even if sometimes she moved across listened to his music in the tree.

"Come into my parlor, said the spider to the fly," Dominic mocked as he walked inside, his back to her, waiting for her to follow.

'Big tool!' Teresa thought, while gazing about at hammers on the wall. 'That's the third nursery rhyme in less than a minute. What's he take me for? A child? What's he think I'll do? Huff, puff, blow his shed down?'

Dominic was used to putting up with her miserable face. Like something the cat brought in.

There were long rows of wooden mallets, chisels, hammers, screw drivers, saws, all in their proper place on hooks or between nails on a makeshift ply wall against the iron. Teresa stared about, as though looking for the bed, frightened that some tool might try effecting a breach. She unconsciously clutched her St. Christopher medal round her neck, as though that would ward off evil, or vampires in the ceiling.

There was no ceiling. Just sheets of iron. She sat solemnly perched on the sawhorse.

'For goodness sake,' Dominic thought, sensing her fear as he sat. 'Damned girl next door! About as unimaginative as our parents. The thought of 'availability' was the last thing on his mind. The shy kid who always refused to sit on Santa's knee.'

He felt like cranking the music as loud as it'd go.

"You want to be a professional boxer one day?" Teresa didn't know what else to say. Her short pleated skirt was covered in yellow sticky pollen. She wanted to dust it off on the floor yet wasn't prepared to in front of him. Boys, she thought. All the same. Baseball capped. Sport shoes. Tracksuits. My team's better than yours. Animation comics. Fart jokes. Looking at girl's boobs . . . their short green skirts! Checking them out. How wrong she was. Dominic just followed her home each day, slow as a funeral, with a job to do. He did it, without complaint.

Dominic barely looked up at her.

"Don't think so. Don't know how good I am." He obviously didn't want to talk about it.

"What you reading at school?" He tried, in his own earnest way, to make conversation. To him, Teresa usually looked pissed off, as though called in for jury duty, or having just been asked to clean the place. He knew that it smelled like a sweatshop. He didn't really care.

"Usual shite. Communist stuff, at the moment. Orwell's 'Animal Farm.'"

"I thought you'd like books about talking animals."

"No. I didn't like The Hobbit, Watership Down, either."

"You don't like much, do you."

"Yes I do. I like Uncle's stuff."

"But that would have to be Communist, too. Wouldn't it?" He smirked.

"No it's not."

"Sharn said you two read 'Lolita.' You like reading dirty books?"

"It's not a dirty book." Teresa looked at him indignantly.

"Just kidding. I like Fergus' music. He's always sending me some over."

There had never been any animosity between them. Only distance. If Teresa asked him on the way home up Edward: 'What was that music you were playing last night?' Dominic would say 'Can't remember. It's still in the cassette. I'll leave it on the gatepost for you.'

If she asked, then she could have it. He shared, shared alike. He just didn't like his sister giving away his favorite boxing vests to Teresa, that's all. (Sharn, two years older than Dominic, was totally sick of seeing him in boxing gear). And, after all, the music was Fergus' in the first place. Fergus shared everything. Having no family of his own, it was as if he'd adopted these two. They'd adopted him, as well.

She'd answered him vaguely while looking blankly round—the punch bag in the corner, weights on a mat beside a speed ball, barbells on the ground. Three sets of boxing gloves. Boxing posters. The place stank of liniment, sweaty shoes, stale beer. There was a rancidness about the room. It smelt like a swamp. The single light gave off a swampy glow.

'Just another dirty boy's room. Trees give off far fresher scents,' Teresa thought primly as she sat, wondering why she was even in there at all.

The room was stifling hot. There was an upright fan in the corner, turned off. Dominic must have needed all the electricity for his stereo. The room seemed to cook like a micro-wave. Fetid smells overwhelmed her. Sometimes Teresa could smell wood being cut by the electric saw here. Maddox and Declan would cut concreting stakes, rails for footings. Dominic always covered his stereo from the flying chips.

"I've just read John Steinbeck's 'The Pearl.' Short story by James Thurber called 'The Secret Life of Walter Mitty.' Want to read them? You remind me a bit of Mitty." Dominic said bluntly.

Teresa stared, wondering if he was being sarcastic. She wasn't taking the chance. "I'll read the Steinbeck."

When Dominic got up to fetch it, Teresa moved across, slipped her shoes off, dusted the pollens off her skirt and legs then began relaxing on his sofa, making it known to him that she didn't care.

'Yeah, make yourself right at home,' Dominic thought as he handed her the book. She was still wearing her school blouse. As he stooped to hand her the novel he noticed that it was now way too small for her, almost bursting at the buttons.

"Thanks." She ignored him, immediately turning to the opening chapter. Dominic said nothing.

"You feel o.k.?" He asked, wondering if she'd hurt herself in fact.

"I'm o.k."

There was a small desk and a chair in one corner, stacks of school books beside them on the floor. He liked school. He saw it as a sure way of getting out of Crone. No way was he ever going to hang round here. It was a dump.

He sat back down to his music. Teresa noticed a singled out pile of CDs belonging to Fergus. She wondered why Fergus took such an interest in Dominic, other than his boxing, yet she didn't feel the least jealous by having to share. Such feelings never entered their heads. God only knew how much money Fergus gave to Sharn. Sharn was a brat. An upfront brat. But funny as a fight. Even Caitlin told Fergus not to give her so much.

Life was not like that with her lot. Whatever the equation was, jealousy did not enter it. She loved Dominic's parents. She always called Declan 'Daddy-O,' as Sharn did. Declan came over to their house most Mondays and Thursdays nights to watch 'Home Improvements' with Maddox. Teresa always made them piles of pancakes before she went to bed. She liked Declan. He teased her, but she knew that he wouldn't hurt a fly. He liked her, too. She never answered back the way Sharn would. But Sharn was Sharn. No hope of ever changing her now.

It was just that . . . well, boys were such dickheads. And slobs. Untidy. No wonder Sharn bossed Dominic about.

But Dominic was a cautiously untidy and deliberate slob, not that easy to figure. At least he was better than those apes up on Hope. He had to have some discipline in order to be such a good boxer, and had received many certificates for high achievement at school. They were nowhere to be seen.

Teresa closed the pages of the book, looked at him as though wondering what made him tick. What sweaty brute force made him so different? Dominic began snickering.

"Listen to this one." He pressed different buttons on the remote. Came the sound of a disc falling, selecting of a track.

"Fergus reckons this is his favorite opening line of any song."

Teresa listened intently. She recognized it. Fergus had played it before at her house, yet she hadn't bothered listening carefully to the words. He'd never shared this thought with her.

It was Joan Armatrading's 'Love and Affection.' "I'm not in love but I'm open to persuasion . . ."

"That's Fergus." Dominic mused, "nice line, though."

"Story of his life," Teresa grinned. "You'd never know with him."

It was a shared moment that they'd never had before. Neither had much to say to one another before this. The neighborly gulf suddenly seemed to close, if only momentarily. Dominic said nothing more as he read the CD cover, then the inside printed history of the artist. When he looked up, he saw Teresa had fallen asleep.

"Shit!" he muttered. He always thought of her as a bit mad spending all her time up in the tree. The tree was almost a hundred foot tall. He remembered how Caitlin always said that she'd fall out someday.

'O, no,' he thought, jumping up from his chair. He didn't know much about girls. He knew his sister sometimes got dizzy spells, got real moody, spent lots of time in the bathroom. He feared that Teresa was concussed. His thoughts were of Fergus in that bar that night while his parents and little sister Teresa were out dying on the side of a road. He didn't know what to do. Shake her? Slap her, like his Pa did to Fergus to stop him from sleeping from concussion after winning his national title?

He didn't want to get too near. Her skirt was raveled up on her thighs. The top button on her school blouse was undone. It must have popped as she stretched to lay down. He couldn't see any cleavage. He didn't particularly look. That didn't annoy him. What did was that she was wearing underneath his favorite old boxing vest, which Sharn had given her. Without his permission. He'd never forgiven his sister for that. He wanted to check her pulse, yet didn't want to clutch her wrist or touch her neck.

He ran cross the yard to Caitlin's, rapping on the front door.

"You better come. It's Teresa," he said with grave concern. He didn't want to give her up as having fallen out of the tree.

"Think she might've hurt her head." He often clipped his sentences of 'I.'

Maddox run down the steps expecting the worse only to find Teresa sound asleep on the sofa. Her face was between the book's pages.

"Teresa. Wake up." Maddox shook her shoulders. Teresa opened her eyes, startled and disoriented.

"Sorry, Dom," she whispered as her father helped her up to her feet. She clutched the open pages. Maddox thanked Dominic, knowing he'd no idea how to handle her. It amazed Maddox to think that Teresa would even venture over to the shed.

The boy stood sternly. Dominic followed them out, opened the adjoining gate for them, hoping Maddox wouldn't see the bower on the shed roof.

Next morning, Dominic slithered the bower off from the end of a rope. After school, he rip-sawed it up for firewood, stacked it for the barbeques, pulled nails from the planks of what had been a tree house, took boards back to Maddox's piles.

Teresa watched, hiding up in the fig tree.

Dominic told nobody anything. He wasn't a snitch. He minded his own business. She watched, then went back to reading the Steinbeck on her lap. It didn't take her that long to finish.

Next day, Teresa placed the novel beside his shed door, with a note. "A boy's book. But very well-written."

Dominic grunted when he saw it.

'She'd have been better off reading the Mitty,' he thought.

A few nights before, he'd turned the pages of old School Yearbooks in his shed. There was Teresa's sad face in each of them, so un-cool, about as lifeless as an old fashioned kid wearing a bonnet, and looking like the one least likely to succeed. She looked like her brain had taken the year off, yet he knew that she wasn't stupid. Different, that's all. He'd always thought of her face as partly hidden behind curtains of green up in the leaves, now scribbling away with her new golden pen.

He placed the novel back on a shelf, then sang along with the Emmy Lou Harris song again

'I would walk all the way, from Boulder to Birmingham . . . if I could see your face.'

The Parable of the Bottle

The following Friday night, Dominic was surprised to see a visitor this late at his shed. He stretched from his chair, turned his music low with the remote when Fergus appeared at his door. He'd always insisted that Dominic not call him mister but by his first name. Fergus immediately feigned the slight stagger of a drunk with a brown paper bag of booze in his hand, grinned at the boy, sat down, making himself at home. Fergus looked a well dressed drunk, winding down on Friday night.

Dominic knew that Fergus was sober. He'd only been home a short while, never drank and drove. He wondered what Fergus was up to, why over here.

Everyone drifted in and out of one another's houses, never knocking, especially Sharn, who ashamedly walked in, took things from Caitlin's refrigerator without ever asking. Sharn used to hit Fergus up for money, Fergus giving freely. Why not ask from the local Communist.

Some years before, Teresa had gone over and asked Sharn what exactly a Communist was. Teresa had heard the word used of Fergus. She knew that Sharn would know.

"They smash up people's cars, don't pay for their drinks, don't dress nice or use deodorant, don't ever get married or go to church." Sharn gave her the lowdown, the whole enchilada.

"Uncle pays for his drinks, dresses nicely, goes to church with us on Sundays." Teresa was not quite convinced. She couldn't remember, because so long ago, whether he'd smashed into Father Kevin that night when racing across the street.

"That's only because he wants to talk to Kevin. They have a smoke and coffee together after Mass in the church hall; Fergus sloshes his whiskey flask in Kevin's cup; Fergus always says 'Let us give one another the sign of peace.' I think Kevin's a Communist, too. They're always giving each other secret signs, like them Masons do. They're a bunch of Communists, as well."

But Dominic always knocked even though he didn't resent Fergus' intrusion this evening.

The shed was Dominic's getaway. He liked it out there, a trick to quiet away from his rowdy sister, who dominated the house. And had answers to everything.

"Had dinner, Dom?"

"Yes." The boy sat up straight in his chair.

"You want to try some after dinner liqueur? It's pretty strong stuff. A thimbleful won't hurt you. I'm not stoo-pid." Fergus emphasized the final word with a roll of the lips, then added as an afterthought, "Kev and I drink it all the time."

Dominic looked at him in a perplexed way, as if drinking with priests made it right. But he'd also picked up something else. Everyone called him 'Stoo-pid' at school. He knew that Teresa must have told this to Fergus.

"Why do they call you stoo-pid?" Teresa had asked him only that week.

"Don't worry about it. Names don't hurt."

Fergus raised his hand, two shot glasses slotted between his fingers. Fergus had particularly large hands which made huge fists. He unscrewed the cap of the bottle within the brown bag, tipped it, filling the shots. "Like a couple of old drunks in the park, aren't we!" Fergus said, then saluted the boy through the disguised bag.

"Smell it. Twenty seven different plants and spices. Trade secret recipe. Like that fried chicken stuff you boys eat. Taste it. Eighty per cent proof. Forty per cent alcohol. I'll tell your father. He won't mind. Little booze never hurt anyone."

Dominic stretched across in his shorts and boxing vest, his standard clothes at home. Sharn always said they were only suitable for a shed. He took the glass wondering why Fergus was there. He, drinking forty per cent proof alcohol with the aging boozer from next door.

He knew that Fergus moved in mysterious ways. And why he was there. Teresa.

Dominic still admired the man's determination and unflinching generosity yet was never sure where they might lead. To Dominic, Fergus was a strange man. He gave not what he had left over but all that he had. He'd worked hard for things, then gave them away on the flimsiest of pretexts.

Fergus and Kevin had recently made the local council remove the homeless from a nearby culvert where two men had been drowned during sudden rains. They'd had it cordoned off with metal mesh, then Fergus insisted that the homeless be re-housed. Fergus held sway in the community. He'd sometimes drink with the homeless in parks. He gave them cigars. Money. Books. Booze. He was a soft touch yet also this same man, according to Maddox and Declan, could strike, hit with the power of four, dislocate a boxer's shoulder in the ring with a single punch. His determination was like that of a disembodied will.

Dominic had been listening to his father's music. Declan liked country music, and played country guitar competently. Declan was not the sentimental type. The music he admired usually had a hard edge to it, a raw simplicity, deep poeticism. Dominic liked it. Fergus brought Declan CDs back from the city.

There was an old TV against the wall, CDs on a shelf above, stacks of videos of old boxing footage. On one wall, between racks of tools, a poster of Muhammad Ali, on another, Sugar Ray Robinson Sharn dismissed the shed as 'boy's zone,' Dominic's 'holy of holies.'

Sometimes on Sunday afternoons Dominic and the three men would watch old boxing films out there. His father always said that Fergus was an astute practitioner, one of the best, and a good commentator on the sport.

But it wasn't boxing but booze Fergus had in mind this evening. So it seemed. The boy sat up respectfully. He was his father's son—straight, blunt, cold blue eyes, unsmiling. His chest was flat, shoulders broad, strong upper legs—ideal shape of a boxer. Long arms. Those low levers necessary to fight.

Fergus gazed about fixing his eyes on the posters. "You ever heard of Ray Charles, Dom? The singer? Frank Sinatra once called him the only true musical genius of our time." Fergus gazed idly, awaiting an answer.

"Yes. Pa's got some of his albums. Somewhere. I've heard him play them."

Fergus clutched his booze bag while casually stretching his legs, looking beyond Dominic to the posters beyond.

Fergus reflected. "His surname was Smith. Simple as that. He changed his Christian and surname to Ray Charles Robinson. A big mistake. He then knew if he was to have any success in music it would be too confusing to keep up with a name like Sugar Ray Robinson, the boxer. He dropped the surname altogether, became known simply as

Ray Charles. Ali admired Sugar Ray Robinson. Rated Robinson higher than any other. Ended up as a dancer in Paris. Great on his feet. Went back to America to fight again when he shouldn't have. Owed taxes. Got beaten. Stayed on in the game too long, as lots do."

There was a short silence. Fergus sipped his drink. "Lots to be said for a name, Dom."

"You're here about Teresa, aren't you?" He asked bluntly.

Dominic never knew quite how to take Fergus. Best get to the point. Like father and sister he wasn't one to hedge, beat round the proverbial bush, yet he didn't want to be rude. Just given to brevity.

"No. But she told us that you're called Stupid at school." Fergus shrugged his shoulders dismissively, fell silent again.

It got no reaction. Dominic didn't seem to care much.

"I've got a friend at school. His name's Karl. He started it as a joke. He's Dutch. Says Dominic means 'stupid' in his language. Not real stupid, more like playing stupid, like playing possum. Name sort of stuck. Karl felt real bad about it."

"That so?" Fergus felt better about that, then edged the bottle up from the paper bag. He stopped when it revealed the word Benedictine, followed by the capitalized letters D.O.M.

"Named after you, isn't it!" Fergus grinned. "You like the taste? It's made by Benedictine monks."

"Warms the throat. O.k., I guess. Ma told me Teresa once wrote in her school essay that you were a Dominican monk who made liqueurs down a cellar. I guess they told you about that one."

"Of course. Made me feel mighty proud having another liar in the family. Even Kev had a laugh. Probably not too far from the truth. I've drank out of many illicit whiskey stills in my time." Fergus grinned at the boy.

Dominic didn't respond in knowing Fergus had something more important to say.

"See these three letters on the label here. D.O.M. People mistake them for 'Dominican Order of Monks.' They're not. Nothing to do with Dominicans. They're Latin. Stand for 'Deo Optimo Maximo.' 'For our best, greatest God.' Something like that. 'For our best health.' 'Doing our best.' That's what it's all about, isn't it!"

Fergus looked seriously at the boy as they toasted the rich liqueur again.

"Sure beats the hell out of the Dutch meaning of 'stupid.' Stick with the Latin, son. They tell me you're very good at your schoolwork. I know you're a good boxer."

Dominic was not that easily flattered. Somehow Fergus reminded of Teresa. They brooded a lot. The whole world seemed to be resting on their shoulders. They both wanted to belt it, tear it apart, bring it into submission. They even looked like one another.

Then there was that taboo subject that no one talked about. That Fergus felt guilty for his little sister's death. Responsible somehow. Her name was Teresa. He wasn't ever going to let anything bad happen to this other one. Dominic knew that, or surmised it. He'd picked up on these vibes, years ago.

"I can take cheek in the street, Fergus. Thanks for your words, anyway."

Fergus got up, collected himself, bottle and glasses, moved to the door.

"You're a good boy, Dom. I'll leave you to your music." Dominic sat stiffly, watching him exit with serious eyes. At the door, Fergus turned.

"You know why boxers first started wearing padded gloves, Dom? Eight, ten, fifteen ounce, even heavier for amateurs? Mostly eight for professionals. They use ten ounce in California." Fergus quizzed.

"Sure. Protect their hands." Dominic said quickly.

"Right. You ever see any of those bare knuckle fighters in old films, beating one another up, all that blood and gore? They wouldn't stand for that kind of fighting today. Except cage fighting. That's mostly wrestling, anyway."

"Sure. Charles Bronson in 'The Street Fighter.' I liked that movie."

"So did I. But it wasn't really like that in truth." Fergus paused.

Dominic didn't doubt him. He also knew Fergus came at opponents from all angles. Dominic wondered exactly what his angle was here.

"The jaw's probably the strongest bone in the body. Cheek bones, almost as hard. Hit them bare-knuckled and you can easily break your hand. Bare knuckled fighters made lots of body punches as a result. Don't believe all you see in movies. Hands are far too important. You need them to write, feed, fight." Fergus paused for Dominic to take it in. "Nobody was ever killed fisting bare knuckled. Only when gloves were introduced did deaths occur."

"Is that right? Didn't know that."

"So. What do you do, son? Two, three boys attack you in the street on the way home from school. Let them. Be patient. Don't wail in. You might break a few teeth, bloody a couple of noses, if you're lucky. Too risky. You dance. Like Sugar Ray did. But the dance isn't an Excuse Me. It's as serious as a Tango. First, you throw sand in their eyes. Second, while they're covering up, bending over because they can't see, you have them expose their flanks. You then aim for the kidneys, liver, solar plexus—they'll go down like a sack off a wagon. Watch out for head butts. Better to punch in the throat. Not the head. All for the sake of the hands. The Marquis of Queensbury rules don't apply out on the street. And when they do go down, kick them with a hard shoe so they don't get up. This isn't pistols at twenty paces, Dom. It's not about honor. You and Teresa have got to survive out there. Cunning's how you survive."

Fergus stared at the boy with serious intent.

"Pa says he won't tolerate me fighting outside the ring. What am I to do? Teresa's a sister to me. But they're not going to make her life miserable. Did you use your fists in South America? They're pretty macho down there. Use knives. All kinds of things."

Fergus put bottle and glasses back down on a table near the door, went back to sit down. He was astounded at the boy's maturity. It was a question to be answered. Answered as only Fergus knew how.

"Your Pa's right. You don't need to prove yourself. It's a brave man who turns on his heel, walks away. But I'll answer you. I worked in a place once. It doesn't really matter much where. Lots of handguns, shotguns on the streets. Bodyguards for the wealthy wore full belts of cartridges crossing their chests. Guards outside banks held shotguns, automatic rifles. Real tough place. My first ten minutes and last of the day were spent shaking hands with all my co-workers, asking about their children, mothers, fathers. Never about their wives, unless you knew them personally. Politeness was everything to these people. You made every effort not to offend. Insults could have real bad results. Yes, boys teased the girls in bars, tried to seduce them while out walking the promenades, but a sense of honor meant they'd never dare touch them without their consent."

Fergus paused, shuffling his feet on the concrete floor. He reflected.

"I was in a bar one night out in the countryside. They call them bodegas, full of low life. It was in Paraguay. I was drinking at a table with others, amongst them the local Chief of Police. He was in uniform. Wearing a handgun. It was a pretty wild place, more bad people than good. Bit like here. Anyway. This big German tourist came in the bar. Real rugged looking guy, carrying a heavy backpack, a long knife in a sheath at his side. He was drunk, rowdy, a little out of control. The Police Chief cautiously called over a waiter, asked him to get the man to leave the knife behind the bar until ready to leave. The German snarled when asked by the waiter, said 'Says who?' The waiter turned, pointed across to the Police Chief, who then immediately stood up, raised his hat to the German, left the premises.

The Policeman was known as a very brave man. Did the right thing. Avoided conflict at all cost. Someone might die. The gun's far quicker than the knife. Anyway, drunks always end up going to sleep after a while. Harmless. The Police Chief didn't want the German to lose face. He let it go. Drunks would always turn up at his cells when he was on duty. He'd give them a cell, bread, coffee next morning, then packed them off home shamefaced to their wives. Bravery's all about calculating the risks. Like a soldier does. If you have to fight, you only fight to win."

"I don't like fighting dirty." Dominic muttered.

"Who does? But sometimes you have to use your imagination. Imagination's more important than almost anything I can think of. There's a hundred ways to skin a cat." Fergus smiled. "Don't you tell that to Teresa."

"How do you mean?"

"What does a boxer do, Dom?"

Dominic wasn't sure how to answer. "Fights. Protects himself." The boy shrugged as though his answer was elementary.

"Exactly. The Romans were great soldiers. They'd learned their fighting tactics from the Greeks. To protect themselves they formed a wall of shields in front of them. Called it a phalanx. Soldiers behind held shields above their heads like a roof. Called it a 'testudo.' Latin for tortoise. Hard shell. No arrows could penetrate that wall or roof of defense. But protecting yourself doesn't have much to do with the winning. They used their imagination for that."

"How so?" Dominic's eyes widened.

"They won a couple of battles with sling-shots of hives of bees at their enemy to break up their lines. Then they attacked. It was the first kind of biological warfare." Fergus shrugged and smiled. "Bee-illogical warfare, if you like. But smart, don't you think? Bees go crazy looking for the queen, stinging anything in their way." Fergus then muttered loud enough for the boy to hear. "Everyone's a soldier, son. Use your imagination. You'll always win, if you really want to."

Dominic sat silently taking it in. "I just don't like to think of Teresa as a sitting duck on Hope Street. Why should a bunch of homeboy-would-be gangsters have her shitting bricks every time she walks down the street?"

"I'll bring Teresa over one Sunday morning. Show you both what to do bare-knuckled. I'll fix it first with your father. If it comes to the crunch you're going to have to find a way to give those homeboys all the fists they can eat."

Fergus stood to go. "Be stoo-pid, my boy, play the game, play possum, like your Dutch friend says, play dead if that will give you an advantage."

"Thanks for the advice, Fergus." Dominic stood, grinning at Fergus as he exited. "And for the parable of the bottle."

"You're welcome, son, think nothing of it," Fergus said as he ambled off home.

The Matchbox Shuffle

Fergus took Teresa, along with his booze bag again, through the adjoining gate next door the following Sunday morning. They had all been to late Sunday Mass. Eleven o'clock. 'Drunk's Mass,' as it was fondly known, husbands hanging their heads, wives with those 'menstrual-red' bloodshot eyes (Sharn's words). They'd all had a big night before. Fergus often looked the worse for wear. Caitlin and Colleen kept urging him to slow down, relax more. Even though he had them believe otherwise, Fergus drank little, always had his wits about him. Teresa was always very quiet at Sunday Mass. Sharn just looked plain tired out.

Sharn and Dominic were already changed into their exercise gear, waiting without gloves for him to arrive. Fergus sauntered through the gate. Teresa and Sharn pulled faces at one another. Fergus. At it again. Often Teresa and Sharn played hopscotch or jump rope here on Sunday. Today things were to be more serious.

Fergus symbolically took out the bottle of D.O.M., tipping the rest of the contents onto a plastic table. He looked at Dominic, making sure that he saw the ominous bottle. There were six large boxes of matches. Fergus took his jacket off, dramatically rolled his sleeves, his biceps bulging. There was going to be friction today, one way or another.

Dominic stood stiffly and quietly awaiting some great meaning to emerge. But it was Sharn who had Fergus' measure. She knew that friction with Fergus was about as useless as trying to strike a match on a one pound rump steak.

Sharn was slightly shorter and heavier than Teresa. She was a mass of runaway blonde hair, her long earrings, painted nails, sparkling cheek stud, nose and lip ring, and often had a coarseness about her that made Teresa wince. Her pastel colored shorts were tight. Teresa feared that she might split them. Sharn didn't have much time for any pomp or ceremony. She liked to call things for what they were. Yet she was never lazy at work or home. Colleen seemed to keep her under control. She was kind, like her mother was, and that was enough to forgive her many faults.

"Take a matchbox in each hand." Fergus pointed to the pile. "Get the feel of them tightened in your palms. I've taken matches out so the boxes will crush more easily. Three quarters full. If you hit with a bare fist, you'll hurt your hand. You need something inside to cushion the blow."

Dominic muttered "Maybe a horse shoe over knuckles would be better."

Sharn paired up with Teresa. Fergus took to demonstrating with Dominic.

"Hit me," said Fergus, relaxed, staring hard at the boy.

They squared off against one another. Dominic was good. He was known amongst other young boxers for his coordinated left hooks. He liked the styles of Dempsey and Frasier. He was quickly acquiring some finesse. He stood firm in front of Fergus, threw his punches straight from the shoulder, getting in a few on Fergus' neck. Maybe Fergus was taking him lightly, purposely giving the boy an edge.

"Again," Fergus said. "Harder."

Pace quickened. Fergus began dancing round him, shuffling, feinting, pulling punches, coming in at Dominic from all angles.

"Dance, dance, dance," he said slapping the boy lightly—his stomach, ribs, under the chin to the throat.

The girls stood back in amazement. They'd never seen Fergus box before. They'd always thought him a soft touch, almost a push-over. He obviously thought that what he was doing was important.

Then, Sharn's turn. She'd watched on with a dropping jaw. Whatever Fergus was doing, she knew that he wasn't showing off. Sharn covered up, boxed, Fergus sticking out his chin to be hit. Sharn threw straight from her shoulder. They breezed past, missing by fractions as he ducked, weaved, her eyes alert and focused. He threw a punch at her, then opened his fist, pulled at her long blonde hair.

Then, Teresa's turn. She sometimes came over Sunday, trained with Sharn, who, to her credit, felt sorry for her brother outside in the yard, especially on Sundays having to train. Declan ran a fruit stall up at the market on Hope Street on Sundays. He trained his binoculars back on the house making sure that Dominic was practicing in the yard.

Fergus crouched. Teresa banged away at him clutching her boxes of matches. "Straighter," he said, "straighter." Teresa suddenly found it funny. She was more used to hitting his leg for being such a big tease. She grinned, started belting at her uncle's knees.

Then, Sharn's turn again. Fergus soon had her puffing. She was missing wildly, fists clenching the boxes. She'd soon had enough of this so rushed in at him with her superior weight, tackling him to ground. She and Teresa capsized on top of Fergus, punching, laughing.

Fergus saw the funny side, covering his face with his hands.

Dominic stood back, un-amused. He stared at Fergus. Declan wouldn't allow this kind of carry on to chaos. Yet he also knew that Fergus was smart enough not to press an advantage.

"I'll watch you three," Fergus said after getting up. "Just don't think this is as easy as rolling off a log. I need a drink."

He sat back passively on a plastic chair with his shot of D.O.M. Benedictine, watching Teresa grit her teeth, her elbows in, striking at Sharn's padded hands. Tall and stringy, Teresa could now weave back and forth, move round the pads with perfect balance.

"Dance," Fergus muttered to the drink in his hand, "Dance, dance, dance."

Fergus sat with some concern. He worried about what Dominic and Teresa might have to put up with on the burning macadam of Hope. He knew that he couldn't throw money at that, as if as easy as settling a bill. As if a couple of boxes of matches could really make them street and jungle-wise.

Teresa was now only two weeks off her sixteenth birthday. What a beautiful young woman she looked, Fergus thought from his chair. Subconsciously, perhaps, he desperately wanted to protect her, protect as he had failed to his own sister, Teresa Bridget the First.

Caitlin suddenly appeared through the gate with two cups of coffee. She sat beside Fergus, confiscating his shot glass, then clutched his hand on the table. He gave her a rueful look as they sat sharing an unspoken thought. Teresa knew what that thought was. She had been looking through her mother's church missal during Mass. She pointed her finger at a page, lifting up an In Memoriam card, getting her mother's attention.

Today was the anniversary of her grandparents and young aunt's death.

Driven up the Wall

Given half the chance, a busload of thirty fifteen year old schoolgirls on day excursion will be as rowdy as they possibly can. They looked a pretty raggedy lot as they single filed onto the bus, dressed down to their sawn-off shorts, boob tubes, crazy hats, outrageous as the pictures of themselves they posted on cyberspace. The long the short and the tall, many of them lumpy, most of them under-achievers. They were also a cliquey lot, who just liked to mill around together, united for survival rather than with a common interest, usually with one central member with a mouth big enough to keep other groups at bay in games of one-upmanship.

They looked hardly off to some glamour photo shoot. Sister Susan watched them sternly as they'd filed on board, vetting slogans on T-shirts, stickers on backpacks. Most had an allergy to school, where truancy was rife, yet a free school trip can create a kind of bonding. Half would probably have taken the day off, if not for this trip. Sister Susan didn't try too hard to correct them. Why should she, two days off end of year, just to hear a whole lot of 'whatever-ing?' Three girls were not allowed to go. Disciplinary issues. None of them was that big on learning. Not so when it came to volume. They were all raring to go.

It was instantly 'the wheels of the bus go round, round, round;' 'Mr. Stubbs takes us to town, town, town' in full voice, then yahooing out the windows with youthful exuberance, Jennifer flashing what she had under her T to stationery traffic at the lights. Another trick, of their creative flow, was that sweet teenage wave, smiling out the window to traffic in the adjoining lane, hands going round and round like a chamois cleaning a car. Once having elicited a reluctant, but benign, wave in return, the next gesture to the motorist was usually an obscene one. They weren't the kind of girls ever to score real good jobs, go to the gym(none of them worked out), the hairdresser's, or have a pedicure—Teresa, maybe—she had her own gymnasium climbing her fig tree, her own home hairdressing perm kit in having Sharn next door. Exercise, to them, was having to do boring chores after school, skateboarding to there rather than walking. These kids were generally here to stay, small timers, never to leave, go away, like to college.

So long as they remained seated, no one bothered too much in correcting them. Mr. Stubbs sat blithely reading his newspaper up front in his blue blazer with gold buttons and grey slacks. Mr. Jacobs, the school bus driver, put on his usual jolly face.

It was now the end of school year, the seniors had left, exams were over. Teresa had a class day trip to the sea and to an indoor rock free-climbing center. Mr. Stubbs and Mr. Jacobs accompanied them.

It was a chance to dress up, or down, let off some steam, grateful school was almost over. Teresa sat primly behind Jennifer and Marcia in her new lilac T shirt, black cotton shorts, sports shoes with the lilac laces, her hair tied in bunches with matching lilac ribbons. She looked as pretty as a picture. She wore a one piece swimsuit underneath. Colleen had bought her the lilac T. "It'll look lovely on you, Tess. I couldn't resist it." Then Fergus noticed some runners with lilac laces and matching lilac fleck socks in the city. Teresa felt so spoilt. She kept them for her casual best. Her black shorts had pleats in the front. They looked tailored and expensive. Sharn had bought them for her, borrowing the money from Dominic.

Almost a year ago now, Fergus had given Teresa a free cutout coupon to the rock climbing center for her fifteenth birthday. Another one of his dumb presents, yet one he knew she'd like. "You've been driving us all up the walls for years now; it's our turn now." She made him take her there that weekend, twice since then. Fergus didn't mind much. "Still cheap," he said, "less maintenance than a pony." "I never asked anyone for a pony," she retorted. Ask Fergus for a bicycle; he'd go out and buy you a picture of one.

Teresa sat by herself by the window. Mr. Jacobs had picked her up on the way on the corner of Edward, and everyone thought how cool she looked as she walked the aisle to her seat. She sat behind Jennifer and Marcia. They'd hung out together for as long as Teresa had known them. Jennifer immediately began moving her long blonde hair, forking it up with her hand, sitting forward in her seat so she could arch back whenever about to speak. She liked to imitate the voices of the rich and famous, worthy families, like Paris Hilton; Teresa listening in, used to snooping on conversation. Jennifer handled the voices well. She had a kind of comic timing. Marcia had recently put red streaks in her hair, spiked it, which was not allowed at school, yet so near to end of the year she'd risked it. Raised slightly at the seats went back, Teresa could look down on them, listen to their chatter.

Sharn knew both of them from Sunday Mass. She'd also done their hair at the salon. She told Teresa that they were just a couple of bubbleheads who wouldn't know an axle from an alternator(Sharn had just bought herself a car), a good example of what-not-to-wear, that they were both about as attractive as two beach towels. Sharn called them a couple of 'try-hards.'

Teresa didn't respond to that. Charity forbad it on Sundays. She liked to keep the peace, anyway. She had been on the receiving end of similar criticism herself, so it seemed, all her life at school. Whenever Jennifer and Marcia saw Teresa they'd smirk as if suddenly remembering a funny joke. Teresa was beyond caring what they thought of her.

Jennifer wore a hazelnut crop top, white shorts over her fluorescent bikini; Marcia, pastels over a one piece. Teresa quite liked the way they dressed. They'd cut the labels off the swimwear so no one could see the make or size. Teresa knew that they'd pinched them from the Mall, for they'd said so once in class; some scam they had going by flashing an old receipt to security at the boutique door. Jennifer was good at flashing. Marcia once gave Teresa an eye liner in class, said it would suit her better. Teresa dropped it down a drain on Hope that afternoon, knowing Marcia had stolen it.

Teresa listened to snippets of their conversation. They thought themselves pretty hip. Models of wellness.

"I've got a FFF today's going to turn to crap. Dad said there's big swells at the seaway. Life savers may close the beach." Jennifer said.

"OMG! Just our luck!" Marcia exclaimed.

"Oh, well. A good Monday to chill-ax, then." Jennifer said. "Really like your hair, by the way."

"Do you! Thanks. I made an effort with it. I usually feel so mol'd out by Monday." Marcia muttered. "Mondays give me a splitting headache. I feel good today." She repeated.

"When you seeing Dave again?"

"Two weeks."

"You grounded?"

"Nope. Waiting for my face to clear up first."

Teresa peered over, counting Marcia's zits.

"Look at Susan over there. She such a povo! She's on Ritalin. Hasn't even got any tits yet. Flat as a ruler. Her father drives an old Nissan. How shit embarrassing is that!" Jennifer said boldly.

"Her skin's pink as a prawn."

"And as full of shit."

"And she's a thumb-sucker."

"And look at her knees. Even they're fat."

Eventually they stopped. It was like suddenly calling the dogs off.

Teresa glanced across at Susan, who suddenly sat up and turned. Teresa read the words on her T-shirt—'No Can Do.' Teresa had bought Susan a plastic digital watch at an Op Shop. It had only cost her a dollar. Teresa had given up on trying to teach Susan to read a clock. Susan was a diabetic. Teresa often kept an eye on her. Susan was miserable, more often than not, always complaining about her weight. Caitlin told Teresa that it might be because of the insulin, just tell the girl to exercise more. Teresa did that, but didn't push it.

Yet it wasn't as if any of them had turned up to the bus in shiny minivans, SUVs or Europeans imports. Everyone knew that Teresa must be poor, for she shopped at Thrift shops, and was always made to walk to school. None of them knew much of Teresa's pedigree, but seemed sure that it didn't amount to much.

Marcia turned, glimpsing across, noticing Teresa was sitting behind them. "Guess whose behind us?"

"Who?"

"Teresa."

"Does she still look like that time of month again?"

"Just looks like she could do with a Happy Meal."

"She always looks like she's out to lunch."

"She looks so-o-o *Brokeback!*"

"What's that mean?"

"Like a trip to the bathroom."

Teresa didn't care what they said. She sat up straight. Nothing wrong with her back. She was used to their carry on, anyway. She sat quietly listening. She then suddenly became distracted by the sound of birdsong outside over the engine noise.

Marcia reached in her bag for her lip gloss, amongst water bottles and small Tupperware containers. "Water to flush, almonds and sultanas to snack. We must eat every three hours, keep our metabolism firing."

"What? No naughty snacks today?"

"No. Did you soak your oats last night?"

"Nope. Skipped breakfast."

"You're naughty. Should never skip breakfast, Jen. That's bad. I'm even going to avoid lifts from now on, take the stairs, keep the body firing. Climbing's supposed to be good for the body." Both were a bit on the heavy side.

"What? Like you-know-who-behind?" Marcia said quietly, then zippered her lips with a finger as though to say that's our little secret.

"Yeah. Wouldn't mind a body like hers, though" Jen muttered enviously.

Marcia pulled out a Tupperware cheese dish from her bag, after taking long gulps of water from her drink bottle. Teresa noticed small vials of what looked like prescription drugs, then realized they were antioxidants and vitamin supplements. "The French make all the best cheeses. They use raw milk. It isn't pasteurized. Their yogurts are real nice, too. They put a dollop of cream in them."

"Greek yogurts are the best,' Jen mused pensively. "You'd think they'd be a real rich country, wouldn't you—everyone eats Greek yogurt."

Teresa could only agree. She and her mother loved Greek yogurt. Teresa often got it discounted from Spiro's store.

"We've got to be real careful what we eat," Marcia added. "We shouldn't even eat any wheat or dairy. There's no food allergies in Third World countries. They don't eat them."

"Where's that then?" enquired Jen.

"Don't know. Where they don't have to go to school."

It was only a short ten mile ride from school to ocean. The weather was mild that day, but it turned out Jennifer's dad was right, that the sea was way too rough for swimming with three meter swells, so everyone, including Teresa, ignored their cut lunches, fed their faces instead on takeaways or got high on sugar at the fudge shop along the beachfront, without much disappointment, then all went off together to the rock climbing center. Teresa had ordered herself a burger with fries, which she ate, then went halves with Susan for a pizza because Susan was a few dollars short. Jennifer and Marcia had stared at them thinking what a couple of losers. Teresa didn't care. Teresa thought maybe Sharn was right what she said about Jen and Marcia, bubbleheads, really up themselves. Teresa knew one thing for certain, that Marcia's mother couldn't spell for shit.

Yet everyone was generally happy and relaxed. One day of school left until the long summer holiday started.

It was not compulsory to free climb. Less agile students were content just to watch, for there were definite dangers involved, in addition to the degree of difficulty. This was not some spit on the hands and up you go. This took strength and fitness. Many just sat it out. The thought of bodies knocking together up a wall, and in full view of the class, brought out a kind of instant homophobia. Any excuse will do to sit down.

It was a free and introductory lesson, the motive being to lure students in over the long summer holidays. There were three walls next to one another: a junior, a more difficult senior, then the open grade. Two female instructors slowly demonstrated the art while another spoke through a hands free microphone.

All the girls sat in a semi-circular five tiered gallery watching the two climbers ascend, noticing their foot and hand holds, how and when to grab, how best to place their feet while suspended by webbing to a safety rope. The junior wall face was covered in yellow, red, green, blue knobs of rock jutting out, of round, oblong or square design. The wall seemed like a full scattering of confectionary; less so the intermediate wall; less again the senior. Jennifer and Marcia sat plugged into their iPods on their waistbands. No way were they going to do it.

Some girls reluctantly volunteered, aided up with the instructors beside them. Teresa took her turn. She said she was prepared to go up by herself, which she did slowly, carefully managing to get safely to the top. She wanted to attempt the senior wall, but didn't ask.

It soon got boring, well beyond the ken of most. The class in the gallery gradually got restless. When given something difficult to do, most were like a bunch of sand-crabs, scuttling back to their holes in hiding. They didn't have long attention spans. It became a drag, time droning on, as if back in class. There were lots of yawns and stretches. They missed the boys. At least playing grab-ass was more fun than busting yours grappling hardened walls. They wanted action. Punch and Judy. Falling marionettes. The instructor soon sensed their unease, then said, reading from a clipboard, that the school record for fifteen year old female climbers was 1:02, sixteen, 1:00, seventeen: 48,: and would anyone like to try their hand to beat the clock. It was better to make a contest of it than put up with the giggling and shuffling of feet in the gallery. Where was the adventure in that?

Two big clocks faced them. They registered 0:00 and 1:02. Some of the girls had now just turned sixteen.

The walls looked so high, sheer and daunting. There was a long silence. Some girls soon turned vaguely to Teresa. They then all began chanting "TREE MONKEY, TREE MONKEY, TREE MONKEY," stomping their feet on the wooden boards as if they were here to get their money's worth, one way or another. "ONE, TWO, THREE, TERESA LIVES IN A TREE, ONE, TWO, THREE, TERESA LIVES IN A

TREE," the girls were now swaying left to right, shoulder to shoulder, as though rocking in a boat on a pond.

They were just words to Teresa. She was used to them by now.

Teresa stood up quietly, sauntered across to the wall with an easy elegance, where she remained at attention They all watched her body move sheepishly, in her usual school daze, noticing her shiny calves, that she not used to vying for any attention. The girls gave her that quizzical look. She was still a stranger to them. And was she pretty, or what? It seemed appropriate that she should just stand there. There was always a wall of sorts in front of her. She stood like a robot. Not easy to know what a robot thinks. And she had those rock hard abs, like those colored rock nodules gleaming on the wall. She did have a nice rack, too. Medium natural, even under her one piece swimsuit.

"You think she got a boyfriend?" Marcia wondered.

"Nah. She's for Display Purposes Only." Jen countered.

"What? Like at the Op Shop?"

"Not today."

"Nice bod," Marcia said.

"Nice threads, too." Jennifer replied.

"She doesn't care very much, does she?"

"Nah. Looks like she's about to answer a telephone."

But the noise then gradually became louder. Teresa didn't care. At least she wouldn't have to speak to anyone, make an ass of herself with words. This was not difficult. To Teresa, playing the recorder was difficult. Climbing was much better than the classroom. It always got rid of her claustrophobia, feeling wedged in as up on Hope Street.

"You have to go up by yourself," the instructor said. "You are completely self-reliant and responsible for your actions. If you're going for a record, we cannot shout instructions."

"That's o.k.," Teresa said with a shrug, then added, "Can I try the senior wall?"

"All right. I noticed you before. You have a sure footing. Just be careful."

They both moved across to center stage, Teresa helping to attach the pinch clip to the safety rope, then rubbing magnesium carbonate in her hands for a solid grip, then looking up to the wall, waiting vaguely for the clock to sound. She knew that real rocks could be sharp and dangerous. These weren't. It was just a wall. Like a tree, really. Nothing to a tree monkey.

She suddenly turned to her audience with the safety rope attached, spread her arms out either side, brought them in, curled her hands inward under her armpits scratching herself with her thumbs. Like a monkey. She puckered up her bee sting lips into a round, went "Ooo-ooo-ooo," then broke out into a smile. She was not being sarcastic. It made no difference to her. Only about one gene difference between a man and a monkey.

Everyone applauded.

She turned her back on them, patiently awaiting the signal to go. She had been up all three walls many times before this.

A gong sounded.

She jumped at the face of the wall, having worked out for herself a predestined route, her long legs and arms stretching out left and right to their maximum, placing her feet in the footholds, rotating her knee so that it pointed downward, climbing with a fury until both her hamstrings felt like they were near to busting, egged on up by the long slow clap, chants of "TREE MONKEY, TREE MONKEY, TREE MONKEY." She knew how to breathe and relax properly, having read up on Pilates books. It immediately became obvious to her audience that she knew the right tactics and techniques. Her lilac ribbons and laces seemed to flash out at them like moving spots of phosphorescence. Her slowness before had been quite deliberate, working out all the harder sections, the exact placement of hand and foot. "SPIDER WOMAN, SPIDER WOMAN, SPIDER WOMAN" came the new chant. She knew where all the holds were, and some of those partially hidden. The senior wall was not a perpendicular climb but a constant zigzag, almost having to throw herself across at the holds. She liked climbing from side to side, giving equal exercise to both left and right arm and leg.(she didn't want one arm bigger than the other, like tennis players have, and certainly didn't want one breast bigger). Up and up she went by going side to side, without once looking down, and in powerful one dimensional moves, increasing her speed until finally reaching the top, slapping her hand on the edge of the highest brick, then kicking her weight out from the wall, quickly descending to ground.

Teresa had no fear of falling. She hit the floor with a sudden thud, her eyes blinking like extinguishing stars from the sudden rush.

The clock stopped. She didn't even look over in its direction, just waited like a robot for the instructor to detach the rope from the webbing.

There was silence in the small stadium. Somebody muttered 'Bloody hell.'

: 46. She had broken the record for seventeen year olds.

There is a rare moment in sport seldom seen. A gradual persuasion, perhaps. Nobody particularly wants it to happen, as if their prejudice or skepticism forbids it, yet, once observed, onlookers are stunned to silence for a short time, then all the spectators stand, as though automatically, clapping with genuine applause.

Teresa stood still at the foot of the wall, then turned to face her onlookers like a Muhammad Ali over a supine and senseless Sonny Liston. She smirked amiably at her audience, as if to say "I'll-do-it-again-if-you-like."

She then spread her legs slightly apart, like Ali did, drew one clenched fist up over her chest, shouting 'YES.' She finished her act by performing the old soft shoe out of her tap classes, did the one foot forward, her arms and hands splayed up and down—"DA-DAAR"

Everybody laughed. It was so spontaneous of her. No one could quite believe it. It was something that they'd never seen before. She never smiled much. Just that inscrutable cocked gaze. She had caught their hearts, at last. Her unquestionable beauty seemed to take on a new character for the very first time. Teresa! Teresa Mahone! That religious chick! A bit of the outdoorsy type, nevertheless. Usually, they thought of her not as a warrior but a worrier, and she was, to them, always about as funny as the Shroud of Turin. Never a barrel of monkeys.

Teresa quickly shook hands in succession with the three instructors, who congratulated her with big smiles, then she skipped lightly, with red faced embarrassment, across the arena to her sport's bag at the edge, only to pick it up, leave the building and go wait outside beside the bus.

A *Step* Too Far.

Mr. Jacobs went out of his way that afternoon to drop Teresa off again on the corner of Edward Street. He and Maddox were friends, and he knew Teresa by name. That name would now be engraved on that sport's center gymnasium wall and be recorded in the school magazine. As she stood up to alight from the bus, walk down the aisle, a new chant went up, this time led by Jennifer and Marcia. "VIVA TERESA, VIVA TERESA, VIVA TERESA." They had remembered back to her assignment on Che Guevara, the one that she had got a good telling off for, for corrupting the class.

Teresa turned to them on the steps and grinned, punching her fist in the air.

She then dropped her guard by dragging her heavy sport's bag along Edward that afternoon, stopping only where the street turned slightly, resting her head on her hand on the top of a strainer post of the eight wire fence. She suddenly retched, vomiting profusely over into the vacant land. The climbing had almost pulled her stomach apart, knowing that she should not have eaten those takeaways before climbing. She limped off home, ran herself a warm bath, tipping muscle relaxant powder in it to 'chill-ax.' She purposely left the bathroom door open. Ballou came in, jumped up, walked along the edge of the tub. Teresa gathered a handful of foam, Ballou striking out at the suds with her paw.

She also knew that her mother had to work late; that Maddox and Declan were concreting that night the levels of a new car park, so she then dressed for bed, made herself some toast, without butter, which she thought was all that her stomach could handle, then e-mailed her uncle in the city telling him of her success.

Dear Uncle,

Take this. I finally nailed it. Today, just when you thought I was on the rocks, I went and blew the local rock climbing record for SEVENTEEN year olds right out of the water. Thanks for that coupon you gave me to go there. And I did it in those lilac sneakers you bought me, too. What you giving me for my next birthday?

Love, Tess.

The next day was the last day of term. Teresa said nothing to her mother about the day before, except that she didn't feel very well that morning.

"But it's prize giving, dear. You have to go up on stage and collect your Christian Instruction prize."

"Can't be helped. Dominic will bring it home for me," Teresa said miserably.

"What will I tell them then when I ring the school office?"

Teresa didn't care. She didn't want to go up on stage that day. She knew that it would be another chant of 'Tree Monkey, Tree Monkey, clap, clap, clap.' She just wasn't in the mood for it.

"Tell them I've got an upset stomach. Maybe it's contagious. I'd better stay home."

She stayed home that day, ate only her feelings, got over the torments of the afternoon before, yet with a great sense of pride.

Background(20 years before).

When Maddox Mahone married his childhood sweetheart, Caitlin O'Flynn, and Declan O'Leary, Maddox's best friend, married Colleen McGuire, Caitlin's best friend—one after the other on the same afternoon in the same parish church after the last of them had turned nineteen—both couples moved north to the small town of Crone. They were not the types for any temporary moves or overnight pledges. These had been two long standing relationships.

In Crone, they hoped to make permanent lives for themselves, a forgotten nook of coastal hinterland in from the South Coral Sea under the Tropic of Capricorn and the stars of the Southern Cross.

Fergus O'Flynn had put them up to it. He'd always been a little left of field, full of wild schemes, a kind of hard boiled Bogart type. In fact, his young life so far seemed to have hinged upon the word Antipodes, that southern region of the world where they lived for those who dwell opposite, literally feet against feet, upside down. Fergus liked the challenge of upside down. He was bold, tough, a born leader, given to excessive generousness. How he had chanced upon his money so far in life, most were too afraid to ask.

Crone, in fact, was a dump. Hardly a window of opportunity. Still, they were fighting tough these O'Flynns, Mahones, McGuires and O'Learys. Ex fighters. None of them had glass jaws. Like those tent boxers of long ago, Fergus led them to believe that north was where the bright pennies were tossed. He was confident. They'd take on all-comers.

However, these nuptials seemed a little too familiar to many, raising eyes of wedding guests, setting tongues wagging, especially when they heard the couples were taking up residence in adjoining houses in an otherwise vacant street. Further to, they were taking Fergus with them. It was only gossip behind hands. Nobody squared off against Fergus and his ilk.

His proposal had been seconded unanimously, even though the couples got the notion that he may have stuck a pin into a map for somewhere less shuttered down by cold, a place where the barometer would soar, fish would jump. Fergus held Crone up as invitingly as the page three pin-up girl in weekend tabloids—fresh, on the threshold, oozing with life, sunburst, not grinding cold like their hometown not far from the Southern ocean.

"It'll be great up there. Just the pig's whiskers. You'll see."

Fergus had always taken control. He was older. And there were reasons. Always are. He pretended to rule like an Old Testament prophet, a bit mad like Malachi, even though ruling unobtrusively as the downstairs maid. He'd have them all marching to Zion in no time. Fergus was right into marching. Everyone followed as he beat the band.

The Double Wedding.

The couples had always been close neighborhood friends, negligibly Irish now, third, fourth generation Australian. The girls were pretty, sweet tempered, sheltered and convent educated. Declan and Colleen evenly shared the same family tree as cousins twice removed. The double wedding reception was to be a grand marquee affair, all paid for by Fergus and Colleen's parents, both as nuptials and farewells.

The weather held that Saturday—windless, warm into a fading twilight. That only seemed fair, for each couple seemed destined for one another, meant to be, two perfect matches.

These were to be traditional ceremonies—no made up vows in open necked shirts, scuffed shoes, fingers crossed hoping for the best, hiding pregnancy bumps under bridal arches down a beach somewhere, then into town for fish and chips leaving behind a hundred empty liquor bottles at midnight. No way.

Traditional music, too. The band(Maddox's cousins), had wanted to play in the church. The priest said no. It wasn't a football match. There'd be no playing The Zombies' 'She's Not There' just because Colleen said that she liked it. It was a wedding, not a knees-up. Wagner would march both couples in; there'd be Schubert's Ave Maria in-between; Mendelssohn to get them out again. "The way it should be." Father Niven had said. "They won't let you play religious music at civil ceremonies, there'll be no rock 'n' roll at ours."

Everyone made a special effort that day, an improvement on usual racetrack attire. Male guests wore morning suits, ladies their best—vintage gold brooches for big occasions, classically styled linen skirts, heels, soft leather bag complements, for there was something unique about a double wedding and farewells. Then there was the sorry memory in proximity for most, a clatter of ghosts from the past.

There was almost a synod of priests at St. Patrick's that day, a small, dignified church with a dwindling congregation. Both brides wore eggshell white gowns without trains: Caitlin's a high neck, Colleen's a low; and lace sleeves embroidered with white roses. Colleen's mother made both dresses to reflect their personalities(pretty much the same, like the Bobbsey twins). Everyone said how much they loved the gowns in the plural, almost unable to tell them apart.

Colleen looked buxom yet a slim-waist, with long runaway yellow straw hair; Caitlin, slenderer with her Irish-Spanish skin and dark eyes, hair blacker than Indian ink. There were no petty jealousies, tears or confusions or bridal moments that day. The two young women even held hands as best of friends while being photographed together. They looked so youthfully cute-as-pie. Guests went gaga at the sight of the slender waistlines, drawn to the eye by ruche lace. The bridesmaids, ten in all, most of whom worked with Colleen at a large hair salon, wore bright pink dresses(so they could be worn again to parties), had ice sugar rosettes, one even sported a high lacquered beehive, much like Madge Simpson. They looked like Avon ladies meant to be, just younger.

All spent the morning with cucumber rounds in their eyes, reminiscing of days when they were Princesses, and that Fergus was The Good Fairy. Providentially blest by him. The gift that just keeps on giving. "Fergus believes The Tooth Fairy's a male," Caitlin said, no hint of sarcasm intended. "Has franchises all over the world. Sells dentures." Everyone giggled, cucumber rounds wobbling in their eyes, while wondering what it was that he did sell working overseas.

"He'd better behave himself today. I told him to. No politics or religion, just like at the dinner table," Colleen said fearfully. "He promised me he would," Caitlin replied, blessing herself hurriedly, looking heavenward then shielding her eyes from the thought. "Don't worry, Cait," Colleen mused, "he's tougher than hairs on a scrub brush. Let's hope that he keeps it as clean."

There was a long double bridle table, the finest Irish linen, a makeshift white trellis of summer flowers behind; a wooden dance floor assembled in the middle of the marquee. There was hired statuary of glistening maidens, leaning Cupids with bows outstretched peering out like little leprechauns amongst the potted topiary. The local bishop, three priests, and two in the making from the seminary, updated the Roman splendor. The sentimentally faux Irish band, formed for the day, wore shamrock-shaped suit jacket lapels, calling themselves 'Guinness and Jamesons,' without apostrophe, and, despite the play list Fergus had provided, warbled 'Danny Boy' and 'Mountains of Mourne' until the cows came home.

Acting dumber than Irish stones, and just about as pagan, they'd suggested playing 'You've Lost That Loving Feeling' by the Righteous Brothers for Caitlin's bridal waltz. Fergus silently disabused them of that by raising a clenched fist.

Everything went sweetly. Everyone drank various kinds of ambers while the brides looked innocently gift-wrapped in white. Pure as the driven. Good girls. Both could cook, sew, keep a neat house. They never cheated in class at school. Honorable men, too. The wedding guests knew that neither would covet his neighbor's wife, even though Declan did play country guitar. All them cheating songs.

There were the standard jokes, lots of hearty Irish ha-ha-ha, promises of Love, Honor and O'Flynn; Colleen's father stating it was 'the happiest day of his life' as though getting rid not of his only daughter but some Shakespearian shrew, while her mother shed tears to think that she was losing her daughter forever to the north.

Fergus' speech had far more panache, tinged with a faint Celtic sadness. He'd always been an enigma to most. Assembled guests hanged on his every word like notes from some ancient flute, laughing nervously, knowing that there was probably humor there yet unable quite to guess it. He'd always looked a most serious man, older than his twenty five years. Many viewed him as a kind of precocious master playing billiards: slim, impeccably dressed, frowning, stroking, stalking the table. Everyone gave full attention awaiting his cue, hearing the clicks, seeing the balls hit pockets while suspecting some mischief as to how they'd got there.

Fergus was all signs and wonders.

He usually puffed on Cuban cigars, smoke rising from his hair, using words much like the prize fighter that they saw in him—assuming a crouch, feinting left and right but really only punching the smoky air. Expecting to pocket wheat all guests got was the chaff.

Caitlin looked to her brother, mouthing quietly. "Keep it all fizz and froth." That he did, mainly for the sake of his sister, whom he loved dearly. He left the homily to the bishop, as he should, despite the odd questionable comment on religion, which hit like a jigger of whiskey into a pint of draft. Towards the end he made passing reference, politely bowing to the august company of priests, to the first miracle of the wedding feast at Cana, assuring the guests that there'd be plenty of booze at this one(mainly house wine, sparkling, and beer). And as free as God's grace. He smiled at the priests as benignly as a reader of evening news, sweetly as though a cocoa before bed.

So he ended. One could almost have heard the sighs of relief from the brides. Perfect. He had shown a sense of decorum. They should both have known better ever to doubt him. It wasn't as if they were lots eighteen, nineteen, at the registry office, or taking numbers at a supermarket deli. This had cost Fergus a packet. He didn't swear. Not once. He didn't make any anticlerical remarks, even come close to calling the priests a bunch of shirt-lifters, as well he might elsewhere. He correctly failed to mention his sister's favorite statue of The Virgin Mary, the one which shed crystal teardrops. That would have turned Caitlin's pearl tiara on her forehead into cold beads of sweat. Nor did he clock the caterer(an Italian), head butt the photographer(a Croatian), knee ball the candlestick maker(a Greek). Not a plate was broken. Nothing went belly up, not in his typically Antipodean way. Nor should it. It wasn't his day. The day belonged to his sister, her best friend. And he did cut a fine figure in his bespoke suit of charcoal grey that afternoon, the darling of the ladies, perhaps the only one there worth gossiping about.

'Let not ... admit impediments.'

Four wedding guests standing together with their fluted glasses of white wine. Older. Wiser. Fifty-ish. Friends of both sets of parents, both present and deceased.

Male#1. "Sure got to hand it to our brother Fergus. Just turned twenty five, putting on this shindig for us. Shelling it all out. Sparing no expense."

Male#2.[quipping behind his hand]. "Probably ransomed off some rich businessman down in Argentina in order to pay for it."

Male#1 "Running cockfights under a house of poor repute in Bolivia."

Female#1 [ignoring them both] "But doesn't Caitlin look a picture! Such pretty eyes. He's always looked out for his sister. If she'd wanted gold leaf and crystal chandeliers he'd have them for her. Fergus the rainmaker."

Male#1. "Not in a marquee. Pretty pair of pots, if you ask me. That goes for both brides."

Female#2.[slapping his arm playfully in coyly randy laughter] "It's us old pots who make the best stew."

Male#2.[ignoring both, raising her eyebrows]. "Had to, I guess. Kind man, nevertheless. True Socialist. Believes in drinks all round. Duty free, when he can. That's about as rare as a unicorn these days."

Female#2. "I don't think Fergus believes in unicorns."

Male#1. "You'd never know with him. Like father, like son. They say Fergus has had his difficulties keeping off the juice, too. Can't leave anything alone. Selling contraband down in South America. Some say even guns."

Female#2. "So that's the word on the grapevine, is it?"

Female#1. "I heard he bought his way out of jail in order to get here."

Female#2. "Never been one to brown nose the world has our Fergus. Wouldn't ever want to stiff him though, would you?"

Male#2[snickering]. "In like O'Flynn, out again. Like a whooshing sound. Giving everyone the slip. He's our 'Man with a Van.' Anything considered. All things Russian beginning with a K."

Female #1. "What's that supposed to mean?"

Male#2. "Kalashnikovs. Things of similar grain. What were you thinking of? Kelloggs? You should know by now Fergus doesn't do flake."

Female #1. "Is that a fact!"

Female#2. "You're being unkind. You shouldn't listen to those rumors. If you believe that, you'll believe anything. They've both had tragic lives. The accident, and all that. Remember little Teresa Bridget? Such a beautiful, sweet little girl. Gone to God. Little angel now. Well before her time. She was only seven when they died. So sad. Caitlin's Sunday missal is stuffed with memorial cards. What a load to have to carry."

Female#2. "I remember it as though yesterday. Poor Pat. Easy as Paddy with the rent was Pat. Only time he ever hurried was in that ambulance. Only on time in a hearse. That was the night after Fergus won his title. What a fight that was. They still talk about it today."

Male#1. "It was a war. Best fight I've ever seen. We used to call him 'Jukebox O'Flynn' because he was the one with the big hits. And he could dance in the ring. Feet more nimble than a matador."

Female#1. "If I didn't have so much junk in the trunk I'd be out there dancing with him now. Couldn't ever hope to keep up."

Female#2. "Who could? He could throw two hundred punches every round, as fast going back as forward. He tore that Nigerian boy apart. Twisted his punches, shut his eyes, broke his skin. Spirit, too. He ended up with three titanium plates in his left cheek. All in three. Fergus could have gone all the way, if not for the . . ." [she tilted her liquor glass shakily, gave a tipsy look].

Male#1.[looking appraisingly] "Not Fergus. Too many brains to carry on. He didn't want to end his career washed up at twenty five, giving after-dinner speeches like this one today, disguising a slur, spending the rest of his life dancing with the stars."

Male#1. "You're right, I guess. Reckon he could've made it, though. Had he stayed."

Male#2. "I'm not so sure. His brain wasn't that good the night of the tragedy. That was the day everything went to hell. They say he was supposed to be home looking after Teresa but suffered a concussion in the fight, was out sleeping it off in a bar somewhere. Maddox kept slapping him to stop him from dozing off, but he'd drank too much as well."

Female#1. "They sent Caitlin over to Colleen's. Thanks be to God. The parents took Teresa with them to the party. Pat got drunk. As Pat did. Violent storm. Shouldn't have driven. Dead in an instant. God rest their souls. Open coffins. All smelling of formaldehyde. All pushing up the daisies now."

Male#1 "Pat was Pat. Father, like son. Fergus doesn't know when to ease up either, but in a different way. He's the stitch in time. Exhausting just to be around him. Won't put off until tomorrow what he can do today."

Female#1. "Colleen said Fergus almost organized the two weddings all by himself but for the bridal wear—he wrote all the place settings in tiffany blue in that beautiful handwriting style of his, did the table arrangements, entertainment, had visual boards for the maids of honor and best men, even did the lighting himself, wheeling and dealing with the alcohol and food. Regular wedding planner with his timelines and running orders. Who'd ever thought he'd a feminine side to him! As for Pat, he would have been hopeless, had he been here."

Male#1.[scoffing] "Everything! But for bridal wear! I can just see him running up a few bride's maids' dresses."

Male#2. "Remember how Pat used to say that every wedding anniversary he'd go out, buy his wife an expensive present then go round to the presbytery, beat the hell out of Father O'Rouke for marrying them? Joke wore a bit thin over the years. He sure as hell belted his wife and daughter that night!"

Male#1. "Sure did. If heard it once, then heard it a thousand times. But Fergus has never been quite right since. Concussed, confounded by fate, he entered his dog days like some jilted lover. He never got over those nights. I think his brain went AWOL. Couldn't tell the sunshine from moonshine. Such a shame. There's a man who's afraid of nothing except putting flowers on his little sister's grave. I'm going to do a quick whip round for the brides."

Female#1. "I don't think he needs anyone's pity. He's so handsome and dashing! You could put him in a Bond movie. He carries himself like one of those Brazilian soccer stars. Did you see him turn up with

Caitlin in that red Alpha, top down, the whitewall tires, twin mufflers, her veil trailing behind like a silk scarf, looking more like Isadora Duncan going to a dance than to a wedding? That fine Italian suit of his, double breasted waistcoat, silk tie, gold cufflinks, genuine Spanish leather shoes? Look at him with his sister. A regular Fred Astaire!"

Male#2. "That was the way he boxed, too. Like Robinson and Ali did. And she's such a looker. Like Colleen is. Pretty as milkmaids. Pity the two boys are about as dull as lavatory seats."

Female#2. "Somebody once told me Fergus went out and walked a thousand miles because he felt so badly about the little girl. Felt responsible, negligent, even though he wasn't. Funny thing responsibility, isn't it!"

Female#1. "Yes, I heard that. Molly reckons walking that way is only done by those wasted and trashed, worried about dying. What a mournful thought. Let's have another drink before we drive. Who wants to end up cold stone soda! Only here for a short time. Drink now, pay later."

[Each, listing a little to starboard, takes a champagne glass from the waiter's passing tray, then another for the toasting].

Female#2. "Molly told me Fergus reckons everyone should cut their milk teeth by going on a walk. He used to step it up to 30,000 paces a day, that's almost a marathon, and under a heavy backpack, for well over a month. He'd lose over ten per cent of his body weight, reckoned that he did it to see the world more clearly. Apparently Fergus' done it a few times. Spain. South America. Energy to burn. Walk, walk, walk, even when full of booze."

Male#2. "Got to admit, he's not the kind of drunk you'd want to try and roll. Get it out of your system, he'd say. Whatever 'it' is. Crammed more into his few years than others have a lifetime."

Female#1. "Queer bird, that's for sure. Nuttier than squirrel shit, if you ask me. Have you heard about the two houses he's bought them in Crone? Fergus just laughed when I spoke of it. Told me the accommodation's about as one star as Che Guevara's beret! To a thousand. Said much of the roofing's missing. That's the loony Communist in him."

Female#2. "What's he think he's doing going up there? Navigating his way to the stars? Bit like running away to Canada, if you ask me, building log cabins in the wilderness. What's that old expression? Home's always found true north? Heaven forbid. Not for me. It'll be like the blind leading the blind up there. Living cheek to jowl. Out in the middle of nowhere. Too close for comfort. Getting on like a house on fire. For crying out loud! Give me a week of that I'd be paging Dr. Phil."

Female#1. "That's our Fergus for you. Tougher than Judge Judy. Skipping all the niceties. Railing against bankrupt values. Given half the chance, he'd make all offenders go out and walk the Santa Fe Trail, he kicking their butts for jay walking. You don't get any laying on of sympathetic hands with him!"

Female#2. "There's something of the puritan about him, don't you think? Straight, true as a church pew. Well, that is for a red-fed."

Female#1. "I'm not so sure about this Communist thing. Look at him. His beard's too trimmed."

Male #2. "And they don't ride about in fancy Alfas."

Female#2. "Communists would pull up to a church in rickshaws."

Male #2. "Caitlin probably pulling it."

Female#2. "Give her a break. Not today. Not in that dress."

[They paused a moment to watch Fergus dancing with his sister].

Male#2. "They reckon he was real tough on those two sisters of his. Pat was never around. Fergus would make them both walk across town to the gym after school, have them both punching the heavy bag, hitting the speed ball while he bench pressed and trained. He'd have those two girls like a couple of combat soldiers in fatigues, singing the G.I. blues."

Female#1. "I guess Fergus had to carry the stick for the family, picking up the slack. As for Pat, he'd always be out playing swizzle the swizzle stick in a bar somewhere."

Female#2. "Yeah. True. But Fergus always chastened the girls with laughter, turned everything into a quickstep instead of a goose. Spoilt his sisters rotten. He even taught Caitlin and Colleen to dance. Strange man."

Male#2. "Got to accept him for what he is, I guess. Just don't expect a kiss from Fergus after he's walked you home. Only kisses he believes in are with snooker balls. And he's sure got the balls. Must be saving his smooches for the kiss-a-gram girl."

Female#1. "The world according to Fergus. His world just doesn't do nice. Shirley Temple's strictly an American cocktail to him."

Female#2. "What's that old Johnny Cash song?" 'My fists got hard, my wits got keen.' That's him. Just when you think you've reached thirty miles of blue skies and light winds he assures you that's about the size of the eye of the storm."

Female#1. "Forget 'O, sweet day, so cool, so right.' He's all 'jump down, turn round, pick a bale of cotton.' Slave driver. Walk 'em 'til they're crippled."

Female#2. "For Heaven's sake, we're almost talking like him now. Full of wise quotations. Remember his speech before? Quoting Oscar

Wilde? Some daft Irish witticism, which I've forgotten already. Fergus couldn't help himself but make a lyrical gob-ful of it, like his cotton picking mouth was running away on him—'As Oscar Fingal O'Flahertie Wills Wilde once said . . .' He reduces everything to jokes. You'd never know where he stands. I held my breath a couple of times waiting for him to have a go at the priests."

Male#1. "He did. Didn't you hear? It all had to do with the food? I cringed when he said it. He pointed to the oysters then to the crayfish, the abalone, then to the turning spits of pork outside in the barbeque pit. 'Everyone must eat shellfish and pork,' he said, like giving a command, 'even if a Muslin or Jew. Ferdinand and Isabella legislated that we have to.'"

Female#1. "Don't get it. Too deep for me."

Male#1. "Ferdinand? Isabella? They sent Columbus off. You know. 1492, Columbus sailed the ocean blue."

Female#1. "Still don't get it."

Male#1. "He was having a go at the Jesuits. Inquisition. Pork's forbidden to Muslins and Jews. All must eat pork or get out of Spain. King Ferdinand wanted to make everyone the same."

Female#2. "But don't Communists want everyone the same?"

[Nobody knew].

Female#1. "Well, at least he didn't sing Danny Boy or Galway Bay. The band's awful! They sound like they've just come off a battery farm. Where the hell did he get them from?"

Female#2. "Wouldn't be of Fergus' doing. He'd have brought in some Mariachi band from Mexico. Bunch of Commo peasants."

[There was a lull until Female #1 started up again.]

"It never ceases to amaze me the men we marry. Declan and Colleen. Second cousins, twice removed. Bit lazy, don't you think? Lack of imagination? And they're all so young. Wet behind the ears. Green as grass. Going up north to the countryside to be amongst the baa lambs, the moo cows and chickadees. Like in one of those Nativity scenes. And living in a rundown barn? Away from it all. Dancing ring-a-ring-a-rosie round the Maypole. Pretty ho-hum, don't you think? The girls will end up a couple of old gray sea turtles up there in that heat, all wizened round the mouth. I like it better down here."

Female#1. "Sounds like something colorful Fergus would say. He'd turn any sonnet into a sonata. Yes. Maybe you're not so wide of the mark. But these girls are such lookers. Gliding swans. The boys? Well. Home grown, rugged, solid, reliable. Lame ducks, nevertheless. Each has a careless grace about him, I guess, but certainly no oil paintings. Not like Fergus."

Male#2. "He's the wildflower amongst the perennials. Even if a bit out of sync with the world."

Female#1. "They all stuck together like glue after the tragedy. I think Caitlin and Colleen have just ducked for cover. For Heaven's sake, they're both nineteen. You won't see our swashbuckling Fergus getting married off in such a hurry."

Female#2. "Guess it takes care of the uncertainties of life. Molly reckons both girls are still 'virgo intacta.'"

Female#1 "Get out of here. I remember when the girls were born. I'm a Virgo. Nowhere near my birthday!"

Female#2. "As for Fergus. He might not be taking it one day at a time just yet, but drunks always have difficulty taking vows. Good man's failing. Like his father. I'm picking he'll remain single. Not all relationships have to end in nuptials, do they? All that Catholic nonsense. Love, bringing forth of children, suffering. Working like a bunch of Irish mules. Only characteristics of a marriage."

There was a long pause.

Female#2. "Speaking of quotes, I once asked him if he'd ever marry. Know what Fergus said? 'Who would keep a cow of their own that can have a quart of milk for a penny?' That's our boy! True Socialist. Spreading it round. Smart answer for everything."

Female#1. [sounding her disbelief] "Pig's ass! Fergus wouldn't say that."

Female#2. "No. Cow's udder! He likes the baa lambs and moo cows, doesn't he? I asked him where he got the quote. Old English proverb? Book of Mao? Communist Manifesto? He just stood there, opened his jacket out by the lapels to display himself, a big grin on his face, said: "'The Life and Death of Mr. Badman,' by John Bunyan. Whoever the hell Bunyan is. Sounds like a big callous to me."

Female#2 "Wrote The Pilgrim's Progress. Come to think of it, he mentioned him to me once, too. According to Fergus, Bunyan's all about walking. Fergus says all the great books and poems are. Dear God in Heaven! You should've heard him carry on."

Female#1. "Load of shite, if ever you heard one. I got his biblical version—Flight into Egypt, Moses to The Promised Land, Journey to Bethlehem. I said 'Not bad coming from a Commo atheist.' Know what he said?"

Female#2. "Tell us."

Female#1. "He raised his eyes, said. 'Thank God that I am.'"

Male#2. "I still feel sorry for him. He's the one with the grit. Only thing he ever lacked in the ring was pity. Then again, the only thing that ever brought him to his knees was his little dead sister. She was his Achilles heel."

Female#1. "What's an Achilles heel?"

Male#2. "Don't remember. It's like . . . like having a glass jaw."

Female#1. "But Fergus doesn't have a glass jaw."

Male#2. "You know what I mean."

Female#2. "Who cares, anyway! They'll get their happy ever after. Find it up north. Especially under the guiding shepherd's crook of Fergus the Elder. He might not have the Midas touch, even a clue about real estate, yet he'll earn good money overseas to provide for them all."

Male#2. "They tell me he put himself through university by working drilling rigs in the South China Sea during his long vacations, got himself a pilot's license, went crop dusting in the shorter holidays. Falsified the documents. Lied about his age. Could talk his way in and out of anything. That's determination for you. Straight A student. He's really a deep and serious man."

Female#1. "Determination to keep off the drink by staying sober out on the rigs. And up in the air. But you're right. Got to hand it to him. And he's sure got a strong hand. They say underneath he's a moral man. Well, for a Commo."

They paused again to watch Fergus and Colleen now dancing.

Female#2. "I heard the university was prepared to discount his boozing, offering him a Master's course at reduced fees, a part-time tutorship, but he turned them down knowing he couldn't be relied on to get out of bed on time each morning. He reckons if you miss out on the night, you miss half your life. Like a zombie. Now there's fighting words of a young vampire. Tough as they come. Some people are just born brave—standing out on those drilling platforms, working the wells, looping the loop in crop dusters, walking the world under heavy backpacks. Sure as hell not the kind of man who'd call in sick. Someone told me once he even moonlighted as a doorman for a tango bar down in Argentina. How macho's that! How romantic!"

Female#1. "I don't believe it. You should know Fergus better by now. He's a Romantic. Believes in the better life. Anything's likely to come out of that lyrical mouth of his. It's all blather. You'll never pin him down. Makes it up as he goes."

Female#2. "My brother calls him Fergus O'Fith instead of O'Flynn You know? One of them acronyms? 'Effed-in-the-head.' [she puts her hand to her mouth in mock horror.] "Just another dingbat Commo."

Female#1. "He's a Communist, all right. Share, share alike. Setting up houses, giving them away. Friends. Family. Speaking of which. So did this good ol' boy." [She cocks an ear. Willy Nelson's song could be heard by the band singing. 'Blue Eyes Crying In The Rain.']

Male#1 returns, interrupting. "Well, I've done the quick whip around. Eight hundred buckaroos. Not bad for ten minute's work. Only goes to show how popular the two girls are."

Female#1. "Give it to me. I'll go crimp it to their bosoms."

Male#1. "Get out of here. Wouldn't trust you with a three dollar bill. If anyone's going to fiddle with those pots, it'll be me."

Male#2 [taking him aside]. "Slide a lazy fifty this way, will you. My brother supplied Colleen's bridal car. It'll pay for the gas."

*   *   *

It was a great night of celebration. The four co-conspirator guests had punched more holes in Fergus' reputation, covered more ground than Fergus had out on the dance floor. Fergus finally made sure that lots of taxis were called, guests spirited away safely to their homes clutching their little Tupperware tubs of wedding cake. Next morning, he made arrangements that all bills were suitably paid, for he'd everything in writing and unalterable(except that they knew he was long on cash, and accepted the discounts he asked), then he was never seen in the town again.

Like the knocking down of tent pegs, Fergus and his circus of boxers had finally moved on.

The Town

Hope Street. Literally the end of the line. At one end, Teresa's school, the other, a dead end of trailer parks, a mish-mash of old caravans with illegal awnings, piles of discarded mattresses, car parts heaped off to the sides. A blissful hide-out for unmarried parents or unemployed dodging the system; those who worked usually cut grass in parks, tidied up leaves and litter. It was the living end. Whoever gave it as their home address always got the sideways glance. It was a veritable hide-out for criminals, as well.

After some bank robberies nearer the ocean the police came straight to here instead of taking time to comfort the distraught tellers. It was here that you caught the robbers before all the money went into a hole in the arm. The local council hounded the place, mainly for safety matters, especially illegally rigged gas cylinders. Fire could ravage it in minutes. As a result, it stood alone like a reservation, fire breaks and embankments placed between it and houses opposite.

Hope Street, Dope Street, Cope Street, Mope Street, end of your Rope Street—Teresa had a different rhyming name for it every day, by age fifteen. She often wished her family was rich, like Uncle. At least the rich don't try and mug you. The rich swan about in luxury, go to private schools of their own choosing, have chauffeurs to take them home. Not even buses round here. School, or otherwise. Every time Teresa entered Hope she felt like a bleep striking the radar, a troublesome blip, something recognized by infrared, identified, dealt with by a bunch of boys with bugs up their smartasses. It was all a game of eat my pain.

The town of Crone was no country village down some pretty village lane. It was a deadbeat, wastrel little town out on the edges of the hinterland, a forgotten nook where no one had anywhere much else to go. It existed as if nobody wanted it. It was not near enough to the beach, not quite enough in the country. It peeved the police who had to go there, reluctantly monitor it from the next suburb—All roads lead to Crone, they'd often say while taking away some witless juvenile who'd just broken into a car with a screw driver.

No bad ass bikers cruised for victims here, just little whippersnapper scooters with pillions grabbing at handbags after mounting sidewalks, unemployed youths 'clothes lining' BMX riders down alleys when nothing else to do. Hope was little more than a single street of kiddy skid row from the overflow from nearby trailer parks of broken families, youngsters stealing aerosol and sealant, selling pot, hardly a scene of drug terror. It was a cheap place to live, full of lanky hard jawed boys, whey-faced girls still with acne, some living in cars, youths out of reform school, unmarried mothers surviving on whatever they could, hardly gang-bangers with cell phones, headphones, pumping their SUVs, or girls with ten inch heels grooving on sidewalks.

Caitlin soon saw the result of its despair coming through Mercy hospital's doors, where she worked as a nurse. There was an infamous off-ramp at the end of Hope known as The Suicide Jump. Below the overpass, deep divots marked the ground where the bodies had fallen, been gummed out, ladled away to the mortuary. Kids from the trailer parks would often lay in them, crossed chest, playing dead.

Then there were the street girls with their lank henna hair, who got hustled into alleyways for just a few cans of beer, a few cigarettes. It was a magnet for young runaways, most of them white, the expelled, pitiable and indigent, those more sinned against than sinning.

The beachfront was far too expensive; that was for the tourists, living there was beyond most pockets. There was no commercial district as such on Hope, mainly burger joints, Thrift shops, a main drag for BMX riders and clunker cars, a hang out for local hoods with inbred dogs with twitching legs on short leashes, too dumb even to fetch a stick. Goods left outside Thrift shops were rummaged through at weekends. Clothing bins weren't placed near. They'd long gone. Louts, in frustration, would light tapers of paper, set them alight inside. Big, old TVs were stolen, carried away, dumped, smashed soon after, boys too tired or lazy to carry them all the way home. Stealing started early morning, anything, drunks stealing newspapers, begging for free loaves from the bakery trucks. No Egg McMuffins, hash browns, hot coffee here. Except for those with cast iron stomachs, most avoided the restrooms and drinking fountains for fear of dysentery, at least.

What seemed to console these kids, the stealing, dope and drink, distressed them as well. There was so little to do. There was a swimming baths where locals hanged out, their change rooms covered in graffiti, but authorities clamped down on bad misbehavior until in the end nobody went there. There was a river, from the hills to the sea, too murky and dangerous to swim in. Bull sharks came up less saline waters to cleanse themselves of barnacles. Nobody swam in it, few fished off it.

Teresa and Dominic had to put up with it on their way home.

Sharn had left school now. Sharn had a mouth on her like a sewer lid. It flapped bad language. She told them where to go—the hobos, panhandlers, drunks, junkies. She'd give them a gob-full, and in school uniform, literally spit in their eye. Despite her Farrah Fawcett runaway hair, Sharn was no cutie to be trifled with. She handled it. It didn't drive her nuts like it did Teresa.

Most people had a sort of conscience about Hope Street. Conscience was not bleeding, that's all. If only it could be swept away, like the hosing off of concrete.

Crone progressively became a public nuisance over the years, a kind of horsefly that authorities were not keen enough to swat—much like the eyesore of the sweating, sulking trees of the Reserve crowding up to the edges of the two houses.

The Reserve

The Reserve was next to and below the two houses up the end of Edward street. No teddy bear's picnic was ever to be had down there. It seemed endless, confused, a sunken pit rather than a ditch, without definite surrounds. It lay beneath them like a canyon, a catacomb of dead bones. It was creepy, like something out of a horror movie The Living Dead. One could easily imagine the zombies hobbling about there at night, stunted, bleeding like the undergrowth. Caitlin would sometimes look out at it and shudder, then recite the old rhyme from her childhood:

> My mother told me
> I never should
> Play with the gypsies
> In the wood
> If I did, she would say
> Naughty girl to disobey.

Yet there were no gypsies down there. It was uninhabitable. Full of venomous snakes, poisonous spiders, bats that carried disease, foxes, goats, swamp hens which came out after rains, cane toads, crawlers and critters, yet also beautiful parrots and cockatoos, full galleries of them circled in for the wild berries. Street kids would light fires down there, sit in a huddle, smoke dope, drink alcohol, looking for some kind of magic mushroom to give them a high, but the ticks and mosquitoes soon got the better of them.

Gypsies, by nature, move on.

They'd moved up onto the bleak moonscape of Hope Street. Both the Reserve and street were often seen as the dead lungs of the district, an old Crone under a heavy load of sticks.

But Fergus knew better.

Give it time, he said.

Time for what!

He believed the Japanese or Koreans would soon move in, buy up the land below, let it drain for ten years then put in a private golf course. That was the plan. What he'd not figured was that developers were more interested in waste land nearer the sea, that bikinis and sunhats drive economies faster than his pie in sky schemes. Coastal resorts, cycle tracks, rainforest walks, excursions to waterfalls, these characterized the civilized activity of beachgoers. Fergus refused to believe, despite his go-get-'em nature, that there were better drugs, smarter embezzlers at the seaside, that they were as isolated up the end of Edward as on The Little House on the Prairie.

The Three Trees

Raised beside the back fence, jutting out into the Reserve, was a wide spreading Morton Bay Fig tree, still looking youthful at over thirty meters high with its tumbling crowns of foliage. It was not a fig fruit tree with succulent berries. An evergreen, some of the lateral boughs seemed as wide as high. It stood alone catching the full rays of the sun in its many canopies, its cable-like invasively subterranean roots holding the embankment. They looked like raised barricades in some places, high enough for a child to hide behind, rising then falling in a serpentine way only to appear again elsewhere. They acted as buttresses on the ground holding the enormous weight above them.

It was a devouring monster of a tree. The roots were now heaving through the thin concrete layer beneath the new fences Maddox and Declan put on the properties. Any thought of placing an in ground swimming pool would be fruitless. Roots would inevitably crush its sides. The previous owners had the prescience to position the concrete water tanks as far away from the tree as possible.

Despite its milky toxic sap it was extremely elegant, its finely layered foliage of brightly ovate green leaves billowing from verdant crowns, cascading its massive structure. At first sight, it was difficult to believe that the trunk was strong enough to hold the enormous bowers and branches. A great source of shade, its infertile fig-like berries from its springy wire branches were a source of shade for birds.

Precipitously below it was the Reserve.

Caitlin went into damage control when Teresa first started shinning her way up at age five, threading through as if to find some hidden cave. She'd peer through the leaves back at her mother like a little black head on a pike, a turning periscope through a sea of green.

Fergus, offering his fearless(read useless) advice, thought it was a great idea. "Children her age are out on motor bikes doing doughnuts and wheel stands. Let her start with the hundred foot jump."

Caitlin couldn't keep Teresa out of it. Always a shy kid, as soon as she was out of the stroller when she'd go to town with her mother, she'd take to walking along short concrete walls with the balance of a jockey, a low center of gravity, the spring of an insect. She liked anything off the ground.

The two small fruit trees front and back, a mango and avocado, were far easier for her to climb. The avocado would give some four hundred fruit; the mango would droop, laden with fruit, often every second year. The trick was to keep the fruit bats away; they'd silently radar in at night, pick the mangoes until they fell, leaving them to rot, bats not foraging anything on the ground. But it was the fig tree which captivated her. No longer ballasted by any sandbags of gravity, she'd now peer over into the abyss below, that deep dark thicket of fallen trees strangulated by cacti and vines amongst all the flowering scrub and eucalyptus gum trees.

Arrival in Crone

The others had all finished High School, therefore were eligible for university, so Fergus talked them all into trying a semester at a tertiary institution nearby. He said he'd pay the fees. He seemed driven himself, and was still earning big money on rigs overseas. He was concerned, particularly for Caitlin, wanting to give her a head start in life. He did not want his sister wasting away in a small town unqualified and unemployed.

He stayed on a few weeks to help out with the roofing, routing, soldering, plastering, buying in two new hot water systems, then he was up and gone. Relocated out of there. Like a ghost. Caitlin was always sad to see him go, fearing that he might not return, lost to her forever like her dead parent and younger sister.

Maddox and Declan were strictly outdoor, practical souls, unhurried by ambition. They'd tried part time once at a technical school, but the thought of being riveted inside in hallowed halls at a draught's man desk studying building plans all day reminded them too much of their schooldays, where they only stayed on to be with the two girls.

To them, a problem in physics was how much force was required to fall over backwards while urinating against the garden shed; how much onion and beans was necessary from the barbeque to gain elevation. The rest seemed dust dry to them in a place where there was much outside work to do. While thankful for Fergus' endless generosity, they liked to play the caricature of him.

They left soon after to go out fence building in the district.

All four were handy with tools. As was Fergus. Colleen may have been a hairdresser by profession, but when it came to hard physical labor her Croatian background could outshine any Irish toil. The girls would work out the patterns, space the pickets, nail them, place joist hangers where the rails aligned, use nailing jigs and cutting scallops. They could replace any fence post, realign a sagging gate, keep up with their husbands in carrying heavy sheets of iron, pitch in with the creosote, tar and paint.

Then the two young brides would arrive at first 10 o'clock lecture in a flat deck pick-up with locked aluminum boxes on board, gently step the stairs of the lecture hall in their stained bib overalls, steel capped leather boots and canvas ankle chaps, still glistening with the salty glows of morning labor from the end of pick axes, crowbars and manual post hole diggers.

To the amazement of other students, they'd then pull Kyobi drills, plumb lines, cartridges of nails from their heavy satchels (for both were licensed to carry nail guns) to get to pens and paper, only then to have to deal with William Wordsworth's 'The child is father of the man,' or John Keats' 'Beauty is truth,' when their real famishment was for the pasta dishes or sausages and eggs over at the university canteen. Toughing it out on a fence-line seemed more enjoyable than these poetic lines. Fergus may have liked these notions. Caitlin and Colleen didn't really care. It did their heads in. They hadn't a clue what they were about. They may have got to learn the difference between a hackneyed expression and a handsaw, but did it really matter in the end? There seemed more frankness in hand saws.

Fergus had the lyrical mind. Not them. They'd rather read their pot boilers than poetry, be outside listening to the lorikeets than inside studying John. They made a quick decision to drop out before the penalty of full fees, Colleen returning to hairdressing in the suburb soon after, preferring hair to intellectual extensions. Caitlin, more serious by nature, began a nursing course at Mercy Hospital instead. Sharn was born to Colleen, Dominic two years later, then, after almost despairing of ever conceiving, Teresa to Caitlin two years after that.

They liked their houses removed from everyone else, the isolation, solitude of it; they liked racking up the yard, laying out in the sun with eye masks on, eating outside together in the evening, burning camphor bombs to keep the mosquitoes back in the trees, watching the sunsets, glimpsing the ocean in the distance.

There was a kind of rhyme and rhythm to picket fences.

Teresa, aged sixteen

Down in the Devil's Garden.

Dominic was late in leaving last class this Friday. It had been a testing week of heat. The school was set in a hollow; no benefit to be had from breezes this far from the ocean. It was humid, sticky, hard to sleep at night; annoying that he had to wait behind to collect a weekend assignment. The unforgiving sidewalk home would be as hot as a skillet. Pigeons often waited for Teresa to feed them the leftovers from her lunch-box as she passed. He doubted that they'd be there today.

Sharn now had her driving license. She was taking him and his friends to the beach that weekend. Maybe Teresa would come. She was a drag round them, gluing herself to Sharn. Dominic's friends were all rough and ready, made nuisances of themselves, a bunch of bozos honey-potting the girls off the short cliffs. Dominic was just as guilty. He'd listen to the sea reports in the morning. Everyone swan within the flags, never away from lifesavers. Rips could be fatal. Fishing off the rocks, fatal. A monster wave might hit, sweep people out to sea. Then there were other concerns. Sometimes they had to swim in netted pools because of the box jellyfish. Their stings could kill you. There were always dangers.

Hope Street didn't frighten Dominic. He'd cope with it o.k.. It just annoyed when they put hurt on Teresa. He couldn't wait to finish school. Get out of Crone.

"You're not wearing that," Sharn would say to him while painting her toenails, giving them and her mouth plenty of air time on the couch. "Won't be seen with you in that retro shirt. Even at the beach. Go and change it. Home's home. Not a gymnasium."

And she always tried giving him goofy haircuts, gelling his hair up for church on Sundays, experimenting styles for her hairdresser's apprenticeship, making him look a real dickhead.

"Don't trust you," he'd say. "Know what you're like. Given a chance you'd leave me looking like Mr. T."

As he turned the corner from school into Hope, Dominic saw Teresa hurrying back towards him. Suddenly she stopped, slipped under the fence rail down the embankment beside the Council's 'No Trespassing' sign to the Reserve.

Hope was a hive of activity on Friday afternoons, without much industry. Street girls assembled, some even carried bin-liners of possessions, hooking up, going through the hoops—Sharn called it 'dick day'—cars with big-ends cruised passed alleys, the pool hall filled with street kids, sly dealers. Teresa called it 'the street of freaks and sneaks,' especially on Fridays.

She often wondered why everyone got things backwards in this heat. She just went quiet. They all got fidgety, worked up, especially over stupid shit. Just to get home, up Edward, up her tree for safety.

Teresa walked with her head down, sulking like her fig tree. She reckoned that she could feel her tree brooding. It sighed. The last few nights after dark she'd let the garden hose leak into its root system. There'd be water restrictions soon. Even the birds went quiet in this. Blue skies seemed to turn to black, spotted with flies. And those flies could bite. Little parrots would come in for the birdseed she'd place up on her shoulders in the tree. Sometimes she'd put seed in her ears. They'd pick it out, then try at the gold studs in her ears. She'd tip seed in her hand. They'd hop down, take it, placidly sit on her wrist.

Even the shopkeepers were happy to call it a day, roll down their shutters bright with grime, pull the metal grills across. Even more so when hot breezes circled the hills. Winds seemed to make the kids go crazy, short tempered, whipping up hostilities. Teenagers from the caravan parks would hang out, pissed off, giving each other the lowdown, calling each other names.

Listlessness took over. Bravery in Crone was going off to reform home rather than do community service. It was their job to spread garbage, not to clean it up. There were no permanent gangs as such. Population was far too transient.

Teresa had been wrestling with thoughts from Father Kevin's Christian instruction lesson that last class of week. He'd told them that they were all gifts from God, their vocation was to testify for Jesus. Yet all she could think about was the walk home. Friday afternoons were like open season on Hope. Here were God's pests. Out in full. Like those biting flies. Why testify to that? Why talk to them? Why shouldn't she maintain her vow of silence? Insults didn't merit any reply. 'Please, pretty please, let me pass.' That never worked. Boys only wanted rewards. Pestered. Day in, day out. It continually tested her charity. Stupid. Stoo-pid! Stupid enough to try getting high sniffing inside the dry cleaners on the other side of the street. None of them walked far. Walked anywhere. She wondered why the parenting had stopped. Often she could smell weed on them.

"Suck it up," she thought, "like an Electrolux. Why don't they all grow up? Life's not a rumpus room."

"Bunch of prongs," Sharn would often say, "just tell them to f-off."

Dominic could see four guys up ahead, two in board shorts, others dungarees. They'd apparently chased Teresa back towards him, whooping, hollering, one cupping a hand under his armpit making farting sounds in timing with his toad-like jumping gait. Another followed up, croaking like a frog. Dominic heard the sounds even from that distance.

He knew these guys, but only by nickname. Reputation. Snot-Nose, Hackett-Face, Road-Dog, Sly. Lost Boys. The indignity of their names hardly suggested any respect for others. Teresa always found them about as unsettling as four miles of rough road. Dominic thought of them as little more than jokes. Tweety Bird, Sylvester, Snoopy, Charlie Brown. Just to get passed them each afternoon was enough for Teresa. Dominic never spoke to them, either. What was there to say!

Obviously, they'd blocked Teresa's passage. Stand and deliver. Deliver what! A game? Teresa said 'Let me pass.' They laughed. One tried to mock hump her leg, like the street dogs sometimes did. She felt like kneeing his privates. The others stood round like a small plague, hand rolling cigarettes, mouthing God only knows. She felt like a lab rat at best of times, constantly observed. Sometimes she hummed a tune under her breath to keep her courage up.

Teresa thought of these boys and their like as pack dogs converging at a junkyard fence, barking, leaping against the wires. She was easy meat, the only young looking bobby-soxer for miles. "Old enough to butcher, old enough to bleed," one of them said. She'd stared at them with her protuberant eyes, tore her school bag away, then decided to make a run for it. The malevolence of the Reserve was hardly the scenic route home yet preferable to these slavering dogs.

'If you want scary,' she thought, 'come down the Reserve. I'll show you who is the wuss.'

But they followed up, stood by the road fence looking down, not content with having pushed her over the edge. They thought it a real blast. One said 'Let's go get the little bitch.'

"Why didn't she cross the street?" Dominic thought as he peered over—for there she was, dragging her schoolbag, her Lycra shorts hanging off her skinny butt beneath the hem of her school tunic, beating a track through the slime and duck cast, not looking behind but up to her house in the distance on the hill.

"It's a wilderness down there," Dominic muttered, "not even one the Devil would show as a kingdom of the world."

He'd heard that expression from Caitlin when referring to the Reserve.

Dominic looked at it with a kind of despair, it looked as inviting as entering a sty. A triple-decker of giant pillars of dead trees. Dead meat. Carrion under a merciless sun. Everything rotted down there. Nothing was spared. That sun sat above it like a tilted axe. A pit, stranded in time, isolated from history.

It seemed that Teresa didn't care. Come and get me, if you can.

The boys were now gaining, trying to dodge the thickness of thistles, avoiding the bramble, blackberry thorns, density of undergrowth. Vines hanged from trees like withered intestines, the ground fossilized with age. Dominic was not frightened of much, but this place gave him the creeps. He got a sudden feeling of nausea. He spat the taste of it from his mouth.

He slid down the embankment, grazing his knees on the whitened stones. They'd looked like crumbled bones slipping beneath his school shoes. At the bottom he cast his eyes round, picked up a long wedge of hardwood, hit it to ground to test its strength, and finding it had not broken followed along the primeval maze, of which no one could make head nor tail. The track was as thin as a thread. He looked for the needles either side.

It was the wrong time of year ever to be down this catacomb of decay. As if there were a right time. Summer's heat burned fiercely at mid-afternoon, fermenting anything which held any moisture, mushrooming growth from yesterday's brief rain. Dominic thought of tropical bamboo growing six inches a day. And it was a place of strangulation. No sight of waves lapping the beaches down here; no bougainvillea, Poinciana, flame trees, the brilliant flowers of local parks and gardens, just a complication of tumbling creeper and vine, some hanging in groups, ropelike as the banyan trees.

Teresa seemed unconcerned. She knew that she'd lose them in it as she stalked out in front. She'd pictured in her mind a map of the landscape from her spyglass up the in fig tree. She knew every nook, every cranny. These boys could now come into her parlor, she'd make burnt rissoles of them, feel the pain of it for themselves. 'Take a good look,' she thought. 'It's where you belong.' She dismissed them.

"Let me pass," she'd said. That's all. Not chill out, clear off, leave me alone. Fat chance of their listening. No meant nothing to them. Nuns at school told the students that they must perform 'random acts of kindness.' Teresa did. Often. But it didn't work here. Kindness was only a weakness. A chink in one's armor. A daydream. Sometimes she wished she lived in the ghastly suburbs with a ghastly mall or two, only because of the walk home. She loved home, the isolation, parties at weekends, uncle stirring things up, winding up the band. Fridays were best of all, full of expectation.

For no clear reason, she remembered again her seventh birthday.

What a disaster that had been.

She'd been full of anxiety, soon to make her first communion. What concerned most was what to say to Father Kevin at her first confession. Her mother feared she'd clam up, say nothing at all. Teresa pestered her mother with questions about her sinful soul: am I bad at home, did I really kill the baby Jesus? Nothing they said placated her.

They brought Fergus in.

He'd sort it out.

Like Ghost Busters.

Or Dante.

He'd give her some decent sins to confess.

Fergus sat with her at the kitchen table. He put her through the hoops, there in his black jacket like some latter day Spanish Inquisitor: do you leave the refrigerator door open, the lid off the jam jar, DO YOU PULL WINGS OFF FLIES?

Teresa remembered shaking her head in disgust.

On the day before her first confession, Fergus took them to a Drive-In movie, made her lay in the trunk in the car, then got her in without paying. "There you go," he said, a big smile on his face, "That's what they call cheating a business out of what's rightfully theirs, a sin worthy to confess."

She just thought that she was doing as she was told.

Fergus told Father Kevin, who shook his head in wonder. What could he say! What else would one expect from Fergus!

Momentarily, she noticed the subtle shades of green, much closer to them now, and for the very first time. She felt no goose bumps on her arms, just saddened to think that these boys seemed as unruly as this undergrowth.

As she stalked on, Teresa wondered if you could see stars in daytime from these hollow reaches. It was like looking up a chimney to the sky. The Reserve ran a sunken path like a dead artery, clogged to nowhere to all. She'd seen these things in her mother's nursing books. She bumbled along, muttering 'dirt-bags,' remembering the small neglected tracks in the cartography of her mind.

She knew that kids off the street had tried living down here under their plastic hump tents; that they'd come to light fires at nights, drink alcohol in huddles, smoke dope, but the area was so full of mosquitoes over stagnant pools when rains came that it became alive with lice and summer ticks. Seasons were barely perceptible, yet they did exist, if only just to trick the snakes into sleeping. She'd trick these snakes, even if it killed her.

It was a hopeless place. There were dead dogs down here. She'd even seen wild goats now and again. Purple breasted swamp hens would sometimes come out of hiding, wade about once it rained heavily. She liked the swamp hens. She admired their determination. Her Pa once had told her that if they were shot or wounded by hunters they'd rather drown themselves than be captured by the bird dogs.

There were also lots of bush rats nested in the thicket, snakes too, most of them venomous. Teresa had been taught at school how to identify the different species, what to do if confronted. Snake handlers had given talks to her class, said how they'd capture them to make the anti-venom, casually referring to their job as 'being out on the milk run.' She could now plainly see beneath her feet the ring shaped homes of the trapdoor spiders protecting themselves against flood. It was not as though the local council had put up the No Trespassing signs because it was a place of any value. Fire was their real concern. It would ravage it in no time. The heat would be so intense that it would melt unlit candles in the two houses. And it abounded with evils. Walled in. Like up on Hope.

She then thought how evil wearied its way into destroying things.

Nuns at school saw it differently. Evil, they said, was nothing, just an absence of good. She was never certain what her uncle thought about that, but was sure that he'd not agree. Nuns annoyed her. How could they see what life was like on Hope having their heads up their butts. Teresa knew that was an uncharitable thought. She couldn't avoid it.

Teresa knew every inch of the terrain. After all, it was her domain to survey. She'd often watched the fruit bats drifting in by radar along its deep funnel at dusk, observed the cheeky magpies becoming more aggressive in nesting season; had once seen a nest of snakes copulating on open ground for what seemed hours. She wondered why this was. She went and asked her uncle.

Fergus said snakes lacked the frills and crests and changeable colors to attract, relied on scent only, which they caught on their tongues tracking the females. Teresa thought how glad she was that Ballou had been fixed. She was much younger when she got her cat, didn't know what 'being fixed' meant when her mother insisted on it.

She went and asked Sharn.

Sharn knew everything.

"It means Ballou won't put lipstick and rouge on at night, play Barry White records, go down Hope Street looking for some action."

Yeah, right, Teresa now thought, fat use you were, Big Sister.

Although it held endless fascination for her, she still thought of this ravine as an actively spiteful and angry place. It was more than a nothing, no absence, so like, and fit for, these boys. To her, they all had spiders in their heads. They'd cultivated them up in the damp heat of Hope. As above. So below. She thought.

The place often filled with dirt and toxin. Cane toads. After rains. This was, after all, sugarcane country. They'd been introduced to the cane fields in a vain attempt to keep the cane beetle population down. Some of these marine toads were enormous with their purring 'pop pop, pop' as they dropped their black tadpoles in strings of jelly in the water. She'd read that a single female could lay up to 35,000 eggs a year. And they always came up nights round her house when there was lots of moisture in the air. They'd eat any food which didn't move, indifferent to human presence. Their venom could kill her cat, if it struck out at them with its paws. They'd infest the whole town when it rained, so much so that the council recently put a bounty back on them. Children would go catch them by the hundreds some nights, for money. The toads were then frozen as the most humane way of putting them down.

They'd always reminded Teresa of the toads up on Hope. Popping eyes. Paralyzing drugs. Ugliness of lives. Ugly, ugly, ugly. They really tested her charity.

She plugged on through the spiteful brush with a thousand such spiteful thoughts.

Many of the trees were long dead in this lowered cemetery pit, tangled in clutches of vines, stretched, strangulated until inevitably falling inward with decay. There were rotten bowers, far too dangerous to consider climbing. They had termite nests inside. There were also gaping shaded holes in trunks, cooler places for snakes to lodge. Yet she was not perturbed by these dangers.

Only the ticks frightened her. They needed a blood source for their life cycle from early Spring on. What frightened her most was their invisibility. Their saliva was full of toxins, causing paralysis, even death for a person her age. They were to be feared more than other crawlers and critters. They were capable of killing a dog within a day, seemed smart enough to lodge only where they couldn't be scratched. People wouldn't feel them entering, burrowing under the skin without irritation. There they'd live without the host knowing.

Caitlin no longer toweled Teresa off after her shower, checking for lice, behind her ears, under arms for ticks. Yet Teresa also knew that her trees held no such dangers, that the mango and avocado trees were more humane, bearing fruit, not disease.

The only fruits she could see down here were all scarred by death.

Ticks invaded the fruit bats. Teresa would sometimes see them comatose down here on the ground through her spyglass. The bats never survived.

One day, a year ago, Teresa saw from her tree Declan collapse in his yard. She was about to laugh. It looked so funny. Declan teased her as much as her uncle did. She'd yelled at him. He didn't respond. She quickly descended, ran inside for her mother. As Caitlin turned Declan over she noticed a small black spot on his neck made by the mandibles of a tick. Teresa rushed back inside for a bottle of spirits, pair of tweezers, a magnifying glass to pull the tick from his neck. Abdomen, thorax, head. It all had to come out, carefully, piece by piece.

She stalked on reassuring herself that she'd be the one to survive this, pulling her leather schoolbag close to her chest to cover herself. She turned to see if the boys were catching. She'd seen Dominic scramble down the bank, noticed that he was carrying a stick like a hickory club, knew that he could not be far behind them. She thought of her cat, so glad it had not ever strayed into this slough.

As she quickened her pace, running an unbeaten track of her own making, her thoughts were again of catechism lesson in Christian Instruction. She tried to remember the passage how The Lord wanted us to lay down in green pastures, lie beside the still waters, how that restoreth the soul. She knew such places could never be found down here amongst the dead and dying. This place was past redemption. Sometimes Teresa could hear from her bed the frantic swamp hens screeching down here at night. As if someone was strangulating them. She said a quick Hail Mary for them.

She then wondered where that damned fox was who'd killed her goose and gander.

She could hear the boys getting closer, still yapping like dogs, talking their filth as she led them further and further into the density of vine. They reminded of kookaburras, Laughing Jackasses, big, ugly kingfishers with their 'Hoo, Hoo, Hoo,' 'Ha, Ha, Ha,' chuckling absurdity of sound. Less absurd than these 'dirt-bags' with their handmade noises under armpits, evolved for no purpose at all.

She'd much rather hear the 'tewp-tewp' soft piping of the little Yellow Robins, had once heard the trilling 'treees' of a tiny Fairy Wren. Nights often disappointed Teresa. She could no longer see clearly through her spyglass.

One evening, as she was about to go inside, a Tawny Frogmouth Owl came up from the Reserve, sat squarely gazing at her on the fencepost. With wings flattened out to its sides it blended with the post. Owls often roosted down here during the day, otherwise they'd be set upon by the flocks of Honeyeaters.

Teresa stared at the owl. It looked back at her from the dark areas around its eyes, surrounded by 'spectacles.' It was molting, old, not interested in foraging. It then suddenly began shaking with uncontrollable convulsions, obviously near death. Her Pa told her that it had probably eaten insecticide somewhere, stored it in its fat, unable to rid it from its body. It would die. She never saw it again.

That night, at dinner prayers, she bowed her head and said "And God look after Ballou and the Tawny Frogmouth Owl, who has just joined my Auntie Teresa."

Teresa stomped her feet angrily into the freshly muddy ground in order to leave a deliberate track. She was not frightened of her pursuers, nor what lived down here. A bush rat suddenly crossed her path. That didn't phase her. It looked cute. It meant no harm. She didn't like killing things. She even often made way for lines of ants. Fergus once told her that he'd seen women in a marketplace in Colombo, Sri Lanka, how they'd wait for the ants to pass in front of them, how women would pick the lice from one another's hair, place them to ground; even make market sellers crack eggs before purchasing, not wanting bad karma from killing live chicks inside. Some religious people wore gauze masks in the streets, not for the gas fumes of traffic, but the bad karma of inbreathing bugs of the air.

She wondered if her pursuers would be too dumb to notice the tracks.

Dominic noticed.

He was looking to ground for her prints. As the bracken and tumbling vines got more dense, the boys grew quieter.

"Let's go back," Teresa heard one say, "bitch ain't worth the trouble."

As Dominic went underneath the darkened bowers, pushing the thorny brambles aside with his stick, he heard a soft voice from above.

"Dom."

He looked up. He saw her black head peering out high in the dying foliage She must have been twenty five feet off the ground, perfectly camouflaged in the middle of a bower.

"Run along the fallen trees." She said softly.

He noticed a Willy Wagtail in the branches beside her, the quick flit of its tail left to right in the sunlight. They always made a din on the ground beside the house, noisy whenever Teresa's cat came near. It was now swiveling beside her as though wanting to perch, as it does on cattle. Maybe she knew this particular bird. Maybe it had sat beside her before in the fig tree.

Dominic never cared much for the trees. He liked to keep his thoughts and aspirations on the ground, never over-reaching himself. Sometimes, in early evening, he'd remember to water the pot-plants, which his mother put in the shade of his shed. He would see Teresa peering down at him from her fig tree. One evening, he deliberately turned the garden hose up on her, giving her a quick spray as it passed the branches.

"For you, Little Irish Rose," he said in mock imitation of Fergus. He liked the lyrical way Fergus spoke. Teresa darted back into the foliage, climbed again, scurrying away from the passing drench. She then reappeared, poked out her tongue at him. The cat was always with her. It hated the drench of water.

Dominic ran up at a forty five degree angle along a fallen trunk. It had lodged itself into the fork of another. He stood on the interlocks, holding his wooden club, staring up, then climbed further until reaching Teresa's level. There he rested, his back against the trunk, looking out to her along the bower.

Teresa faced him, squatting with perfect balance, hands on knees, enough foliage around not to be seen. Dominic gripped his stick like an Irish club. Teresa didn't seem the least concerned. Her schoolbag was slung across her chest. She crouched like a little panther. Dominic noticed two boxes of matches which she'd taken from her satchel. She'd placed them on the bower. She was ready to fight.

They could hear the boys' voices getting closer, coming back out of the entanglement.

"Let her be." One said.

"She'll keep." Said another.

"Another time." The third.

They walked underneath, swearing in annoyance, stepping over the brush which looked tighter than herrings in a tin, then brushing the pollens off, webs from shoulders, stickiness from clothing, then they quickly headed back to their track before hoofing it back up the hill again.

Teresa peered down. She felt sad. They'd looked like a line of little ancient men beneath her, nothing much to do or say to one another in a Neolithic world. They looked beaten, white, bathroom sick, bewildered, worse for wear having encountered a nature greater than they could ever hope to wreck.

Dominic noticed Teresa, too—maybe for the first time—the blue black sheen of her hair spread out in disguise freed from her bunches; her eyes so sad, her lips thick with a kind of savagery. When the satchel slipped from her chest he noticed her breasts like rounded young bull horns, so firm under her strong shoulders.

But she quickly picked up the match boxes, then stood, began running back towards him along the bower in a light skip, her brown leather schoolbag clutched to her white shirt. He was amazed at her balance and agility. She moved as quickly as a mud stripper over water.

She went ahead, quickly descending to ground.

"I know a fast track to home up the hill."

She looked so clean, hardly a spot or web on her clothing. She spoke as though just another day up a tree.

He followed, as he always did, without speaking, all the way up a rough path to beside both their houses. She knew every twist and turn. Unhindered.

"Don't tell my Ma we've been down there. She'll flip if she finds out," she said in passing at the fence, before going their separate ways.

What's One to Do with Her?

Caitlin often talked to Fergus about Teresa. Fergus wasn't ever much help.

"She's such a oddity. She's like Little Orphan Annie wandering round all day by herself" Teresa heard Caitlin say to him one night.

Teresa was snooping from up the mango tree when supposed to be in bed. Everyone sat outside on Saturday night.

Fergus said. "Well, she isn't. Better than being a doe-eyed princess. The kid costs you nothing. And this family's better than none. Let her mouth off. Don't worry about the lip and the back chat at nights. She's just rehearsing. She's only saying what other kids say at school. She says it at home. To you. She's a good kid. She's happy here. She's never gives you any trouble, or is into self-harm. Let her get herself studs in her chin and a dozen nose rings, if she wants. Who cares! It'll stop her from sniffing glue."

"I know she's good. It's just sometimes I wonder if her day-dreaming is a form of depression. Always by herself. Dreaming her life away up in the trees."

Caitlin was clearly disappointed.

"Maybe just dreaming up new ways to be smart. Don't worry about it."

"Teresa says the girls at school get on computer together, talk of date rape drugs, anal sex, write things as disgustingly as they can. Even Sharn does it. Teresa won't have a bar of it, so she tells me."

"So what! It's only bravado, Cait. Encourage bravado at home. Thank God she likes it here. You don't ever have to correct her. She'd rather kick about working with Maddox and Declan on Saturdays than hanging around the Mall. Be thankful for it. She'll find her own way, soon enough."

"But her school reports. They're appalling."

"Encourage her to learn at home, then."

"Well she is not going to be home schooled, not for religious reasons. Imagine that, dear brother," Caitlin grinned at him, "You'd be showing her pictures from South America of some Communist Jesus with a rifle slung over His shoulder."

"I think He's coming back. It'll be an Israeli Uzi."

"I'll ignore that. She's going to stay where she is, even if she has no friends at school."

"She likes Sharn. Her friends."

"That's not enough."

"Let her leave then. Get her a job in the hosiery department at the Mall."

Caitlin playfully slapped Fergus' hand. "It's not your department to help. She hates Malls. You know that. And there isn't much need of hosiery in this heat, is there!"

"Don't worry, Cait. Be glad she can read and write, use a knife and fork. Let her be away with the birds. No one's ever going to stop them singing or imprison them. She's not the sort of kid to grow up and sit in bars, doing nothing."

"But the school reports, Fergus. They're atrocious."

"Just be glad we live in a cul-de-sac. She'll escape it soon enough. You never have to raise your voice to her. Let her go to Samoa, get tattoos from head to foot, sit on a beach, split open coconuts, pour half a bottle of rum in them."

"I'd be raising my voice to her if she does that. I don't like her slopping around in rags."

"Whose to see? Whose to care! It's just a phase."

"I wish she liked boys more. Sometimes I wish she'd get one, fall in love."

"Forget it. She's o.k. as she is. In half the world it would be considered shameful for a sixteen year old girl to fall in love." Fergus offered. "Let her find her own way."

"Only that half of the world that you know, dear brother."

Teresa didn't care what they said about her, but her eyes did widen when they mentioned that the 'dancing teacher' was coming over on Saturday night. The dancing teacher was Fergus' 'girlfriend.' All very hush-hush. Who was she? Was she loony as Fergus? Surely, she'd have to be.

The dancing teacher. Teresa told her parents one evening at dinner that she's seen Fergus with a pretty woman outside the town library. Her parents immediately clammed up. They didn't want to talk about it. All she got was 'she's a dancing teacher from the city,' and 'mind your own business.'

Teresa thought little more about it. Probably one of Fergus' passing fancies.

Teresa slipped down from the tree, went inside to bed.

All Grown up (and shaving)

"How come you never tell me off or tell what to do, Uncle?" Teresa asked Fergus that Saturday afternoon. She was feeling badly about her school report, and perplexed why Fergus didn't really seem to care much about it.

They'd had lunch outside. Caitlin was inside preparing for festivities for the evening. Declan and Maddox got gone away to cost out a job.

"I'm your uncle. Not your grandpa. Not for me to say."

Teresa thought about that. Uncle. Grandpa. There was a sense in which he was a Grandpa, too. He had raised her mother.

"You never hug me much, do you? Or kiss me." Teresa pouted then grinned.

Fergus put his arm round her shoulder, gently kissed her cheek, immediately drew back.

"The only things you should ever kiss are billiard balls, Tess. Then there's always dangers of bird flu, of course. Kissing can be very dangerous."

"Ha, ha, ha. It's pretty dangerous down in the pool hall on Hope."

"Is it? I'll take you in there one day, if you want. I'll show you how to play properly. A great way to misspend your youth."

"No, thank you."

"Suit yourself."

"When will you bring your lady friend round to meet us?"

"So you've heard about her, have you? Tonight. If that's o.k.?"

"Do you kiss her?"

"Only after we dance together. Both cheeks. Bird flu again."

"Yeah, sure, Mr. Whiskey Tango Foxtrot." Teresa smiled. Fergus would often answer his telephone with those words.

"I want to meet her. Does she have any tattoos? In strange places? You can tell me. Now that I'm all grown up . . . and shaving."

Fergus grinned. "I don't know."

Teresa leaned across, slapped him gently on the arm. "Liar, liar. Yes you do. I've now decided what kind of tattoo I'm getting. A permanent hickey. I'll tell the nuns it's a birthmark. Say they just haven't noticed before. Where'd you meet her, anyway?"

"Marseilles."

"Where? Mars?" Teresa grinned back cheekily.

"Marseilles. France." Fergus looked back at her straight faced.

"Do you like French people?"

"Of course not. A big bunch of sissies, if you ask me. Only good at cooking. Only capable of writing menus. Big words about food that we can't understand."

"But you like her?"

"Yes."

"What the hell's she doing here then?"

"She doesn't live here. She lives in the city. She has a dance studio."

"So I can meet her tonight?"

"Sure."

"What's her studio called? Does she have any calling cards? Phone number? Do you think she'd put me up if I decide to ran away?"

"Do you want to run away?"

"No. Hope Street's full of runaways. Nobody's got parents anymore."

"Does that make you feel sad?"

"Sometimes. They're a bunch of losers up there. They don't represent anything."

"Maybe that's because nobody's ever represented them."

"Why do those girls have sex for money? Why don't they get a real job?"

"It is a real job. Maybe they're saving up for a house? Go to university?"

"Doubt it. They can't even spell university."

"Then maybe it's because they can't concentrate. Do you concentrate on anything, Tess? That's what life's all about, isn't it? Concentrating on something?"

"My attendance record's perfect. That takes a whole lot of concentration."

"Have you spoken to any of the street girls? You should. Cross over the street. Ask them why they do it. Ask them to answer you seriously."

"Yeah, right. Says you. You never answer anything seriously. I'm not allowed to cross the street. Full stop. Ma won't let me. I guess I could if I made it into a school survey. I'm sure the nuns at school would love that. I could present it in economics class. I could have perpendicular graphs about how to make money on the horizontal."

Fergus said nothing. He knew she picked up these expressions from Sharn. The two girls would text one another on their mothers' phones, leave it there for their mothers to see, butchering the language as much as they could: full of 6, 4play, Dom is a big 2L, Sharn's ass looked like crap—on and on and on.

Teresa didn't like his silence.

"Why don't you give those street girls money then, like you do for the homeless people?"

"Because those people had nothing at all. Some say they want money for books. Ask me what to read. Feed their souls. Food only sustains them."

"What? A whole bunch of stories which mightn't even be true?"

"Doesn't matter if they're true."

"What? Like, say, the story of Adam and Eve. Do you believe that one?"

"Doesn't matter what I believe. We're still better off for having the story."

Teresa went silent.

"What sort of a dance studio has your girlfriend got, anyway?"

"'It's called Sister Pauline's Studio of Pole Dancing . . . For Runaway Teenage Girls.'"

"Ha, ha. She'd better not be a nun! Or an ex nun. That'd be awful. I've never heard of a dance called The Penguin or The Shuffle-Bum. How boring that'd be!"

"You shouldn't call nuns penguins, Tess."

"Why not? Have you heard the one about the guy up on Hope Street who asked the policeman if there were any penguins around here? Policeman said no. O dear, said the man, I must've just driven over a nun on the zebra crossing."

"Yes, Tess. I've heard it. When I was a kid." Fergus looked at her glumly.

"Well? What's wrong with that?"

"Penguins probably have a harsher life than almost any other living creature on this planet. They suffer badly, all huddled together protecting their young in the Antarctic winds."

"Nuns don't suffer. They lock themselves away in cloisters."

"Are you sure of that? There's a tradition about penguins. They pierce their own breasts with their beaks to feed their blood to their young. They have to put up with you, don't they? And all the Paulies of the world. And help Ian with his Down's Syndrome. And the rest of them."

"I help Ian, too. In the library."

"I know that. And it's good that you do. But nuns also wait at the gate for him. Wait and wait and wait. Every morning, afternoon. They see him safely on his way." Fergus hesitated a moment then muttered under his breath "Along with all his Christian baggage."

What Do I Do?

It was now much rarer with a sense of bravado that Teresa performed at home. She began to discuss things more seriously with her mother, things which concerned her.

"Sister Agnes says I should get myself a job. Baby sitting, something similar. Working part-time at McDonald's weekends for chump change. She says it'll bring me out of myself. It's not for the money, Ma. I just don't want to do it. I'd rather help you here. Colleen and Sharn down at the salon, if I have to. Or Pa and Declan weekends. Pa lets me screed and trowel off the concrete driveways. He says I'm good at it. I've got a good eye for levels."

"The discipline you learn at McDonald's does look good on a C.V." Caitlin said sharply. School was not going easily for Teresa.

"I just don't like going out. I don't want to hang out with friends at the Mall stealing clothes, CDs, like some girls do. I have all the clothes and CDs I want. I'd rather go to the library. Nights and weekends are fun here. There's always a party. I'll do more chores. For nothing. Clean uncle's room. Do the lawns next door. Just say it, Ma, I'll do it." There was a hint of desperation in her voice.

Caitlin relented, putting her arm around her shoulder. "I know you would, dear. You're a great help to us. Your Pa and I really appreciate what you do. But you must get yourself friends of your own. You can't stay at home all your life."

"I like all creatures, Ma. Great and small. I like Ballou. Birds. They don't tease. I don't tease them. I don't mean like the way Uncle and Declan tease." Her answers seemed to hit Caitlin like a blackout.

"But these things mostly live in trees, dear. What about Dominic's friends? They have nice girlfriends. They come over here at weekends. You must know them. They go to your school. Why don't you take time out, talk to them?"

"Most are in the swimming team. They're all into fashion. Wet T-shirts." Teresa looked at her mother, turning up her nose, lowering her head. "Boys only like things clingy and wet. I don't like water balloon fights. Boys are revolting. They should grow up. I'd rather listen to Uncle's music than the stuff they listen to. Weekends are happy here. I like seeing you and Pa happy. And Colleen and Declan. I like dancing with Sharn. Her friends. They're fun. Even Father Kevin has a good time when he's over. Am I just being clingy as well? Wet?"

"It's ok. No one's going to make you go out to work." Caitlin hesitated. She didn't want her daughter forever innocent, isolated from the world. "Don't you like boys, Tess?"

"No. They're like that old rhyme—frogs, snails, puppy dog tails."

"Thought you liked frogs."

"Make it toads then."

"What else don't you like?"

"Girls." Teresa grinned inanely at her mother.

"Doesn't leave much to be desired, does it?"

"Uncle gets on ok without either. I'm going to live alone. Like he does."

"You don't know that for sure, do you!" Caitlin said softly.

"You mean he lives with that dancer woman?" Teresa's eyes lighted up.

"I said you don't know that, FOR SURE! Tess, you have to lose your attitude."

"That's what the teachers say at school. That's so dumb. How can I lose my attitude when I don't really have one?"

"Sharn has lots of friends." Caitlin said.

"They give her lots of bad hair days, too."

"So what."

"Bad hair days make mine stand up on end. Real hairy-scary. Who wants that?"

"There's lots of bad hair days in life, Teresa."

"I really like Sharn, but I sometimes think boys only like her for her big tits. I heard one of her boyfriends say he can support two of her watermelons under one arm. That's real funny, isn't it!"

Caitlin didn't reply.

"Dominic's friends call them 'airbags.' I feel like saying to them that's about right, they were given to us for a bunch of airheads like you." She reflected a moment. "I just want to be myself. By myself. Is that so bad?"

"No, it isn't. But you don't have to be about as unlovely as a car battery, Teresa."

"I don't feel unlovely. I feel good here. I need more time. I'm working on it."

Caitlin almost said 'more time to waste at school.' She didn't. She let it go.

Teresa got the last word in. It was with a phony workman's accent. "I'm going to work at a job that's off the ground. Like up a tree. Roofer, scaffold worker, firefighter, cleaning high rise buildings. That'd be different."

Caitlin laughed. "I can just see it now. All the passers-by will be wolf whistling you instead of the other way round."

Home Ten. School Nil.

Fergus went south to the city every Monday morning for his liquor selling business. He was a good salesman, welcomed in places for his business acumen, famous for his boxing past, humorous as a kind of 'loose unit.'

"You do what you know best," he'd often say. He was a very sociable man, and making plenty of money. Despite buying the two houses here, he seemed to have the Midas touch. He now drove a brand new S type Mercedes, but what really impressed Teresa, whenever she rode with him, was how he'd do his paperwork, toting up lists of figures with a pen while stationary at traffic lights. He was smart. Organized. And she secretly admired the way Fergus kept moving on. Driving all day meant he kept off the drink. He never spoke of where he stayed while away.

Another thing that Teresa liked was that Fergus always brought home all the wrong things. There was food, and plenty of it, enough to keep them all week, not quite dag-woods and fairy-floss but there was party foods for Saturday nights. Old habits die hard. He had brought up Caitlin in her teenage years. He kept feeding the families as if their lives, and his, depended upon it.

Teresa would wait up the tree for him on Friday evenings. He'd arrive regularly around five. Teresa could distinguish every vehicle coming up the street by their engine noise. Few cars ever came up Edward. Fergus' car purred noiselessly as her cat. She always made sure that the house gate was open Fridays. Fridays brought with it new surprises. Caitlin would stand grinning at him from the kitchen window while Teresa would stand open-mouthed up in the fig tree.

Fergus would pull in, the music still blaring from the car stereo. One Friday he got out, opened the rear door, bent over disappearing momentarily into the back seat. Teresa stared down, as if expecting some monstrosity to appear. His hand reached up, placing a green apple up on the car roof. The hand disappeared, reappearing shortly after, feeling for the fruit on the bonnet. A suckling pig's head then reared with the apple in its mouth, a little trotter waving to Teresa in the tree. Fergus then danced up the garden path to the music, the pig cradled in white muslin in his arms.

Other weeks it would be a ham in a bag, a dressed lamb, a large salmon. His car trunk was always filled with goodies. Teresa would immediately drop to ground, rushing over to help. Weekends were fiesta time. Like the birds in the trees, he filled her with curiosity. He was smart, bold, free, venturesome, returning regularly each week like some magnetic field beckoning him back home.

She liked to think that this was his home, not the dusty motels he lived in during the week. After all, he'd bought both the houses.

There were often other surprises half hidden somewhere in the house: mantel-piece, next to her drink bottle in the refrigerator, outside her bedroom door.—an interesting book, a CD, a new pair of walking shoes, a fashion labeled T-shirt—something he'd heard her speak about. Teresa never ever intended them as hints. She preferred to be round him than be handed his goodwill. But everyone got gifts. He'd leave CDs outside the shed door for Dominic. Caitlin called Fergus' Mercedes his 'gypsy van.' It yielded anything you ever wanted.

Fergus would turn a firing spit outside on Saturday afternoons with Maddox and Declan after they'd watched football in the shed. After eating in the evening, Fergus would throw hot coals out on the ground. He'd produce bags of marsh-mellows for the young ones to toast in the embers. Everyone sat round or stood talking. Everyone danced. Sharn and Dominic were always encouraged to bring their friends over.

Nobody ever argued. Fergus treated everyone the same. He came, he went, he did as he pleased, and was just as likely to have breakfast with Sharn and Dominic on Saturday morning then go off shopping with Colleen. He and Colleen would often walk along hand in hand. Fergus would often hold his sister's hand. They were a weird family. Teresa thought that she knew the reasons why, but couldn't get anyone to open up about the past as to what made them the way they were.

"I reckon he holds up banks during the week. Different ones on Friday on his way home." Sharn confided once to Teresa, "He'll have us all shitting bricks soon. We'll probably go to jail as Communists for receiving. I'm not going to ask him for money again."

Fergus the Pastor

Then there was the thorny question of religion. Teresa only excelled in her Christian Instruction classes. She'd been first in class since the age of nine. When she was ten, at the dinner table one night, she asked Fergus if he would teach her 'religious things,' in her own words, for him to be her 'pastor.'

Caitlin immediately kicked Fergus under the table. She then mouthed 'Holy Mother of God, NO!' Maddox could all but smile.

The Gospel, according to Fergus. Teresa thought her uncle could do anything, short of turning loaves into fishes. He was pretty good at turning wine back into water again. Religion it was to be, filtered through the liver.

"Yes, I'll do that," said Fergus, unfazed.

Teresa and Fergus would sit up at the dinner table in the evening before the meal was served. Teresa would have had her shower, sitting right beside him in her terry cloth robe, quietly imitating his actions. He'd be toting up figures on a notepad, entering in telephone numbers, crossing off filled orders. Teresa would have similar notepad and pencil that Fergus had given her, making notes of her own.

This evening Fergus began scrawling on his notepad. When he finished, he tore the page off, handed it to Teresa. She read:

'One idle damn Sunday Dad killed a cheating thief and lied to cover it.'

"You shouldn't say damn, Uncle." Teresa looked at him crossly.

"Says who?"

"It's in the Ten Commandments."

Fergus pointed to the paper that he'd just given her. "They are the Ten Commandments."

"Liar."

"Look at them."

Teresa looked to the page, pondering it for what seemed ages. Suddenly she grew excited.

"I've got it. One . . . there is only one God. Two . . . idle, there are to be no idols before Him. Three. Damn . . . you must not swear, or take His Name in vain. Four is Sunday, you must keep the Sabbath. Five is Dad, so Honor your father and mother. Six is don't kill. Seven is adultery is cheating. Eight is no stealing. Nine. Lying is giving false witness. Ten. Do not covet things."

"Very good." Fergus said. He nodded across to Caitlin, then to Maddox. No false witness given. Not so far.

"Are you sure you know the meanings of those words?" Caitlin asked.

"Yes. Sort of. Does honor your father mean you have to do as he says?"

Caitlin wasn't quite sure. At least she didn't ask about adultery.

"Not really," Fergus said. "It means more that you should provide for your father and mother in their old age."

"Can I have another one, then?"

Fergus scribbled on his notepad again. He handed it over.

It read 'Pews 'Ave Glu.'

"What's that mean?"

"You know what church pews are. They're covered in glue."

"Liar. What's it really mean?"

"They're The Seven Deadly Sins."

Teresa eyed him with instant disbelief. She went away and got her catechism. She checked them.

"Pews. I get it now. It's just the letters. Pride, Envy and Wrath and Sloth. 'Ave. Glu. Avarice and Gluttony and Lust. I get it now." She felt pleased with herself.

"Do you know what the words mean?" Fergus asked this time.

"Sort of. My catechism explains them. Can I have another one?"

"After dinner."

Caitlin grinned then shook her head, partly out of relief.

After dinner, Fergus said seriously to Teresa. "You know how parables are interesting stories to illustrate a moral?"

"Yes."

"Well, we will need an illustration for this one." Fergus left the table. Typically, he returned soon after with an Irish Jameson whiskey bottle and two glasses. He explained to her that whiskey was a generic name, a trade usage, spelt as whisky in Canada, pointing to a bottle of Canadian Club whisky, and whiskey with an extra e in Ireland. Originally, it was spelt whisky in Scotland. Not so today.

A spelling lesson, thrown in for good measure.

Caitlin wondered where on earth this was taking them.

He then poured out two large glasses of Jameson for Caitlin and Maddox, which they then sipped, religiously. He himself abstained.

He then handed her another note.

'Bart And John Fill Matt with 2 James, 2 Simons, 2 Judases.'

"Where's the parable there?" Teresa asked.

"They are the names of the Twelve Apostles. Two James." Fergus pointed to each of her parents' whiskey glasses.

"I can only count eleven names here."

"Include 'And' as a name. Don't use your catechism this time."

Teresa thought for a while, trying to recall them from memory. "Bartholomew, Andrew, John, Philip, Thomas, Matthew, James, Simon, Judas."

"That makes only nine," Fergus said.

"Where's St. Peter in this?" Teresa asked.

Fergus said nothing.

"Wasn't one called Simon Peter, the other one just named Simon?" Caitlin said.

Fergus didn't respond.

"Weren't there two Judases, as well? Judas Iscariot. Judas the Greater?" Maddox added.

It was then that they all were stuck.

Teresa reached for her catechism. "It's James the Less and James the Greater. You didn't even know yourself, did you, Uncle? You wanted us to find out and tell you."

Fergus smiled, and said nothing.

*   *   *

Yet to Teresa's surprise, it turned out that Fergus did know the answer. It was the following Saturday night. Teresa was supposed to be in bed. Unbeknown to anyone, she was snooping on the adult's conversation hidden up in the avocado tree. She heard it all. Fergus. Father Kevin. Having an argument. It all had to do with the Apostle James the Greater.

Teresa didn't understand much that was said, only that Fergus didn't like James The Greater much. This was politics. Adult stuff.

She saw Fergus charge Kevin's glass, just like he had her parents a few nights before. She only heard bits and pieces. James came in for a real hammering. Fergus was up on his high horse. He was obviously teasing Father Kevin about religion.

"James went to Spain for eight years. Returned to Palestine where he was beheaded. They then took his body back to Spain. They came to call him The Moor-slayer. General Francisco Franco was a big fan of James. Both of them were from Galicia in the north."

Teresa knew that the Moors were Islamic people, because Fergus had told her that. Fergus, Kevin and Spiro had helped out these Sudanese men in the district. They had once come to the house to see Fergus. They looked frightening, like white ghosts in their long robes, but with black faces. She had also seen them at Spiro's shop, where Fergus had sent Halal meat for them to collect. Teresa stopped, stared at their black, large pink veined hands. "Fergus's girl," Spiro said in an aside to the men, "her name's Terese." The men stopped and stared at her. Teresa immediately moved on, muttering "my name's Teresa."

But she didn't know who this Francisco Franco man was. Maybe he was a Franciscan. Probably just another Communist.

"Franco and his devils would give their stiff arm fascist salutes to effigies of James The Greater from the balconies as he went past them in religious processions. Alongside them on the balconies, of course, would be all the archbishops."

Kevin said nothing.

Fergus would often salute Teresa up in her fig tree. Hello soldier, he'd often say, an open palm up to the temple. Teresa would salute back at him with her Che beret on. She didn't know what a stiff arm salute was.

"Spain's troops in Iraq today still wear the Moor-Slayer symbol of St. James on their uniform." She heard Fergus say.

Teresa could tell that Fergus was angry.

Kevin asked. "Franco's dead. Times change. Do you tell Teresa about these things?"

"Of course not. Times don't change. The whole damned world recognized Franco as being legitimate, except for Mexico and Russia. And he was a brute. James is still out there too, very much around, riding his pure white horse, appearing in miracles for the Christians against the Moors. I swear I'll send her over there one day. She can find out these things for herself."

Teresa climbed down from the tree and went inside to bed.

Enters the Dancer

There was a light tapping on Teresa's bedroom door that Saturday night. At first she ignored it. She was expecting Sharn over. Sharn never knocked. She'd brazenly throw pebbles at her window while walking through the yard, yell 'Ground Control to Miss Mahone,' 'Here, kitty, kitty,' or more usually 'Hey, Bitch!' at the top of her voice. Often they'd get out the bedroom window, lay down on the roof, look at the stars, talk for ages until the music and hunger finally took them outside.

Teresa was brushing her hair in her terrycloth robe, wondering what to wear to the party downstairs. Ballou always hanged round the spit Saturday nights, taking in smells, Fergus throwing her out morsels. Teresa had put up a sign. 'Beware Of The Cat.' The men would stand round talking. She didn't want anyone standing on her.

She never worried as to what to wear. Jeans, grunge, T-shirt over T, but her mother said she was to wear something nice this evening. Sharn always gave Teresa her old clothes, bigger and loose. Colleen had showed her how to stitch patches on her jeans. No butterflies. Sunflowers. Nothing too cheesy. Fergus suggested a Communist Hammer and Sickle. Caitlin said 'Don't you dare. You're not walking round with that for all to see.'

Sharn often treated her sister as a model Saturday nights—face paint, make-up, earrings, scarves from mothers' wardrobes; sometimes Teresa wore a red rag in her hair. Sharn poked and prodded her with hairpins, painting her fingers, toenails ten different colors

"You could be a model one day. You have really beautiful eyes and lips, and you're tall, Tess. And got a nice smile. When we can see it." Sharn would say with tinges of envy, "you're looking hotter every year."

"Wish I was thinner," Sharn said that last Sunday beside Teresa at the mirror.

"You look great. Like Britney. You'll get taller. Thinner."

"Right. If I was taller, I'd look thinner, wouldn't I! More in proportion. Don't want to look like a big heifer."

"I wouldn't say that."

"You'd better not. How 'bout you, Juicy Lucy? What you wish for?"

"Be a bit stupider. Not think about things so much. Be a pest at school. Suspended. Get in trouble. Stupid."

"But you don't do mad things, don't like rocking the boat, do you!" Sharn said continuing to gaze. "Dominic's stupid. You don't want to be like him."

"Why do you always say that? He isn't stupid."

"Yes he is. He's a dickhead. He plays air guitar in front of the mirror."

"What are we playing then? Mirror-mirror-on-the-wall?" Teresa gazed in beside her. She slumped her shoulders, scrunched up her face, lolled her tongue, poked it sideways at Sharn.

"You're nuts!" Sharn hesitated "Can get us drugs, if you want. Drugs make you stupid. Want to try? I'm going to get some, make me thinner."

"Nope. Might want to be stupid, but drugs aren't clever."

"Do you think I should go to Weight Watchers?" Sharn asked seriously.

"No. But there's enough fast-food wrappers in your car to run the bar-b-q Saturday night. Lay off that stuff. You go at it like Pac Man."

"I know. Work. Eat on the run."

Teresa said nothing. She knew that Sharn worked hard. Sharn was next to Teresa's shoulder. "One day you're going to have real big hooters, Suzie Q. Like me. Your Ma. Mine. We'll be known as sisters. Dolly. Pamela. You'll just have to have 'em. It's in the family. No one cuts it today without 'em." Sharn always made references like that, as though actually sisters.

Teresa reflected. "I didn't really mean stupid-stupid. I meant that other word. More . . . super-something."

"Super what?"

"Super . . . fickle?"

"You mean superficial?"

"That's it," Teresa said, "Wish I was more superficial."

"Just be a bit crazy, then. Guys like crazy chicks. Crazy chicks are good in bed."

"Is that right? Good for them. All I want is to leave school."

"Leave, then."

"Fat chance of that. Ma won't let me."

"Hit Fergus up for a job, then. He must need some help."

*   *   *

"Come in," Teresa said tentatively, now realizing that someone was there. Sharn would bowl in Sunday mornings, go straight to Teresa's wardrobe, choose a dress for her to wear for Mass. "Come on, Little Sister, get your lazy butt out of bed." She'd slide the hangers, banging them together, then despair. "Not that, not that, not that. Take this crap back to the Op Shop. It's ghastly. Hit Fergus up for some decent city dresses. This is such retro shit."

But this was a timid knock. The door opened ajar. Teresa moved across. "May I come in, *ma cherie?* Do you mind?"

It was the dance teacher, the one she'd seen from a distance with her uncle. Teresa stood back staring, holding her hair brush in at her side like a bat. She was tall, willowy, much prettier now up closer, her dark hair tied high in a swirling knot. Deep brown eyes danced gently on her face. She smiled sweetly from the small features of her French face, not wishing to intrude. It was a soft voice. She guessed the teacher was round her mother's age. Yes, Teresa thought, my breasts ARE bigger than hers, as she looked her visitor up and down.

She wore blue stretch jeans, an off-white embroidered top with puffed sleeves, soft black satin shoes. Teresa stared at her top. It looked Spanish. The lady clutched a multi-layered colored cotton skirt under her arm as she stepped inside. She extended her hand. Teresa took it. It was a nice hand. Tender. There was a quiet graciousness about her, such a contrast to Sharn, who'd blaze in as if on a mission. Teresa imagined Fergus and this lady sitting, sipping quietly in some urban coffee house. There was a mystery about her. There just had to be. Anyone would have to be a little left of field ever to put up with Fergus.

"My name's Maria Gonzalez. I'm your uncle's friend. He told me that you're very pretty. You are. He was telling the truth. For once." She then bit her lip in a comical way as if having just said the wrong thing.

Teresa grinned, relaxed by the sudden lack of seriousness. "Uncle tells lots of fibs, doesn't he!"

"Only things worth fibbing about. May I change in here? I bought a skirt for dancing. Your uncle's a very good dancer. Will you dance with me, tonight? We can have fun. Not serious dance. Just kicking up our heels. I'll show you how to swish a skirt to 'La Bamba,' samba to 'Esso

Besso.' Would you like that?" Maria kicked out her long legs low and slow, then from side to side, swishing in timid imitation of a can-can.

"I'd like that. Uncle told me you're French. Your name's Spanish."

"He also said that you're clever. You're right. My father's Spanish. Mother's French. Mother calls me Marie. Father, Maria. They live in France for part of the year then Spain, when they can. My mother works for Cirque du Soleil in Europe and Canada. She's a trapeze artist." Maria then began rocking back and forth, rolling her eyes in unison while looking to the ceiling.

Teresa giggled. "I once wrote a story at school that my Ma worked for the circus. I'm a fibber, too. Like uncle is. He said you teach pole dancing to teenage girls."

Maria smiled, put her hand up to her mouth in mock horror. "Come on. I have something for you." Maria walked across to Teresa's bed, put the skirt on it. She took time to pat the cat, which remained undisturbed on the bed, then lifted the dress. "Voila! A small skirt for you. Same as mine. You can keep it. I want you to have it. I have them made up for my students."

Teresa's eyes widened. It was so pretty: the browns, yellows, red-white stripes for Spanish dance. "Thank you." She said softly. "I'll keep it for best. I'll wear it to church Sundays."

"Why don't you wear it for us now?" Maria implored gently.

"O.K."

Maria gazed about. It was a brightly peach colored room. Teresa and her father had painted it together. The only thing that dulled was a large dark wooden crucifix over her bed. There was a crystal Madonna and Child lamp on a side table; two Raphael cherubs either side in small photo frames, tubby, pink and bright. One had its chin resting on its fist. There was a bookcase mounted on the wall: Harry Potter books, Alice In Wonderland, tatty teenage novels which Teresa bought from Op shops, then older hardbacks with neat dust jackets that Teresa had obviously borrowed from Fergus. No schoolbooks in sight. Those she left downstairs by the front door.

She had her own stereo on a raised table, a rack of CDs rising from the floor, and, of course, her writing desk, polished and shut. Marie noticed the key in it. No secrets to be locked away. There were two porcelain black cat ornaments with shining golden eyes, a large Johnny Depp poster on one wall, The Blues Brothers on another, a Ricky Martin album enlargement with the words 'Livin' La Vida Loca,' next to it

"Do you like Ricky Martin?" Teresa asked. "Uncle says those words means 'living the crazy life.' Do you think it's a bit cheesy? The music, I mean."

"I like it," Maria smiled benignly. "Cheese, maybe, but very tasty. It has melody. Lots of beat. Gets to the heart. Does Uncle ever play you Latin music?"

Teresa rolled her eyes. "Does he what! All the time. One night when Ma and Pa were at a party we sat downstairs. He played me 'La Paloma' over and over, but never by the same artist. He has it done with vocals by an older woman, a young woman, by trumpet, by harmonica, by xylophone, by a single electric guitar. I really liked it. Especially when Artie Shaw played. He sometimes dances to it with Ma and Colleen, I never get sick of it. He says that he'll get me versions of it by Elvis and Edith Piaf one day. Then he played Carlos Santana. I like him, too. Does Uncle ever play Santana's 'Maria, Maria' for you? 'Love Of My Life?' He plays them here."

Teresa never meant it to probe, just an association by name. Maria was touched, and clearly embarrassed. She leaned across, kissed Teresa's cheek.

"Yes he does, my dear. You have such a romantic heart. I hope no one ever breaks it. Did uncle ever tell you the story of 'La Paloma?' If he has, then may there never be a white dove sitting on your windowsill."

"Of course. I understand that expression now. Maybe there is a dove there already. My Auntie Teresa."

Marie sat calmly. Maybe Fergus was too embarrassed ever to tell about his dead sister. He never mentioned her to anyone else. So Teresa thought.

"Will you tell it to me again?" Marie ignored Teresa's answer. She patted the bedspread for Teresa to sit beside her.

"It's about a sailor and his true love, set long ago in Cuba. It was written in 1863. I even remember the year. Uncle talks about Cuban music a lot. That's because he's a Communist, I guess."

Teresa looked to Maria, who did not register any dismay.

"The sailor thinks he might drown out at sea, never return to his true love. She will know if he'd drowned if the white dove, La Paloma, comes and sits on her windowsill. That white dove would be the soul of the dead sailor. Uncle says the song suggests that the sailor will drown one day."

"Does the story make you feel sad?" Maria asked softly.

"It did. Only at first. Uncle said the dove is meant to bring all our hearts together at the end, so it's really a happy song. The guitars are cheerful, everyone's dancing. He said the dove is the final link to love which overcomes death and separation. I remember how uncle laughed. 'It's a killer tune, isn't it, Tess?' That's what he always says. He always says that about the tunes he likes."

"It is a 'killer tune,' my dear. It turns what could be sad into happy. Your uncle likes doing that. The man who wrote it died two years after the song was written. It became one of the most popular songs ever recorded."

"That's sad." Teresa looked grimly to her bedspread.

Maria clutched Teresa's hand. "No, it isn't. Just look at what he gave the world. A most beautiful song. And such a pretty name. Like yours. Picasso called his daughter Paloma. The original story goes back thousands of years. Do you want to hear it? Do you like listening to stories?"

"Yes. Untrue stories are the best."

"It started back in 492 B.C. Darius' Persian fleet was dashed against the shore rocks of Mt. Athos in northern Greece. The Greek soldiers then observed these white doves being released from the ships. This was really strange; for there were no white doves in Europe at the time. The Greeks believed these birds brought back home messages to loved ones lost at sea." Maria held Teresa's hand throughout. She then let it go patting it gently. "That's because 'Love Conquers All Things,' as they say. Nothing stops it. Not even death. You must see it as a happy story. They will be united again. If not now, then one day."

Maria immediately stood up.

She'd stood quickly as though just having overstepped the mark. It seemed not right for her to remind a young girl that there are a hundred ways for love to fall apart, especially by death. She'd told the story with a cheerfulness, as though imagining it on a postcard yet unable to express its real beauty.

Teresa hanged her head. "Like my dead Auntie." She looked up. "How can sad ever be happy?"

Maria could not ignore this, but she did not want their first conversation to be a sad one.

"Last week your uncle played me a Cuban American country band called The Mavericks. It's really good. They play mostly old or popular songs, in English and in Spanish. Great fun, but often in a peculiar way. It has these sad country songs—a woman falls out of love, leaves the man; takes the house and car, all the furnishings. But the songs are done with a full orchestra, lots of brass. You find that you just want to dance to it, because it's joyous, funny. Like one of uncle's jokes."

"Love gone wrong." Teresa pondered. "Some country songs are so sad. Dominic plays them out in his shed. Does she take the children with her, as well?"

"No. They purposely avoid ever singing that. That's never funny."

"My Ma would never leave my Pa. Colleen would never leave Declan. How can leaving be funny?"

"It isn't. But it does happen. Point is, we must refuse ever to be sad. Life goes on. There's always song and dance to cheer us. Come on, let's get changed and go outside."

They changed into their skirts, chatting about this and that, less heavy thoughts, as if the story of doves was now told and gone, stored for future thought. Maria purposely played with the cat, chucking it under the chin before she and Teresa went out hand in hand, dressed in their identical skirts. Ballou followed.

Fergus had set up the stereo beside the plank tables on the lawn. Sharn and Dominic and their friends were over.

Sharn immediately moved across, began whispering in Teresa's ear.

"Hey, spoilt bitch! I wanna skirt like that."

"It's got an elastic waist. We can share it." Teresa whispered back behind her hand.

Everyone sat round; they ate, they drank and they danced. Caitlin had cooked fish that the men had caught in the boat earlier that day; Colleen made bowls of barley and capsicum-bean salad, sweet potato patties. Fergus had shown Teresa how to make open sandwiches, dishes of eggplant. He'd made antipasto with Teresa earlier that day, then jaffles and banana damper for the younger ones later in the evening.

Maria danced with everyone that night, to all kinds of music.

Teresa was amazed how she moved, so delicately yet un-forced in natural movements as if extensions of the beat. It seemed to Teresa that Caitlin and Colleen were glad to have her here, at last. Teresa noticed that Maria was no stranger to them, relaxed in their company, purposely making mistakes with her dance steps, pulling faces so the younger ones could laugh at her.

Later that evening, Fergus took off his barbeque apron, put on a trilby hat. He and Maria danced a tango to accordion music on the lawn. Everyone cheered and clapped, especially when Whiskey Tango Foxtrot Fergus made purposeful mistakes. His mouth opened to his audience in acknowledgement. Maria gently kicked him with her soft shoe. They danced cheek to cheek, forehead to forehead, Maria's hand up on his short ponytail under his hat.

Teresa stared at them. She'd never seen dancers this close before. At a certain point, the most strident, the grand finale, Fergus bent Maria over his leg then looked out to his audience, said 'I'm not well' then continued on till the end.

When it finished they kissed one another's cheeks. Maria put her hand over her breast(smaller than Teresa's) announcing to all "He is my dancer, my very heart of Argentina."

Fergus bowed in acknowledgment, scraping the ground with his trilby. A loud cheer went up. Everyone, including Kevin, threw out crusts of bread and empty beer cans at him.

Teresa observed that Father Kevin and Maria weren't strangers, either. They had spoken to each other informally.

Teresa suddenly began to feel cheated. Why hadn't she met this woman before? Everyone else had. Why had they kept her away from her?

Maria later took Teresa aside.

"Come on, my dear. I'll show you some dance routines. I have them on a CD/DVD. I'll leave it here with you, if you like them."

Fergus put the CD on.

She and Sharn and the other girls lined up, did Cha Cha Cha with attitude, Salsa steps forward and back, moving their arms, then a Mambo tap, moving to the beat. Sometimes Maria would ham it up, as only Fergus would. Afterwards Maria and Teresa went and sat with him. Nothing much was said. Fergus filled two wine glasses for Marie and Teresa. The three sipped in silence. Teresa could tell from the expressions of their eyes that they really liked one another. Caitlin came and joined them. Colleen went and sat briefly on Fergus' knee. Teresa could tell that her mother was happy in having Marie here. They clutched one another's hand on the table.

"Tell me another story. About another song," Teresa asked Marie.

Marie thought a while. She then spoke softly to Fergus. Fergus got up and went away.

"I've asked him to play it for you." Marie smiled.

It was a serious smile. Marie did not tease. Only men teased. Maria then began to tell the story.

"Once upon a time there was this girl, not so long ago in 1962, and she's still alive today, but back then, around your age, standing five foot eight, a brunette and golden teenager, she'd go for a walk in the morning, often just to buy her mother a pack of cigarettes. She was so light and full of grace that she inspired the second most recorded song of all time. Second only to the Beatles' 'Yesterday.' She'd walk along the seashore through a fashionable district. All the men watched her from outside coffee tables as she passed by. Many would wolf-whistle her. She was that pretty."

"That's horrible," Teresa pouted.

"Not really. No one would ever dare touch her. She was quite safe. They just wanted to see her beauty. No more than that. A man wrote a song about her. Stan Getz played it. Bossa nova. It became a hit worldwide. The ultimate in cool. It's called 'The Girl From Ipanema.' It won the Grammy for Best Song back in 1965."

"I know it. The Blues Brothers had it in their film. Robbie Williams and Nicole Kidman do it. Is it Spanish?"

"No. Portuguese. They don't like people to think it's Spanish."

Fergus began to play the song on the stereo. It was the original version.

"What do you think of it?" Marie asked excitedly.

"I've always thought it sounds sad." Teresa said softly. She didn't want to disagree, make statement more about herself than the song.

"Yes," Marie could only agree. "You are clever. There is a sadness there, but there is beauty in that sadness. That's what makes it such a haunting song."

"Why is the girl sad, then? Is she unhappy? Do the men just annoy her? The writer says 'She looks straight ahead not at me.' He should be the sad one. Not her." Teresa wanted to know.

"We don't know the answers. It's a mystery. The men are sad because they know they're too old ever to court her. They'd never win her heart. Maybe the girl's shy, sad too. We're all sad because we know beauty fades. It may be as simple as that."

"I still really like it," Teresa smiled back.

*   *   *

Early next morning Teresa ran downstairs to the kitchen, made two big mugs of coffee as quickly as she could, as she often would for her parents on Sunday mornings. She felt emboldened by the night before. She wanted to go in, sit on Fergus' bed, personally invite Maria back every weekend to dance, be happy with them. She had loved the stories, sad or otherwise. She knew that it didn't matter how big her breasts were. If only she could tell stories like that, move like her, dance the night away, despite unhappy things in the world. Teresa thought of Saturday nights of the past, how she and Sharn would clown around, swing their hair to the music, show off, yet that wasn't dancing. Maria could dance. The music and movement were one. Teresa could not tell them apart. It had been the best fun having her here.

She quietly opened Fergus' door.

He and the lady weren't there.

Flown away.

Like two white doves.

All that I *Survey*

It was now home for the long summer school holidays. Summer seemed to hit early as late October this year. Porcelain blue days tingled with heat. Muck up on Hope Street seemed to turn to instant rivers of slime. Workmen were replacing the bitumen with concrete on a hill nearby to prevent tar running off the naked stone. Teresa was glad school was over, not having to walk home each afternoon in this humidity, louts taking up her space, dishing out hell in installments.

Walking home seemed as uncertain as spinning the bottle.

Teresa worked the two busiest days of week, Thursday and Saturday, in the salon with Colleen and Sharn, taking bookings at the counter or on telephone, working the cash register, sweeping the floors, a general dog's body in training. She was still shy, a little too morose ever to face the public, yet customers liked the silent youngster, all commenting on how pretty she was.

Sharn was fun to be around. She made Teresa laugh, so loud and comical that she often had clients in stitches. Everyone said she ought to be on television. Colleen made little effort to shut her up, seldom telling her to 'Knock it off!' The girl was diligent and very good at her job.

The salon was not far from the Mall. Colleen would sometimes cover for them while the two girls lunched there.

Fergus had picked up three near new pairs of roller skates at a jumble sale in the city, and, as the council had recently repaved the sidewalk on Edward, Teresa and Sharn and Dominic would tear down both sides to the corner of Hope in the early evenings, screeching their wheels, yahooing, honking like geese under street lights, competing for the lead. Even Caitlin and Colleen had turns. Some nights the temperature never fell below 28 Celsius. Physical exhaustion seemed the only way to sleep in late December's torpor.

Teresa would have preferred to work outside, away from the public with her Pa. Maddox and Declan would've gladly had her, Dominic too, but there was little work late December through to January when most building shut down until end of month. Teresa stayed home by herself the rest of the time, cleaning house and yard, preparing meals, getting a few extra dollars. Some nights she'd prepare salads and cold cuts for both families while Colleen and Sharn coped with the holiday rush. And the fig tree always beckoned as a means for staying cool.

Dominic was now to be in his final year. He suddenly decided to move away with his friends to work in a slaughterhouse down the coast, all saving money for university. When he came home weekends he'd skate with them in the evening. Teresa was determined to beat him, even though he had the edge without practice. She'd try until she did.

It was a Friday afternoon. Temperatures were soaring. Birds in the sky looked like distant glitter under the constant sun. Nestled in the hills where they were, their houses were too far inland to be affected by sea breezes. Hotter in summer, cooler in winters, one could literally have fried an egg on the tin shed roof next door this day. Teresa noticed the wilting leaves. If she had any friends, they'd all have gone to the beach. Between daytime hours of ten to four the ultra violet rays were extremely dangerous at the seaway. As for friends, that wasn't an option. She'd wait until Sunday when Sharn wasn't working, kick round with hers.

Dominic's friends had an old car amongst them, and were coming home most weekends. She wouldn't go with them. Why would she? To have to listen to their puerile talk—sports, comics, animations, computer games, fart jokes, while Dominic drove, for the others to stare at her titties in the back seat. No way. She'd wait for Sharn.

Teresa had cut the lawns with the mower, raked the leaves and dried husks and stalks into piles to compost, then barrowed them there, then thought that that was enough for the day. She was wearing her fatigues and beret, green T underneath, her steel-capped boots, which she had to wear while fence building or concreting. Fergus had bought them for her last birthday to keep her out of her tree, be more useful. Another loony present.

She'd tied back her hair with a band then stuck her ponytail up under the beret.

She was pleased with her effort. The yard looked spotless. It smelled like freshly mown hay. Teresa headed for the fig tree. It would be cooler in the foliage.

Ballou stretched out on the front porch, but did not answer her call. "Come on. Let's go climbing." The cat opened an eye, shut it again.

Like a ship's captain coming on watch, the first thing Teresa always did was survey her domain below through her spyglass. When Fergus came home Fridays she'd always raise the glass to her eye from the tree. Fergus would stand to attention, salute her, then raise his own imaginary glass to his lips. That meant time for her to come down, go inside. Fridays nights were fun. Next door would come over. Declan would bring his guitar. Fergus would wind up the band.

Teresa would always look to the ravine then up onto Hope, back and forth with the glass like the passing traffic. She'd learned to focus minutely on things, sometimes imagining herself a sniper pinpointing with cross hairs. She never wanted to kill bird, beast or fowl, yet had mixed feelings about some of the dirt-bags on Hope. Especially those who gave her a hard time. From the tree she could clearly distinguish faces.

Sometimes the Reserve made her shudder. She remembered the day she'd been down there, how it had been like walking along the basement of the world, sinking to rock bottom. She remembered how she'd held her school bag so close to her chest, her school insignia on the leather like a coat of arms to ward off evil. Some evenings at dusk she wondered if lost souls ever wandered out in its darkness, hoping some raging fire would engulf them, purify them for release. Dominic sometimes played a couple of songs from his shed—AC/DC's Highway To Hell, The Eagles It's a Long Road Out of Eden—they seemed appropriate thoughts to Teresa.

Her Ma and Fergus had bought her books on trees, scrubs, bird identification, reptiles, animals, snakes to avoid, spiders which bite yet not poison. Maddox would regularly turn over the long form-like dining table in the yard checking for red-back spiders underneath. Black Widows. They could really make you sick.

Sharn recently told Teresa a story she'd heard from work, how a guy with long dreadlocks had gone to have them cut off at a city salon. It was almost closing time. The hairdresser said she'd cut the cornstalks only, that he was to come back next morning for styling. He agreed. She cut them. The guy walked from the salon, promptly dropped dead on the sidewalk. The hairdresser unwittingly disturbed a nest of red back spiders in the locks.

Sharn reckoned the black widows ate the smaller males after mating. Teresa went to her books to confirm it. It said it was probably that the males became so enfeebled after several mating that they then died. The male fang was too small to penetrate human skin. Sharn made some rude comment on that when Teresa told her. Teresa blushed.

She preferred to think about ladybugs anyway, and would often sing the rhyme in garden or tree. 'Ladybird, ladybird, fly away home, your house is on fire, your children all gone.'

Fergus told her the rhyme dated from times when hop fields were set alight at the end of season, killing off the ladybug larvae.

Teresa allowed the big hairy-backed Huntsman spiders to crawl up her arm in the tree. It was usually only the little ones of bright color she had to be wary. Caitlin crossed fingers, touched wood that the cat was still alive. It too knew it was on dangerous ground, always close to Teresa when outside. Two weeks ago, Teresa had found two black pythons curled up in the lower reaches of the fig tree. While Declan fetched a ladder to get them down, Teresa raced inside for two pillow slips.

"Don't kill them, Declan. Put them in these. I'll empty them back in the Reserve."

Declan wound her up, as he customarily did.

"I'll kill them, make a couple of leather belts, give Sharn and Dom a darn good curry up."

"O, no you won't, Daddy-O!" Teresa replied. "We're putting them back where they belong."

One morning, not long before as Teresa set off to school, little birds came in wing-whirring at her, fluttering in her face. They brought her to a standstill. Only then did Dominic notice a red belly black snake slithering off the camber of the street beside them.

Teresa could now distinguish the changing seasons through the glass, not easy to do in the Tropic. Often there were six seasons, even more, barely perceptible. She observed how the leaves do fall, degrees to which they turned color. Pinks, greens, oranges, reds. Even the gaudy birds were difficult to see below in blossoms and flowers. On very hot days birds seemed to twinkle in shimmering skies. She'd watch bigger birds displace the smaller ones. Birds would annoy one another, Teresa guessed, for the fun of it. There was this one particular fantail which continually annoyed a hawk, even sitting on its back in the sky. Sometimes she'd be kept awake nights by the lorikeets jostling down the ravine. She'd watch birds and bees for ages, long interlocking tails of birds mating in trees below. Rainbow lorikeets could be seen pulling flowers towards them with their feet, holding them in place while taking eucalyptus pollen out. It held endless fascination for her.

Suddenly she heard distant yelling emanating from below. It seemed to come up from these catacombs as though through a chamber of echoes. Teresa focused through the foliage while standing on planks of her tree house at the beginning of a limb. She did not venture out too far along in steel capped boots. She shouldn't be wearing her boots in the tree. Her father warned her about that before.

There was an indistinct haze of humidity rising from ground below. Two big men in heavy boots, blue jeans, army camouflage jackets, were pushing a young woman down the slope off Hope. Their feet looked as big as clown's shoes as she focused from ground up. They both had shaved heads glistening in the sun, sleeves rolled on muscular arms. They wore desert fatigues, light brown sand with blotches, not the green jungle type like hers. It did not quite blend with the thicket beside them. They were big men, twice her size, and brutal-looking. They looked like Storm Troopers. They'd kicked the girl down in front of them. A third, much younger, maybe Teresa's age, was tagging down after them, frequently turning, looking back to the street.

The girl was wearing a pair of denim cut-offs like a loincloth sacking, white sandshoes, a brief halter top. She was a waif compared with her attackers. Teresa could hear her plaintive cries as she toppled end over end. Teresa focused on each of their faces. She knew them all by name and reputation, knew that these boys never sat round playing Scrabble. Teresa had neither pen nor paper, nor need to take notes.

The boy behind was Guy Rowland. He'd been expelled from St. Ignatius' at age fourteen, a recalcitrant kid no one could handle, in or out of school. He'd gone on light duties at a iron foundry out of town. That didn't last. He came back soon enough to make a serial pest of himself on Hope. He'd sometimes mouth off at Teresa. She'd never lifted her head to him. Dominic said 'Don't answer, Teresa. You'd be wasting your words.'

Guy now had a distinct spider tattoo, web draping throat to neck. Teresa could distinguish it clearly. She looked in horror. It was as if the barometer suddenly dropped, the winds died, the storm clouds circled the hills about to dump rain.

The two soldiers were Billy 'Bad mouth,' Guy's elder brother, his friend Tom Piper-Vickers. His name on the street was 'Viper.' Billy had scorpion tattoos on each shoulder. She'd seen them before on the street. Billy always wore a green soldier's vest, his tattoos visible. Teresa only ever saw him once in a shirt, his shoulders so big that the garment was split at the back. Teresa remembered how younger boys on the street would chant 'Billy's hanging loose. Billy's gotta screw loose.' Teresa saw him as a big, ignorant man. He had bare gums, would bolt down his food, could break your neck in a half-Nelson. Piper had a long snake tattoo on one arm.

Thugs, Teresa reflected.

Even Sharn never answered them back.

They'd once ruled the street before going off in the army together, bullying the squatters and winos, themselves often drugged to the eyeballs. No one ever messed with either.

The girl was Gloria Lang. She worked the shady side of Hope. Sharn knew her. She was a slight, pixie-faced girl with a reputation for being unable to keep her britches on. Teresa always felt sorry for her. Gloria had more nicknames than a high school quarterback. None of them was nice. She used to hang round the salon, complaining she hadn't enough money for a cut. Colleen often took pity. If free, she'd cut her hair, give her a shampoo. Gloria Lang. Sharn said boys called her Glorious Gangbang. Teresa knew what that meant.

Teresa had always associated these boys with the magpies. They'd sniff her as she passed, check her out, yet smelled no fear on her. Magpies attack in nesting season, swoop low, cut tops of heads, even attempt to take out an eye. They'd never attacked Teresa from the trees near school. They had with others, and cyclists. She always kept her head down anyway, blanketed in hair. Some kids would paint crude faces with eyes on plastic ice-cream cartons, wear them back to front to confuse the birds. Or they'd put on dark sun glasses, in reverse. That was so cool to do. Shooting magpies was against the law, but sometimes the council was forced to send a shooter in to destroy one or two menacing birds.

Magpies had lots of nerve.

Teresa knew that these two soldiers were menaces, in or out of season.

Teresa looked steadily at the scene. Mad magpies peeking at Gloria. They looked more like a murder of crows.

Billy wasn't really that brave, or very bright. Teresa remembered how Declan had scratched his head wondering how the boy ever got in the army. He was big, hairy, his eyebrows so thick and out of control that he looked bull-blind. Sometimes he dribbled uncontrollably, like a beast. Even now, with a shaved head, Teresa could clearly distinguish his thick joining brows. He'd fight on the street by rushing in like a bull, bunting guys out of the way with his superior strength. Those brows reminded Teresa of bullhorns. Inexplicably, they also reminded whenever her teachers said, 'Teresa, you have to take the bull by the horns.' How? So wild. So fierce. Strong. As if she, anyone, could wrestle a bull to the ground.

She knew little about Piper, except that the two of them had been inseparable for years. Guy was the runt of the litter. He always wore board shorts, selfsame black vest emblazoned with the skull and cross bones. His arms were now tattooed, giving life to his puny muscles and scaly skin.

Teresa hated skull and cross bone T-shirts. One night she'd looked up what cross bones were. Femurs. Her Ma said they were thigh bones. They seemed appropriate for the ravine. Skull and cross-bones were standard symbol for poison on industrial drums.

Fergus was there that night, had heard the conversation.

Next Friday he brought Teresa a T shirt back from the city. It had two femur cross bones on it, a cupcake mounted on top. They had a good laugh about it. Teresa liked the shirt.

On a silted patch tucked in from the street above, Teresa now had full view of what was taking place. She broke away the obstructing twigs. It was so hot. The street must have been melting above.

Billy and Piper stood over and began belting the girl viciously round the head and mouth with closed fists until she slumped to ground like a rag doll. Teresa had witnessed male rage before on the street but nothing quite like this. Billy then bent over her, poked his boot toe into her midriff to test for reaction, then ripped off her top in one strike, tore down her cut-offs, pulled her white underwear out from her belly. They stretched like a piece of chewing gum until finally snapping. Billy hit her again to stay down, then got on the ground himself, opening her legs out like a pair of scissors. He then fumbled about at his groin.

White crested cockatoos alighted from the trees around them, squawking to the air. Teresa suddenly thought of those white doves of La Paloma.

Teresa stiffened on the planks of her tree house. She took the spyglass away from her eye and frowned.

She didn't want to watch this, began fearing for the girl's life. Teresa knew that if she screamed or shouted from the tree her voice would only drift above the canyon. Traffic noise up on Hope would drown it out. What other option did she have? She'd try anyway.

LEAVE HER ALONE! She screamed, again and again and again. She didn't want them to know from where the sound was coming. If she climbed higher, would they then hear it? POLICE, POLICE, POLICE! She yelled, loud as she could. She picked up a metal dish for the birdseed, began hitting it hard with a stick, still thinking of what other rackets to make.

She reluctantly watched again as Billy pumped roughly at Gloria belly. Teresa then turned the glass to Piper. He stood at attention, his back to her like a soldier at muster. She knew what he was doing, playing with himself like a hand crank, awaiting his turn. Beating off, Teresa thought, doing what boys do best.

Billy drew back. Guy was now jumping up and down, whooping with glee, egging Piper on.

Piper turned Gloria onto her stomach as though no more than a rough sack, then pulled her limpness over and up, squatting her on all fours. Suddenly he stopped, looked up. He must have heard the din. Teresa beat the dish as hard as she could, screaming out in intervals. Viper was now straining her back by her hair. He held onto it as a rodeo cinch, reeling his free arm as if riding a wild calf.

Then he stopped. The noise was disturbing him. He moved back on his knees. She slumped forward. It looked like two beasts uncoupling. Piper turned her over with a clout to her back again. He spread her legs, then threw a handful of silt from the ground between them. Billy and Tom then roared with laughter. Guy was furious with them.

But the noise was overwhelming them. They reluctantly began to fear being sprung. Teresa could hear Gloria cry out in pain. If I can hear them, then they must hear me, Teresa thought. That only made them more angry.

Guy threw himself on top of Gloria wrestling with her limp body. Billy stood back, idly began taking the laces out from Gloria's sandshoes. Tom began pushing Guy off then tying her feet then hands behind with the strings. He picked up her cut-offs, top and underwear, carrying them off with him. Guy got up reluctantly, then kicked her in the thigh before ambling away, yelling 'slut' at the top of his voice, as though he'd been the one who'd got the raw deal.

Before Tom and Billy walked away they too put the boot in, several times.

Teresa was down from the tree in an instant. The girl would die down there in this heat. She ran straight to the house, the spyglass in her woven bag over her chest, then quickly tossed her cat gently through the front mesh trap, locked the house door, then moved along the veranda to the coat and hat racks. She changed her steel-caps for high rubber boots, grabbed an old brown raincoat, which nobody wore any longer, as an apron for the thorns and the three foot nettles, then surveyed the shelf beside her until finding a box cutter kept there with other small tools. She put on the coat, slipped the box cutter in a pocket, then ran out the front gate along to the nearest track.

She slid down the embankment, the rubber grips of her boots pushing the loose stones down in front of her.

It felt so strange being down there again. It gave her an eerie feeling. Small birds alighted at the sight of her, then flew alongside from above, sensing danger. Half way down the bracken slope, sliding on the loose, crumbling earth, Teresa stopped, steadied herself, pulled the spyglass from her bag, shaking it to extend, focused again on the three men. They must have moved away quickly up the other side. They were now standing in a huddle along Hope. Suddenly, a few yards north of the No Trespassing sign, she saw Billy toss the torn clothes and shoes over the side into the thicket below.

Teresa sliced through the narrow breaks of thorns, protected by her long oil-skin coat. It dragged on her rubber boots. Head down, the beret giving her some protection, she continually watched for correct footing, as she did up the trees.

Once to the bottom, she ran across the more open ground like a wild cat on a full tank of gas. She could hear clearly the girl's whimpers, faint cries for help. Teresa had the momentary thought that she wished she could fly like an angel. As she drew nearer, she saw Gloria's body quivering with shock. With hands tied behind her back her body was now heaving, then it went into spasm. Teresa knelt down beside her.

Gloria's bloodied face winced at the sound of the extending blade. Teresa turned her on her side, sawed at the laces on her wrists, then the ankles, then quickly retracted the razor. The girl's eyes were now no more than swollen slits, her face enlarged in masses of contusions. Her small breasts twitched on her concave chest. Her skin was as white as whey. Her brown pubic hairs were covered in soft silt. It looked vaguely like cinnamon. Her hair was dank with perspiration, mouth bleeding at the corners. Gloria's two front teeth had been knocked out. Teresa picked them up.

"We must get you out of here. This place's evil."

"They threw sand at my pussy. That bastard tried to do me from behind. Shit, shit, SHIT!" Gloria kept shaking her head trying to relieve the pain.

"I saw it. Come on. Stand up. You must go to hospital. Here's your two teeth. They'll keep them alive for you. Put them back in. But you must hurry."

"How can I get there?" The girl sobbed, awkwardly scrambling side to side, testing for feeling, seeing if she could move at all.

Teresa had always been made to carry a billfold, a ten dollar bill in it. "If you use it," Caitlin always said, "replace it from the money tin in the kitchen. If it ever gets too bad up on Hope, get a taxi home.

You, and Dominic." That was the rule. There was a taxi ramp at the beginning of Hope between the school and the No Trespassing sign.

Teresa took out her wallet, took back the teeth, wrapped them in the ten dollar bill, then placed it back in Gloria's hand. Gloria couldn't see anything. The blood on her face was now mixed with the silt and spores from the air.

"Ten dollars. Your two teeth are wrapped in it. I'll get you up the hill to a taxi. There's one waiting. Can you make it? Wear this coat."

Gloria raised her limp head. The sudden movement made her retch. She turned her head, vomited profusely onto the ground. She tried to sit up, clutching her left side where they had kicked her. All she could manage was a squat. A pressurized spray of urine suddenly hit the earth splashing up soft mud to her legs. Her bottom was caked in blood.

"You think your ribs are broken? Be careful in the taxi. Lay on your back in the rear seat. You could pierce a lung." Teresa covered the girl's shoulders with the coat. "Come on, put your arms in." Teresa lifted each in turn, then buttoned her up.

"Can't. Can't see. They'll kill me if I go to hospital." The girl sobbed. She tried to move forward testing her legs, then finally managing to, shuffling along slowly like a convict in manacles.

"No they won't. They're gone. It's down here that'll kill you. I'll push you up the hill. Where's it hurt most?"

"Where do you think, man?"

Teresa wasn't sure, wondered if that was just an expression, or if Gloria actually thought she was a boy. Gloria looked to the sky. The sun was obviously stinging, burning her tears to salt. Her walk was lop-sided. Teresa feared Gloria's ribs might be cracked

"Come on. You can do it. Be careful." Teresa badgered her, pushed her, shoving her from behind to get her up. She thought of giving her the rubber boots, but then saw that Gloria's feet were larger.

"Sure bin shafted today," the girl muttered. It was spoken without any anger. A kind of resignation. As if a fault of her own.

"Hospital, hospital, hospital!" Teresa reiterated to get the thought in her head. "That's where you're going." Teresa moved on in front at the highest part of the rise, grabbing her hand again. Pushing became pulling. Near the top, Teresa took back the money note, opened it out then put the teeth into the coat pocket. "Teeth in pocket. O.K.? Remember them. O.K.? Money for taxi. Taxi to hospital. You must, you must, you must!"

"I'm in trouble. Big time!"

"No you're not. I'll tell the police. There'll be no reprisals. They'll put them away. I know who they are, even if you don't. You must tell them what happened at the hospital. They'll take care of you. Don't wipe yourself. Let them get the D.N.A. Those guys are just a bunch of animals."

"I feel so hot." The words seemed to stumble from her mouth.

Gloria had felt as hot as a furnace door. "Good," Teresa replied, "I'd be more worried if you were cold."

Teresa knew that her mother was still on duty at the hospital that day. That was in Pediatrics. Caitlin had little to do with Emergencies and Admissions. She didn't want her mother knowing anything of this, to be upset, worry even more about her being by herself, and certainly not down here in the ravine.

The girl's eyes were now two constricted slits. Her breathing was heavy. Even the rain coat must have been hurting her. Gloria shrugged, pouted, sighed. Her purple lips ballooned.

"Breathe through your mouth. Your nose might be broken." Teresa knew that it was. It looked plastered right across her face. Teresa felt for her, fearing for her looks, even though she knew that this was no Homecoming Queen. Teresa thought of her as the kind of girl dancing by herself at the School Prom. Maybe with the other wallflowers. 'Guys wouldn't touch Gloria with a barge pole. Except after dark.' Sharn had once said of her. Her facial features were so light and thin. Her hand felt like a helpless paw. Teresa noticed the nicotine tobacco stains on her fingers. There were also small black blotches in the crook of one arm. Teresa thought that she must be using. Her hair was mud encrusted. When she'd pushed her from behind Teresa noticed the thick tickles of blood stopping at the calf of a leg.

At the top by the railing on Hope, Teresa went under first, then pulled Gloria underneath one handedly, pressing her head down, then stood her up again. Gloria panted desperately while straightening up on the sidewalk. Teresa buttoned the coat again, took the money out from the pocket. There was a waiting taxi ten yards ahead, facing up Hope.

Teresa ran ahead, opened the back door, threw the ten dollar note over the seat at the driver.

"Hospital. Quick!"

The driver protested with a grunt when he saw Gloria shuffle awkwardly across the back seat. Teresa said. "Lay down. Your ribs. Don't move. Teeth in pocket. Go to Emergency. Call for a doctor."

"This isn't an ambulance," the driver objected.

"JUST DO IT!" Teresa yelled at him in a bent position.

"All right, soldier," he said, putting the automatic into gear.

Teresa slammed the door once sure that Gloria's stiffened legs were in. She hit the car roof repeatedly with her hand. "Go, go, GO!"

She watched it move away before heading back down the bank again for home.

A Truly Ignorant Place

No birds guided her back that afternoon. Teresa felt her eyes so dry, the shock of the scene meant all the heat had left her body.

She got that sudden feeling that she was now all alone in the world, but she adjusted her beret on her head with determination thinking of what Fergus might say about this.

"It's your watch, soldier. Do what you have to do."

She then remembered how Sharn and she had once passed Gloria up on Hope. "Skinny little hoe," Sharn muttered in an aside to Teresa. Teresa had watched as Gloria walked by, noticing the girl had pretty lime green eyes. She had a care-free confidence about her. At least she didn't feel out of place on the street.

Yet she was still a skinny little hoe, destined for no more than to walk the other side, for the slam vans on Saturday nights. No cheese with her. Teresa kind of liked Gloria, exactly for what she was.

As she scrambled through the bracken up the other side, the densely knotted root system suddenly reminded Teresa of a Saturday night when she hid up the mango tree snooping on adult conversation when she was supposed to be in bed. Her uncle was talking with Kevin. Her Ma and Pa were there. Fergus had been graphic in his details of an incident that had happened once somewhere in South America.

"The wife had been raped by soldiers after they'd murdered the husband. The woman was already pregnant. The mother vowed after that that was never going to happen to the daughter she bore five months later. So she put a potato up the girl's vagina to prevent conception occurring when she'd grown to a teenager." Fergus paused for a moment. "The ignorance, the ignorance of it."

He then continued. "The tuber grew, as tubers do, breaking the capillaries inside her, infecting her with dirt, agonizing the girl with constrictions which made her faint at work, pulling her insides any which way."

At this point Teresa had blocked her ears. She didn't want to hear anymore. She had climbed down the tree and scurried inside to bed.

She now thought of the Reserve as that potato. Tendrils crushing. Soldiers and animals in their mammoth skins.

A truly ignorant place.

The Truth Will Out

Teresa sat at her writing desk, fountain pen poised in her hand. She clicked the joints in her fingers. They felt so tight, like knots in a whip. She then relaxed enough to head up the page "Attention: Crone Police," then wrote "Rape and Assault of Gloria Lange in the Reserve off Hope Street" below.

She could hardly call it an 'incident.' Police always called everything an incident, then only an 'alleged' one. She tried to be as exact as she could, giving the time, day, month, even the year it happened. She wouldn't sign her name at the end, wishing to remain anonymous. She shouldn't have been down the Reserve, anyway.

She said nothing about it to Sharn. She could not trust the reaction. Sharn didn't like the little 'slag,' anyway. 'I was there. I saw it. I must do this myself,' she thought boldly. Liking had nothing to do with it.

She also knew that the facts should speak for themselves. Two plus two made four. They had to. All she wanted to do was to confirm, as a witness, what Gloria must have told the Police already at Mercy; name the names, remove any doubt by her knowledge of where the clothes had been dumped, 'corroborate' what took place that day. She thought that that was the right word, yet wasn't too sure.

Teresa wrote it in her best hand, believing that style would make the Police believe that here was a person who was careful and exact. She kept it simple, numbered the times, as best she could remember, that they belted and kicked Gloria, and did not blanch from writing that dirt was thrown at the girl's anus and vagina.

Her mother always used the correct medical and anatomical terms in front of her. It was only Fergus who used words differently. He never spoke of sex in front of Teresa anyway.

Her Ma always said that the Police were often called to the hospital, especially Fridays and Saturday nights: accident reports, beatings, alcoholic poisoning, hotheads with broken hands from hitting someone in a bar. These stories fascinated Sharn. They horrified Teresa. Fergus always listened, without making comment.

Sometimes the right words just would not come. She'd never seen humans having sex before. Teresa knew that the act could get real rough—animals holding the frightened females down, clawing at the napes of their necks. But knocking them out? She'd once watched two goats through her eyeglass humping in the Reserve. She didn't think that animals ever did it face to face, or ever change partners. Maybe 'change partners' was not the right expression to use. That sounded more like a dance after the music had stopped. She pondered what to say, finally settling on the term, 'did the switch-a-roo.'

Teresa wrote it out in full, read, reread it aloud, folded it up in an envelope, addressed, sealed, stamped it, then took the letter down to the postbox outside Spiro's 7/11.

Done, she thought, over with. These boys would have to go to jail for a very long time. Nurses would have their DNA. Done and dusted.

Teresa sometimes watched forensic programs on T.V. Nobody ever got away with this sort of crime anymore.

There was a book in the school library, now all grubby and dog-eared, which boys looked at for the forensic pictures. Teresa wouldn't ever touch it.

She remembered once overhearing Marcia and Jennifer talking, laughing how the boys at discos would pinch at their nipples through their camisoles, ping their G strings from behind. Teresa was horrified. They carried on in front of her like pet ponies being allowed out for a run.

Sharn would have smacked the boys in the mouth for that, told them exactly where to go.

It took until Wednesday before Teresa saw the Police from her tree. They put a plastic rope cordon round the area Teresa said Gloria's clothes had been thrown.

'Yes,' she thought. 'Gotcha! They must have dossiers on them, anyway. Must have. Getting away with rape and grievous bodily harm doesn't cut it anymore. These guys must have offences dating back to the Doomsday Book.'

The incident was not reported in the local paper as rape. Teresa started reading it every day after her Pa brought it home after work. An assault 'allegedly' took place. That appeared in a small insert. No more. Nothing for anyone to get upset or concerned about.

Declan and Maddox sometimes took Dominic to the local Police Club where the boys boxed. Teresa once heard her father say that the Police often filed reports as quickly as possible, unless the media demanded explanations. Things conveniently went out of sight. Suicides and burglaries they refused to disclose, because of the possible copycat nature. Things racial were rarely reported, for they might be seen as 'inflammatory.' Community standards had to be protected. She remembered her father scoffing after watching items on television news; how a Police superintendent was quick to assure viewers that there was no racial intent on a taxi driver being attacked, when the following item proved, by both the victim's statement and the witnesses overhearing, that there definitely was.

Teresa remembered how her uncle would often say 'it's a complicated world out there, Tess.' She could never understand why that had to be. She saw things in black and white. She clearly understood that if a fox got in a henhouse, it'll eat your poultry. A fox kills cleanly. It takes its prey away to devour. But it doesn't half beat it to death, then couple with it, then leave it alone to die.

Next Friday night, Teresa sat on the top stair in her pajamas after saying she was going to bed. She'd do this, not really being tired, cradling her cat, still wanting to eaves-drop on adults' conversations. She'd learn things.

This night she distinctly heard her mother say.

"The girl was in a real mess when she arrived. Hysterical. Especially when they convinced her she could easily have died down there. Press charges, the nurses said. She said she didn't know what to do. The nurses said that didn't matter. Charges would be laid. She was badly beaten, left there to die."

There was a short silence. As Teresa stood quietly to go inside her room she heard her mother continue.

"If it weren't for that young Chinese soldier boy the girl would never have freed herself. He cut her hands and legs free with a box cutter. She'd shivered when she heard the sound of it. The taxi driver said he was a young soldier."

Teresa went and looked at herself in the mirror, swiveling her face from side to side, pulling her hair up high. Chinese? Do I look Chinese? She remembered that she'd been wearing the beret, her hair bundled underneath. She also remembered Che had once been to China. Chinese wore similar hats. Maybe Gloria was a Communist. Knew about these things. Communists were always getting beaten up. Some of the nuns at school thought them a godless bunch of heathens, therefore probably deserved it. Fergus would never say anything like that. But he was different, a kind of Christian-Heathen-Communist. He used to belt people up in the ring, but never spoke of being beaten as a Communist.

It was all getting a bit confusing.

Teresa recalled a story her Pa told about her as a young child. The adults thought it funny. It'd embarrassed Teresa—how they'd take her out in the stroller as an infant, how she'd cover her eyes up whenever people gawked at her. Maddox told them she was Chinese. It all had to do with the eyes. She couldn't take the full rays of the sun, squinting as from a papoose on her mothers' back while working in the rice paddies. He was going to buy her a Chinese parasol as soon as she could walk.

She remembered how her Ma cuddled her when the story was told, said that Pa had only been kidding, that she had beautiful eyes, that it was only a silly naughty joke that workmen tell.

Them Lazy Cops

Caitlin bought Teresa a mobile phone soon after. Previously, Teresa used her mother's, for she'd only ever text Sharn at the salon. Teresa had been indifferent about having her own.

"Gee, thanks Ma. Is it for my protection? Kind of rape whistle in case I get knocked up on Hope? Can I photograph it myself? Now that would be a real good Kodak moment, wouldn't it!" Teresa said softly, then kissed her mother with gratitude.

She didn't want to sound sarcastic, or give any hint of what she'd witnessed.

Maddox looked at Caitlin. Fergus looked on. The rape off Hope was exactly the reason why.

"You can now dump your boyfriends by sending them texts," Maddox offered.

"Ha, ha. Fat chance of that. I'll send one off to school now." Teresa fiddled round with the key pad. "I'll give THEM a multiple choice. "Wont b @ school b 4 May. Have problems with a) technology b) syringes c) razor blades d) tying my shoe laces."

"Don't be smart, Teresa. They're made Dominic a Prefect at school this year. He's going to have to do duties after school. You're going to be more on your own from now on." Maddox was clearly worried.

"That's o.k. I can look after myself." Teresa answered back blithely while pressing the digits competently, sending a text off to Sharn. Sharn dumped her boyfriends by text. Teresa shuffled her bottom coquettishly on the chair. "Especially now that I'm . . . textually active."

Caitlin put her arm round her. "I know you can look after yourself."

She also worried about Teresa's bravado. Was it a kind of whistling in the cemetery? She'd never ever been the happiest tent in the camp. Older now, that was becoming more apparent.

"First thing I'm going to do is put blocks on certain numbers. Stop the school secretary ringing here." She fiddled again. "And them lazy cops," she muttered to herself under her breath.

Communist Conspiracy

She heard her mother say to Fergus and Colleen that next Friday night.

"The girl's still in a mess. She doesn't have a very good reputation round town. No one denies what happened to her. Hospital reports were clear. One only had to look at her. She'd have died down there, that's for sure. She'll be back on the street in no time. Just didn't like losing her front teeth that much. Stupid girl. That Chinese boy told her the hospital would put the teeth back in for her. Quite smart for Hope."

Colleen continued. "She comes in the salon. We had to get rid of her in the end. I took to shampooing her with two pairs of gloves on. She had sores on her mouth, always complaining of a sore jaw. I swear she had chancres. Too dangerous. But, pity has its limits. I tried, but she's just another drop kick. The owner told her not to come back."

Fergus then spoke. Teresa was listening up in the mango, but his voice was too soft with his back to her. She couldn't hear a single word he said.

"I was speaking to Spiro the other day. He'd been speaking with the police. Those boys are going to get off Scott-free. Vickers and Rowland are going to Afghanistan in a few weeks time. The Military stepped in. Took the Police reports away. Young one's underage. Police had a sealed file on the elder Rowland. The Military hadn't done their homework. Knew nothing about it when accepting his enlistment. Sealed files on juveniles usually go way back. And always for serious crime. Manslaughter. Grievous bodily harm. It's all going to be swept under the proverbial carpet."

Another Bad Report

"You're not going to make it through school with reports like these, Teresa." Caitlin expressed her disappointment with vehemence. "Two more years. Don't you have any ambition? Dominic has ambition."

"Don't compare me with him. We're not alike. He's like uncle. I'm like Sharn. You. Pa. Colleen. School bores me. Nothing interests me there. Uncle's going to look after me. Just like he did for everyone else here."

Caitlin ignored that. "It says here that in Science you may as well not have sat."

"I did sit. The examiner sat. I rolled the exam paper up, looked out the window through it at the birds, like through my spyglass. Boring, boring! I only like Christian Instruction. Sit and listen. Sit and listen. That's all we do. It's so non stimulating. I feel like jumping around like popcorn in the microwave. English books bore me. 'Animal Farm,' 'Lord of the Flies.' Boring. No sex. And the teacher's such a dick-less sack of . . . whatever." Teresa put her hands to her head in despair.

"The Headmaster sums you up at the end on the report as being 'oblivious.'"

"What's that mean?"

"It means forgetful, therefore dreamy. Unable to concentrate."

"When I'm eighteen I'm going to change my name by deed poll then. I'm sick of being known as Mahone. I still want an Irish name, though. Maybe that's a good one for me—Teresa O'Blivious. What do you think? Would that suit?"

"That's enough, Teresa!" Caitlin was almost yelling. She didn't correct the bad language as she usually would. She was trying to deal with her own anger.

"I'm too old for school . . . Hope Street beckons. I'd rather cut sugar cane in Cuba for a peso a day."

"No you wouldn't. You have no idea how hard that would be. And don't get smart-mouthed with me, young lady. You have no idea what you're talking about."

"Why can't I stay here, work for uncle? I can do his computer work, answer calls for his business. I hear his fax machine chugging away day and night. You help him with his paperwork. And you do your own job. I can take the pressure off you."

"He wouldn't allow it. Neither will I. You have to be eighteen before dealing with liquor."

"No I don't. I have to be eighteen to consume it. I don't drink alcohol, anyway."

"Out of the question. Get the idea out of your head."

"I come from a family who work like Irish mules. Why can't I be a drug mule on Hope then now I've got a mobile. Everyone else's doing it."

"You've been watching too many bad movies. Get a grip on yourself. And stop being smart-mouthed. It won't get you anywhere."

"I have a grip. Only movies you ever let me watch are cheese, anyway."

"Teresa, you've won the Christian Instruction prize each year so far. You can do it again. It's just you must apply yourself in other subjects."

"Then I'll run away, be a preacher then. Have my own church. Make lots of money. Do pole dancing on the side." Teresa shuffled restlessly on her chair.

"Stop talking like a tart. You'll end up beaten senseless in a ditch."

"No I won't. No one's going to rape or beat me up." Teresa then muttered under her breath. "Not this little Communist Chinese boy."

"What was that?"

"Nothing."

Caitlin was becoming more furious with her insolence. Heartily sick of the backchat.

"What's wrong with you, Teresa? Why have you become so nasty? You have nothing to be sullen about, nothing to regret. You only have to make a few real decisions in life—right career path, where to live, who to marry. You make bad choices now you'll end up . . . you'll end up in HELL!" Caitlin couldn't contain herself any longer. Maybe fear of damnation might get through to her.

Teresa thought about that a moment, then smirked.
"Hell sounds real good to me. At least I'd have it all to myself."
"And what's that supposed to mean?" Caitlin glared at her.
"It's empty down there. All the devils are up on Hope Street."

What Makes Proof?

One night at dinner Teresa wheeled the conversation around to suit herself.

"Uncle. What's 'cor-rob-o-rate' mean?"

"I'll show you." Fergus took a bread roll off Teresa's plate, put it down on the spare chair beside him. "I steal your bread. You then accuse me of stealing it. I say 'prove it.' You ask your mother if she saw me do it. She says 'yes.' That's corroboration. Proof."

"Is it always as easy as that?"

"No. It often depends on the reliability of the witnesses. Suppose the witness was not your mother but Dominic, and he lied about it."

"Dominic wouldn't lie. He's far too straight."

"I said 'supposing.' All right. Take Sharn then. She lies, sides with me, just for the fun of it. Sometimes you need two unrelated witnesses. Proof must be certain. You need a smoking gun."

"What about me as a witness. To murder. And Ballou. Can Ballou ever be a witness? Cor-rob-o-rate what happened?"

"No. It always involves language. Cats can't give evidence."

"What about a dog, then? Suppose it was there with me, sees a killing take place, then tracks the killer back to his house by sniffing the trail. The Police are called. Evidence is found. Is that the same as two reliable beings giving evidence?"

"Good question. Excellent proof. But I don't think it'd be called 'corroboration.'"

"What do they call it then? 'Clever dog?'"

"Most would argue that. The judge would likely call it 'canine instinct.' Do you wish you owned a dog now, Detective Teresa?"

"No. Happy with having Ballou. Things will have to remain mysteries forever, won't they? Like with the Catholic church."

Teresa said no more.

Fergus then told her(she assumed he was talking about places in South America) that some corrupt lawyers hire professional corroborators as witnesses to car accidents in order to sue. Miraculously, these witnesses capture almost every traffic accident there is to see.

Teresa took it all in, holding out little hope for her case. Trust Fergus to throw another haymaker in the ring.

What's It All About?

Teresa was now regularly reading her Bible up in her tree houses. She'd bought herself a large Concordance from a Thrift shop, spent endless hours cross-referencing on her haunches in the tree. Now straighter than straight, purer than pure, it gave her solace—especially the books of Isaiah, Jeremiah and Job, more prophetic the better, not her usual poetical books.

One month elapsed. None of the boys had been charged yet.

It began to concern the others that the older she was getting the more she wished to be by herself.

It was a Sunday. Both families had gone to Mass that morning, except for Declan who'd been working at the market. They'd invited Father Kevin back to the house for lunch. Teresa excused herself to eat inside with her cat. She'd rather snoop than listen, and had always been wary of Kevin at the house. Apart from her classes on Christian Instruction, Kevin knew how badly she was faring at school. Schoolwork was slow, tentative, always of insufficient length, a perfunctory effort. Once Kevin had gone, Teresa went and sat with Fergus. She clutched her Bible, then placed it up on the table, opened it out, began reading from a bookmarked page.

"For out of the heart proceed evil thoughts, murder, adulteries, fornications, thefts, false witness, blasphemies. These are the things which defile a man . . . Matthew, chapter 15." Teresa paused and looked at her uncle. "I don't see much love out in the world, Uncle. The Bible says the heart's evil. That doesn't hold much hope for us down here, does it!"

Fergus thought carefully before speaking. "Even less forgiveness out there, Tess."

She hated it when he agreed with her.

Fergus shrugged. "There's lots of quotations about the heart, Tess. 'A merry heart doeth good like a medicine, but a broken spirit drieth the bones.' That's from Proverbs. I thought you preferred the wisdom books. You have to turn off whatever it is that nourishes the disease."

"What? Like a valve? On, off, like trying to hide the truth?"

"Why not? A doctor would say that's good medicine. A good attitude."

"Like good comedy?" Teresa spoke sarcastically.

"Why not? You'll never learn all that much up in the trees, Tess. You can't live your life wrapped in cotton-wool."

Teresa looked at him with a hard stare. She almost said 'How would you know? Where are your wife and children? In a bottle of booze?' She didn't want to tell him that every day on Hope felt like a near miss. Some days the misery of it tore her heart out. She felt as eviscerated as a dead chicken.

"What's love, Uncle?" Teresa slumped morosely, staring across to the avocado tree. It was now bursting with fruit. Too many ever to consume themselves. Declan had been selling them at the market that morning.

Fergus could not help but notice how pretty Teresa had become. Almost in spite of her sadness. He also saw the way Dominic's friends would watch her at the house on Saturday nights. Even Sharn's boyfriends seemed to be sniffing round, swarming to look like jumping jacks over the fence. All she gave back was her indifference, scowling when anyone came too close, as though she'd like to take out their eyes with a spoon. She didn't want to know their friends. Senior boys from the football team were continually offering her rides. She'd rather trust the openness of Hope than the confines of their cars.

Caitlin told Fergus that Teresa often related stories she'd overheard of boys' weekend sexual exploits. Frankly, Teresa didn't believe them. They were just shooting off their mouths about what they'd like to do, as they did up on Hope street.

Yet her hourglass figure seemed so ripe, as fruitful as the avocado tree beside them. But there was a blight there. She didn't like the world much.

That didn't stop Fergus from teasing.

"What's love?" Fergus reflected, now giving his full attention. "Love is like a rebellious bird that no-one will tame, a roaming Gypsy child who had never known any laws. Love is far off, you have to wait for it.

It flies away." Fergus fluttered his eyelashes and fingers in unison, in a silly way.

It wasn't the answer she wanted.

"Good one, Uncle. Can you give me chapter and verse? Sure ain't in Proverbs. Maybe it's from one of Ma's Romantic novels? Sounds real creepy to me. Like something crawling up the legs of my shorts. Something that won't go away."

Fergus laughed. He liked her wit, mordant as it was, but he wasn't going to be much help to her.

"They're lines from Bizet's 'Carmen.' You remember it? We saw it on T.V. the other week. Subtitles were on the auto-cue. You said you liked it."

"Well, she sure made a mess of love, didn't she? Can't you do any better than that?"

"'Afraid not. That's about the best I can offer. You'll love the world one day, Tess. You'll have to. You've got no other option."

"I want a job, Uncle. Give me a job. Please! With you. Any job. I want to quit school. I really, really, really want a job. You're busy at work. I can answer the telephone, type in the credits and debits, profit and loss. You're making heaps. You must need help. I don't want much for myself. Just to quit school."

Fergus frowned. He'd never undermine his sister. Caitlin was insistent Teresa stay on. He wasn't going to say that.

"There's plenty of jobs out there without qualifications—pumping gas, pizza delivery on a bicycle, giving blood, walking people's dogs, even their cats. Everyone wants their carpets cleaned." Fergus paused then looked away. "Give it another couple of years. You're pretty. You could get a job on TV as Weather Woman at best—you're always watching the weather from your tree—or work as a waitress, even instruct at an indoor rock climbing school. It doesn't really matter what you do. Jobs are just different hats people wear. Life's all about getting three regular meals a day. You don't eat much, anyway."

"I don't believe you mean that." Teresa's disappointment seemed to compound. Fergus dismissed her question, throwing it away like an empty peapod. She hated his understatements. Why should everything from Fergus elicit just a smile or a guffaw. She was beginning to see her schooldays as being without end. Entering Hope each day was like cutting off the Hydra's head, another one immediately appearing. Hope was Hell with a big hoarding 'Abandon All Hope Those Who Enter Here.'

She hated her own prettiness. Carmen would've been better off hating hers as well.

Fergus purposely drew a cigar from his pack on the table. "Carmen worked in a tobacco factory rolling up these things week in week out, year in year out, like lots of women still do in Cuba today. They have readers who help the workers pass the time by readings from imaginative books, even poetry. Sounds pretty good to me."

"How useless is that!"

"I disagree. Why don't you go out more, Tess? With Sharn. Her friends. They're good girls. Dominic says his friends like you. Your Ma says you should get yourself a boyfriend. Get out. See the world around you."

Teresa quietly thumbed the pages of her Bible. "I feel badly about that. Dom told me his friends like me. He asked 'why don't you come out with us?' He thinks I'm pretty—pretty weird. I should have told him, no thanks, I'm a lesbian. I didn't. I quoted him John 9:10 about The Good Shepherd instead. I said I'd rather stay here. With Him."

"Where's that, Tess? Up the tree with your cat?"

"It's clean up there." Teresa always said that. She truly believed it.

"There's another meaning to the word 'shepherd.' It's not in the Bible. It's used as a term in sport. Rugby union, for one. 'Shepherding.' An infringement block. And it's illegal. You purposely stop the opposition coming through. But the opposition has the right to come through. Isn't that a bit like what you're denying?"

"I don't like the opposition. Why get knocked round by them? Do you mean I should give up reading the Bible?" Teresa was almost thumping her hand on the pages.

"No. I didn't mean that." Fergus looked away and asked softly. "Why have you gone so sour on the world?"

"Because of love. Love, love, love. It's so hard to take. I don't believe in it. I listen to girls' endless chatter about love at school. They love the world. One hundred per cent. Love's going out to dumb parties, doing drugs, having sex, bouncing up and down at discos, seeing fireworks displays, they even believe in the advertisements they see on TV.—the man selling second-hand cars is great just because he looks good in a suit. They believe in EVERYTHING—it's such a bunch of shite. I think a life of those things only is worthless. How can you believe in everything? Come on, Uncle, you tell me."

"You're not the first Christian ever to say that. There are Christian philosophers who believe you only begin to live when you see life as pretty much worthless. Best you have these thoughts now. Get them over with. Life's not short, Tess. It's long. You'll find meaning in it, soon enough. If you keep thinking about these things all the time you'll find life's useless. Like music's useless. Books are useless. But they're a different kind of useless."

"What about life in the meantime? I don't believe you when you say a job's nothing. Would you like me to work in a cigar factory? Like Carmen did? They were a bunch of bad girls in a bad town. Just like this one."

"No. They were poor. She didn't have much of an option. You have. Point is, she did have a passion. She craved for something more than her work."

"What was that? Loving lots of different men? Making them all jealous of her? Getting killed while still young?"

"I don't think so. What she loved most was to dance. As much or as little as song. That was enough for her."

"Like your girlfriend, Marie?"

"She's a beautiful dancer. Her mind becomes transported by dance."

"Do you sleep with her, Uncle? Come on. You can tell me. I liked her. I know you'd never get married. Being a Communist, and all that. Che never married. Had lots of children, though. I'm not ever going to marry, either."

"I believe falling in love's good. Sex's bad. Like in those Bollywood movies from India." Fergus smirked at her childishly. Teresa hit his arm. He then turned more serious. "Che got killed as a young man."

"I know. But he did look a beautiful corpse, didn't he! All those pictures you have of him laid on a slab. Soldiers standing around. Like rock singers who sing about dying young, looking good in a coffin."

"Tess, don't have these thoughts. Steer clear of them. I don't think Carmen or Che thought much about death. Find a passion of your own. A passion's the only thing that will stop you from being lonely."

"I have my Bible. That's my passion. Passion enough for me."

"That's ok. Nothing wrong with that. There's lots of religious scholars in the world who don't know anything about the things of this world—geography, politics, mathematics. They've never watched TV, been to a basketball game, never gone to the beach to swim. They can only count out sufficient change for the next few stops on the bus. They can't even tell you exactly what's over the border. They don't want to know. They don't allow their wives to vote, nor vote themselves. And these are good people. Genuinely good. We shouldn't doubt them. All their knowledge is derived from their sacred texts. They believe there's nothing else they need to know. They believe in a different scrutiny of order. It works for them. We've no right to question it. Their society allows, even encourages it. But do you want to live that way?"

"Like Father Kevin. He believes in order. Do you believe in order, Uncle. Tell me, truthfully. Tell me what you believe."

"Of course I do. One has to. I just won't belong to an Order, that's all. And I believe tree houses are hiding places. You're not going to get knifed and stoned in the street, but you've got to find ways of coping with it if you do get threatened. That's life."

Fergus gently clutched her hand then got from his chair and walked away.

Fergus the Secretive.

Dominic was made a school Prefect in his final year. Considered an honor to be one of the seven chosen from the senior class of forty five students, the criteria were academic, sporting, an unblemished record for discipline and moral rectitude. Father Kevin had some input with final selection. Dominic's obligations meant that he was now given a roster of duties, sometimes during lunch hours, less often after school. He was achieving well academically, confining his sport's activity to gymnastics and running, which helped with his outside interest of boxing. There was a group of Central American boxers visiting later in the year. Dominic had been selected to fight one in his weight division. Now in training four nights a week, backyard Sunday mornings, he was becoming extremely fit.

Teresa would sometimes wander over, put on the gloves, take up the pads and spar with Sharn. She'd take to the punch bag like a righteous soldier, morose and angry, pummeling her fists into it.

"Go for it, Little Sister," Sharn would say, "knock it off its hook."

"I'm trying!" Teresa would yell back.

"Move your hips, hit straight from the shoulder, protect yourself at all times." Sharn would correct her. "The last thing you want to do is break a hand. Fergus said so." She and Teresa would giggle over that. Even Dominic would smile in recognition.

Fergus would sometimes go over next door, correct Teresa's stance, quietly guide the three while he sat on a chair. He said little to Dominic. Caitlin would bring him over a cup of tea. They'd sit in the morning sun at weekends and chat, more often ignoring the exercisers.

They talked business. Caitlin was now doing more and more for him, even though he tried to confine his work to weekdays. His days were long, with much travel. Sometimes he'd not come back for three weeks. He only answered his telephone between six to seven each evening when at home. Nobody else was allowed to.

"Secretive old devil," Sharn said to Teresa one day. "Truth be told, he's probably selling guns again. Anyway, he's got this woman on the side. I heard him talking to her on his cell. 'Hello my sweet.' 'Yes, my darling.' He sounded like a lovesick schoolboy. I didn't think he'd have time to juggle sex. Her name's Elena. Must be his 'secretary.'"

Sharn wrapped the vital word in parenthesis with her fingers in the air.

"I should ask him." Teresa said disappointedly. "I liked that dancer. Tell him to get rid of her, give me a job. What happened to Maria?"

"Search me. Better not ask. I heard my Ma talking about Elena with yours. I think it's real serious. All pretty hush-hush. Probably got bigger tits. That wouldn't be too hard." Sharn reflected. "Anyway. Let's get you someone, Little Sister. Let's mock you up a dating site."

They went away and sat at Sharn's computer.

"Purchased at a slave auction. Drop dead gorgeous tree climber from Africa, virgin, 16, dark hair, black eyes which will break your heart, 5'6" 46kg, looking for a not-quite-too-sure-yet. Straight-meat lumberjack. Gay social climbing girl. Must be a Jesus freak. No pic, no pussy." Sharn offered. Sharn looked to Teresa. They were both perspiring profusely from the exercise and heat. Sharn added "Warm and sticky and sweet to eat."

"Ha, ha. Try—16, 5'6" 150k, looking for outings with tow-truck driver. Must have big wheels, large hoist. No digital pic poss. Text me at blah, blah. Go figure. Maybe looking for quick encounter."

"Like who?"

"I don't know. Maybe the postmen, meter readers."

"Be serious, Tess. You know you're going to have to start sometime. You don't want to die a virgin"

In the Dunce's Corner, again

Teresa now began getting regular lunchtime school detentions—Work Not Done, Did Not Sits, which staff said amounted to insolence. She dragged herself corridor to corridor, one musty classroom to another. Dominic choose to be in charge of these lunchtime detainees, for that meant he could leave early for boxing training. Teresa chose lunchtimes.

He would read out the roll, call "Teresa Mahone?" The word "Present" would come back in a barely audible reply. There would be a long silence before he read the next name on the list. Dominic would look to the walls, up the ceiling, as if up a tree, to see where the sound came.

"Ha, Ha. Jerk!" Teresa would mutter into her desktop.

Dealing with detainees, some of them his own age, was a duty Dominic didn't relish. Some prefects abused their powers by bullying. Dominic found that distasteful, and would always take off his Prefect's badge the moment he left school grounds. There was no need for prefects to be up on Hope.

Payback Time

Dominic followed Teresa down Hope this Thursday afternoon. She'd suddenly stepped out off the sidewalk in front of him, staring across to a group of girls standing near the steps opposite. She then began jay walking through the traffic to the loiterers.

'For crying out loud. What the hell is she doing now?' Dominic scratched his head in wonder. Even Sharn never walked over there. It was a grimy, unregulated area, lots of bantering, gossiping, arguing, sometimes fights over territory, and always someone trying to look official. There were cat fights, bickering as to who minded the youngsters in strollers, who to hit up the café for free hot water to warm a baby's bottle, none of them with discipline enough to form a line on the sidewalk. Some took to the alleys for shade, sat on dustbins. One or two of them were slightly crazed, their eyes swiveled, others looked like they needed to be hosed down, sponged with alcoholic wipes.

Teresa felt sorry for them. Some had a disfigurement. Teresa might not have liked boys much, but she felt sorry that no boys even liked them.

Caitlin would see them come through hospital doors. "How have we got to this?" she would wonder out loud.

"You must get out of here. It's far too dangerous" came a voice at Gloria's shoulder. Gloria turned her skinny elfin-like body in her flat shoes and sling on dress with cheap buttons, instantly recognizing the tone of the person fronting her. She looked Teresa up and down with surprise, least expecting some uppity convent girl asking her to do anything, and the person she'd thought was a Chinese boy.

Teresa stood firm, glowering at her gelled up hair, thinking what Sharn would say of that. 'Hair should always look relaxed, Little Sister.' She noticed Gloria's front teeth were back in, her nose straightened, yet her face still looked slightly lopsided. There were visible marks of plucked stitches one side of it.

Gloria immediately put her head back as though Teresa might head-butt her, almost tottering on her flats. It seemed she hadn't got her balance back. Her pixie face reminded of a chicken, head back, ready to pick, sucking in her stomach as if to strike an insect in the air. Gloria seemed vulnerable, certainly no swishing piece of tail imagined on a bar stool. She'd lost weight. Her chest seemed to freeze, breasts no bigger than dog's testicles, perhaps fearing some do-gooder's click, smile for the camera for a newspaper.

The girls beside her looked a raggedy bunch of nose pickers; even the children in push chairs all seemed to have runny noses

Teresa looked away, not wanting to seem overpowering.

She then began rooting through the mish-mash of her schoolbag as though hunting for lip balm. She shoved things aside, pulled something from the bottom, showed Gloria the gilt star beret. Teresa immediately put it back, then placed her two hands behind her neck unclasping the St. Christopher, which she'd dutifully worn for eleven years now. She handed it to Gloria.

The girl looked down to the medal. It meant nothing to her. She didn't need some mumbo-jumbo amulet for protection. Damage was done. She'd had it coming. She'd accepted her lot with resignation as being her own fault.

"Wear this. It'll protect you." Teresa wasn't too sure that it would. She just wanted Gloria gone from there. The other girls looked on with bemusement, puffing cigarettes closely together like smoke rising from a slag heap. They weren't used to some prissily dressed dark convent girl their side of the street. 'Get out' was the look, but no more frightening to them than a black cat crossing their path. To them, convent girls were rudest of all. Saving their vaginas for marriage. Doing other things. And, given half the chance, they'd nick anything. That was a standard joke with them, if not the truth of it.

Sharn would have had them all down in the salon in an instant, getting fungal rot out from fingernails, beating them over the head with curling irons. They looked awful together. A shabby corner without decency. The girls didn't even seem to like one another as they stood on their bony legs, puffing their small trays in front like peddlers. One wore a pink hat, another fake blonde, another streaks gone wrong from so many previous layers of dye. They looked as if they could do with a solid meal. Fat use that would be, Teresa thought. One would spew it up in this stench. They looked frail, pigeon breasted, easy to trip up.

Teresa had seen most of them before, somewhere or other, mostly over the street near the slot machines beside the pool hall. This was the shady side. The alleys behind looked almost as dark as a cinema. Right behind was a public convenience. The sign read 'Ladies only.' Teresa could smell the reek from it.

Teresa suddenly recalled her Christian Instruction last class. They had discussed The Seven Spiritual Acts. It occurred to her that most of those didn't apply here. She wasn't this side to instruct the uninformed, counsel the doubtful, admonish sinners, have them bear wrongs patiently, forgive offenses willingly, but she was here to comfort the afflicted, at least help this girl. She didn't see her as morally diseased. She felt genuinely sorry for the beating she'd taken, maybe the misplaced courage in not ratting on her attackers.

Unlike Sharn, Teresa didn't care much how they looked, and was certainly not going to suggest acts of confession to put it right. Neither would Sharn's new perms or manicured nails. She thought maybe Fergus was right, that they don't represent anything only because nobody represented them.

This side of the street reeked. There were a couple of dirty men with starved looks standing around, as if for a peepshow to start. Or freak show. One had a flattened body, a bullfrog face. Had they seen the report of Gloria's rape in the paper it would have read as just another everyday story to them.

Gloria had to be sick, Teresa thought. Scared sick. She pretended not to be afflicted in any way. Those three males were going to get their comeuppance, whether Gloria liked it or not, otherwise they'd only do it again to somebody else, and without remorse. Teresa thought the only remorse the two soldiers would ever feel would be in getting found out. That was not Teresa's problem. Getting found out, she'd make sure that they would.

"So it was you," Gloria said without hint of thanks, puffing her chest defensively as though accosted for some wrong. "What you care," she asked rhetorically. "I'm back. To stay. Guy Rowland's down the street. I'll wait. His day'll come. I'll get him. One day." She ladled her words out slowly, shading her raggedy fringed eyes with her hand. Teresa noticed again that Gloria moved back with a slight limp.

"I'll go speak to him now. Are you coming with me? Come on, Gloria, let's go tell the whole street what happened that day. If the Police won't take action, we will. Let's have some fun. He won't hit you again, too many witnesses around this time. He wouldn't have the nerve."

"What! You crazy? He'll beat you half to death." Gloria screwed her face up. Her skin stiffened like plastic from the stitches. It was not a pretty face. Her hair was lank, hiding most of it. Her lime green eyes were half shut, reduced to a squint. Her thinness made her look like the homeless runaway that she was. Yet, for reasons unclear, Teresa somehow preferred Gloria to her namby-pamby classmates at school. Gloria wasn't the kind to make snide comments behind her hand like they would, belittle others, and obviously she wasn't self pitying.

"Not if we beat him first." Teresa stared back.

Gloria idly tossed the St. Christopher medal up and down in her hand as if it were a stone for a beggar to throw if a person got too near. She smelled of cheap shampoo. Teresa thought how that would offend Sharn.

"Are you coming, or not?"

"You're a crazy bitch!" Gloria yelled back as Teresa retreated. The other girls laughed. They knew the score. Just another uppity convent bitch, nose in the clouds. They weren't too sure what the conversation was about. Nobody told them what to do, anyway.

But Gloria's mouth had fallen in amazement when Teresa turned. She headed back the other side as if on a mission. Dominic was waiting, leaning up against a closed roller door, fiddling distractedly with the padlock as Teresa passed him, she gritting her teeth. He'd heard Gloria's final words.

Teresa could now see young Rowland up ahead, rattling close together with others on the sidewalk like a pocketful of loose change. She was sick and tired of these dickheads. It was as if they only existed in numbers. She opened her satchel again, fumbled within before stalking up, fronting Rowland with his friends. Dominic immediately quickened his pace

"You're a goddamn rapist, Rowland. You're a dirt-bag piece of shit!"

Guy turned, facing her in silence. Teresa stood over him, inches from his nose.

"I saw you, your brother Billie, his friend Vickers belt up then rape Gloria that Friday afternoon. I've got all the details. I wrote them down. Sent them to the Police." She began to yell at all those about her. "Look at the rapist, everybody! Rowland's a lowdown rapist! Rowland's a rapist! A dirt-bag rapist." That word seemed to ring in the street.

Dominic could hardly believe what he was witnessing. Teresa's Lycra shorts suddenly seem to bag round her knees, her school skirt askew. She was ruddy cheeked. She didn't care how she looked. Her face was filled with fury.

Guy pushed her back so as not to be within earshot of his friends. He turned angry, face flush with rage, and embarrassment. Teresa noticed the veins in his neck began pushing out at his spider-web tattoo.

"Take it easy, Rowland." Dominic edged towards them. He didn't know what else to say, not knowing what provoked it. Rowland's friends stood their ground, one folding his arms on his chest. They looked a bunch of face pullers, little barking dogs. They didn't want to mess with Dominic, or any of those mad Mahones, just closed ranks and did their usual sniping.

"Get this crazy bitch out of here." Rowland stared at Dominic.

"You're a coward! Rapist! Woman beater!" Teresa blurted before moving forward in his face again.

A crowd was now gathering, as for a car crash.

Teresa yelled "I saw you. Rapist! Rapist! Rapist!"

Dominic wondered what exactly Teresa had seen. How could she have?

Guy lashed out at her, knocking Teresa's unlatched satchel to the ground. Schoolbooks spilled everywhere. Dominic saw the beret then caught sight of a metal object near his foot after it slew from the bag. He stepped back. It was a box cutter. Only then did Dominic suspect it was Teresa who'd freed Gloria in the Reserve.

"Enough, Rowland. Back off." Dominic stepped forward, gently pushing Teresa aside. Rowland's straggly, unkempt beard bristled on his Fagin-like face. His youth had nearly gone. His face looked hollow as his skull and cross-bone T. Dominic wondered what kind of drugs were flowing through his veins.

Guy drew back. He knew Dominic was handy.

"It's you, Stoo-pid. My brother and Viper go to Afghanistan next week. You don't want to have to deal with them."

Dominic realized now that the two soldiers must have been the ones with Guy that day. Why else mention them? Rowland was uneasy, shifty, resenting the pedestrians gathering.

"I do," Teresa said loudly. "There's rapists, too. Bring them here so I can tell them myself." She turned to the crowd. "Guy Rowland, his brother Billy, Tom Vickers—they raped Gloria Lange down in the Reserve. I saw it. The Military's covering for them because they're soldiers."

Teresa didn't know that, not for sure. It was no more than surmise. But Dominic knew. He'd heard about it from his Pa.

"Just might bring them here, you crazy bitch. You don't want to have to deal with them," he repeated.

He then turned to Dominic. "They'll belt you too. Scared?" Guy's friends laughed derisively, wedging themselves together like badly parked cars.

"You don't scare me, Rowland. Or that big oaf brother of yours. Things Rowland usually go downhill. You leave her alone. You lay a hand on her and that's where you're going." Dominic added "Come on, Teresa. Leave it."

They all backed off. The crowd slowly began dispersing. Teresa's eyes flashed round. She caught sight of Gloria further up the sidewalk. She'd followed them. Heard it all. Teresa turned back. It was then that she noticed Spiro backed up against a building. She saw a baseball bat tucked in at his side.

"You sure of what you're saying?" Dominic asked as they turned into Edward.

"I'm sure. If I see those animals again I'll front them. I mean it. You don't have to be in on this with me. It's my business."

"You'll need a whole lot more than a box cutter to put those big brutes away."

"I don't care. I'm going to make them aware that someone else's aware of what they've done. Why haven't the Police acted? Why didn't Gloria press charges?" Teresa shook her head despairingly.

"Military did step in. They didn't want a sandal with their boys going overseas. The Police got out-ranked on this one."

Teresa muttered. "All the more reason to front them. Don't you dare tell anyone at home."

"You have to tell me everything. If Billy and Vickers turn up tomorrow then you'd better have some kind of a plan."

Teresa ignored that. "I'm sick of it. I'm sick of feeling like a hen in a henhouse just waiting for the fox to arrive. Those pieces of shite—standing round, working out the proper way to rape girls. I don't care what Gloria does. She didn't deserve to be beaten. I prefer her any day to those throwbacks."

"You're not in a henhouse. You're out in the open yard. Ever tried catching a hen in a yard. It sure ain't easy. It's an old trick they make us boxers do. Few ever manage it. Just see yourself as that hen out in the open. You've got to be the one to outfox them."

Showdown on Hope Street

Dominic never mentioned the incident at home. He thought long and hard about it while twiddling with a remote control without sound, brooding out in his shed. Nobody ever suspected Teresa freed the girl that afternoon. But Spiro had seen them. Fergus was bound to find out. There was little point in bringing out the Ouija board, having a séance, it was Dominic's job to look after her in the here and now.

Dominic remembered that his father once mentioned Billy and Viper. "How they completed basic training in the army is beyond me. Two big ignorant oafs. A couple of body building pumped up woman haters with their death head tattoos. Billy's so dumb he broke a jar one day by screwing the lid the wrong way. His brain bulges like an inflatable raft. Full of air."

Billy had lots of nicknames. Dominic remembered hearing one of them was The Bulldozer, thought that was about the best classification one could give him. The sound of Billy starting up gave everyone the shivers.

"You don't have to walk with me, Dom." Teresa said quietly, her head down in her loose hair on Hope the next afternoon. "I can take care of myself."

She moved on doggedly as a tram sparking on rails. Dominic could not brake her optimism.

"These guys are dangerous, Teresa."

"I'm passed caring."

Friday, traffic was always heavy Fridays. Workers finished early for the week. Everybody—truckers, manual workers, light industry crews—demanded early starts to escape the mid afternoon heat. Fridays, to Teresa, made the world up on Hope Street angrier, nerves tighter than catgut knowing the rage and disappointment, boredom of weekends.

'Pedestrians, far too many,' Dominic mused to himself, thinking of necessary room to maneuver. He wished Teresa would slow down so he could buy time. Time to think. Maybe there was nothing to think. Billy and Piper weren't big in the thinking department. Dominic had boxed wide necked boys before, big like them. He just worked on shutting their eyes. But two together. That was a different prospect.

Many settled up on Hope on Friday afternoons like bluebottle flies bloating on beer and dope, hoping maybe to get a girl for nothing.

"Three warriors ahead. Just before Edward. Careful, Sister. You say your piece then run like they haven't seen hide nor hair of you."

"I'm not running away, Dom. Look across the street. Is Gloria there?" Teresa asked without caring much for an answer. She was going to finish this today, one way or another.

"Sure is. And staring right at us."

"I'm fronting them, Dom. I don't care anymore. They have to be told. I'll let the whole street know what they did." Teresa then came to a standstill, swept the hair from her face with her hand, tied it back with both as she did before practicing boxing. She looked to Gloria, beckoning her across with movement of her head.

Gloria frowned, then skipped lightly through heavy traffic, giving the finger to a motorist who'd blown his horn. "Save it for your wife," she yelled. Dominic looked at her grimly as she came and stood beside Teresa.

What now?

"Friday. People everywhere. Here's the plan. Why play talk and tell again? These guys don't understand. You're just going to have to rush up, belt hell out of Guy, like in a moment of madness. Ignore his friends. I'll fix Billy and Viper."

Teresa's mouth dropped.

"You're crazy, man!" Gloria shouted at him. "We'll need THREE taxis to the hospital this time."

"Maybe. Maybe not." Dominic muttered.

"Guy's got three friends. Billy and Tom make six. Three of us. Not good odds, Dom." Teresa stared ahead. "Think again."

"Just start it. Take the initiative. They won't know what hit them. You'll need room to move. Strap your schoolbag up on your shoulders. Keep your hands round your chests to block punches coming in. Don't break 'em. Don't underestimate these numbskulls, either. They're only half ignorant. A bad day on the street's still better than a good day ever was at school. You want to teach them a lesson, don't you?"

"I want to shame them. But is that a plan, Dom?"

"Let's do a Fergus. Only way we can win this is to fight dirty."

Teresa adjusted her leather bag on her shoulders. Her face seethed as though her life had suddenly come to this, willed and determined by the street. She looked to Gloria, so slight, timid in comparison. She then thought of Che. His fearlessness. She didn't care if fighting was right or wrong, or Christian. Today she'd be a Communist. Was there difference? Did difference matter? When Father Kevin came round to their house Fergus would always stand, shake his hand like two soldiers. They'd hug one another. Embrace of friends. They'd then joke together. Fergus would always say "Greetings, Comrade Kevin," "Greetings, Comrade Lenin," Kevin would reply in mock rhyme.

She put on her Che beret. She remembered Fergus once saying Che was simply more 'intelligent,' 'tenacious,' more 'capacious' than others. His life was about making 'brave decisions.' Teresa had gone away, looked up those words in her dictionary. She remembered back to one picture from Fergus' books, a large hoarding on the side of the road in Cuba, words "Queremos que sean como el Che." Fergus translated for her. "We all want to be like Che."

Dominic purposely turned his back on the soldiers further down the street. He pulled out two pairs of wrap round plastic sun-glasses from his pockets.

"Put these on. Today you're going to look like The Blues Brothers."

Gloria screwed up her face. "This ain't no dumb movie, man. It ain't Ghost Busters. This is for REAL."

"Yes it is," Dominic then pulled a round canister out from his bag, took off the lid, cupping his hand over it to stop the breeze from blowing it.

"Gloria, your turn now. We're going to throw silt back at them. Black pepper, white pepper, cayenne, chili powder all in a mix. Teresa, you're the concrete worker. You've got a good eye for levels. Sweep it out in front of their faces. Aim for the eyes. This'll make them care more than a pinch of pepper for what they've done to Gloria. Keep your mouths tightly shut. Take a deep breath before you do it. Soon as it settles, toss the glasses, wade in, boots and all. They won't see a thing. Are you on for it, or not? You'll have to cover your nose and mouth with your other hand. It'll confuse them. They'll think you're in kind of fancy dress. Let them try shaking this off like a bunch of wet dogs in the rain."

"Can you handle the others, Dom?" Teresa looked to the canister, adjusted her shades, then pushed wisps of hair from her face to behind her ears.

"Bigger they are. Harder they fall." Dominic muttered as he turned to face them. "Let's start it."

Teresa strode forward as though finally ready to beat the drum of Revolution on the street. Fed up with years of grime, spittle and filth, how even the brick buildings seemed held together by dirt, she vowed she'd eat it no longer, take their joking at their own disgrace. The street smelled rancid as last night's cigarettes. She was sick of the street smelling like a zoo. Her heart was not racing, as it was that afternoon in the Reserve as she ran across it, raincoat whipping her boots. She now had a canister of vitriol of her own. She'd spoil their looks, even if for a moment, as they had Gloria's. She'd resolved to bow her head to this barnyard no longer, make them feel sorry for the day they were born. "Dance, dance, dance," she muttered under her breath in imitation of Fergus, as if that controlled her sense of havoc.

"We're plumb crazy!" Gloria drawled as she dragged her half gammy leg, laughing at the thought of ever forming this lunatic pact.

"Too late now," Dominic replied.

Billy was in his fatigues, military boots, and wore a gray vest. Even from a distance his eyes seemed to bulge under his thickened brows. Then Viper beside him, similarly dressed, upright as a soldier standing with his strangled rage. They seemed to tower above everyone else on the street.

"No more than scarecrows to scare a bird," Dominic said loudly, "All we need is them at a standstill."

Teresa's mind then went back to that day in the canyon. At least down the Reserve was a tumulus of flowers flaring bright, nettles alongside blossoms. Birds tumbled on the wing, but all Teresa could see here was deadly nightshade.

Their turn now. She and Gloria would take to Guy like mastiffs to a bear.

Up ahead they first spotted Gloria limping in front. Teresa suddenly slowed, turning to Dominic.

"You'll lose your prefect's badge if you fight on the street. You don't have to do this, you know that."

Dominic wasn't listening.

Teresa smirked as they continued. "You got Fergus' boxes of matches to cushion the blows?"

He didn't hear, staring ahead with wild boxer's eyes as one billed as a prizefighter. He looked to Gloria instead, slight and helpless, a fragile doll someone failed to dress properly, thinking of her birdlike blinking face, noticeably pock marked.

To Dominic, Billy and Viper reminded somehow of two giant pairs of Dutch clogs. His friend Karl had clogs. Soldiers' boots looked similarly heavy. Noisy. Wooden. No left. No right. He hoped they too hadn't.

"Do this properly, Teresa. If you fall, get up quickly otherwise they'll kick you on the ground. Whoever pushes must expose a flank. Wade in from the side, aim at their kidneys and livers. You can win this. Just make sure you pepper their eyes first." Dominic said loudly.

Teresa caught up, smiled faintly across at Gloria, then looked up to Billy and Viper. They seemed huge, twin peaks, giant volcanoes, but she now doubted, from what they'd done to Gloria, if they were really fearless at all. Her thoughts drifted back to Che again—frail, weak in the chest yet fearless, of indomitable will. She then thought of David, not the classical statue of Michelangelo's but the Biblical runt boy pictured pitted against the giant Goliath. They too now had a slingshot of their own.

"Don't miss, Teresa." Dominic ordered from behind

Gloria rushed towards Guy and his friends, ignoring those behind. Teresa went in stride for stride then stepped in front, put her hand over her mouth and nose fanning pepper mix across their faces. She waited those few moments for it to settle then both tore off their shades letting them fall to ground, grabbing Guy by his hair.

The pedestrians immediately stood back, turned to watch the fray, just as surprised as Guy was. The three boys yelped, covering up, foolishly rubbing their eyes, lowering their heads, blinking with tears. The girls wanted Guy only. They belted him with one fist repeatedly while making a tug of war of his hair with their other. It looked a typical cat fight, two females ragging a tom.

When Viper moved forward Dominic sprung out to the side of him. As Viper attempted to shove Gloria aside Dominic loaded up a bricklike fist, crashing it hard into Viper's kidneys. Viper staggered sideways. As his legs began to scissor for grip Dominic delivered his trademark right cross to his jaw. There was a loud cracking sound. Viper fell to the sidewalk. Dominic wasn't going to let him get up. He lined him up, punched him square in the jaw as he tried straightening on all fours, momentarily severing nerves to his brain. Viper flopped unconscious beside him.

Dominic winced with pain, knuckles tingling. He spun round for Billy. Billy stirred, noticeably dribbling from the mouth. In that single moment everything seemed to stop for Dominic, like the end of the world. He realized he'd broken his hand. He briefly caught sight of Teresa over Guy, shoulder blades rising like heavy wings beating down on him. He caught flashes of Gloria's hair billowing in the air as she kicked repeatedly at Guy's legs.

A hand suddenly pushed Dominic's shoulder. It sent pain all the way down to his fist. Dominic quailed as though having caught a cannonball in a mitt.

Fergus.

He rushed passed him, hit Billy moving forward. Billy shuddered on the spot, trying to shake Fergus' punches like a long lashed bull flicking flies away from his eyes. Fergus kept throwing. Stinging punches. Fast as a jack hammer, peppering his face, intended to keep Billy upright. Billy failed to keep his hands up yet still kept moving forward, trying to bunt Fergus out of the way. Finally he reeled then stumbled. Fergus locked his legs into the sidewalk, round housing him. It was a fierce punch, belting Billy like a police baton across the face. Billy fell. Out cold.

Spiro stood watch as Fergus went back between the two girls, grabbing Guy up to his feet by his T. The other boys fled. Gloria kept yelling abuse, kicking Guy for all it was worth. Fergus hauled him aside. Teresa pulled her back then stood adjusting her school skirt, tugging at the waistline of her shorts.

Fergus yelled in Rowland's face. Teresa looked to Dominic then back to Fergus. She'd never seen him angry. She feared he was about to kill him.

"Can't hit me. I'm a minor," the boy simpered from his bloodied mouth at the end of Fergus' hand. He spat a tooth from his mouth. Fergus twisted the T at his neck like the screw of a tourniquet. It looked as though Teresa or Gloria had broken his nose.

Fergus purposely spoke loud enough for all onlookers to hear.

"You, or your friends, ever touch a hair of any of these three again, this is what I'll do, Rowland. I know who you are. I know your father. I'll come round to your place. I won't touch a feather on your little chicken-shit head because you're a minor. I'll belt your father for everything you and your brother are. You hear me!"

Fergus then pushed the boy off on his way. Guy stumbled, clutching his sides.

There was gloomy silence on the street. Most locals had heard of the rape down the Reserve, indifferent to it as just par for Hope street's course. They cared as much as somebody just having ran a red light. Someone just had their front end banged in.

*   *   *

The same silence could be said of the car as Fergus drove Dominic to the doctor's surgery. Teresa and Gloria grinned with pride at one another in the backseat. Dominic could now forget about the upcoming fights with the Central Americans. He didn't seem fazed by that.

Fergus moved aside at the surgery to ring the local Police. They said that they'd just heard about the incident, didn't want to know, that the soldiers got exactly what they had coming. Fergus snapped his phone shut.

They all went home to Caitlin's.

Viper and Billy both had their overseas tours delayed. Both had their jaws wired. Still nothing was said, done about it, shoveled aside once again

"Good riddance," Dominic said when he heard. "Closed for demolition."

When word finally got out, Dominic lost his Prefect's badge for fighting in the street, for—in the words of the Headmaster—'hurting our soldiers who bravely give their lives for this country, and you dare go injure them.'

Dominic made Fergus promise that Father Kevin wasn't to know the truth.

"I'll bat for myself, Fergus. I'm out of here soon. Sooner the better. And the other thing, Fergus," Dominic said as the car pulled up at the house, "you never round house an opponent, it seldom works, better just to punch straight from the shoulder."

Fergus and Teresa laughed.

Was it Worth it?

Gloria stayed over that night. "Wow," she said, "was that fun or what?" She could not contain her excitement of revenge. It was a thrill, certainly better than dry bumping one another up a rock climbing wall. Teresa said little but gave Gloria warmer clothes to wear as the evening went on, an invitation to come party here any Saturday night she choose. She said they could all sing and eat, roller skate, even climb her trees. Gloria said she wasn't that keen, was not really the outdoorsy type, yet that she would call her.

The adults threw them a party that night.

"Viva Guevara," they yelled, toasting their bravery, passing Teresa's beret round, wearing it in turn, part as jest, part downplaying the incident. No one asked how Fergus knew, why he'd come home early that afternoon. It was obvious that Spiro rang him. Teresa always suspected Fergus had an inkling she'd witnessed the rape. It all had to do with the beret.

Gloria, Teresa and Sharn took turns in belting Dominic's good arm that evening, writing 'Stoo-pid' in black felt on his plaster cast, signing 'Sore Winner,' 'Captain Hook,' 'Cool Hand.' Sharn got the last word in, as usual. 'Dickhead! Should've listened to Fergus.'

Yet Sharn was kind to Gloria, bringing her plates of food, giving her shampoos, cosmetics, telling her to get off the street, not to be such a 'dickhead.' Like her brother.

Spiro and his wife came. He still brought ice cream and confectionary for Teresa to share with Dominic forgetting they'd now grown up. He still said to Teresa that she was to share them with 'the boy.'

It was a happy night. There was music. Greek dancing. Declan played country guitar.

* * *

Teresa and Sharn took Gloria up to her room. Gloria had asked to see it. She said she could never remember having had a bedroom of her own, having spent most of her life in trailers. She eyed the walls with a kind of awe, cringed at the sight of the crucifix over the bed, then ran her hand over the bedcover while ogling at the antique desk and chair.

"Ma said we can throw mattresses from the shed in Dominic's tent. We'll grab some blankets downstairs, sleep outside tonight."

"Wow!" Gloria ignored her, pulling out the carved chair, sitting uninvited at the writing desk. For the first time, Teresa remembered Gloria's eyes looked bigger. They were pretty eyes. They came alive at the sight of the desk.

"This is so cool. I ain't dumb, I can write. Can I use that ink pen? I've never used one before."

Teresa unscrewed the gold cap then handed her some writing paper.

Gloria sprawled over the pull out wooden leaf. "You think I'm stupid, don't you!"

Teresa looked to Sharn, who shook her head.

There was silence as Gloria wrote slowly in a shaky cursive, her beaklike nose almost to the paper.

"I know words. I read them vampire books." Gloria repeated then pulled back proudly showing off what she'd written.

'The quick brown soldiers jumped over the lazy whore.' All letters were conjoined. Teresa read them then looked to Sharn again. Gloria continued with a smile. "Only joking you. I can do computer. I've had fine things. Ate caviar once. Fine things are no big deal. Tastes like everything else. Crap." She reflected more seriously. "I help girls fill out forms. Do crosswords with them. Gets boring on the street sometimes. It cools the sick out. But Hope's o.k. No crime bosses, leg breakers, stuff like that. Sometimes guys pay me on pay-day. I can wait. It's kinda like family up there. Common ground. Ain't no devil's playground. Hope's been o.k. to me. I don't have expectations. Only lead to disappointments. See, I know big words. We have fun. It kills me some days. Even though those three guys hurt me real good."

"Real bad," Sharn corrected.

"Really badly," Teresa corrected again, giving Gloria a horrified look.

Sharn was curious to know more. "What you do with money from sex?"

"Smoke. Drink. Rent for caravan. Give most of it away."

"To who?" Sharn wondered loudly.

"Winos. Bag ladies. It costs to live in a trailer park. Everyone's greedy these days. I give money to the girls. For their babies. They suffer too, you know."

"What! Even old Black Charlie? You give him money! What's he give you?"

Black Charlie was the prize serial pest on the street.

"Charlie's mad, that's all. Can't panhandle no more. Drops his trousers in the ally sometimes. Moons at us. Got bitten on the butt by a rat the other day. I gave him some bucks, made him go to the doctor, said 'go moon at him for a jab in that ugly black ass of yours.'" Gloria laughed. "Don't like being stingy. I ain't no Scrooge. He came back later with a bottle of whiskey. We laughed at that."

"Do you ever get bored?" Teresa asked tentatively.

"Sometimes. Everyone gets bored, don't they! Mostly Sundays. Nothing to do Sundays. Hate Sundays. Nothing happens. We know where some of them church people live. Jillie and me steal flowers from their garden when they at church. Not many. Just some so they don't notice. We love flowers. Put them in the trailer. Only thing we steal. Pick flowers. They come home, not notice, go out, cut the lawn. Kids wash the car. They think lawns are pretty. Cars are pretty. I think flowers are pretty. By Monday me and Jillie go stir crazy. Jillie shares a van with me. She's a trick-bag, too. I don't do sick like Jillie does. She likes bottom feeders. Not me. I tell her she's being too kind. But we both want more than just a sofa and T.V. That's not life."

"What you do Mondays, then?" Sharn's curiosity was burning.

"Go out to the prison. Pick up guys. Early releases Monday."

"Are they bad boys?" Teresa asked.

"No. Mostly just guys who had arguments with their bitches. Bitches like winning. They ring the Police, say their guys threatened them Friday nights. Cops lock them up for the weekends. Have to. For bitches' safety. Just in case. You know how it goes. Everyone just plays games nowadays. Some girls are out there Mondays crying their eyes out knowing they overstepped mark. Boo-hoo, I'm sorry. Stupid cows. Everyone likes visitors, too."

"What say the girls are right?" Teresa asked coldly.

"Some are. Then those guys take it out on us."

"What? Smack you round?" Sharn was horrified.

"Yip. We deserve it. Sometimes we do. We get on their nerves talking shit, spending their money. Best way to stop boys hitting you is getting them stoned first. But I still like boys. When you're hot you're hot. Know what I'm saying?" Gloria turned to Teresa. "You like boys, Teresa? Plenty to choose from up on Hope."

"She doesn't," Sharn answered quickly for her. "She likes church Sundays."

"Does she?" Gloria sounded amazed. "Hate church myself. All them flash cars on Sundays. All talking together outside. All them fine suits. Fancy ladies. Kids so clean looking like Heidi going home to cups of hot chocolate. Hate hot chocolate. I think sin's just a big trick they play on the poor. The poor don't have tickets on themselves like rich folk have. We get preachers come talk to us on the street. Jillie talks to them. Jillie believes in Jesus. I don't. She likes the idea of a good and gentle Shepherd. Scares me. I don't want moral trouble."

"Do the preachers help you?" Teresa asked.

"Nope. Bunch of molesters, if you ask me. One or two put the hard word on Jillie. They're the purest of scum. That's my opinion. I tell Jillie it don't seem right to me."

"Do I know Jillie?" Sharn asked.

"Yeah, you do. Got pink Champagne hair. No brains under it."

Sharn raised her eyebrows to Teresa. "Is she the one who did her brains in off a skateboard when she was a kid?"

"Sure did. I look after her. Her care giver. Government wanted to pay me to do it. I said didn't want them to. Don't get paid. Don't want government anything."

"How can you care for her on the street?" Sharn asked.

"She has horror days at home. May as well be out spending them with me. Sometimes on Thursday Jillie and me go watch the magistrate's court. We stand at top of the stairs, look through the glass panel at those waiting to be called up. Makes us feel real good. They all look like shit, smell like shit, think like shit, not like those fat cat church people on Sunday with all their money. These guys have nothing. Jillie reckons court day is Judgment Day when the poor enter the kingdom. The kingdom's the slammer. It's them fat cats who like to hog Jesus to themselves behind money, crim-safe screens. Flash things." Gloria turned to face Teresa. "Like your uncle's car."

"He still helped us today." Teresa defended.

"I know. I'm grateful. And to you. They got what they had coming. But why give money to them churches? Church's rich enough already. Everyone rich gives to churches. That's because everyone's just jerking everyone else off, one way or other. Me? Rather give to the poor. Even sex. For nothing. Make someone poor happy. Get rid of frustration." Gloria reflected. "If there's a God then He sure put me last in the queue."

"Queue for what?" Teresa asked.

"Dunno. Things. Good hair days." Gloria comically forked her hair high in her hands. "You know about hair, Sharn. But I'm also front of the queue for getting bashed, ain't I?"

"Like from Billie and Viper?" Sharn scorned.

"No. They're just a couple of mean mothers. I don't care if I get hit by them if it stops them bashing some other kid against a wall. They wanted sex that day for nothing. Said soldiers deserve it without paying. I said no. Then they say 'What about a discount for veterans, then?' I say 'You ain't no veterans. You bin nowhere. You both done jack shit 'cept making people unhappy.' Only then did they get real nasty. Guys don't like being told the truth. But soldiers lose their heads sometimes, too. Heat of moment stuff. Fizz up like a soda pop. Me and my big mouth. But I ain't sly. I tell the truth. Lying is a kinda weakness. Always gets me in trouble. When Billie hit me that day I called him 'Coward-y, Coward-y, Custard.' Then, boy oh boy, he didn't like that. Belted the shit outta me."

"They could've killed you down there!" Sharn raised her voice.

"Still here, ain't I! It's spilt milk. No point crying over it."

"Thanks to Teresa."

Gloria suddenly put her face in her hands at memory of it, yielding to a kind of fear for the first time. "Yeah. Guess I wanna die peaceful like everyone else in the end. Not down there. I'm grateful. And to your brother, Teresa. He sure got a couple of good mitts on him. Hope it heals ok. I have."

Teresa's curiosity did not abate. "Why wouldn't you press charges? Were you frightened of them?"

"Nah. Ain't scared of nothing. Just felt sorry for Billie, that's all. Billie's like Black Charlie. Can't help themselves. Both should be in a loony bin, if you ask me. Just can't help being mean. Didn't want to sell Billie out. Billie's a big, hairy throwback. I ain't no Squealer. Ain't no Scrooge. Ain't no Stooge." Gloria counted the statements out on her fingers. "I ain't no one's bitch, either. Rather be hit than be a bitch. I got a conscience. Jillie and me try to do one good deed a day. If I hated all them who done me wrong up on Hope I'd have no fun. I like it up there."

"So you wouldn't give it up for anything?" Sharn wanted to know.

"Why would I? Then I'd miss out on what's happening, wouldn't I?"

*   *   *

Teresa was the first to wake in the tent next morning. They'd slept in their clothes on the mattresses up in a figure T, heads transecting at the top. They talked and talked until sleep overtook them. Teresa had woken to the smell of pancakes in the yard. She stuck her bleary eyes out the flap, saw Fergus cooking on the griddle, Caitlin laying the outside table with pineapple, mango, maple syrup, eggs, rashers of bacon. Fergus beat a dish with a metal spatula calling them out for breakfast.

Teresa and Sharn giggled as Gloria gorged her food down like a dog, wolfing it, licking and licking, then almost barking with delight. It looked comical to watch, especially to Teresa who always tried to imitate Fergus' manners. Yet, to Teresa, there was little about Gloria which seemed pitiable. She wasn't a creature to whimper. Gloria slurped her coffee only to light a cigarette, but then felt time had come for her to move off. It seemed good manners not to outstay one's welcome.

"Thanks, Missus," Gloria said to Caitlin after entering the house, still not quite sure who exactly was who. "Never eaten so much. It was nice to stay here. Thank the man who helped us. Say thanks again to Teresa for me." Gloria smiled then joked. "Convent girls ain't so bad, after all."

"Come back and see Teresa any time. Eat with us again. Do you want a ride anywhere?"

"I'll walk. Need to. Stomach's so full." Gloria turned to Teresa. "Thanks for everything."

She exited without turning, muttering 'will be on my way,' moving off with her pigeon toe limp yet not showing any sign of agony, and with a bag of Teresa's old clothes. She'd thanked her for them.

"Still plenty of fight left in that young dog," Sharn said to Teresa, then shook her head in amazement.

"Nobody's bitch," Teresa said.

They grinned grimly at one another. Gloria did not seem to deserve ridicule of laughter.

"Notice something, Sharn?"

"Notice what?"

"Gloria was wearing my St. Christopher."

"No. Didn't see it. Well, hope that can keep her mojo working."

They both crossed their fingers, finished their breakfast in silence.

More Bad Marks

That year came and went, slipping by slowly for Teresa. She'd gained some respect up on Hope. Pedestrians looked differently at her now as she walked passed them, but she was, to them, still that girl who walked with her head bowed. The incident did little to alleviate her pain. She still felt like a shadow dweller there. The street spooked her as much as the Reserve did. As above, so below. Why should she look up at them now, smile while sweating it out in her soul? Years of staring faces would not go away, as though they were all counting the freckles on her arms. She had no freckles on her arms. Boys still panted as she passed, barked at her, expecting her to wiggle her butt. She'd wiggle for no one. Senior boys at school, almost in competition, offered her rides home. She'd glower at them, hide behind the rules that they were not supposed to go down Hope, if ever answering at all. She'd rather dwell up her trees, protected by garrisons of birds, for they'd sing to her, sit on her hand or shoulders, placidly pick at her earrings. That world did not overwhelm her. Up the tree was like down the rabbit hole for Alice.

She'd sometimes wave across to Gloria, not expecting much to change. All the same. Day in, day out. Sometimes Teresa wondered if it had been worth it. Everyone has their rules. Gloria's rules were not that bad. "She's a trollop," Sharn assured her. After putting up with Sister Care and Sister Compassion all day at school it crossed Teresa's mind maybe Gloria was an Angel of Deliverance on the street. After all, Angels, by definition, were not creatures who were severe.

Dominic got back his Prefect's badge after three months. It meant little to him now, as did boxing. The Central Americans won 5-0. They were far too experienced, much more hungry for success. His hand mended. He took to helping his father out in the gym but his heart and mind were on leaving town.

Teresa remained, slogging it out in the classroom. Months dragged by with endless schooldays. She did not have the patience for science and laboratory work, the exactitude required for mathematics with its proofs and certitudes, preferring those of her faith in Christian Instruction class. There she'd sit front of class, as she did elsewhere, sometimes answering Father Kevin's questions, especially if the answers could be short. Teresa learned how to waste time, dreaming of days when school ended.

At home she hovered over Fergus' library of books downstairs like a bee buzzing a bloom. If only to settle. If only to fly away.

*   *   *

Teresa didn't like boys. She'd said it to her mother so often. 'God awful boys,' she'd call them, nearest she ever got to blasphemy. What made it worse was everybody now said how pretty she'd become. Pretty has expectations. Not so to Sharn. Sharn told her the God awful truth, that she 'looked like shit.' 'Get off your lazy butt, Tessie girl, go out, have some fun. Stop being so highfalutin'. You'll get afraid of ever being happy. Look on Teresa Mahone and despair.'

Teresa would scowl at her. Boys thought of her as a foxy looking chick, said how her body looked buffed, chiseled, her abs great, as if they could see them. Teresa could never quite understand why. She knew the trees probably made her that way, years of continual climbing making her nimble and strong.

All she wanted was to drop out, be by herself. Invisible. Being by oneself was better than moving in a tight pack, speaking street language few could understand, selling themselves short. Yet she too had C-grade reports. She wondered if she had wasted her life sitting up front of class, maybe there'd have been no difference sitting at the back with the wasters, tilting her chair up against the wall. Front or back, school bored her to tears.

She didn't think about sex. The idea of it filled her with loathing. All those creeps on Hope standing round like bookmakers figuring odds as she passed. A kind of strip poker game, girls legs eleven. They'd gawk as if saying 'Attention: Code Blue and White coming up.' All they wanted was sex. She'd seen sex. Once. Where was the love? The 'honorable estate?' 'Highfalutin' stuff they taught her at school.

'Get used to it, Tessie girl,' Sharn would say, 'times change. People have given up on Christian instruction. They're out acquiring carnal knowledge. Don't be such a freaking princess, Tess, get out there, even if it means slapping people round.'

"Princesses don't slap people round."

"That's what I mean. Time they should," Sharn replied.

Teresa wouldn't waver. Nor go out. She knew Sharn was probably right. It worried her that she had to get real.

One night at dinner.

"Uncle. What should I read?"

"Read what you like."

"Give me something. Short stories. Nothing too long."

"Sure. After dinner we'll have a look at the shelves downstairs."

"I don't want The Teddy Bear's Picnic, like we get at school."

"We'll find something."

"Something gay. Written by women. It's got to be real." Teresa paused to eat before resuming. "Sharn and I watched 'Brokeback Mountain' the other night. That was gay. It was good. So-o-o real!"

There was a kind of sadness in her voice, a struggle as what to do, how to behave. She knew they wouldn't move mountains but perhaps books would help. Fergus immediately left the table, went downstairs. He returned moments later.

"Here. Read them. Just don't leave them up the tree."

Teresa picked up 'Brokeback Mountain And Other Stories,' and 'Heart Songs,' both by E. Annie Proulx.

"Are they good?" She asked.

"The best. Good as it gets."

"Says who?"

"Not just me. Critics. Readers. Read the one of the movie. See for yourself."

"I want something else, Uncle. Give it to me! Bet you won't."

Teresa would sometimes play grumpy demanding games at dinner.

"Try me," Fergus continued nonchalantly.

"You won't give them to me because I know you can't."

"Try me."

"I want a book on female painters of the time when, say, Leonardo was painting. A feminist. There weren't any, were there? Why was that? Go on, tell me!" Teresa grinned at him in a mock paddy, shuffling her feet back and forth on the floor in annoyance.

Fergus placed his knife and fork, leaned across, gently put his arm round her shoulder. He brought his hand round, clasped it over her mouth.

"Because they were muted by men, weren't they!"

Fergus let go. He resumed. "There was one I can think of. A feminist, I guess. She was as good as the men were. I'll get her for you."

*   *   *

Caitlin and Teresa were driving to the Mall. This time it was a Thursday night.

"Ma?"

"Yes."

"I read 'Brokeback Mountain.' It was good. I read some other stories, too."

"I'm glad."

"Is it o.k. for Sharn to read it?"

"I guess so. Why?"

"Because Uncle loaned it to me. I'm responsible for it."

"Uncle won't mind."

"I said she has to finish it by Friday so I can return it before he gets home."

"That's the proper thing to do. I'm sure she will. You always return his books in mint condition."

"Ma?"

"Yes."

"Gloria told us she's 'no one's bitch.' You're not Pa's bitch, Colleen isn't Declan's, are you?"

"No, dear. Whatever made you ask? I love your father. Colleen loves Declan. That's the way it is, always was. Who wants to fight all the time!"

"I know."

"Why ask, then?"

"Just wanted you to say it."

"Ma?"

"Yes."

"Who should I listen to? Uncle or Father Kevin?"

"Why don't you ask your uncle that?"

"I did."

"What did he say? I know he wouldn't have teased on a question like that."

"He didn't."

"Well?"

"He said Father Kevin is my pastor. That I must listen to him."

"That was it?"

"I said 'And what about you, Uncle?'"

"He said 'All I ask is you think about things.'"

"Doesn't that seem fair?"

"Yes. But . . . and I know it's my own fault . . . I wish now I hadn't asked him for that feminist artist."

"Why?"

"Uncle gave me a book. There were all her paintings there. I looked her up on Google afterwards. Horrible things happened to her. She might have been as good as the boys but she sure suffered more than they did because of it. Women had no say back then. They were always somebody's bitch. I'm not going to be. Life's so unfair."

"Time's change, Tess. And for the better."

"I guess so. I studied her for my Art Assignment. Will you read it when we get home?"

"Of course, dear. What's her name?"

"Wait until we're home. I can't pronounce it properly. Don't you say anything to Uncle, will you?"

"I won't. Promise."

"I was right. There were no women painters recorded in history. When this one came along the men hated her for her talent. Only men painted. They went to bars and inns. She had to paint in a convent. She couldn't do anything openly."

Caitlin said nothing.

"Ma?"

"Yes"

"I'm always going to live alone."

"You'll get married one day, dear. You're very pretty. Some nice young man will come along."

"No, it's just not going to happen."

"It's not good to live alone, Tess. Unless you're Father Kevin."

"You mean to tell me Uncle lives with someone?"

Caitlin was silent.

"I'll go and ask him, then."

"Don't. Mind your own business."

*   *   *

Artemisia Gentileschi, Baroque artist, purported to have been friends with Galileo and Michelangelo's nephew. Teresa's assignment was all too brief. There were some black and white photocopies of the artist's subjects, all women—Judith, Susanna, Bathsheba, Magdalene—an emphasis on 'Judith slaying Hologernes,' her most famous work, circa 1614-1620. All her subjects were of or about women.

Caitlin read Teresa's account of how Judith got to the Assyrian General Hologernes in disguise, made him drunk, then hacked off his head with a sword. She and her maidservant had brought a basket for the head, a mop for the blood, then they both ran away, vindicated. That was it.

Teresa had read the Biblical Book of Judith, then read elsewhere the opinion that it was sometimes referred to as the Book of Revenge. She told her mother this.

"She didn't like men. Neither do I."

"Why didn't she?"

"Because her patron set her up, had her art tutor rape her. His name was Tazzi."

"Was he charged for it?"

"Yes. The last pages of the trial have been lost. It took over seven months. His defense argued she deserved it, that her family were prostitutes, kept brothels. Lies. All tales. None of it was true. They just said anything to win and discredit her."

"At least they didn't win, did they," Caitlin said softly.

"But they tortured her in the process, Ma, she had her thumbs pulled back almost ruining her hands forever for her art."

"Why?"

"To prove her side of story. The logic was, if she could tell the same story under duress, then it must be true."

"Why didn't you say this in the assignment?"

"Why should I? Enough sick creeps on my way home without writing about them. I tried once. It never really got me anywhere, did it!."

"But it did. You don't know, but you were probably the only one who ever stood up for Gloria."

"She didn't want me to stand up for her."

"But you did. And she will always remember you did."

Battle of the Sexes

Her assignment mark was barely average, once again. Teresa persisted instead in turning the glossy pages of Fergus' art books downstairs, examining voluptuous nudes of traditional art and sculpture. She would stare at their sexual embraces. They weren't exactly rude. They didn't show that much. Teresa knew that sex regularly took place in foreign films on late night television. She had her own television in her room which she'd turn on late, sound down, read subtitles of films, especially when she couldn't sleep. Her mouth would be agape—boys/girls, boys/boys, girls/girls; once she saw three on one. It changed 'mid delivery.' She didn't think that was the right term. It sounded more like something happening at the hospital.

'But they've only just met!' She'd think, incredulous. 'No love there.' 'Why'd he leave her?' 'Why not take her with him?' It seemed that everyone just puffed then parted.

Sharn was a bit like that.

Sharn once told her. "Sex's over in no time." She liked talking about sex. Boys would call on her on their motorbikes or in their muscle cars, flying up the vacant street with a keen sense of anticipation. Teresa saw them from the tree, knew they'd not come for a hair-cut. She had to be having it off. 'Having it off' was Sharn's expression. Sharn said that she'd sometimes lay there, look to the ceiling hoping that one day she'd meet someone who'd 'take her breath away.' 'Yeah, right,' Teresa would answer, 'take your breath away and you die.' Sharn often talked about 'soul mates,' how she wanted someone 'in tune with her

224

own thoughts,' like their parents. That didn't seem very easy anymore. Teresa thought that Sharn was asking far too much.

Sharn gave up after a while, writing Teresa off as too slow on the uptake, a 'very late bloomer.'

Teresa told her that she'd once seen snakes having it off down the Reserve. They'd looked like they were just laying about in the sun. The act took place over half the day. Teresa couldn't quite see how they did it.

"They rub chins. Get a scent." Sharn said. "Males cluster round a female forming a heaving ball, trying to work themselves into the right position."

"Yeah, right," Teresa said, "that sounds like the Reserve."

She discovered, quite by chance, from Fergus' art books, that Leonardo didn't do it either, nor did Michelangelo. Or so she thought. Michelangelo just lay on his back painting ceilings instead of just looking at them, like Sharn did. Father Kevin didn't do it. Teresa had no idea whether Fergus did it or not. She was not game enough to ask.

Yet ask him she did.

*   *   *

"I don't like boys, Uncle. Life's no more than a prank to most of them. They scare me half to death. Sticking their noses into your business. Do you like women?"

"NO!" His answer was so quick and definitive. He spat the word out with a vehemence and disgust. He was downstairs at his work desk this Saturday morning. Teresa had been hovering about, offering him coffee, perusing his bookshelves. He could tell that she was uncomfortable, just about to explode. He got in first.

"Why not?"

Fergus didn't answer. He placed his pen, got up, moved over to put a CD on his stereo. He held up the remote, pointed to the screen, put the song on hold.

"Women are like March," he muttered again, dismissively.

"March?"

"Yes. Month of March."

"Who says?"

"Lots of Italian singers do."

"Why's that?"

"Because it's wet, then it's cold, then it's warm again, always unsettled. March is the one month that can't ever be trusted. Too moody."

"I'm not moody."

"Course you are."

"Are you talking sex here?"

"Course not. You know I don't talk about sex, just about women in general."

Fergus paused then raised the remote control. "I don't like women because of this song."

Fergus handed her the album cover, pointed to song five. Teresa read the sleeve. Verdi's Rigoletto. Songs sung mostly by Mario Lanza.

"Forget about March for the moment. Get a load of this. This really gives women a bad wrap."

"O dear. Another damned opera. Thought you only liked 'Carmen'?"

"Can't stand the woman," Fergus said unfalteringly, "just somebody's bitch."

Teresa now knew that Fergus must have been talking to her mother.

"Bomp-bomp-bomp, bomp-pee-day," he repeated, fingering his desktop to the beat. At least she had his attention. The music played.

"You know it, 'La Donna E Mobile' Lots of people have used it in movies and TV. What you think the title means?" He turned the sound lower to background music.

She feared a trick here. So wary of him, she decided get in first.

"'La Donna' means a girl. 'La-Donna-E-Mo-bill-lay' means . . . it means that . . . that every girl has . . . a mobile phone?" She grinned inanely at the album cover.

"Good one, my dear. But you're wrong. Try again."

"I don't know. Every girl is . . . mobile? . . . moves about? . . . gets around?"

"That's more like it. Literally it means 'Woman is flighty.' All women. No exceptions. Women are dreadful creatures, Tess. We all have to live with that." Fergus went back to his paperwork. "Can't paint, they can't . . ."

"I'm not flighty!" Teresa was suddenly enraged.

"'Course you are!"

"And Ma?"

"Even worse. Always sticking her nose in things where it doesn't belong."

Teresa knew that was not true. Truer of Fergus.

"How 'bout Colleen, then?"

"Worse than your mother is. Can't keep her big mouth shut."

Colleen could keep her mouth shut. Especially when it came to correcting Sharn. She didn't have a big mouth. Sharn had the big mouth.

"Sharn?"

"That's a no-brainer. Nutcase. Disturbed. Leaves a trail of disaster wherever she goes."

"Speak for yourself."

"She'd be better off living up the trees with the squirrels."

"We don't have squirrels here. And you like Sharn. Deep down you do."

"Only to keep the peace round here."

"And the nuns at school?" Teresa thought that no way would Fergus call them flighty.

"Flighty and ignorant. Mother Teresa came from Albania. They wouldn't even know the capital of Albania."

"And you do? What is it then?"

"Can't remember. But they should know it. Women just don't know these things. Too flighty. Too busy buying clothes at Op shops Saturday morning, things like that."

"How do you know that?"

"Because the song says so. Therefore, it must be true."

He pressed the volume up on the remote.

"Ha, ha. A killer tune, Uncle. What's it all say?"

"It says that women are oh so sweet and pretty but all of them change their minds. They lie, they deceive, they act as light as feathers in the wind—woe is the man who should ever trust one."

Fergus then slapped his hand on the desk to punctuate his point.

"And boys are not?"

"No. Boys are just fine." Fergus leaned over, picked up his coffee that Teresa had just made him, raised it to his nose for the bouquet, poked his tongue out at her sideways before sipping.

"Just a minute, Buster. Opera goers wouldn't fall for that crap. Half of them would have to be women. They'd kick Verdi's ass. Woman haters. It's . . . moss-og-genly."

"Misogyny."

"That's what I said."

"Where did you pick up that word?"

"I read stuff."

"You've asked the right question. You're right. Opera goers wouldn't stand for it. The man who sings the aria is very flighty himself. Therefore, it's intended humorously. It's supposed to be ironic."

"What's ironic mean?"

"When something is said—sung, in this case—but the audience knows the opposite is true; that the singer's not a reliable critic."

"Yeah. That figures coming from you. All said with a straight face but the answers real crooked."

Fergus continued. "It all hinges on the end when he sings the words 'who on that bosom does not drink?" He raised his coffee cup to that.

"There you go. Typical male. Breasts, breasts, breasts. How stupid. Like ass-kissing. I still don't like boys, Uncle."

"It's ok, Tess. Me neither, when it comes to women. Best a man can hope for in a woman is one who won't smash his CDs when he's late for dinner." He pointed to a pile of CDs. "I've tried to understand them. The trail always goes cold after a time."

"But you like the song."

"The song's great."

"You like Marie, the dancer."

"Not really. She's French. They're disgusting people. They eat snails. Hermaphrodites, for heaven's sake!"

"Only half French. She's Spanish, too."

"That half's all right. They eats bulls and pigs."

"You like my Ma."

"Only because I have to. She's my sister. Only family I've got left."

"And Colleen."

"Have to. Your mother's best friend."

"Good one, Uncle. True to form. No help to me at all. Do you like me?"

"I don't have much time for young people. You should know that by now. I only like Dominic, that's because he's a boy. Do you like Dominic?"

"Yes, but . . ."

"There you go. You do like boys, don't you!"

*   *   *

One day Teresa read in one of Fergus' books that Leonardo said the human race would become extinct if every member of it could see themselves having sex. There was something ludicrous about the sight of lovemaking. Teresa couldn't remember the exact word he'd used. All that thrusting, grinding like animals out in open fields. Nothing beautiful about that. It looked absurd. She pondered how Gloria could have enjoyed those brutes. How could she let them belt, punch, control her the way they did? 'What you care!' Gloria had said to her. Yet Teresa did care. That act hardly took place on some French Impressionist's carpet of picnic grass. The thought of it made Teresa shiver. Tampered with. Seized upon. Drugged, lamed so as to have no chance to win. Handfuls of silt scraping her uterus. Like a hobbled horse. Horses are beautiful creatures. Not like those bull-dogs up on Hope, squinting, twitching, barely contained. And it was a sin. It had to be. An act which took place between enemies. She pondered these thoughts for hours.

She knew that her uncle had been kidding her. Sometimes up town Fergus would hold Caitlin's hand. It was as if he did it out of fear. He did it to Teresa, too. As if not wanting to let go, as he had to his little sister. Fergus didn't like being beaten. She often got the impression that he was out on a mission.

Yet perhaps he preferred those different movements from side to side. Dance. With Maria. He obviously didn't care how small her breasts were. Her dancing was neither a grind nor a thrust. She was an 'artiste.' Like Leonardo. All his women had clothes on. Or so she thought.

So who was this Elena woman that Fergus had on the side? Maybe Fergus used her for sex. Verdi should have written 'Man loves breasts,' instead. Some bigger girls at school refused to diet, for that's where the weight would drop first. Maybe, as Sharn suggested, Elena simply had a better set. And, as for that Carmen woman from the opera, she would have had to have a big chest in order to sing like that. It just didn't seem right, or fair.

Exits Teresa

"Ma, please, let me leave school. I'm so sick of it. I just can't take it any longer." She was almost at her wit's end.

"Yes. You can leave. But not without some horse trading first."

The answer came as quite a surprise. It was Amen to that. Her dreaming was now over. She felt like applauding. Teresa paused then thought, if in for a lamb, why not a sheep.

"Ma, I've grown up. I'm no skittish filly, even if Uncle says so. What's to be traded, anyway?"

Caitlin grinned. "He told me about that one."

"Be serious with me. Don't kid me along like he does. He sometimes treats me like a little princess. I don't want to be a little princess. I want to abdicate the throne. And I think he wants me to. I'm stuck in a rut here."

"I know, but you're not going to be silly. You're not leaving school without first having a plan. We've already discussed it. Your father and I. If you're that unhappy, then you can leave. What do you want to do with your life?"

Words now tumbled out. She had thought hard about it. She did have a plan. "I want to go and live in the city. I have to grow up. Maybe Sharn's right. I have to get out more. Get away. Uncle can keep an eye on me. I'll share an apartment. I don't mind living with a couple of like-minded girls. I'll get a job at a rock climbing center. I see those jobs advertised in newspapers all the time. I'll take night classes, if you really want me too. I'd like that. I don't want to end up a dead head. I'll be o.k. City life can't be as bad as up on Hope. I can organize myself. Cook and clean. Pay my own way. Uncle can bring me home some weekends. It's not as though I haven't thought it through. I'll e-mail you. Often. I'll be right. It's not like I'm going to Baghdad or anything like that. Just to the city."

"All right. We'll work something out." Caitlin could not disguise her disappointment. "I want you to know that it's your own fault you've got no life here. You've sold yourself short. There's no one to blame but yourself. You've missed your chances. They might never come again unless you continue with some education. And remember, the city can be a dangerous place. You're going to have to have a plan. We're not allowing you to be all lost and bewildered."

"No more dangerous than crossing Hope Street."

"You were never asked to cross it."

"I know that. But I did, didn't I! I want to put it right. I JUST DON'T LIKE SCHOOL. It's cold soup. I hate cold soup. Why can't I go live with Uncle? He's on the road a lot. I could keep house for him. Work for him as well. And do night classes as well as that, plus do a job.."

"Not possible." Caitlin turned away.

"I don't care if he has girlfriends. Boyfriends. No friends. Why has no one ever told me where he lives? I know he owns a house in the city. Does he live with a bunch of Communists? Maria? Who's this Elena woman, anyway? Sharn heard him talking to her on the phone. Is she the new girl on the block?"

"Mind your own business. Uncle would rather you fend for yourself. He'll never be far away. I know he'll keep an eye on you. And don't go looking for answers rummaging through his things downstairs."

"I don't. I'd never do that. Who's Elena, Ma? Sounds like an East European prostitute? Does she use Maria's pole dancing studio as a cover? Do you know her?"

"Cut out the cheek! Yes, I know her. And you're barking up the wrong tree, young lady."

"Tell me, Ma. I want to know. I liked Maria. Why'd Uncle dump her?"

"No. Definitely no."

"All right," Teresa walked away muttering. "Nobody tells me jack shit around here. Don't ever expect to get the truth out of me, either. I'll just tell everybody a bunch of fibs. Like Fergus does."

Teresa, aged seventeen.

E-*mails, to and from home:*
Teresa To Caitlin
Subject: I'm ok, you ok?

Hi Ma,

I'm missing you all already. I've only been away two weeks. The city's o.k., I guess. So many men and women in dark suits, carrying umbrellas. Such seriously legal faces. I'll get used to the noise over time. There are so many nice places to see. I love the Botanical Gardens.

I like my evening classes, too. We're studying modern poetry at the moment, but it will be mostly song lyrics we have to analyze. The work isn't very hard. I'm going to do really well this year, you'll see. I won't let you down. Don't worry, I won't become a rapper or break dancer, send home pictures of me spinning on my head for loose change on the street. It's going to be head down, bottom up, work, work, work from now on.

I have my own room and we're not far from buses and train station. The girls are real cool. They're both so interesting. We get on famously. I held my breath when I asked if they'd met Uncle. They said they hadn't, only the rent agent who fixed everything up for me.

At my first evening class this guy next to me blew a paper whistle right in my face, then yelled 'Surprise!' I thought for a moment I was back at kindergarten. 'Like your sweater!' he said, staring at me like a big dork. Mr. Check-You-Out. Felt like putting my feet up on the lecture desk, asking, 'Like my shoes, too? Size 10. I'm a policewoman!' Then blow him a raspberry myself. Can just imagine the mouthful Sharn would've given him. Guys are such jerks. Why don't they grow up!

How's Ballou? Is she missing me? I know she's getting old now. Hope she doesn't die from pining. I automatically look for her on the end of the bed when I wake up in the morning. A pity I can't have her here with me. If I let her out, she'd get run over. And she'd go nuts in the apartment all day by herself.

How's Pa? Make sure you have plenty of bran in the house for when I'm home next. I'm going to make lots of muffins for him and Declan. Say hello to Colleen and Sharn.

Love, Teresa.

P.S. Tell uncle there's a great bar nearby called The Crown and Anchor. Us three girls go there most nights, eat, drink, gamble until the wee hours. Mainly with a lot of bad-ass bikers, girls in latex. I like wearing see through clothes, as see through as the vodka I drink. They have pole-dancers, too. I think I'd be real good at that. But we're cutting it out soon. We only drink vodka because it's the least calorific. It's the mixes that are sweet. Putting on far too much weight!!!

*   *   *

Caitlin to Teresa
Subject: You'd better not be!

Hi Tessie,
I'll ignore your postscript. You'd better not be, you cheeky brat!!
Are you settling in o.k.? Uncle tells me you're with an Arab and Jewish girl, and that they're both devout religious students, a regular little United Nations you have up there. Are they nice? You make sure you do your fair share round the apartment, won't you. I know you will. I did ask Uncle what the girls were like, not realizing he hadn't met them. He said they looked like 'a couple of bitchy blonde cheer leaders with big busts,' so he knew you'd get on well. Isn't he hopeless!
When do you start your job at the Indoor Rock Climbing Center?
We miss you heaps! Ballou races to the door each time it opens to see if it's you. Make sure you're eating properly. Colleen says hello, Declan says hi, Sharn says little sister must keep 'hydrating.' (I won't even repeat other things she said). Remember, Fergus says he'll bring you home any weekend, take you back Mondays, fit his schedule in with yours. Please take him up on it. Pa misses you. Says the house's not the same since you're gone. Has to make his own work lunch now, and misses your muffins. I think what he really misses most is the backchat. Please take care.

Love, Ma.

*   *   *

Teresa to Caitlin
Subject: Calling you from the United Nations.

Hi Ma,

Thank Fergus for the offer. I'll take him up on it soon, but I'm now working Saturdays and Sundays at the Climbing Center. Plus two days during the week. We get lots of school excursions here, but weekends are when work's at its busiest with adults. I have to take the work when I can get it.

Fatima is an Arabic girl from Jordan. She spends much of her time studying at her school and mosque. She wears a headscarf, but not round the apartment, and is lots of fun to be with. She's very pretty. And very kind. Always thoughtful towards others, no matter who. She thinks and speaks differently, often ending her sentences with 'If God wills it.' I told her what uncle said about her. She laughed. I told her on purpose. A warning should he call. She said she has an uncle who teases her, too.

Fatima is betrothed to marry in a year. I've met her man. He's nice. They're well suited. She does not like to go out much by herself, so we go together to the supermarket and mall. We have lots of laughs, but she's also very serious. Her religion has made her wise. We are both trying to believe in more things. That's hard.

Hester is studying at a yeshiva. She's serious. Like me. She is orthodox, and intends to live in Jerusalem one day. We often only see one another in passing. Friday is Fatima's holy day, Saturday's Hester's, and I go to Mass early Sundays because of work. (The only three days when we don't go to the bar!!!) We have great religious discussions. Mostly about things our religions have in common. They both said the prayer 'Our Father' could almost be their own. I think I'd like to study Comparative Religions one day. Maybe. Although I do like what I'm studying at the moment. When I get stuck on things I e-mail Uncle. He replies immediately. He is helpful with his insights.

Food's a bit of a problem here. I have to be real careful what I put in the refrigerator. Hester's food, even her Coca Cola, has to be blest by her Rabbi. When she breaks eggs into a bowl she must check for blood spots. She eats lots of smoked salmon and herring, and makes great orange and almond cake. It's so-o-o-o nice!

Fatima's meat is Halal, butchered facing Mecca. The girls politely asked that I don't put any bacon or shellfish in next to theirs. Or camel. We have an eco-religious freezer(mostly vodka—isn't it funny how vodka never freezes!!). I sometimes eat on my way home from lectures. I get home late Wednesdays. Fatima always prepares food for me that night. She does not go to bed until I arrive. She's so sweet and kind.

Fatima does not believe in putting her money in the bank to gain interest. Hester and I reckon she hides it somewhere in the refrigerator, but we're yet to find it! We tease each other like that.

Don't worry, Ma. We won't become a terrorist cell. Hester makes sure Fatima's friends leave their guns and grenades beside the front door. We don't have to examine our underwear for lead shot. Hester makes Fatima's friends sit and watch old episodes of Seinfeld. We have a good laugh. They like to be a bit crazy. I say to them 'Just wait until you meet my uncle. You don't know what crazy is!' We're all for Truth, Justice, Western ways. We're liberals. We recycle. Dispose carefully as we put in the refrigerator. If we had a garden on the roof, we'd be composting. And they both like my poster of Che.

And I now have lots of TATTOOS, as well! Just like Sharn's. HA, HA, HA! Got there at last. I can now run away, join the circus, like Maria's mother. Whatever happened to her, Ma? Has Fergus ever brought her back home again or did he give her the flick? I liked her. I know you won't tell me.

Miss you lots.
Love, Teresa.

*   *   *

Sharney to Teresa
Subject: Get off your butt.

Hey, little B-I-T-C-H,
still sitting with your head down up the back of the freaking bus, are you? by the time you're twenty you'll be looking like the back of one! any boyfriends yet? no point swishing your tail along the park when you have a backside like a rhino. Seize the day, why don't you. you'd have to be best looking hottie in class. Met any guys, ON-LINE? so you don't have to face them? try Lonely Heart's—must like cats, climbing trees, reading bible, no sex. I'm not asking you to be the city pump but are you even dating yet? come on! skank it up a little—miss muffin basket! don't want to hear what's happening up the apartment. Tell me what's happening downstairs. anything. even if it is your broken heart being hauled home at the end of a tow truck.

Your two room-mates sound totally boring! Hardly hip hop, house music and DJs. sounds more a conspiracy theory to me. Hardly Cameron Diaz. Natalie Portman. I'm concerned, that's all. just want to make sure your butt's in the right hands. someone's got to put it to bed!

Dad says he only misses teasing you. And bran muffins. Dominic still looks fit as a buck rat but is as big a nerd as ever. after a shaky start, he's getting straight A's at university. Ma says kisses, kisses, I say big kick in the rear. do you wear those slinky tights at climbing center? you got boys climbing up walls after you yet? now got myself ten ear-rings and a couple of studs in my left cheek. Only hurts when I blink. got a yellow Mohawk as well. no kidding. got on a bus the other day and the driver tried to charge me extra for the parrot! cheeky devil. felt like smacking him in the mouth.

Luv, big sister,
Sharn.

*　　*　　*

Teresa to Sharney
Subject: Birth Control!

Hi Sharn,

If I wanted bad advice I'd only have to go to uncle. Don't you start on me too.

I started my job at the climbing center the other week. This guy came up to me after an hour, dropped to the floor and started giving me ten press-ups! All I could do was giggle. He thought that I thought he was FUNNY. What a jerk! Felt like saying 'Give me a thousand!' You might go to sleep then. Dork!

I went out with this other guy after work the other night. He seemed o.k. From England. He turned out to be a regular Mr. Hugs with his Come-here-you-hug-hug-hug. Nearly crushed my freaking ribs. He said he'd buy me TEA. I thought for a moment he meant English High Tea. Thought I was in for a treat. But he meant it. A green tea with a peppermint chocolate beside on the saucer. He thought at least I'd get dressed up for the BIG occasion—short skirt, boots, something a little OFF THE SHOULDER. Wrong! Dickhead! I listened to his shit. Full of innuendo. Know what I'm saying. In-your-end-o. (My God! I'm beginning to talk just like YOU!) The moment my back was turned he replaced the chocolate mint with a big fat condom in a fancy plastic wrapper. I looked at it, said: 'Let's go Dutch.' Paid for the tea. Walked.

Anyway, must sign off. The bar's just opened down the street. The girls are pestering me to join them. I like the barman there. He asks nothing of me except 'Another double?' I'm putting on so-o-o much weight!!!

Love and kisses,
Little Sister.(a.k.a. Ms. Not Interested)

*　　*　　*

Sharney to Teresa
Subject: OMG!

Tess,

I didn't mention the bar to anyone, you cunning little cow, but your ma wants to know—whatever happened to that condom?

Sharn.

*　　*　　*

Teresa to Sharney
Subject: Dork!

Sharn,

I told him to pull the thing up over his head and go rob the cashier! Because he was such a CHEAPSKATE! I don't like the thought of people bringing me gifts, anyway. Too used to Fergus' loony presents. A dozen red roses is like giving me ten press-ups on the floor. I want a thirty meter TREE!
Idiots!

Teresa.

*   *   *

Teresa to Caitlin
Subject: Sisters.

Hi Ma,

I don't know what's wrong with me! I've gone all quiet again, and eating like a bird, but when uncle rang the other night and took me out to dinner I ate like a horse, babbling on like a chatterbox all evening. I said I only wanted a 'bite.' He hardly said a word all night. Just listened. I don't think I let him get a word in edgeways, anyway. Hope he didn't mind. He should have put some duct tape over my mouth. A few years ago he would have! Guess I'm growing up, getting too old for that. He treats me differently now. Still teasing, of course. He bought me a big box of really nice pastries to take home to share with 'the Turk and the Greek.'

I'm doing ok. I guess. I really do like my course work. I'm going to get very good marks this year and win my way into university. Be like Uncle. If I can keep my standard up on internal assessments I'll be heading for an A+.

Hester's well. She's quieter than Fatima. Whenever Fatima and I walk down the street together everybody looks at her sideways in her long skirt and headscarf. I often wear my Che beret, sometimes my army fatigues, on purpose. I don't like looking like a piece of Grade A Prime. And, wait for this. We often hold hands as we walk, like sisters! Sometimes we ham it up, kiss continental-style with the one-two-three. Nobody casts a second look at that or my clothes. That's good. It's ok to be a Communist nowadays. Just not a Muslim. Fatima told me that Arab women wore veils for six hundred years before Islam was even born. I'll stick with my Guevara clothes. Hide my money in the refrigerator.

Fatima and Hester are real good to me. Because I'm a bit younger, I guess.

When uncle came to pick me up for dinner the other night I warned them both: 'Please, don't mind my uncle. Anything's likely to come out of his mouth.' But he was fine. He stood at the door, thanked them both for being kind then *offered to take the girls to dinner with us. I held my breath when he asked. Thank God they declined. He probably would have taken us all to The Porky Pig, sat outside in the car, made them sweat it out a bit, then move away, laughing his head off. Imagine how big a puke that would have been for them!*

And just when I thought he was getting worse he left me a couple of bottles of kosher wine to give the girls before he went. I checked inside the bag. Just in case. Knowing him, it could've been a couple of bottles of holy water and a big bunch of garlic, couple of vampire movies thrown in for good measure. He knows me like a book by now. Knew that I'd check. There was five hundred dollars for me there in an envelope. I did e-mail, said 'thanks' after I'd found it. Bought myself some nice new clothes. You tell him he doesn't have to spoil me. I'm coping well, financially.

Anyway, it was so cool riding around the city with him in his new Mercedes. He says he's going to send Father Kevin round one night for dinner, sleep over on the couch. I said 'Don't you dare. You're as bad as one another.'

Work's good at the Rock Climbing Center. I can now go up the wall, across the ceiling, down the other side. In record time. Aren't I clever! I mean, few other people achieve that in a day at the office. Literally.

Love,
Teresa.

*   *   *

Sharney to Teresa
Subject: what's going on!

Little Sister, have you become a lesbian or something. Nothing wrong with that if you are. May go that way myself someday. Lots of jerks round here too. The gays at the salon say you have 'Sapphic' tendencies. all you ever talk about is girlfriends! failures with boys! we're all going to buy you for your 18th birthday CDs of K. D. Laing and Rufus Wainright.

Sharn.

*   *   *

Teresa to Sharney
Subject: My goldfish died.

Sharn,
I'd rather listen to Rufus' parents. Loudon, his mother Kate McGarrigle. Uncle listens to them. Anyway, just when I thought I was emotionally unavailable

I met somebody. Parents not only have big bank accounts but land as well! They're into concrete, bricks and mortar. I am onto a good thing here. He says my breasts look like 'perfect teardrops.' Only bigger. That's with my sweater on, too. Someone from out of town. I'm in love. I'm not like you, always bringing things home then sending them back. I'm in this one for the long haul. He makes the hairs stand up on the back of my neck. I said 'Get me jewelry!' I'm expecting an engagement ring in a couple of months for my eighteenth. In the range of 100 to 150. THOUSAND! Don't tell anyone, will you! Keep it a secret for me. But I know you when it comes to secrets. You only ever tell no more than four people! Bitch!

Teresa.

P.S. He's really romantic! The other day he bought me a beautiful blue goldfish in a plastic bag of water. Unfortunately I fed it too much. It died. O, dear. All gone.

*   *   *

Sharney to Teresa
Subject: Ms Lost Innocence.

Tessie, you horny little cow! You've been having us all on. it's only the scared dogs that bark! slept with him yet? why'd you throw that condom away? your Ma wants to know whether you're using birth control! you say 'he's from out of town.' you be mighty careful there. boys being boys. you know the old joke, little sister. best form of birth control is having it off with girls from out of town. We don't want you in the family way! how can you do this to . . . Ballou!

Big Sister.

*   *   *

Teresa to Sharney
Subject: Don't be silly!

Sharn,
    Of course I use birth control. Yes. We've slept together. Twice. In our JEANS!

Teresa.

*   *   *

Sharney to Teresa
Subject: Prayers at Mass

    Tess, at Sunday Mass I got Father Kevin to ask the congregation to offer up their prayers for TERESA. He understood. I said there's something wrong with her medically. She has YEAST in her vagina!

Big Sister.

*   *   *

Teresa to Sharney
Subject: I'm in love!

Sharn,
    Ha, ha! I haven't, but I sure will have soon. Especially if I keep sleeping with him in my JEANS! Mind your own business. I'm ok. Just sick of the ginseng! Green tea! Double A batteries! We're now talking real serious.
    I'm in LOVE! O.K!

Teresa.

*   *   *

Caitlin to Teresa
Subject: What's going on?

Teresa,
    What's going on with you? Your father and I are really concerned. Sharn tells us you're 'in love!' Let you out of our sight for a moment and you run amok! I didn't think you even liked boys.

Your Mother.

*   *   *

Teresa to Caitlin:
Subject: You want the Truth?

Dear Ma,
    Don't worry, Ma. I was only kidding her. The truth's different. In the four months I've been away I've put on over four stone, that's 56 pounds, over 25

kilos. My doctor says it's because I'm on the pill, plus having given up smoking uncle's cigars up in the trees, but she says I should lose most of it when I have a baby. So, I'm now off the pill, smoking cigars again, dating every night. Should be back in shape, after the pregnancy, in about a year.

Love, Tess.

*   *   *

Caitlin to Teresa
Subject: Fibber!

Tess,
    I didn't believe a single word you said.

Love, Mother.

*   *   *

Teresa to Caitlin
Subject: You tell me the Truth for once.

Ma,
    I was only trying to quell Sharn's curiosity. You know what her mouth's like. I don't find anything sexy in a bunch of beered-up boys in bars. I think I really am a lesbian. Believe in impossible love. Or love's impossible. Girls are easier to understand. Ballou's even easier to understand than most boys. Life doesn't suck. It just sucks to be me! I decline everybody. Like an heiress. I don't like boys, at all. I tell them I have 'issues.' If I talk to them at all. I tell them my mum lives with the man next door, the woman next door lives with my father. My neighbor's daughter, therefore, is my sister. And uncle can't for the life of him sort it out. Boys soon get sick of that kind of baggage. And I tell them I'm a Communist. Tell them anything, just as Uncle says I should. It's all just a big game in the city. I tell them I'm going to have lots of children, one day. By DONORS.
    Why don't you tell me who that Elena bitch is? You tell me the truth for a change.

Love,
Teresa.

*   *   *

Caitlin to Teresa
Subject: Sorry, no Truth here.

Teresa,

    If you want to tease us then we will give it back to you. Father Kevin is here at the moment with uncle. Fergus says 'you must just concentrate on your studies and not let the family down, that we're a respectable family here, like Michelangelo's family was—they were so disappointed when he decided to go work with his hands.' And Father Kevin's advice: 'Please, Teresa, don't listen to your Uncle!!!' The men are having a good laugh. You're right about men, dear. They're irresponsible creatures. They should grow up!

Love, Ma.

*   *   *

Teresa to Fergus
Subject: I want dinner!

Dear Uncle,

    When are you taking me out to dinner again? I know a really nice Italian place. We can talk. I'm feeling miserable at the moment. Fatima and Hester are so kind to me, but that's also part of the problem. All these religious discussions are so unsettling.

    Religion has got me thinking: how am I expected to account for myself when I meet my Maker—in a harness, helmet, goggles, rock shoes—when all I've ever done in my life is play climbing games. He'll see the chalk on my hands. I just know it. I know I'm not going to die yet, but my life seems so useless compared with Hester's, and Fatima's. They believe they can make a difference to the world. Me, I just climb up walls. My life's all about toeholds, right rotation, traversing, whether to use two fingers or three. It's like playing children's games of stone, paper, scissors. Just a game. Then, what do I go and do after that? I go off and study song lyrics at nights. I study how many syllables there are in a line by counting them, work out a rhyme scheme, that only goes ababab, then I waffle on about some image I see as beautiful. (It isn't all that bad, at times. We had to study the songs in Shakespeare's plays. Most of them were really interesting). Yet how useless is that! It seems so selfish of me. What is any of that going to qualify me to do? Be a bingo caller down at the church? I know that Hester and Fatima must think I'm nuts doing the job I do, but they'd never say anything. Write to me. Don't tease. I want you to tell me what's the MOST IMPORTANT THING IN LIFE. Certainly not anything I do.

For once in your life, counsel me wisely!

Love,
Teresa.

*   *   *

Fergus to Teresa
Subject: Here's something to eat.

Dear Tess,

Don't have those thoughts. You'll do lots of different things in a lifetime—gas-fill, pizza delivery, bicycle courier, check-out, janitor. Some people spend a lifetime in a job in local government, retire on a huge severance without ever really being able to explain to others what they did at work. For goodness sake, you're only seventeen. Yours is not a selfish life. Your job's to look out for the other climbers under your care. And it's dangerous at those heights. I'm going to tell my Maker, as if He doesn't already know, that I was 'a drug peddler,' selling liquor. Maker's Mark! In memory of Him. Because I'm good at it. As you're good at climbing. Not everyone's put here to rappel the drum, call the soldiers to war. Like Che. Thank goodness for that. Just be strong. One thing at a time. Do your climbing. Do your course work. Do it well. That's all. Just like Hester and Fatima do.

Everyone's up on a balanced beam in one way or another, so you may as well smile. I'm not suggesting you stop being serious, but a job isn't one's fate. Treat it rather as a fete. Treat climbing walls like you're on the swing boats and roundabout horses on carnival day, or at a shooting gallery, just mindful of dangers to others. Life's often about finding an 'avoidance' to suit. I suggest you try your hand at writing song lyrics. Good song lyrics. Pen one good song and it could set you up for life. You remember how you and Sharn sang the parts of Lee Hazelwood and Nancy Sinatra in the song 'Something Stupid.?' Now there's a 'silly romantic song.' Only until you realize how clever it is, the run on lines, the lilt and lyrical way it was written. The writer of it has not really needed to work since. Everyone has recorded it! Same too can be said for the song 'Yesterday' or 'The Girl from Ipanema.'

So if you want me to tell you what I consider the MOST IMPORTANT THING in life, then, I'd have to say, in all honesty, no more than a great poem. A well written song. And I can't think of anything more 'useless' than those things. Go and ask Hester and Fatima if they think 'The Song of Solomon' is 'useless.' For the most part they're just love songs. Go on. Quote them 'Your lips cover me with kisses, your love is better than wine.' They'll recognize it. Instantly. They won't laugh at you.

Love,
Fergus.

* * *

Teresa to Fergus
Subject: You've got to be joking!

Uncle,

Recognize it? They'll think I'm a lesbian if I quoted them that! They'd throw me out of the house. And if I did write a bunch of lyrics then they'd be all sad songs, anyway. I've spent too much time alone in the trees. Anyway, when are you taking me out to dinner again? I'm starving!

Tessie.

* * *

Fergus to Teresa
Subject: Tell them Nothing.

Tess,

Tomorrow. At seven. And. Gotcha, didn't I! Sharn's convinced you're a lesbian. Tricked you into telling us the truth! But who cares! Who cares if you are! Tell them nothing, Tess. After your last e-mail to your mother she called an 'extraordinary' meeting with Colleen and Sharn. Your Ma says that the city's 'corrupting' you. She wants to bring you home. Your Pa says just lay off, wait until you're eighteen. I know I shouldn't be saying this, but it was so funny watching them getting all worked up and worried. The reason I'm telling you is, it gives you two months to think about your life, where to live, what to do, those sorts of things. Of course, at eighteen you can do as you please. Just concentrate on getting yourself an A+ in your course work. Don't worry about life. One thing at a time. The rest often takes care of itself.

Love, Uncle.

* * *

Sharney to Teresa
Subject: Big Trouble at home.

    Dear Little Tree Climbing Sister, your Ma's gone into damage control. wants you home. says you're 'depressed.' 'the girl thinks too deeply about things.' 'what she needs is the 'psychiatrist's couch.'
    'you just need a weekend banging on the couch.' SAYS ME. but, that's me. crude, ain't I!

Big Sister.
P.S. Your Ma really believes the city is just not SAFE for you!

*   *   *

Teresa to Sharney
Subject: I'm staying put.

Sharn,
    Tell me what else they said. Come on, out with it! The city ISN'T dangerous. No more so than Hope Street is.

Teresa.

P.S. By the way, Hester disappeared two days ago. She'd been down the Synagogue praying for peace. We suspect terrorists.

*   *   *

Sharney to Teresa
Subject: We're sending Father Kevin up to see you.

    Tess, your Ma says she's worried about you, mentally and sexually. your Pa says he's not worried at all.
    Fergus says 'get rid of the cat, rent out your room.'
    Kevin says he's coming up there to splash you all with holy water. Is going to bring Ballou. (he and Fergus had a big laugh about that, acting it up. 'Hester!' says Fatima from your apartment door. 'There's a Catholic priest at the door. And he's holding a BLACK CAT!' (Kevin's as useless as Fergus is). i say you're a lesbian. my Ma's worried about what people will say at the salon, gossip-wise.
    Dominic was home. he just grunted when we told him. what else would you expect from him!

Pa says it's 'different for girls.' 'things change in a year.' what a goose of a thing to say. no wonder Dominic's such a dick-head!

Sharn.

*   *   *

Teresa to Sharney
Subject: Just the facts.

Dear Sharn,
For once in your life, be serious. What does Fergus REALLY think? I know they'd never rent my room out. And he loves Ballou. He knows me better than everyone else since I've been in the city. Tell me the TRUTH. Bitch!

Teresa

*   *   *

Sharney to Teresa
Subject: You want the TRUTH!

Tess,
Fergus is home. I went over next door, showed him your e-mail, asked him. 'what you think, Fergus? Teresa wants to know the TRUTH.' Typical Fergus, he just put on his best Jack Nicolson accent and said. "Truth! She couldn't handle the truth." Then he looked at me and said matter-of-factly. "I think your little sister has come down from the trees at last. I think she's IN LOVE." he says he can tell. that you babble on like a babbling brook because you're all nervous about being found out. that you then get all dreamy, distracted. he can see the tell-tale signs. everyone should just leave you alone. you're a good catholic girl. he said. even Kevin says so(so long as you keep using protection!). there you have it. i say, forget protection. you're just a naughty LESBIAN! you don't like boys. must like girls. it must be real hard for you after a lifetime believing in the Virgin birth and St. Joseph was celibate. We just got to get over it, don't we!
You're like Robinson Crusoe climbing the highest tree, looking out to sea for a ship come rescue him. Truth is, ain't going happen. We all know he's going to end up with Man Friday, don't we! Ha, ha, ha. Big Sister knows.
And so she wrote.

Sharn.

Teresa, aged eighteen: Her Coming of Age

Colleen said that she'd go and collect Teresa from the early train while Caitlin made final preparations for the 18th birthday party at the house. Caitlin was so excited to have her daughter home. She'd not seen her for over six months. Expectation was a gangly girl in floppy T-shirt and sweatpants, hair down in her eyes. Perhaps she had been drinking in bars in the city. That was what Fergus led them to believe. Fergus was right in his element.

"Thank God she's coming home. Frumpy little cow. Gone to seed. She's urgently in need of a makeover. I'm telling you, it'll keep Sharn busy."

"Is she really!"

"She's got all puffy round the throat," he said. "Vodka. Keeping up the family tradition. Dancing on dingy dance floors, shaking her hair, drinking into the small hours, going home with . . . whoever."

"I thought vodka was the least calorific," Caitlin replied.

"It's that fortified sugar energy stuff they mix with it. I know. I'm in the business. I've got a vested interest in ruining youth. Only thing that excites them dulls them as well. She needs a fix to climb walls, social climbing in the city."

He quietly reflected. "So our little star pupil's coming home at last." Fergus was dismissive. "Just open a can of spam. You haven't seen her for ages. I'm not kidding, you're in for a surprise. She only earns pin money. Don't be upset if she looks like she's been eating from the garbage. Well, maybe getting all her takeout from mobile food trucks. Lovesick. Thin, city trollop. Wearing a mullet. Bloodshot eyes. Skinny as a migrant laborer. Young people don't seem to sleep anymore. They blackout. It's the drink. It's all a big frolic. Nothing more shameful than a daughter gone bad. What else can you expect but for her to spurn us?"

The list seemed to go on and on.

"Is she fat or is she thin?" Caitlin asked in horror.

Fergus ignored her "Big mistake ever letting her leave home. Sending her off to the city with only a third grade education. You should have your heads read. Probably fallen in love with a sailor. I reckon she'll end up as silly as a wet lettuce like you-know-who from next door."

"Go away," Caitlin ordered, not knowing what to think, fat or thin, "organize some music and wine."

Fergus slunk off, chuckling to himself. He knew how to annoy his sister, press the wrong buttons. He purposely selected a Rolling Stones' number at the stereo. 'The Girl With The Faraway Eyes.' So slow. So countrified. So corrrr-rupt.

"Spending her time in bars with a bunch of roughnecks and pipe-liners, listening to this kind of hillbilly stuff. What else can you expect from a kid whose been abused on the street all her life?" Fergus muttered loud enough for Caitlin to hear. "She'll probably want to spend the day with you and Sharn down the pool hall showing you how to set up frames. Meet The Fockers has nothing on us lot."

"Cut it out, Fergus. I'm worried." Caitlin could not imagine Teresa talking to boys, let alone in pool halls.

But what really worried Caitlin was Teresa had been staying away on purpose. It also annoyed to think Fergus was probably right. They shouldn't have let her go. She was withdrawn enough at home, overwhelmed at school. Maybe the city was just too much. Maybe you had to be like Fergus, a joker, who saw it all as comic, ever to cope with urban life.

Teresa had been unable to make it home that Christmas. There'd been gloomy sighs at the end of the telephone. They came up like a bank of mist, vague excuses of indifference, none very convincing or encouraging. One after the another. Worse than that, Teresa, it seemed, was unsure of herself, not knowing what to do. Even Maddox worried. Their daughter, who once refused to leave the house or safety of her tree, now seemed gone from them forever.

The house was empty without her. Ballou lay round all day, barely touching her food. No one fed the birds outside any longer. Even they seemed forlorn, ignored whenever the front door opened. The two houses—'mi casa, sui casa'—formally my joint's your joint, didn't seem the same any longer. Sharn missed her most of all.

"I'll have my Christmas here." Teresa said in muffled tones without any gaiety or warmth on her cell phone. "I have to work Boxing Day. There's a rock climbing exhibition in the park. I wouldn't be able to eat much, anyway. Climbing all day really rips my stomach. I'd be retching. No other sport uses all muscles like rock climbing does."

At least the train was on time. Few passengers alighted. Most commuters had reached their holiday destinations long before New Year's eve.

Although surprised that Colleen was the one to greet her, Teresa offered that same sweet smile from her kindly heart at sight of her, then it vanished. Her brooding eyes had that old look of religious resignation about them, which she once had up in the trees. She carried it like a wound. Colleen could immediately tell something was wrong. Teresa was wearing an old bulky coat that she'd bought years ago in an Op shop. Colleen wondered what bulk it disguised.

Then there were all those vaguely pointed questions asked of her while driving back to the house.

"Where'd you spend Christmas, Tess? Synagogue? Mosque?" Teresa muttered she'd gone to midnight Mass, pronouncing BY MYSELF, then got a taxi home. The answer had such strongly defiant inflexions as though this line of questioning was far too boring to explain, and invasive, that she'd only gone to church to arrange altar flowers. And, of course, mind your own business. Strangely, she wouldn't even look at Colleen, staring quietly out the window.

It was not as if anything changed in the town. Colleen could plainly see how depressed she was. Wrapped in a coat, like self accusation. City life. Doing her down 'Poor little fool,' Colleen thought. Her face looked sad, yet it was a different look from those grimaces of distrust after having walked Hope to home from school. There was clearly something on Teresa's mind. Buttoned up. Weighted by sadness. It seemed deep and enduring.

Like love.

Surely, not love.

"Something wrong, Tess?"

"No. Why should there be?" She snapped back, turning in from her window gaze.

It wasn't as if Colleen had asked 'who you making out with?' as Sharn would, or 'show us your heart tattoos?' to get such an abrupt reply. There'd be no tattoos. They were only a long standing joke, anyway. And she didn't give a city look of being stuck-up, snooty. Just sad. Colleen remembered how Teresa would always walk into her house with a big 'hello, it's me,' her protuberant eyes sparkling with mischief, knowing either Declan or Sharn would be at the ready with a mouthful of cheek to return

It had only been a faint, forced smile on the station platform. It was a beautifully clear summer's day, blue and golden, but Teresa's head seemed away in distant clouds.

She'd got the glooms back.

Fergus had chosen the song correctly that morning. He was right. She did have faraway eyes. There was a kind of reprimand in them for having to return. In another world. Certainly away from this town.

'O, sweet Tess. What's happened to you?' Colleen thought as she tried harder making conversation. She said Dominic had rung the night before, said 'Happy birthday Teresa,' formally as ever, that he'd recently graduated, that he would be home in a few days time.'

Teresa seemed indifferent.

'Maybe Fergus' right,' Colleen thought. 'Here's a young woman who is in love. O well, Fergus will sort her out. He'll see things differently.'

"We'll have a party for Dominic. You'll be staying on for it, won't you?" Colleen entreated.

"Don't know," Teresa answered vaguely. "I'll see how things turn out at home first."

Turn out! Why would anything ever be different? She was certainly no dear sweet child any longer, in fact, her face looked becomingly beautiful as she stood by herself on the platform that morning. That was all Colleen could see. Pretty, she'd always been, not quite a kewpie doll but not yet beautiful. Teresa said she had changed on the train for her homecoming. Changed into what? Colleen couldn't see. Yet it turned out nonsense about drinking in bars, just part of her daring; for her face shone with beauty. She wondered if underneath that long coat Teresa's body was ripped with fitness.

Colleen had expected a tall girl numbed down to a flower print dress, maybe horn rimmed glasses to keep the world at bay, and probably clutching a Bible. She could only ever visualize Teresa with a young man, if ever together, selling bibles door to door. Either that or Ala Vera. Teresa would stand there, distant, pure and virginal, probably blowing bubbles of gum. How wrong she was.

After the car pulled in at the house, Teresa suddenly became alive again, quickly unbuttoning, slithering her coat off to the seat before alighting from the car, strutting up the pathway with her single carry bag. She stopped momentarily to view the tinsel sign 'Happy 18th Birthday, Tess' over the front veranda.

Everyone was there, all dressed up, waiting like a chorus line.

Sharn couldn't believe her eyes.

Teresa was wearing a short black leather skirt, high black boots, a cerise colored top with plunging neckline, shoulder length hair now done in an expensively city cut. She looked the typical city vamp, long legged, lean, curved, eyes shining with clarity, body at peak fitness. Her skin shone like a filament shaded in olive brown. Her nails were sharp, perfectly manicured. Colleen had noticed them instantly. How did she keep them like that rock climbing all day? They had to be false.

Yet Colleen knew better. She may have progressed on surfaces. She'd just seen that face in a fit of melancholy. She understood. A lesbian thing. Having to come home, at last. Tell the family. The truth. Coming to terms with what she was. Spending all her money on clothes(Fergus had to be topping up her pittance earnings). Heart in denial. Probably playing with divining cards in the evening, seeing what an uncertain future holds. She'd seen it so often down at the salon. So, so pretty. Yet depressed.

'I feel so sorry for you,' Colleen thought. 'Women are difficult enough creatures as it is. But two? Two together! Holding hands. Continental KISSING! Girls laying all over one another like kittens. To think, boys would be kneeling at her feet like the Magi to honor one pretty as this. That's the privilege of depressed, pretty girls, giving boys the cold shoulder. She had said so in her e-mails. So pretty for so long. So pointless. City's fault. Paying the earth for everything. Expecting love thrown into the bargain. At least she hadn't acquired some false city accent, taken up smoking those disgusting herbal cigarettes.

Why hadn't Fergus shown more concern while noticing these changes? She should never have left home!

Then, it happened. Teresa couldn't see, but she knew it was Fergus acting behind the scenes. The stereo suddenly blasted. Everyone began dancing spontaneously.

'Listen to this one, Tess,' he'd often say to her, 'a real killer tune.'

Peeling from the speakers was Sam Cooke's 'Oh my baby's coming home tomorrow, Ain't that good news, man, ain't that news!'

She and Sharn used to rock their souls to the reworking of this old spiritual number Saturday nights. Old as the hills, maybe, yet the girls got off on it, clowning with broomsticks as microphones, painted faces, uninhibited, having a hoedown of fun.

Teresa immediately grinned at memory of it, put down her grip bag, began dancing the pathway in a kind of flamenco-rock, hands outstretched, fingers clicking like castanets, stomping her new boots, turning in a circle to show off her new clothes, just as Fergus would in displaying goods and meats in his arms on Friday nights.

She'd shed her raggedly years like old skin. Everyone faced her swaying, clapping, cheering her on. What a splendid looking young woman she'd become. Signs and wonders. It was miraculous.

Fergus wasn't to be seen. Teresa began to wonder. For most of her birthdays Fergus turned them into disasters. She could not think of him inside carefully wrapping something in pale pink tissue, delicately placing it in a box She suddenly felt strangely fingered by her audience, like they were pretending to be a bunch of librarians going through a card index yet about to spring a surprise. She wasn't taking the risk. She'd get in first.

Teresa stopped, reached down into her carry bag, pulled out a single sheet of crisp, white paper, began flashing it up to the balcony.

"And the award for best academic achievement goes to . . . I got an A+. I can go to university now. Top of the class of thirty five by whole ten marks. This soldier's now ready for service." She then stood straight to attention, arms firmly in at her sides.

"Well, just look at you, Bitch Face. So, you finally passed military medical," Sharn broken ranks, running down the steps like hell on wheels, putting her arms around little sister. "The big bend over, now cough. Straightened up with an A1 rating."

Teresa tittered as she hugged her.

Trust Sharn to come up with something crude. Sharn at her wackiest.

Teresa then ran up the steps to embrace her mother and father.

It was hugs and kisses all round. Caitlin finally handed her the cat. How it had aged, sullen and listless now. It no longer got perky in the evenings as it had years ago. She remembered how, after dinner some evenings, she used to put a cardboard box on the living room floor. Ballou would jump into it. The box would capsize, this way and that. How they laughed. How she would study its balance and agility. She now cradled it tightly in her arms. Teresa too, seemed happy to be back in home's cradle again.

"Where's uncle?" She asked nonchalantly. Somebody motioned inside.

It was then that she heard the voice of Raul Malo of The Mavericks, Teresa's favorite group. It was the dance teacher who'd first mentioned them to her.

"Just want to dance the night away/With the senoritas who can sway." Teresa loved the big brass country-Miami sound ever since Fergus bought her the CD two years before. She ran inside, kissed him, knowing only he could be playing it for her.

"What you giving me for my birthday, Uncle? I got the A+ I wanted." Teresa asked, not caring much for an answer. She hoped just another useless present. They made no difference to her now. After all, he'd spoilt her most weeks in the city. It was achievement enough to have finally done well at something.

"Good to hear. Thought you would. We knew you were able enough. You deserve a reward. I've got you an old pair of worn-out running shoes from a Good Will Shop. About time you got away from the walls and outside again." Fergus muttered gruffly, then grinned while checking out more discs out for the stereo.

But she caught his mischievous smile.

Teresa laughed. She remembered his advice. "You can do it, Tess. Don't sell yourself short."

Despite his uncaring exterior she knew when he was pleased. She had never expected any astonished voice from him. Maybe there was something else, maybe up in the fig tree. She remembered back to one Christmas day when she was six or seven, she couldn't quite remember now, how excited she was at Fergus' present, the most expensively wrapped under the tree. She tore the wrapper off with great expectation—a one pound bag of birdseed. Yet, more than happy with that, she ran out to climb the fig tree, fill the ply boxes with seed for the birds. There, in her tree house, was a bulkily knitted shoulder bag, inside an expensively retractable spyglass. So excited at the sight of it she ran back inside and hit him. 'Liar, liar,' she said. 'You're a big liar.'

She wondered what he might be up to. One's eighteenth birthday, she assumed, deserved better than a pair of worn out shoes. She'd gladly wear a blindfold in the meantime.

That would be later. Climbing trees. She wasn't climbing today. Not in these clothes. Climbing had now become a difficult and dangerous chore.

Yet she still didn't quite trust him. He did not even look at her clothes and think 'so that's where the money goes.' Fergus looked beyond. She never expected treachery but knew Fergus was like those Russian dolls—out they'd come, small to larger, larger again, all just as empty as before. It was only then did she begin to fear he knew more than he was letting on.

There were bottles of chilled white wine on the dining table, the smell of percolated coffee, no cheap checkered plastic but Caitlin's Irish finest linen; there were bowls of fresh fruit; pancakes, syrup, and she could smell the barbeque firing up outside. It was a beautiful day, doors and drapes wide open. Nothing slatted the room in shadows. And party time again. Teresa was home, at last. Things finally back to normal

Teresa had giggled at her uncle's gruff reply. The others were now inside, right behind her. Colleen smiled, if only forcefully, happy that she may be wrong. It seemed Teresa had got her old self back. Sharn was most amazed. Little Sister, no longer. What a difference a year makes.

"Hasn't she grown! Blossomed overnight." Maddox said quietly in an aside to Declan.

"Told you so. Girls change. Matter of moments." Declan replied wryly.

Then, present time. Small gifts. The women had made other plans for the day. They'd all go to the Mall. There were cosmetics, hand towels, winter blankets for the apartment, if she were to go back to the city. No one was quite sure.

The first thing Teresa did when she got from the car was look to her trees. How splendid they were this time of year. The mango, full of fruit. Most had now turned green to yellow. Ripeness filled the air. There were also small avocadoes shining yellow-green in sunlight. She seemed, to the others, to look as fruitful as the mangos themselves

"What've you done to yourself, Teresa? You look stunning! We never thought you'd ever care enough." Caitlin held her daughter's arm with such pride. No one expected this, especially from such a dour apartment. They expected a long skirt, carefully hidden hair, a sense of flight from the world.

Colleen and Sharn had taught her to apply make-up. 'Not too much,' they'd always say. 'Accentuate your lips, Teresa. They're your best feature. Lips are everything.' Teresa never cared much back then. Sunday Mass only, fooling around Saturday night. That was only because Sharn was over, insisting upon it. Today it was tubular lips in dark mauve. They looked as pretty as a night sky full of rain. Mascara. Eyes. Just right. Gold hoop earrings. And she looked great in her high leather boots. She'd always had such nicely formed legs. Beautiful hair. Slender waist. How her boobs had grown. Every detail. Everything so correct.

Yet something was amiss. The women surreptitiously peered for tattoos, as if some trump card lay somewhere under her thigh, if only they could see it.

She just had to be courted by someone.

'Perhaps Fergus' to blame. Filling her head with all those soppy songs,' Colleen thought as she looked to Teresa's hand for some kind of commitment ring. She then looked to her wrists, tell tale signs of self harm. 'Things go wrong. Living with a bunch of religious fanatics. Filling her head with . . . other creeds. Girls should stay at home. With their parents. Cities only confuse them. Better they have common social skills, remain rough around the edges.'

"So metro-sexual!" Sharn chimed in, almost lost for words. "Who'd have thought you'd turn out looking so HOT! What a change from that old refrigerator magnet photo over at our place. So HOT you should now go in it! But I don't like that lipstick much."

"What's wrong with it?" Teresa turned defensively.

"Better a nude look. Touch of gold on it. Better for . . . kissing."

"Ha-ha," Teresa quickly turned away again.

"Anyway, who cut your hair, Bitch! Why couldn't you have waited for us? We'd have done it. City cuts like that must cost a fortune."

"It did. I feel bad about it, too. Ninety dollars. Uncle rang and said he'd be late picking me up for dinner. I wasn't game to stand round waiting on Elizabeth Street. He said 'go get your hair cut instead,' because I'd said I felt a bit raggedy. He said he'd pay. When they finished, I had to sit back down for ten minutes before he arrived. They looked at me as though I was going to do a runner. It was so embarrassing! Anyway, mind your own business, Bitch! Where's my K.D. Laing and Rufus Wainright CDs?"

"You said you didn't like her."

"No I didn't. Of course I like her."

Caitlin broke in. "We're taking you down to the Mall. You can have anything you want. I thought you told Sharn not to buy those CDs for you. Anyway, you should be listening to Miley Cyrus and Taylor Swift at your age. Wholesome country stuff. How long have you had the leather skirt, dear? That top's rather revealing. I mean, for you. Don't you think? Do you wear them in front of the girls at the apartment? They make you look rather . . . leggy."

Teresa could feel everyone's eyes set squarely on her.

"A couple of weeks. No way. Dear Lord in Heaven, no! Fatima and Hester are strictly skirts to the floor. It's the first time I've worn them. I was going to wear them out the other night, but Fatima was home so I'd have to have worn a coat. It was far too hot for that."

"You're telling me!" Maddox muttered.

Teresa noticed Fergus grinning. He sat quietly chuckling in his chair.

Teresa glowered at him. Love him as she did, she still couldn't trust him an inch. 'He's going to have to think of something other than a scallop shell this year to cover my bosom,' she thought defiantly. That was another birthday. Her fifteenth. Fergus gave her a St. James scallop shell at the end of a pink silk ribbon. He'd picked it up overseas somewhere. "It will make you look half decent down on the beach," he'd said.

They sat round the dining table. It was too early to open champagne. Maddox poured Teresa a glass of light chilled wine. He kissed her cheek as he handed it to her. He felt so proud. No longer his little kid in overalls. Gone too the nights of cheek, endless backchat. He actually hoped she'd come up with a mouthful. She'd grown into such a beautiful, serious young woman.

'Where've the years gone?' He thought wistfully.

Teresa smiled back at her father appreciatively, then nervously fingered the stem of the glass. She was hardly the kind of party flapper who giggled insensibly over a single glass. Everyone began to wonder exactly what she was.

"What kind of wine is it?" She asked, trying to make conversation during an embarrassing lull.

"Don't know. Label says," Maddox squinted myopically to read. "Caution: Wait four hours before driving . . . or climbing trees."

Teresa leaned across to smack her father. She'd not be climbing today. Too grown up for that. Maybe she might. Maybe Fergus had another gift in a tree house. She'd wait.

As she'd bowed across to slap her father she revealed her dark red lacy bra and cleavage. Fergus noticed. He looked away modestly, then instantly did a double-take. He chuckled to himself then began fiddling again with the remote, watching song numbers come up, flashing green on the system. Teresa wished he'd leave the damned thing alone. Say something. Tease her. One could have cut the air. Teresa could've killed him. He was up to no good again.

She just knew it.

Caitlin had noticed the thin gold chain around Teresa's neck as she'd leaned forward. She could no longer contain her curiosity.

"What a beautiful gold chain, dear. What's on the end of it?"

Colleen noticed, too. "That's so pretty. Who gave it to you, dear? Is it a Star of David? Islamic Crescent? Crucifix?." Teresa immediately clutched it to her bosom.

Fergus laughed at their impudence, then pointed the remote to the stereo like a gun. It blasted with the voice of Raul Malo again. This, he knew, was Teresa's favorite song—The Maverick's rendition of Bruce Springsteen's 'All That Heaven Will Allow.'

'I've got a dollar in my pocket
There ain't a cloud up above,
I've got a picture in my locket
That says 'Baby I love you.'

Fergus hit the remote to silence. A glumness took over the room. Fergus gave Teresa THAT look—Go on, Teresa, answer them. What's in the locket?

"You're right, Fergus." Caitlin said, amazed. "It IS a heart locket. Come on, Tessie, show us who's in it."

"Leave me alone," Teresa scowled at Fergus as she squirmed uncomfortably in her chair. It was a look to kill. Silence. Maddox and Declan felt embarrassed for her.

Fergus then spoke. He couldn't contain himself any longer.

"Here's this year's present, Tess. Part of it, anyway. Happy 18th, my dear."

He casually handed a bank check across the table. Sharn's eyes popped as it passed hand to hand. She'd noticed that it was made out to the bearer for $10,000.

Teresa looked at it sullenly. "No, Uncle." She hanged her head. "Thank you, I don't need this. It won't help."

"Yes, you do. We're sending you away. You're not staying here. Only the cat stays. We're not putting up with your misery any longer. It just isn't going to happen. Adolescent rubbish! Longings. Lu-u-u-v."

The others sat horrified at his heartless catalogue, the callousness, cruelty of it. What on earth was going on? Fergus then laughed at them all, ridiculously.

"Only teasing you, Tess." He then, almost contemptuously, threw a large, folded packet across the table. Teresa picked it up, took it down, opened it out on her lap so no one else could see. Sharn craned her neck to snoop. Teresa thumbed the pages slowly then stared up at her uncle.

"How'd you know?"

Her hands trembled as though caught red handed, her voice barely audible through her mauve and quivering lips.

Fergus put a clenched fist up to his nose. He then spread out two fingers next to his thumb making a V, pointing in at his eyes.

Teresa burst into tears, throwing the folder up on the table—there were airline tickets, itineraries, passport, visa applications—they slew along the linen surface. Caitlin was first to notice. There was two of everything. Teresa tore the heart locket from her neck, breaking the chain, throwing it over her shoulder into the corner. She stood clumsily from her chair, flushed and agitated, rushing from the room.

The women straightened like vultures, sensing a kill. It was as if menacing vapor trails had suddenly torn a clear blue sky. Sharn was first across to it. She seized upon it, opened the locket out, then screamed in horror.

"O, no you don't, you little bitch! This is sick. SICK, SICK, SICK! No wonder she was hiding things from us. Get back in here, Little Sister. Cunning little cow. Cat's finally out of the bag, isn't it! YOU JUST CAN'T DO THIS! Get Father Kevin round here. This is worse than being a Communist!"

Fergus hit the remote again, then got up slowly from his chair. He slow waltzed to the music around the women at the table. He'd purposely moved the song list along to a Spanish number that no one else would understand. 'Besame Mucho.' Kiss Me Long.

Sharn stood stunned to silence. It was as though their little tree-climbing-Jackie-in-the-Beanstalk had just given away the family fortune. Wasn't it a cow Jack bought with it? What'd the world come to? How was she ever to face her best friend, her SISTER, ever again?

Sharn stared at Fergus. As sure as God made little green apples he'd had a hand in this. How green they all were not to have seen it.

The song ended with a single line in English. 'Love me forever and make my dreams come true.'

The 'Punishment' For Secret Love

All the women went shopping at the Mall that day, as planned. Teresa came out of hiding soon after, face airbrushed white as marble. Caitlin clutched her hand. Colleen shrugged. Sharn never said a word.

But Fergus knew better. He'd noticed the signs. They were like invisible rings of truth. He proved the only one who believed love cannot be stopped, only approved. After all, he'd filled her head with songs of love and romance for years now. He avoided the subject, anyway.

Yet that didn't mean love wasn't to be tested. Love was not going to moon round the house all day in sloppy Ts, looking for soft places to fall. Teresa, if anyone, knew he didn't believe in soft mats at the foot of climbing walls. She stared at him warily, in full knowledge those tickets to a European holiday weren't going to be four weeks in a Swiss spa, lazing about southern beaches in Spain.

She feared another of his novel forms of punishment

"You're both going away." He tapped his fingers seriously on the outside table, relishing the moment, like some kind of mock King Solomon about to chop a child in half in order to prove who the rightful owner.

"Is it going to be hell?" She was back in old jeans and T shirt.

"Certainly going to be a hell of a long way."

Fergus then gave one of his puckish grins.

They were both sitting outside under an awning from late afternoon sun. There was a large paperback bookmarked with strips of white beside him. From its size it looked a thousand pages. Teresa turned it towards her viewing the cover: James A. Michener. 'Iberia.'

"For me to read? Another gun-toting Communist like Che? Will this one get me into trouble, too?" She touched it charily.

"Only read the last hundred pages. No. He is a famous writer and peace-loving walker. He reckons the walk you'll both be taking is one of the two or three finest walking journeys in the world."

Teresa reached for his wine bottle, poured herself a glass. She drank it down in a fierce gulp, poured another.

"Go easy on that stuff," Fergus ordered, "Punishments are only designed for the sober."

"Whew! Good one, Uncle. Certainly need this after this morning. And a good long walk. I like doing hell. I come home from work each day already feeling like a martyr. I ache from fingertips to toes. My stomach feels like a ball of granite. I've used every muscle in my body climbing those walls all day, and all you want is to give me something harder? Where're you sending us? It's not going to be easier, is it?"

"Santiago de Compostela. To a cemetery. Tomb of the Apostle James."

Teresa grimaced. "Sounds real gob-ful to me. I don't want to pick a bone with you about cemeteries but where in God's name is it?"

"Northern Spain. Galicia. Above Portugal." Fergus spelt it out, poker faced.

"Why?"

He lent across the table reducing his voice to a whisper. "So you can get away from our lot for a while. It's an eight hundred kilometer walk. Five hundred miles. A pilgrimage. To get you to a cemetery."

"Yeah, right. I can do the conversion myself, thank you. More like something else to test me."

"Maybe. Let's see if you're really done with quitting."

"Is it like the South of France?" She intoned sarcastically. "Will people call me 'pilgrim,' just like John Wayne did in those western movies?"

"Of course. 'Peregrina.' Like a peregrine falcon drifting over great distances. Don't worry about it. You'll be doing it along with 100,000 others. And you'll be going onto the South of France and Greek Isles after that with your mother and father. You just won't have mother's hospital linen and packed lunches along this part, that's all. It'll be hard. Lots of flies in outhouses along the way. You'll be washing in buckets each night because there's no hot showers. You'll be doing it without your harness or goggles. Don't worry. People are nice to pilgrims. They'll never refuse pilgrims glasses of water."

"Liar, liar. Same old, same old Fergus." Teresa sloshed down her glass. "Great!" she then said dismissively, "so long as you don't sugarcoat anything for us. Didn't Che go on a long route march to Santiago? When are we going?"

"That was Santiago de Cuba. All booked for April." Fergus relented. "Look forward to it. You're going off to view higher hills, broader valleys, lots of trees under sailing clouds. It'll be easy. You're fit. Life's easy when you have little to come and go on. You'll come home so positive you'll be believing in miracles. Signs. Wonders." He cast his eyes heavenwards.

'A cemetery. A CEMETERY,' Teresa thought, viewing him sideways, 'the only place my mother told me Fergus was ever too afraid to go.'

Let's Go Now

"Yeah, yeah. Why wait 'til April? Let's go now. We'll travel day and night. Walk till we drop. Just get it over with."

"No. April. And why? April's the onset of northern spring and the traditional beginnings of love." Fergus put his hand sentimentally over his heart. "Lots of people have written songs about that month. April love. Riding high in April. It's always been considered the best month for tranquility and reflection on northern pilgrimages. One month. Walking with heavy backpacks. Five hundred miles. You can still have your lattes and cocktails at night. Up bright and breezy next morning. Off again. Whistle stopping with your . . . new best friend."

"Cut it out. That's it? No choice about it?" Teresa looked at Fergus with vague horror.

"No choice."

"Why?"

"Why? Because all great journeys began in April. You're heading west, young lady, just like Johnny Apple-seed. West. For another certificate. You're my prize pupil, that's why. But. No A+ given for this one."

"Yippee! I've lived most my life up a tree, like Jane. Moment I come down I'm being sent off again into the jungle just to reach a pile of dead bones." Teresa shuddered at the thought.

Fergus sat smugly. "There's an old joke about Tarzan and Jane. You like jokes. They came down from the trees, too. They knew they had to, one day. They took an apartment in Manhattan. Jane bore the brunt of it by having to get a job. She'd come home nights, find Tarzan sitting in the easy chair, drunk as a lord." Fergus hesitated a moment then looked to Teresa. She was getting a bit that way herself. "If I remember the novel correctly, he was made an English Lord in the end," he said as an aside. "No matter. 'Tarzan!' Jane said crossly. 'You've had SIX daiquiris already!' He looked at her with delirium tremors. "But don't you know? It's a jungle out there." Fergus trembled at the table. The planks began to shake.

"Ha, ha. I get it. But is it really a jungle?" Teresa always got his punch-lines. It was the points that she feared.

"Of course it is." Fergus shuffled on his seat relishing the moment. "There's been street girls on this road for over a thousand years all tempting pilgrims from their piety for their money. That's life. Everywhere. Someone once said it's better to travel than arrive. Forget it! Journeys are far worse than arrivals. Five hundred miles, much of it rough terrain, yet all so beautiful. You'll lose about ten per cent of your body weight, have to put up with lots of kooky clap-your-hands-Christians, bad water, cold showers, bedbugs, blistered feet, shin splints, sore hips, then a whole lot of crack-pot healers out there to fix them. There'll be heavies and lager louts along the way who think they can perform miracles with women. And bigots, who hate all races other than their own. That's what people do when overseas. Like children, everyone comes out to play."

"Like on Hope Street."

"Why not! And here you'll meet lots of cyclists on their flash bikes, lots of gears, goggles, helmets, all in snazzy Lycra, like you rock climbers wear. But these ones are in a hurry, even running you off paths. Some do the thousand kilometer pilgrimage from Seville up to Santiago in as little as ten days. Speed has nothing to do with it. Take it slowly. That's the way love is. How else are you ever meant to contemplate love?"

He spoke his final sentence with full seriousness, staring at her with hardened eyes.

"Gee! Thanks, Uncle. Thanks for making some allowances."

"You're going to hear lots of fantastical stories that will make not a word of sense to you. Be careful. You'll be tired. Kept awake half the night by thieves and snoring. You'll all be sleeping in together. No sex, either. Single beds. It's a religious pilgrimage. Creaking springs only keep the other pilgrims awake. Keep your libido in check."

Fergus was loving every moment of this.

"What's libido?"

"Sex drive."

"Is that right? I thought it had something to do with swimming."

"That's lido."

She poked her tongue out at him.

"Just watch out for those filthy French pilgrims. They have sex almost anywhere." Fergus shuddered dramatically in his chair. "It's a jungle out there, Tess. Man's a terrible creature. A beast. No more than an animal."

"Bigot yourself. Hang on a minute. Maria's French. Who's this Elena woman anyway?"

Fergus ignored her.

He immediately changed the subject by pointing to the near empty wine bottle on the table.

"You'll need plenty of this to get to sleep at nights, even though you'll be exhausted. Better get used to it now."

"Are you trying to get me drunk? I know you. Creeping me out again? How are we supposed to put up with all of this?"

"Put up with it by making it fun. Accept it for what it is. Learn to say no to people. Be strong. You'll have plenty of money, all you need, and all the time in the world to do it. When you finish you'll feel so confident you'll never walk along talking to your shoes again."

"I'm all for going slow, Uncle. I burned my Lycra shorts along with my school uniform ages ago. It'll be a walk in the park. A cinch." Teresa raised her eyebrows, staring to the sky.

"But why do it at all?" she then asked, puzzled. "You want me to think about what I'm doing? Contemplate love? I've never been more sure of anything in my life."

Fergus leaned across again with a whispering voice again. "I know that. Just get out of here for a while. We're all come over, see you both when it's done. Have a good time." Fergus gave a forced smile. "If you're too frightened to be together now, no one will know over there, will they? Let's see how grown up you are."

"Yeah, right. Come back looking like a couple of scarecrows. Pa will be calling me 'Stick-Insect' again."

"More like a couple of greyhounds. Thin as whipcords. Fighting fit. Soldiers. You'll be ready for anything after this. It's not hard. Twenty miles a day. Lots of mountains. It shouldn't still be snowing in April."

"You really expect me to wear those second-hand shoes? Will you be sending us onto Everest after France and Greece?"

"No. We'll get you some proper walking boots. You'll have to break them in first in hot places, out on the open roads, through lots of puddles before you go. Plenty of talcum for dryness. Lots of pairs of socks. You'll have to learn how to pack, cinch a waist-belt. Keep the backpacks off your shoulders. It's a great circuit-breaker. Do you both the world of good. Inwardly, you'll feel great."

Fergus got up, moved off to fetch a cigar.

The Detail is in the Devil's Guide

Teresa immediately reached across for the Michener tome, opening it out to a bookmarked page. Fergus had underlined some passages. The ink looked fresh. His words 'Dirty French Liar!' stood out boldly in square brackets heading one page. Another of his jokes. Curiously, there was no paper strip here, but a tarnished looking white feather marking the page.

She began to read. The author quoted the finding of an ancient book, generally regarded as the first known travel guide ever written, circa 1170, describing how more than half a million people moved along the pilgrim roads, the glories and hardships of it. It was written, at the request of the Church, by a French priest, Aymery de Picaud, who lived along one of the pilgrim routes. The priest spoke badly of the Spanish yet not of the French, especially the peasants of Navarra, on the exact route mapped out which Teresa was to take.

'These people are badly dressed. They eat poorly and drink worse. Using no spoons, they plunge their hands into the common pot and drink from the same goblet. When one sees them feed, one thinks he is seeing pigs in their gluttony; and when one hears them speak, he thinks of dogs baying. They are perverse, perfidious, disloyal, corrupted, voluptuous, expert in every violence, cruel and quarrelsome, and anyone would murder a Frenchman, for one sou. Shamefully they have sex with animals.'

Teresa turned. Fergus was at her shoulder, reading with her, grinning inanely. She slammed the book shut in disgust.

Teresa shook her head. "I sure hope human nature's changed a bit since then."

"I wouldn't ever go so far as saying that."

"No, you wouldn't, would you! So people walk the pilgrimage unprotected?" Teresa said grabbing at her refilled glass.

"Some used to take knights with them for protection from the French and German rogues, so Santiago built a contingent of knights of their own. Then, of course, what happened? Knights would challenge one another along the way, jousting to see who was the best and bravest. It's a different world today. Just lots of pickpockets and a bunch of drunken fools. Go to bed early at night. Nothing much good happens after midnight." Fergus paused, then muttered sententiously. "Early to bed, early to rise."

"You really do enjoy geeing me up, don't you? Like a horse. You won't beat me, you know that. I won't fold. For you, or for anyone else."

"I'm sure you won't. That's exactly what I wanted to hear. You'll be safe enough. Have lots of fun. You'll see splendid churches which took over two hundred years to build. Marvel at the beauty of the human spirit." Fergus was all serious again.

"Explain that St. Jacob's shell to me. The one you once gave me for my birthday. It's all to do with the pilgrimage, isn't it? You showed me that painting by Carravagio once. There was a man wearing that shell in the headband of his hat."

Fergus idly opened the book to a marked page.

"You'll sometimes see the word 'scallop' on fish menus in restaurant written as 'peregrina.' Same as the word for pilgrim."

There was a short poem by Sir Walter Raleigh. He turned the book towards her. Teresa read it aloud.

> 'Give me my scallop shell of quiet,
> My staff of faith to walk upon,
> My scrip of joy, immortal diet,
> My bottle of salvation,
> My gown of glory, hope's true gage.
> And thus I'll take my pilgrimage.'

"So you remembered the scallop shell, did you?. You'll see that symbol everywhere on the Roman milestones along the way. Jacob's Hebrew for St. James. Santiago is a contraction of Santo Diego, Saint James. The grooves in the shell are supposed to signify the many roads to be taken, all pointing towards Santiago. James was once supposed to have saved a knight from drowning. Legend has it when the knight resurfaced he was covered with scallop shells."

"Was it a miracle?"

"Signs and wonders."

"But you don't believe in miracles, do you?."

"Doesn't matter what I believe. You believe. You must see things for yourself, make up your own mind, separate the true from the fanciful."

"Why? To doubt them, like you do?"

"Not at all. Many things you'll see will be most worthwhile."

"So, poor little silly Dorothy here has to go trouping off five hundred miles along the yellow brick road to Oz, does she, just to get herself another certificate?"

"Not at all. Sixty two miles, one hundred kilometers, on foot will still get you the certificate; twice that for cyclists. Some still do it today on horseback, others have a donkey for their bags."

"Where do we stay?"

"There are lots of hostels which house forty to one hundred and fifty. They cost a donation only. It may have changed by now. Walkers get preference. They give you a three course meal plus bread at nights costing about eight euros for pilgrims today. Cheapest holiday in the world. It will be like you out shopping at your Thrift shops on Saturday morning."

"And we're both going all the way."

"I don't want you to miss anything."

"No, you wouldn't. Why not just do the sixty two miles?"

"There's a town, Sarria, about seventy miles out from Santiago. Lots of pilgrims line up there to make their start. Even school children. It's the shortest distance for pilgrim's travel. Up to 10,000 children walk it some years. Remember, at this point you'll have just trudged over four hundred miles. This will be a true measure to test your charity. Some days you'll feel like murdering somebody—christened with dirt, shoulders tighter than a vice, feet probably covered in blisters, while these pilgrims here will all be spotless, full of vigor. You'll be aching, using your pilgrim staffs as crutches, and all you'll see in front of you is happy faces doing less than one fifth the distance and achieving the same goal. A certificate." Fergus chuckled to himself.

"I don't care. I like certificates. We 'Shell' Overcome."

"Nice pun. Yes, you can. I'm sure of that. I just don't want you going off ill-prepared thinking it's no more than a walk in the park."

Teresa grinned. "You're the limit. I feel like an outcast coming home only to be sent away again. The Prodigal Daughter returns. No fatted calf for me. Just sent out on another journey."

Fergus lit a cigar. "Harsh, isn't it! Fun, too. You were the one who wanted to go off to the city. But what an adventure this will be. Go visit the churches in the evenings. The paintings will astound you—these figures are real human beings, there's laughter in many of them, a multitude of angels, Jesus standing amongst it watching, finding it good. You like that sort of thing. Watching."

Teresa sighed, still not convinced. "Isn't there something easier we can do?"

"Sure. Go off to charm school for a month, drink whisked vegetable juice with a stick of celery in it. There's month courses you can do to learn to be a debutante. Full days of dress-up, fine dining, good manners, learning to dance properly, then you have a formal ball at the end with an introduction to some figurehead of state. That'd be much easier, wouldn't it! Sheltered. Probably more healthy too, if truth be known."

"You'd hate anything fancy like that. But why should everything be so hard, Uncle? Wave after wave of it. You go and buy me a pair of roller skates then expect me to be doing triple axles, figure eights on thin ice within a week."

"No I don't. Whoever said anything worthwhile was easy? This journey will have you both tempered like steel by the time you return."

"Is it all to do with your boxing, or is it that Communist stuff you picked up in South America? You should've been born back in biblical days. They were prepared to sacrifice their first born. Don't you think I'm tough enough?"

Fergus laughed. He refilled her glass. "We don't have any real idea what tough is. I've meet people on the plains of South America who had so little they believed to have anything is to lose."

"If they have nothing in the first place, how can they lose? Nothing tough in that."

"Yes they had. They had a spouse, a child, a pig, a chicken or two to spare. That's about it. They know what it's like to lose."

He began making light of what he'd just said. "It'll be tough. Even for sex. You'll be in pilgrim hostels along the way. You can't book them. First in, first served. It is easy to get beds in April. Singles. Some hostels are unisex. Others not. There will be guys strutting their stuff in front of you, no clothes on. Further to," Fergus said pompously, before puffing his freshly lit cigar, "at the end of the day, when all's said and done, after just having walked thirty miles, even more, you'll find your feet so sore, shoulders aching. You'll feel more tired than a couple of baggage handlers. But you'll be at it again next morning. Walking, that is." He giggled before the smile suddenly dissolved. "You've always liked climbing trees. Walls. Try your energy on mountain passes. One must progress, never stagnate."

Teresa hit his arm.

He then dismissed the subject with a flick of the hand. "You'll find plenty of haystacks, lots of shaded wooded places, even disused cattle shelters along the route. You're both to have a real good time. Plenty to see. Just get safely from pit-stop to pit-stop. All the rest's been done for you It's safe, much safer than the cities. There'll be thousands of you, all with a similar purpose. No one kills pilgrims anymore. But watch out for the horses, too. People ride it. And quickly. They send a pack animal ahead with another rider. It will open your eyes to life. Eat, drink, be merry. You'll have plenty of money. And you're not to live on bags of crackers, either. Don't eat the pilgrim diet of pig knuckles and blood sausage. When you're hungry, stop at a trucker's restaurant. Eat red steaks, lots of ice cream for sugars. Rest up. Don't overdo it. Take your time. We'll wait. Someone will bus out, walk you back into the city. If you want us to."

"We'll be ok. We'll do this, even if it kills us."

There was a long silence. Teresa's face turned serious.

"Will there be bad men out on the roads, Uncle?" Teresa asked with the jitters.

"Women, too. Always will be. Pilgrims have always misbehaved themselves. Many are still refused beds at the refuges today. Drunkenness. Drugs. There's most interesting jails along the way, especially in Santiago, all designed for bad pilgrims. Still today, locals are very wary of rascals. You behave yourselves. Be polite. Offer them small gifts at hostels. You're going to have to learn lots of polite expressions. Don't demand anything from anybody."

"I never have."

"I know that. And that's why you'll make it. Pretend you're poor. Don't flash your money about. Still today in Flanders one prisoner a year is made to serve out his or her custodial sentence by walking the pilgrimage."

"What will the weather be like?"

"Like life. One hopes for sunshine, prepares for rain."

"Yeah, right. Sounds real cheesy coming from you."

"Weather often disappoints people on holidays. You're going to be cold for the first time in your life. There'll be mud, rain, mist. Mist sometimes closes in on you. Some days up in the mountains it's so misty you can't even distinguish the numerals on the way-markers. You might see snow. There can be hurricane winds which will tear the things hanging from your backpacks."

"What hangs from our backpacks?"

"Last night's washing, which hasn't yet dried."

"No Laundromats?"

"Yes, in the cities. Often only buckets in the towns."

"I'll handle it. I'm a soldier. It'll be far easier than handling those druggies up on Hope. The Church will protect me. Do you think I'll achieve enlightenment along the way?"

She was not being sarcastic. Not quite. Just wary of his signs and wonders.

Fergus laughed out loudly. "If only you knew what you were saying. There were more drugs on the way to Santiago than you can ever imagine. All medieval pilgrims got high on LSD. I mean, all. Every one. They were our first real 'road-trippers' in history. And it gave some of them gangrene, no less. They became convulsive with an illness which brought on hallucinations. They thought they were being 'possessed.' Or achieving enlightenment. Don't think you can ever get away from drugs."

It appeared that he found this amusing.

"Good one, Uncle. Typical. Sending me out into the jungle. Am I really supposed to believe all that?"

"Yes. Better believe it. It's what they called St. Anthony's Fire. Medieval monks would touch the afflicted with their sacred specters believing that was the only cure for the sickness. And, lo and behold, it worked. Praise the Lord! A miracle. As they approached Santiago the pilgrims began to lose all symptoms of illness. Cured. Completely." Fergus cast his eyes heavenwards. "Signs and wonders," he said again, look of amazement in his face.

"You don't believe that. You don't believe in miracles. Where did they get LSD from way back then?"

"Ergot-ism—an intoxication brought on by eating rye bread infected with ergot. It's a fungus which produces the same alkaloids found in LSD. It was an illness prevalent in Europe in those years, especially France where rye was more abundant. It caused painful eruptions of the skin. As they progressed towards Santiago out on the plains of Spain, rye became less and less. Wheat was the staple. Wheat's not susceptible to ergot. They ate different bread. Symptoms fell away. It wasn't the Church which saved them at all."

"Those dirty French again." Teresa pondered.

"You're right. Deserved it."

"I bet you tease Father Kevin over that one." Teresa grinned.

Fergus smiled. "Sometimes at Sunday Mass as Kevin faces the congregation reciting the 'Our Father,' when he comes to 'Give us this day our daily bread' he sees me with a drugged-out look on my face, nervously holding up my hands, fingers crossed, mouthing 'gluten-free.'"

"Please! No more jokes. What say one of us gets sick?"

"I'll pay your medical insurances. But hospitals are free to pilgrims—feet problems, hanging toe nails, blisters which get infected, so forth. There'll be plenty of that. But hospitals are not free for drug abusers . . . pregnancy."

Teresa rested her head on her uncle's shoulder. "There's no chance of that now, is there! Anyway, what other wonderful religious surprises are there in store for us?"

"There's lots of religious stories which will make your head spin. Just accept them for what they are. There's also a church along the Camino that's worthwhile seeing, only for its pornography. It's unique. It's down from Basque country in Cantabria. Go there by bus when you get to Brugos, then return. You'll not be cheating. It's often called the 'naughty church.' Catholic clergy have never condemned it. Visit it. Go and ask the sexton to explain it to you. Find out why."

"PORNOGRAPHY? Explained by a SEX-TON!" Teresa reached for the bottle again.

"Yes. A church minder. A kind of sacristan. Just below the eaves outside is a running frieze of carved animals and people having sex. You won't see pictures like this in the Bible."

"I don't believe you." Teresa looked at him aghast.

"You'd better believe me."

"Then I wouldn't miss it for the world, would I!"

"That's my girl!"

Give Me a Break, will you?

They took a long break, at Fergus's suggestion, so Teresa should eat something, rest, lay off his bottles of wine. She came back to him, soon enough. "Back to the pulpit, Uncle. I'm here for your supernatural skills." She pulled a childish face before speaking impatiently.

"Tell me. Seriously. I want to know. Why make a pilgrimage at all?"

"Everyone should." He answered as though it were self evident.

"What? Religious pilgrimage?"

"Heavens, no!" Fergus threw his hands in the air. "Any kind of pilgrimage. You can make it for a song, a rock group, a painting, a book, a play, a piece of sculpture; go to Gracelands, Broadway, Nashville, people even make a kind of pilgrimage to Silicon Valley. Broaden your horizons, but do it with purpose, not just traveling aimlessly. Lots of people go to Ibiza in the Balearic Isles, Mykonnos in Greece for sex and booze; that's fine, but I don't think it's for you. Do you remember that song by Paul Simon? Taking his son down to Gracelands?"

"Sure do. 'The Mississippi Delta was shining like a National guitar.'" She quoted the opening line.

"I reckon his pilgrimage was worthwhile for just giving us a song lyric like that."

"Do people really make pilgrimage for a painting?"

"Of course. People go to the 'Vincent' Museum in Amsterdam. They play the Don McLean song there every day. Vincent was a kind of religious pilgrim himself. He'd suddenly decide he'd had enough of life. Pack up a few things, take off, walk for hundreds of miles. He was a religious man."

"Didn't he cut off his ear then shoot himself in the chest, then die?"

"Sure. Doesn't mean he wasn't religious. Not for us to judge him."

"Do people really make a pilgrimage to see a piece of carved stone?"

"Absolutely. You remember Michelangelo's 'Pieta'?"

"The one where Mary holds Jesus in her arms down from the Cross?"

"That's it. When T.S. Eliot first saw it at the Vatican he immediately fell on his knees. His brother was with him, thought he was nuts."

"That's Catholics for you."

"That's just it. They weren't Catholic."

"What about me, then? Why do I get to slog it out on the road to Santiago de Compostela. What's the word mean, anyway?"

"No one's absolutely sure. Santo Diego's a shortening of St. James. They reckon Compostela's Latin for a field under the stars. Or a 'compostum.' That field could mean a cemetery. They believe the cathedral there was built over a large burial ground."

"So, let me get this straight. We're going to go five hundred miles, and by skanks's pony, to get to a cemetery that's over a thousand years old? Gee, thanks, Uncle. You're a real pal. That should really get our endorphins going."

Fergus grinned back wryly. "Don't worry. The last few hundred miles are much flatter, far easier to walk. Anyway. Walking has always been the better way to go to a cemetery, hasn't it?"

"You're sick in the head."

"And it gets even worse, my girl. That's if you're looking for purpose. Sir Francis Drake once wanted to attack it, sack the city believing it was a center of dangerous superstitions. And Martin Luther once remarked about the Compostela shrine 'No one knows whether what lies in the apostle's tomb is a dead dog or a dead horse.' But who cares! In the end. You'll meet people of all persuasions. And of none at all. Everyone likes taking Sunday strolls, don't they?. After all, it's the day of rest!"

"You're impossible," Teresa said abstractedly. "No one's ever going to pin you down to anything, are they? What is the purpose, then?"

"Purpose? Point? If there has to be one, then it is that you walk five hundred miles to form a queue outside the Oficino del Peregrono in Rio do Vilan. When you reach the office upstairs you'll present your pilgrim passports with all the daily stamps to verify you've completed it. You'll be asked questions about your purpose, and, if you say it's spiritual, you'll be presented with a parchment certificate. No A+. Just a pass. Like life. You get up each morning. Yawn. Tip the blood out of your boots. You then get on the road to work. Are you on for it, or not?"

"I'm for it. We'll do it just to spite you."

"Good girl. That's the spirit. Wouldn't want it any other way. But it will make you talk to lots of different people. You'll have to, and struggle to make yourself understood. You'll meet people of every faith, even Muslims. They are not pilgrims. Why would they be? Just observers and tourists. Centuries of fierce battles between Christian and Muslim were fought along the Way. They've every right to be there. Talk to them. They'll wish you no harm. The Moors and Jews were ethnically cleansed from the country. Find out about it. Nobody's asking you or anyone else to take responsibility for it now. Just responsible enough to find out."

"How are we supposed to do it if we can't speak the language?"

"Guide books. Read histories. You're going to have to learn some Spanish. Spaniards like politeness, not just straight demands for beds or meals. It's their country, their house. It's pointless to dislike them because you don't understand them. You'll have to talk to get what you want. Many are kind, refusing to take money, even for bandaging your feet. It's considered a Christian duty and reward to help pilgrims. Be confident. Expect the best. You'll be astonished. The churches and architecture and paintings are awesome. You'll see Romanesque, Gothic, Baroque, Corinthian from Ages when much was achieved. Designed just for you, Tess, the pilgrim. To fill you with awe."

Teresa looked at her uncle with a mixture of disbelief and dismay. The ultimate trickster.

Yet she also knew that she had to get away.

*   *   *

Fergus changed the subject back to his original, that of April.

Teresa had now far too much to drink, steeling herself for what was to come. She felt under the pump while Fergus simply talked more with alcohol. She wished more simply.

"Why don't you stick with your designer waters today? Or just a splash of wine."

"Fat chance. I'll take what comes."

Fergus started again. A pompous mouthful followed. Teresa kept quiet, waiting for it to end.

"August is Spain's hottest month. It's crammed with pilgrims, too uncomfortable for you to travel. April's best time to go. Springtime.

Winters are bitter, but its thawing traditionally created a wanderlust in people when all the black trees turned to green again. Chaucer began his Canterbury Tales with the line 'When that April with his[its] showers soote'[sweet]. Those tales are all about pilgrims going from London to Canterbury on a pilgrimage. His Wife of Bath spoke of having done the Santiago trail, too. That was around 1260. Then T.S. Eliot began 'The Waste Land' six hundred years later remembering Chaucer with the line 'April is the cruelest month, breeding Lilacs out of the dead land.' That's also about a journey. April's the right time to go, Tess. Right time for pilgrimage. Don't treat it as a walking event with lots of way stations." He repeated with a smirk. "Everyone's got to make a journey someday. Straighten out their ideas. May as well get the penances done now before the real sins start."

"I haven't committed any sins. Not yet, anyway. But you're right, Uncle. April's the best time to go. It's just like you. Sweet. And cruel."

Fergus did not know what to say to that. He waited a few moments before backtracking. "Only teasing you about the sins. I used to argue this out with Kevin all the time. Protestant Reformers were against such pilgrimages. I liked to take their point of view. They said pilgrimage is neither a Christian duty nor was is it devotional. They wrote it off as childish, just a useless work."

"Why did you go, then?"

"Go? I went to AVOID miracles. Beat the booze, live on loaves and fishes for a while, make sure my drinking bottles never changed to wine. Point is, I truly believe you two won't get sick of one another over there. It'll give you something only you two can share. Have fun. Dance it."

"Why do something that's childish and useless?" Teresa countered.

"So you can learn about the true meaning of useless. It's like your night classes of poetry and song. Not everything has to be useful, not in a practical sense."

"I once remember you telling me. 'If you want to be really happy, don't ask for too much.' Thanks, Uncle." She leaned her head on his shoulder. "Guess I ought to count my blessings. Hundred years ago I'd be sleeping on beds of straw. We wouldn't want to be caught laying on any beds of roses now, would we!"

"Think nothing of it." Fergus extinguished his cigar out in the ashtray. "And you're welcome. After all, it's a Christian pilgrimage, you're supposed to suffer. Most mattresses in the hostels are still pretty lumpy today." Fergus chuckled.

"I'll ignore that. You've never ever showed me your certificate. Is it downstairs? Did you have it stamped by two churches at the end of each day?"

"Yes, I had it stamped. No, I didn't collect the certificate in the end." Fergus gave a soft smile.

"You headed straight for a bar, didn't you? Whiskey on the rocks?"

"More like hobbled off for rocks of ice to pack my knees for the tendonitis. No. I didn't drink again for a long time. I took aspirin. Anti-inflammatory tablets. I had more fleabites than a camel's armpit because of the beds along the way. But it's ok, I'm on my feet again. And the drink." He saluted her with his glass, then turned away.

"Then you're not only hopeless but useless as well, Uncle, aren't you?"

"Yes, my girl. I hope so. About as useless as a song. I wandered about so I could wonder less, be more aware. We should all have an aching suspense for something."

Signs and Wonders

The day passed. They were at it again the next day. Fergus began singing from the Psalmists. 'Thanks be to God for wine that maketh glad the heart of man.'

Teresa felt like tanking herself on another. She couldn't hope to keep up. Yesterday she'd become decidedly drunk. It didn't help any. More she drank, more it kindled new fears.

"What am I really in for? How crazy are the religious stories going to get?"

"Signs and wonders! You'll get more magic here than in any of your Harry Potter books. The only difference is these churches and castles are for real. They're magnificent, in their own way. But the stories! They're about as dodgy as some of the bars along the way. Some miracles you'll hear about are just stories rehashed from other countries, spun by foreign pilgrims over the centuries. They're like fairy-tales. Barbarous, gruesome, evil, but all's well again by morning. Remember, in order to be canonized there must be proof of at least two miracles. Here's one for you."

Fergus paused and reached across for the James Mitchener book on the table.

"Here's part of a miracle." He pulled the white feather out from a page. "There's a church you'll come across called Santo Domingo de la Calzada. It means St. Dominic of the Walkway. This one can really test your belief. This miracle is known as 'pendu dependu'—the hanged man un-hanged. The town has a cathedral of its own. It's full of treasure and has a magnificent tomb. For five hundred years it's had a permanent chicken coop inside the west transept, which houses a live white hen and cock. You go inside the church. You see lots of porcelain figures of chickens. Often, you'll hear a cock crow. There's a garden nearby where you can visit these fowls. They all make their appearances in turn in the church. These chickens are said to be the direct descendants of a miracle."

Fergus waved the white feather back and forth at her.

"Like my goose and gander?" Teresa remembered them sadly.

"Not quite. A miracle didn't save them. They were road-kill. Taken by a skulk of foxes. This one is more like a near death experience."

"Go on, creep me out with it." She raised her glass, sipped it, swiveled her lips, imitating Fergus's voice. "Tell me what amazing signs and wonders occurred in the aforesaid town. Tickle my beliefs with your feather."

She knew that Fergus was just revving her up. Another one of his tricks. False expectations.

"Is this going to be another of those violent once-upon-a-time-story, like in fairytales? I get the feeling you're the fox in the hen house this time."

"Decide that for yourself."

"All right.. Hit me with it. I'm putting my faith on the line here. Give me this day our daily drug of bread. Once upon a time . . ."

"Once upon a time there was a handsome young German pilgrim traveling to Santiago de Compostela with his parents. They stopped off at an inn at Santo Domingo where the innkeeper's daughter fell hopelessly in love with him, but the pilgrim boy rejected her advances because of his rigid piety. He was free of carnal thoughts . . . just like you, Tess."

"Get on with the damn story," Teresa muttered drowsily.

"So angry was she at being scorned by him, she secreted a silver goblet in his backpack, then had him accused of stealing it. She had the Constables go out, stop him from continuing along the pilgrimage. Found guilty by the local authorities, he was condemned to hang. His parents were not aware of this as they continued on to Santiago, thinking their son was on the road ahead. On their return through Santo Domingo they found him hanging from gallows, miraculously alive on the gibbet."

"Chickens, Uncle. I wanna hear why there's all those feather bearing chickens in a church." Teresa slurred.

"Be patient, girl. You can just hear them clucking away in the sacristy, can't you!" He waved the feather again. "I have the feather to prove it."

"Yeah, right. Like the bats up in your belfry."

"The parents rushed off to the local sheriff, a big, rotund man they found seated for his dinner. They informed him their son was still alive, demanding he be cut down. The sheriff jeered at them with disbelief. He said the pilgrim thief was no more alive than this cock and hen he was about to consume off his platter. Whereupon, hey presto! The cock and hen stood up, flew off his plate. The cock began to crow. It was a miracle!"

"Whoa! Just a moment." Teresa said in accusatory tone. "This is Detective Colombo speaking here." She raised her finger in the air. "Did they have their feathers back, or did they not?"

"One can only presume. Fully re-fledged, I guess. They would have to have been in order to fly." Fergus laughed.

"Yeah, right. Can just imagine the cock. 'Give us back our feathers or put us back in the roasting dish again—it's too darn cold out here.'"

Fergus gave her a stern look. "You mustn't ever question miracles, my girl. Anyway. The pilgrim was cut down and received a full pardon. That's it. Amen."

"Hang on a minute, Buster! How did he survive the gallows?"

"That's the question on which theologians disagree. Either it was St. James the Apostle who caught and held him by his feet as he fell, preventing him from strangling, or Santo Dominic, the local town saint. Take your pick." Fergus struck out his neck three times, swiveling side to side like a chicken. "Pick, pick, pick."

Teresa mulled the question over a few moments. Suddenly she gave him a cheeky grin.

"Wouldn't that be so-o-o funny! You go to Sunday Mass there, and when the priest intones 'In the Name of the Father'—all you can hear is cluck-cluck-cluck, 'and of the Son,'—even louder cluck-cluck-cluck—'and of the' . . . then you get this horrendous COCK-A-DOODLE-DOOO!"

Between action of blessing herself, Teresa stood, flapping her elbows at her sides doing the Bird Dance. She and Sharn loved doing that. Fergus snorted laughter.

"Anyway," she settled then asked more soberly, "whatever became of the innkeeper's daughter?"

"Good girl, Tess." Fergus smiled at her benignly. "You've certainly grown up at last. That the only real sensible question worth pondering."

"No it isn't. It's a sad story. Too sad even to think about."

"Why's that?" Fergus was curious.

"I'd never let love ever turn to hate."

Fergus reached over, took her hand on the table.

"I know that, Tess. That's why you deserve only the best we can give you."

"You really are the limit, aren't you? You're an apostle yourself. My Uncle Fergus, the Doubting Thomas."

Fergus didn't answer. He picked up the white feather again and waved it back and forth.

The Pilgrimage

El Camino de Santiago—The Way of St. James. Everywhere there are statues of the Apostle to remind you—by roadside, in towns and cities, plazas and cathedrals, depicted either as Apostle, fellow Pilgrim, or warlike Moor-Slayer, Matamoros. As a Pilgrim, he is depicted in traditional garb striding along in a brown cloak, floppy hat, with walking stick, wearing the symbolic shell, gourd for water, and scandals. Then often seen among other pilgrim statues, distinguished from them as carrying a book.

That month of April came around for Teresa soon enough. From the French Pyrenees they girt their loins like two rooky rickshaw drivers, heads down to pricking winds, black clouds under blue as they began their trek across the top of Spain following the emblem of seashells to Santiago. There was to be no countdown of kilometers. They rose early with sunlight, walked all day, judged the distance to designated hostels before darkness set in. They felt as delicately moist as the new Spring blooms, rugged up in colored jackets before high summer heat would see pilgrims dried as bookmark flowers.

The bulk of pilgrims form a moving caravan one direction, but that's much later in July-August. Twenty per cent of them now are cyclists traveling the mishmash of paved roads, byways, ancient routes, alongside open fields, up narrow paths with their stone fences of gray slate. Pilgrim buses and cars abound. Many modern supplicants still trudge en masse, trimming their backpacks down to basic woolens, blister kits, phrasebooks, memory chips, often to ten kilo and under.

During Holy years, the July of every five, numbers dramatically increase. July 25ᵗʰ is the annual Feast of St. James.

Whatever the reasons for taking it, Fergus assured them that, other than 'a plenary indulgence for remission of sin,'(his tongue in cheek), it was a be a front-row seat history lesson. Teresa read all the books she could, finding that Goethe once wrote 'Europe was formed on the road to Santiago,' an exaggeration perhaps, yet still mindful of its importance. Charlemagne marched armies along it. El Cid is buried along its Way. Pilgrims from Eastern Europe, England, France, Portugal, Nordic, Adriatic countries, to name but some, have made the journey throughout the centuries.

By order of King Herod Agrippa, the Apostle James was beheaded. His followers then brought his body back to what became Santiago de Compostela, where he'd once preached. There it remained unknown for eight hundred years.

They picked up their permissions to walk at the French Pyrenees, paid for their credentials, the same one given to kings, nobles, saints, soldiers, clerics, man, woman and child before them, then trudged through the regions of Navarra, La Rioja and Castilla y Leon onto Galicia, kicking over stones similar to ones Fergus had once given Teresa as pets to talk to up in her tree, wore scallop shells round their necks on pieces of red silk thread, carried pilgrim staff in hand. They came across cairns of stones, sometimes rugged piles where pilgrims placed a rock or stone in silence as a votive prayer to express intention or need. Traditionally, this was the only reward, the first to make placement had the right to then tell a story of saints and miracles from their country to the other pilgrims.

There are now some three hundred simple refuges along the Camino with the principle of first in, first served. Things had changed since Fergus' day. Hostels now stamp the concertina passports of pilgrims, for convenience. Travelers arrive late. Churches are locked. For fifteen euros, or thereabouts, pilgrims are fed, given a bed. Hotels can cost up to one hundred euros a night. Teresa didn't have either the money or wish for them. They would tough it out in poverty. As uncle said they should.

Some days they'd both goof along seemingly endless roads, red fallow fields under heavy backpacks, their feet now padded with bandages. Pilgrims are still given traditional herbs to soothe blisters at hostels. They're offered fennel boiled in milk as an energy drink; vinegar mixed with salt for tired feet.

They'd stop, speak English or broken Spanish phrases with other pilgrims—young travelers, lovers, bookish aesthetes, epicures there for food and evening pleasures, historians, priests, and many who looked like vagabonds—all wishing one another well. Whether the reasons for being there were personal, emotional or spiritual, that did not seem the right question to ask. Perhaps it was just the challenge of achieving a reachable goal, testing ones stamina and fitness, a walking holiday.

Teresa recalled how Fergus said. 'Don't care much about reasons. Reasons don't matter much. It clears the mind. I walked it in sandals. Often bare-footed. To this day I'm still not too sure why. A reckless man back then, I guess. And it makes you learn to take only essentials of life with you. Your mother will have new clothes for you when you arrive in Santiago. Take your spyglass. See the beauty of the world. Stained glass windows. Church ceilings. Walk with your anorak hood down in order to see wildflowers, smell herbs, hear birds sing. Imagine it as if from up in your trees. A place where nothing can harm you.'

Teresa sat on ancient gates, rested up against Roman milestones, climbed various trees—birches, chestnuts, even the poplars—went past lush meadows, across fallow fields, alongside dusty hedges. Like Spring itself, they felt they were pushing their way through. Sometimes she felt like scaling the ornate Gothic frames of city gates. They sought out shade of haystacks in fields, oftentimes rolled in grasses before touching down for life giving waters of fountain springs in town squares. They heard of one fountain spring in Estella(locked up at night) where pilgrims could fill their water bottles with wine. They did, as they took in fragrance of sunflowers, saw fields of new maize bursting through beside grapevines; talked to pilgrims who'd walked for months on end, as though days didn't matter, holding out for nothing better. They did not avail themselves of donkey or horse rides, have their backpacks taken ahead by pilgrim buses. Teresa gritted her teeth, lost a full stone in weight over that month, began looking more like a gypsy tramp while stalking doggedly on. 'If Fergus could do this to beat the booze, I'll do it for the glooms.'

*   *   *

Basque country seemed a land more ancient than any postcard could ever depict, a region of people who'd existed even before Indo-European tribes arrived. An old saying goes "Before God was God and boulders were boulders, the Basques were already Basques." From the Pyrenees to the end, they'd come across farmers beside their docile, cream-colored cows, piebald pigs, men who'd offer fresh apples to the lone couple with their pilgrim staffs passing their gates. Others offered them hand pressed curds, small cubes of sheep's milk cheese flavored with anise. The farmers did not speak English, yet always refused taking money. The people in Basque country seemed so old, shy, timid men of such ancient ways.

Fergus had shown Teresa a copy of her grandmother's school catechism. It stated that one of the acts of Christian charity was give alms to traveling pilgrims.

Chaucer, so it seemed, was right—gray skies did turn blue in April, black trees slowly turned green. Teresa would stop on pathways to view the orange spotted mushrooms of Springtime. Sometimes they'd shelter from flurries of winds under trees, where they'd find protected clumps of crocuses. She'd dreamily place flowers in her hair. They'd stop to view tractors spraying vines against mildew from winter rains, stare at pots dripping with new Spring flowers on village windowsills whenever they entered a town. They'd eat simple foods at night, not chancing the hanging sausages but tried octopus, salted anchovies, fresh bonito, thick soups and cheeses, quince jelly, even the famous almond tart of Santiago. Avoiding local water, they'd wash their food down with cheap house wines. The spirit of Spring moved them along. Teresa began to sense meaning from new experience.

They'd stay in dormitories yet to be filled by rush of summer travelers, sometimes pushing their beds together, turning on their sides, looking into one another's eyes, stretching their arms across, holding hands out from their sleeping bags. They'd rest up for next day when they'd move off again, happy as though off to a feast.

Fergus had given Teresa an ultra sonic whistle to scare away wild dogs. There were none. No wolves either, nor bandits in wait today for the devout or naïve, nor plagues, contaminated water of long ago. Yet there were still long days of drumming rains up the mountains. They got shin sore, tired, grateful to have their pilgrim staffs for the steep descents.

They talked. They talked all day. There were no fights, bickering out of tiredness; arguments as to what to eat, who to carry the artifacts, wash clothes out at evening while the other e-mailed home. They were not used to fighting. Neither was in any spiritual pain, gnashing their teeth for sin. They'd not sinned. Yet this journey seemed no punishment to them either as they continued happily on their way.

Some small towns seemed almost empty. A beaded curtain kept the flies out from what was less obviously the local store. Some places offered no more than plates of greasy beans and boiled chicken at evening. They didn't complain. They'd passed bountiful fields beneath velvety hills glistening with vines, rows of cherry and apple trees.

There'd been black-faced sheep, short legged pigs free ranging; they'd once sheltered from the sun under giant heart-shaped leaves.

Teresa would stop and gaze in shop windows of upscale village boutiques which awaited the tourist buses. There would be thousand dollar leather coats, sweaters, skirts, belts, shoes, blouses and jewelry. She'd grin to herself. If only Fergus were here. And Sharn. Sharn would find her way with him.

Sometimes at evening, perhaps from tiredness, Teresa felt herself suddenly slipping back into childhood when offering some of her food. 'Want some?' as she'd often say outside Spiro's store. This time Dominic said 'yes.' Their hearts were satisfied, marching like two soldiers at peace.

They'd fight, kid one another, act up, just for the fun of it. They'd outgrown childish tantrums long ago. Used to years of silence at home around his bossy sister, Dominic found it no effort to talk now. Competition between them was always friendly and relaxed. Dominic was the fitter for walking. He'd sometimes walk backwards, pretend to thread water, provoke her by feigning complaint. It was like a continuation of childhood, uncomplicated, as if still too young for opinions. They resorted to playful banter. There was not much to learn of one another. No secrets. Nothing to cause pain. They complained while not wanting this to stop. There were no risks in saying anything. No mistrusts. They each had an iPod, loaded with songs, which they swapped about. They talked about writing songs together, often stopping and jotting lines and ideas down on notepads.

Walking the Blues

Dominic would feign tiredness, tap dance in his boots beside her on the road

"Screw this. I'm cutting loose. Taking the bus tomorrow. Then finding a shortcut."

"No you're not. We've never taken buses. We walk. That's why we're here. Only shortcuts home are down through the Reserve."

Or when the roads seemed endless to both "Sick of this. Joining up with the next monastery soon as I can."

"Fat chance. They wouldn't have you."

"Why wouldn't they?"

"Because you're STOO-PID!"

Or she'd then complain. It relieved the long hours of tedium:

"Want lunch. I'm hungry. Get me lunch. Now."

"Nope. Only ladies lunch."

"I'm a lady."

"No you're not. Ladies don't climb trees."

Or, with permanently aching feet. "Need a pedicure, then."

"Settle for a perm. Your hair's in your eyes again. Looks awful."

Or Dominic would sometimes imitate Fergus, strutting along walkways like some kind of Spanish caballero, a man who doesn't do lunch.

They'd ask one another the questions they'd somehow failed to ask before, yet without seriousness, for it seemed they were never that far from home. They shared music through headphones on their long route march.

"Who's your favorite composer, then?"

"Mozart." Said Dom.

"Don't believe you. Bet you can't tell me a single thing he wrote."

"Yes I can. 'Twinkle, twinkle, little star.'"

"Yeah, sounds about right coming from you. You were always big on nursery rhymes. Favorite painter, then? Don't say Norman Rockwall or that Campbell soup guy. Someone classical."

"Reubens."

"Don't believe you. Bet you can't tell me a single work he painted."

"I can't. But he liked fuller figures. You're losing too much weight."

She'd poke out her tongue at him. "Have to for the climbing."

"Guess you do. We both need a pretty strong stomach for Fergus' stories, too."

Teresa mused. "They're always in small courses. Like Campbell's soup. Served cold."

Or he'd ask:

"Can I still tell bad jokes after we're married?"

"Guess so."

"Mother-in-law jokes?"

"Yes . . . NO! Leave my mother out of it. Anyway, I'm in charge from now on. Of everything."

"How so?"

"Because. My most famous person in history is Che. He was a Major. I've got the beret to prove it. You're just the son of a Drill Sergeant. You'll never outrank me on anything."

"Yes I will. My most famous person in history's a Colonel. Colonels outrank Majors any day."

"Don't believe you. You're making it up. You wouldn't know a famous Colonel."

"Yes I do."

"Who?"

"Colonel Sanders."

She flicked out her hip at him, then went to Google it that evening to prove him wrong, only to find that she was.

"Don't worry," Dominic murmured at her shoulder by the computer, "The military haven't been much good to us so far."

Or those deep resentments of childhood would suddenly resurface.

"You still got those old boxing vests of mine Sharn gave you?"

Teresa reflected. "Yes."

"I want them back."

"Get lost. They're mine now."

Then came the subject closest to his heart—Sharn.

"Ma e-mailed last night. About Sharn. She's completely whacked!"

"What? Out of control again?" Teresa grinned. So what was new!

"Ma got stuck into Fergus because he still keeps giving her money. Says Sharn won't be happy until she sees the whites of his pockets. There was six of them there when she mailed, our parents, Fergus, Father Kevin."

"What came of it?"

"Fergus said Ma was right. Said he wanted every cent of it back. Said the girl's no good. Won't walk anywhere."

"Fat chance of that."

"So what did he do? He put it to a vote, put the motion that Sharn is ruthless, cold-hearted, happy, amoral, therefore should be sold into slavery, TRAFFICKED. He said the money would get you a good dowry." Dominic tittered at the thought.

Teresa asked the obvious with a grin. "How did the vote go?"

"Carried unanimously. Five to none."

"You said there were six of them there."

"Yeah, Ma said Father Kevin's vote was an abstention."

Teresa shook her head in despair. "What chance have we got with families like ours? Even the clergy's hopeless."

"Fergus is only trying to . . . help!"

Yet more often than not they cooed along together like birds following each other on a bower. Old habits die hard. Dominic knew nothing other than looking out for her. If the food was bad, then so be it. If she felt lonely, then he'd ask other pilgrims 'may we walk with you?' He'd constantly ease her into conversations, never teased her faith, subtly provoked her not be afraid of her own heart. Because her Spanish phrases were better than his, he'd elbow her forward to do the asking for beds at refuges in the evening. She'd nod politely to staff, always be gracious, act almost flirtatiously, speak of the weather before asking anything, patient, smiling.

There were no squabbles over money. They had plenty. Fergus made sure of that. Teresa did what every other young pilgrim did—look for cheap CDs, trinkets, clothes in marketplaces. Who cared if they looked disheveled! There were so many young pilgrim couples like themselves.

They'd also traipse down two naves of churches at end of day to have their credentials stamped, if they could. Fergus warned them that procuring two stamps was a purposeful inconvenience to prevent pilgrims stopping off in cars for a quick stamp before moving on. Things had changed since then

When they were much younger, if Fergus was at home, he'd drive them to and from school in his car. "In the back, Troopers," he'd always say. They'd buckle up, sit quietly, Fergus would drive, say nothing while glimpsing them from his rear-vision stealing glances at one another. Sharn would be unaware, sitting in the front. He knew. Always did. He knew what it was that they themselves couldn't quite explain. They'd been in love ever since they were children, perhaps not even knowing it, a kind of young love like for a rabbit or cat. They did not know why it was that each of them left the house precisely each morning at 8:30, not wanting to hold the other up walking to school. Fergus did. There had never been "Where have you been, I'm not waiting all day, why are you late?" They'd always walked together, anyway. Fergus knew that. So what was new in any of this!

Sometimes, separated at nights by single sex dormitories, Dominic would wait by her door next morning, just as he did her front gate when kids. This time she'd rush out into his arms. They'd kiss, grab at each other's hand like teenagers. Her knight errant without reproach. Then they'd breakfast together, maybe just a cold bread roll, cups of tepid tea before the challenge of yet another road. As if anything else mattered. Hope Street was worse than this.

A Marriage Made in Childhood

One evening Teresa asked Dominic a question plaguing her. They were sitting on a park bench across from their dormitory refuge watching a village come to rest.

"Dom, how much do you think Uncle had to do with pushing us together?"

"He knew we were sweet on one another. Probably more than we knew it ourselves. He knew you were listening to his music up the tree near my shed. He used to come over, give me CDs, songs he knew you'd like. Gave them to me. Not you."

"He's a cunning old devil." Teresa smirked at the memory of it.

"Before we left the airport he said to me. 'Buen Camino.' Have a good walk. Then he said something strange. 'You waited, Dom. Waited long enough. Waited at the gate. Like a dragon who guards the gold.' What you think he meant by that?"

"I know. That you've waited by my house and school gates every day."

Dominic reflected. "When I turned seventeen, Fergus began bringing me over pictures of naked girls to the shed. I think he wanted to know how interested I was." Dominic raised his eyebrows in mock horror, copying the antic from Caitlin.

"You're kidding me! I don't believe you. Fergus isn't like that. Was he drunk?" Teresa was suddenly outraged.

"No. Sober. Usually Saturday mornings. I've got two of them with me. Take a look." He delved into his pocket for his wallet. "They're pretty battered up now. Fergus would grin as he handed them over. I remember once, he started singing that old Charlie Rich number. 'Hey, if you happen to see the most beautiful girl in the world . . .' Little did I know at the time but they were. Then he'd turn all serious on me. From The Silver Fox, I then got the wily one.

"'Dom.' He'd say. 'Wanna see some dirty postcards?' I didn't answer. I never knew how to take him. He'd show them, anyway. One by one. Only thing was, none of them had arms or heads. No, that's not right. One had a head."

Dominic spread the wrinkled postcards out with his hands on the bench. He gave them to Teresa one at a time, just as Fergus had to him. Teresa seized upon one, like Sharn had the heart locket. Her eyes boggled.

"What's this supposed to be?"

Dominic lightly fingered it. "That one goes by two names. The Winged Nike and Victory of Samothrace. Fergus said she's the centerpiece of The Louvre in Paris. Walking up the Daru staircase leads tourists straight to her. She's considered the ideal of beauty, therefore, according to Fergus, deserves such a prominent place. She once had arms, a head that shouted 'Victory' from the sky to the Greek fleet below her. They'd just beaten Ptolemy of Egypt. Fergus said: 'Look at those wings, Dom. Held back in such defiance. Aren't they magnificent! So compelling.' Dominic spoke with same mock lyricism, tapping his fingers on the card in imitation. Fergus said it supposed to show the divine and triumphant spirit coming face to face. They all had statues of her on prows of their ships back then. He rambled on for ages about her. Raved, I guess. I think he wanted someone else to appreciate her. He said there's a copy of the statue outside Caesar's Palace in Nevada, Rolls Royce has it as their figurine on their cars, the first FIFA World Soccer Cup was based on her model. He said lots of things. Then he dismissed her with a flick of his hand. 'Not a woman, Dom. She's a Muse.' I didn't even know what a Muse was back then."

Teresa ran her finger down the artful drapery of the statue.

"Show me the other one."

Dominic handed her a postcard of the Venus de Milo. "Fergus said they found her on the island of Melos. He said Spiro was born on one of the neighboring islands. Greeks call her Aphrodite. Fergus said 'Look, Dom, even with that broken nose she's beautiful. The epitome of love and beauty.' He said he'd once spent hours staring at the originals. Then he dismissed her, too. 'Not a woman, Dom,' he said. 'A Goddess.' 'You keep them.' He went on. 'Couple of nude female torsos never hurt any boy.' He used to always say that. Like that night he brought me over that heavy liquor. He always had a reason for doing it."

"Cunning old fox," Teresa muttered, both alarmed and amused. "Always playing his games, isn't he!" She then pondered what Dominic had said.

"I remember one Saturday afternoon. I was bored. It must've been around the same time. I went downstairs, asked Fergus if I could look at his art books. He was doing his paperwork at his desk at the time, as he always did. 'Help yourself,' he said. I sat in a chair looking at a book on Michelangelo. He turned, caught me looking at the nude statue of David. I felt embarrassed. He got up, took the book off me, like he was being all prudish, went across, got me a picture of The Mona Lisa by Leonardo. 'This one's got clothes on,' he said. 'Put your fingers over half her lips, then the other half. What do you see?' I saw one half of her mouth was serious, the other smiling. I told him. 'Just like you, Uncle,' I said. He ignored that. 'Now do the same with the David, best you can.' He gave me back the first book. 'Look at the two profiles of the statue. Just the face. Tell me about the face only.' I found that hard to do. I stared at it for ages. The profile you usually see is one of youthfulness and curls, his arm up holding the slingshot over his shoulder. The other side's different—a sort of scrunched up face. I finally said 'Young man. Old man?' He hit his hand down on his desk. 'Precisely! Two people in one statue. Young soldier. Old and serious King.' Then he poked out his tongue at me, said. 'Just like you, Teresa!'

I had to think about that for ages before I saw what he meant. He always provoked me to seriousness, then mocked it. But it was what he said next I found baffling. 'Go away. I've got lots of work to do. Take the books, go over, look at them with . . . Dominic.' Why didn't he say with Sharn? He knew I wouldn't be game to look at pictures of nude statues with you. And he'd never ever told me to go away before."

Dominic shrugged. "He knew we were in love. I know he caught us making faces at one another in church. I think he wanted us to know he understood. He always bought three of everything so you, me and Sharn would be together. Like those roller skates. He loved watching us haring along Edward street at weekends. I think he liked to see the both of us competing."

Teresa went quiet. Dominic continued. "There's something else, Tess. Another two pictures."

"What pictures?"

"Fergus told me I'm not allowed to show them to you until tomorrow. Just before we reach Santiago."

"Show them to me now. You're stringing me along. Just like him."

"No, a promise's a promise. Anyway, if I showed you them tonight you'd never go to sleep."

Later Dominic unlocked his hand from hers from their adjoining beds. "Go to sleep, Tess."

She grimaced. "Show me the pictures. NOW! Stoo-pid!"

"Name's Dom."

Before drifting off to sleep she muttered into her pillow. "And you're always to call me Teresa."

"You want to know something else?" Dominic turned back over.

"Yes."

"Fergus had his spies watching us. We were under surveillance."

"WHAT! In the city!"

"No. Up on Hope Street."

"Ma said Fergus bought Sofia and Theo, Spiro's kids, a mobile phone, long ago. They followed us home after school. Their bus dropped them off up the top of Hope at the same time we walked it. They still had to walk the street, too. They were to ring their father if any trouble occurred. We were being followed. We were safer than you think. Fergus knew you were chased through the Reserve that day."

"Fergus the spy." Teresa hanged her head in thought.

"Communist spy," Dominic added.

"Do Communists wear suits everyday?" Teresa wondered.

"Doubt it."

"Do Communists really hate the French that much?"

"That was his biggest bluff of all."

"What do you mean?"

"Go to sleep. I'll tell you tomorrow."

*   *   *

Over the last four weeks Teresa and Dominic trudged through rain, hail and shine, their lungs often on fire over mountain ranges, mist rising like smoke from a crucible, then it was onto the long floodplains, along countryside, which often looked so picturesque or barbarous, before delivering themselves into towns and cities where they'd stop to view the churches, so magnificent or austere. Some nights they slept without eating. Neither of them got sick. That had been their only real worry. The rest astounded them.

Teresa never thought that she'd ever see long lines of ancient statues standing side by side creating successive biblical scenes for the once illiterate churchgoers, each in itself a relief or single page of a story. She'd squat on her backpack trying to interpret the stained glass windows.

They'd surprised themselves as to how fit they were, refusing to cheat by busing in or out of bigger towns, as some pilgrims did. They walked. They walked. They walked. Teresa refused to be round the flytraps of liquor and narcotics in the evenings, waste nights as some did, preferring to walk next day clear headed. Dominic did what she did. This was the only time in their life that they'd been alone together. Fergus knew that they had been seeing one another in the city. He knew. How he knew, they did not know. He also knew that they were fearful of what their families might think. Fergus had not been so crazy after all in sending them away.

One day they caught up with some Argentine walkers wearing their Che and Mao caps, and while Dominic kicked a soccer ball with them along a road Teresa reached in her backpack, put on her matching beret before joining in. A loud cheer went up. It was a serendipitous moment. Two continents meeting. They told her that they weren't believers. They were Communists. They'd come only to make the walk. She told them that her uncle had given her the beret, that he was a Communist too, but her Spanish wasn't good enough to explain fully. That mattered little, for now she wasn't too sure that he was.

Teresa and Dominic often walked with a definite rhythm, holding hands, lingering now and again to look with longing into one another's eyes. Sometimes she walked ahead, for he'd always liked to follow. Dominic recalled how Fergus had shaken his hand at the airport, gripping it fiercely as did his eyes. The women were crying. Even Sharn shed a tear. Teresa was sad. Fergus didn't say 'Look after her, son' 'Make sure you do this, that,' 'Go here, there,' 'Avoid these, them,' just 'Buen Camino.' Have a good walk. It was as though there was nothing left for him to say, as though yet another day at home seeing them both off to school. He'd then turned to Teresa. "Don't try analyzing the walk too much. You'll see so many crosses along the way you'll feel like you're being tortured on a rack. Just let the beauty of the images transcend it."

Nearing the End

It was not as hairy out there as Teresa had expected. She felt protected by the weight of pilgrim numbers. There were genuine beggars in towns, many of them solitary, yet offering her no harm. Teresa didn't feel afraid of putting a euro in a beggar's cup, as if they'd give in return a clout, an STD, as she always assumed that they would up on Hope Street.

They were now out on the home stretch. There were big rigs, long tourist buses, articulated refrigeration trucks bounding along with their fish catches from the Atlantic. Speeding cars, motor bikes, whizzed past them into Santiago. Both of them were not used to city smells, nor those whiffs of aviation fuel as they neared the city airport.

Earlier that day the sky had been overcast. Sunlight was now filtering through. It looked so strange, a kind of beatific light or like whisperings in the wind drawing the pilgrims towards their destination. Excitement rose as scores of walkers glimpsed the airport on the outskirts of the city.

"I want to finish this properly," Teresa said firmly. "As much as I want, I'm not sleeping with my Ma tonight. Fergus' booked us in at the eight hundred bed 'alberge' on a slope of the city. There's a picture of it in the guide book. It looks more like a military barracks. But we're soldiers. We'll handle it."

They were now almost ready for anything after long days of swirling rains up the mountains. Some nights they'd eat huddled together in stone restaurants beside orange burning hearths. They'd rug themselves up for next day's walk, never having known the cold before. Few hostels or mission stations supplied pilgrims with sheets or blankets, unless explicitly asked for. Everyone slept in sleeping bags, pilgrim staffs beside bunks, scallop shells sewn into clothing or to backpacks, or tied round their necks. There'd been communal kitchens, communal bathrooms, pay telephones, internet facilities, lots of laundries. Conditions had improved vastly since Fergus made his journey. Occasionally, there were single rooms with central heating for the cold. Fergus said that there was to be none of that. "Everyone will be watching you. Even the insects." He'd joked in front of her parents before they left. "Only thing biting your bottom at night, young lady, will be the bedbugs!" Then added "Only those dirty French have sex almost anywhere. Watch out for them."

Teresa had put her hands up over her eyes. Everyone laughed.

Pilgrims were now amassing on the highway. Way-markers indicated just how close they were to completion. They chattered one to another with relief, many of them elderly, some clearly exhausted. Cyclists dismounted to make the final walk, closing ranks in good cheer as they crossed the Rio Lavacola where medieval pilgrims would cleanse and purify themselves before entering Santiago. Soldiers were once placed there, forcing the pilgrims to wash.

With now only two miles to go, it became a slow climb up Mount Gozo(Mount of Joy). At the summit Teresa and Dominic rested, glimpsing the cathedral's towering spires for the very first time. They were ahead of schedule. They knew that their families would be waiting for them as they huffed, stopping to stretch their aching limbs. They'd carried their backpacks like a cross. They'd finally run out of blister cream for their feet. They both felt about as tough as leather. Tough as Fergus. Tough, like when you have nothing else to lose.

"All this for a parchment certificate rolled up in a cardboard cylinder, names listed to be read at midday mass tomorrow in the cathedral," Teresa said wearily.

"Someone said the names of those who've traveled furthest get read out first. Good. Hear our names. Get out of there in a quick step." Dominic smirked.

"Fergus was right. Anything must be a quick skip from now on, Dom."

"Fergus' always right. You know something. He's even worse than Kevin. 'By the power invested in me,'" Dominic parodied Fergus. They laughed at that.

"Where's those other two pictures Fergus gave you? Why the big promise?"

Dominic hadn't forgotten. He was about to produce them, putting his hand in his pocket, opening his leather wallet. A recent photo of

Teresa graced the inside plastic. It was taken in a photo booth in Paris. Smiling. Happy. In love. He reached behind with his fingers, pulled out two photographs wedged together. One was an old snapshot. The other was shining new.

Teresa stared. "They're Auntie Teresa. Why'd he want her with us?"

"Fergus mumbled something about taking them with me to holy places along the way. He was embarrassed about it. But look closely. Only one's your aunt. The other's Elena. She's four years old. Fergus' child. The mother's Maria, the dancer who came that night to your house. Fergus is having a house built next to yours. They're all moving in once complete. Remember he told you we're going to Marseilles after this. Maria and Elena are there with her parents. Your Pa says we can get married in Marseilles. He and my Pa are turning the shed into a flat for us in the meantime. You want that? It'll be o.k. For a while. I guess. Won't it?"

It wasn't ever meant as a kind of marriage proposal. He was not on bended knee. It was like asking for the inevitable, the meant to be, just as it had been with their parents. Teresa knew that Dominic had been busily e-mailing back and forth with her father. He and Declan wanted him to work with them. Fergus had given Maddox and Declan a liquor franchise to share, that Dominic could take over the concreting business while Teresa studied an extra-mural university course from home. That was the plan.

"Yes," Teresa said as she reached up and kissed him. It was no more than a simple affirmation. She knew these things already. She'd been in on the horse trading with her mother over the last four weeks.

"Just you, me, Ballou." She grinned.

"You sure of that? We'll be sleeping on futons. Won't be enough room to swing a cat."

"Stop it! Poor Ballou hasn't got much time left."

But the photos in her hand still perplexed her. "Why, Dom? Why have they kept this from us so long? Fergus' so crafty. Why, why, why? To think that I called Elena a 'bitch.' I thought she was his mistress or something." She smirked. "The liar. Always ridiculing the French. Was it just to put us off the scent?"

"Who knows, Tess? They're not married. Your Ma reckons he didn't want to give you any bad example, so he kept it from us."

"But we've just walked over five hundred miles together. We haven't lost our way, have we! I've missed out on so much by not having Maria and Elena there."

Teresa was visibly annoyed. She stared again at the photo of her little cousin. She looked such a lovely child. Dominic shrugged.

"And there were plenty of signposts to keep us on the straight and narrow. Don't try figuring Fergus. Only your Ma and mine knew about the child. And Kevin. Your Pa, mine. Remember that weekend four years ago when they all went to the city to Kevin's sister Joyce's birthday party? Elena had just been born. We weren't told. Fergus lives with them during the week. He still has business to do up our way. He does it weekends. That's why he stays. I don't know anymore than that."

Teresa put her hand under her sweater tucking the photographs in her bra cup over her heart. They turned, trudged on silently, hand in hand.

*   *   *

Teresa thought about a myriad of things as the two giant Baroque flanking cathedral spires beckoned them into the city: how they'd passed through valleys of mist in low places; sat placidly in town squares at evening viewing photos taken on their cells, saving or discarding them; how they'd watched old men with nothing to say to each other sitting on park benches or open plazas; how they'd seen Jai alai players with their curved woven bats, once used as wicker panniers to gather apples, strike at balls at over one hundred and fifty miles an hour on courts incorporated into church walls. Dominic was invited to chance his arm. It was fun.

They'd seen many things. They'd walked beside concrete blast walls manned by the military up in Basque country, shopped amongst the bootlegs and fakes in many marketplaces. They'd spoken to young daredevils who'd run with the bulls for three years on end up in Pamplona. All these things made them feel more eager to live their lives with more abandon, enjoy the hard won efforts of each day. Fergus was right. They should give themselves over to whatever came their way.

You've Got Mail

Then there was the 'naughty' church up in Cervatos in Cantabria, which Fergus insisted they visit. Teresa e-mailed back home.

Dear All,

I've never written a dirty e-mail before. (Not like you, Sharn, but you've always been a rude cow!) I've had to get Dominic help out with some of the words. We went, as Uncle insisted we should, to view the Collegiate Church of San Pedro de Cervator in Cervatos. I blame you, Uncle, for this—a load of 12ᵗʰ century pornography. The guide book said it is an 'unprepossessing-looking' building—whatever that means. Looked like a whole lot of 'possessing' going on to me. There is a long line of erotic carvings near the roof outside. We went and asked the sexton to explain them. The outside upper reaches have this long, sheltered ledge adorned with ugly gargoyles all wrestling in 'sexual embraces.' There are lots of strange figures in masks—fornicators, phallic beings masturbating, animals mating, even a couple of horses and octopuses giving each other the what-for, hard at it—figures as tight as my kitten was wrapped in a ball. Dominic says the correct term to describe one is 'in the act of auto-fellatio.' It was male, of course.

They reminded me of those fierce mating I once saw through my spyglass down the Reserve. The lady sexton said these gargoyles were in the act of congress—how's that for a new word, Sharn?—that they're supposed to depict an explosion of life. It was supposed to get the population 'randy' again. The lady said nobody really knows exactly why these obscene statues came about. The Church just let them be.

Some say it was a call for the villagers to procreate in times of plague, get the population back. Others say it depicts life just as it is—the sacred right next to the profane. Good one, Uncle. Just like you.

Thanks for the sex lesson, anyway.

I thought Spaniards only wrangled bulls! Learn something new every day, don't we!

Heaven help us! Church will never be quite the same again.

Love, Teresa.

There had been frequent e-mails home. Fergus promised he'd reply every day at 6 p.m. Spanish time, then send the contents onto their mothers. He was his usual help. None at all.

Dear Uncle,

I stink! I need a bath! Urgently. It rained most of today, then got real steamy. We covered almost thirty miles. All those sprigs of lavender and thyme I picked along the Way, put in my clothes, they have finally lost their fragrance. It's going to be a bucket of water or cold shower tonight.

Love, Tess.

Fergus replied immediately, taking on the tone of an irate parole officer: She only asked for simple hygiene. He gave her a full history of it

Dear Tess,

Of course you stink! Whatever did you expect? You're not Hester! Fatima! Jews and Muslims are the ones who have strict rules of hygiene. Not us Christians, who've always ridiculed them for it. Christians stink! Live with it. Don't worry about it! Hindus may swim in the Ganges to keep clean, we stink.

When Christian pilgrims used to reach Santiago, first thing they did was go to Mass. Some days eight priests would, and still do, swing a heavy smoking crucible by pulleys across the transept of the cathedral. It weighs over a hundredweight, swaying almost ninety feet to the ceiling. The incense is meant to counteract the stench of the pilgrims. Then there used to be what they called The Cross of Rags outside the church. Pilgrims would burn their clothes there, purify themselves in fountains, then be given new clothes. The Cross is now up on the rooftop.

So. The long and the short of it is—it's ok to stink!

Love, Fergus.

Dear Uncle Cupid,

Still stink. Urgently want some new clothes. Get me some new clothes. Now. And I feel dehydrated. My jeans feel like sandpaper. I swear I'll disgrace the lot of you by skinny-dipping in the cathedral fountain if you don't come up with them!

Teresa.

Tess,

We'll have you new clothes. Anything to keep yours on, and to shut you up. Make you happy.

Fergus.

Uncle,

I've never been this happy in my entire life. It's been like an epiphany to me. We've both walked home safely through mystical places once again. Thank you, Uncle. I feel so confident now. Dominic and I are really happy.

Love, Tess.

P.S. We'll be there in a few days. Our parents will be with you, but where's Sharn? We have enough money left to fly her return to France. She MUST be at our wedding.

Fergus chuckled. He shot off a quick reply, feigning his usual melancholy in the blood.

Dear Tess and Dom,

How many miles must we send you out on before you finally get fed up with being happy! Be rest assured, the worse is yet to come! Don't you start getting all sentimental on me now in thinking life will somehow improve.

And what's this Uncle Cupid 'remark'? What have I said? What have I done now? Only trying to help.

P.S. Sharn's still working. But it's all organized. Did you really think she'd ever miss out on a wedding? She'll meet us in Marseilles. She now has a shaved head, according to her mother. She thinks it makes her look 'thinner,' for crying out loud! Colleen insists she'll be wearing a wig for your special day. I said some duct tape for her mouth would also be a good idea.

Love, Fergus.

Every Reason to Hope

They were now almost passively moved along the city sidewalk by constant gathering of pilgrims. They could hear a welcoming troupe of street musicians up ahead, strange sounds of bagpipes, girls dressed in motley playing fiddles and clarinets. Sight of them made Teresa think back to men playing Spanish guitar while serving in marketplaces along the way. How they'd reminded her of Fergus: staunch and macho, yet these men were noticeably poor, dressed as everyday laborers, some of them even reading books of verse at their stalls or idly playing guitar for free.

They asked nothing of her. They didn't seem to care much for her presence. Yet they had a dignity and nobility about them, trusting and calm, moving without impatience, a kind of fatalism learned over hundreds of years. They did not look at her swollen sweater, cast their eyes to her denims as she turned, as they would up on Hope. Nor, like Fergus, would they ever want to nurse her like some innocent bird. Their stare was that of a knowing look, as it was of Dominic—just another young, handsome pilgrim couple finding their own way out in the world.

These men could tell that she was shy. They knew. She was not sure exactly what it was that they saw or understood, only that many like her had passed this way before. These men had eyes a thousand year old. Especially in Basque country.

Once she asked one at his stall '*Quiero comprar, por favor?*' She said the words softly, wishing to buy. At the beginning of their journey she'd tried so hard, always searching for the right '*palabra en el libro.*' Dominic purposely left the complexities of language to her. That was the way she wanted it. He'd be of little help anyway, dismissing most things with the universal '*No hay problema.*'

But this day at the market it was a religious trinket that she wanted to buy, a small adorned prayer card by St. Theresa. She almost did not bother asking 'How much is it?' holding coins in her hand for him to take, remembered clearly how the man had looked to her palm then replied with firm grace in English. 'You can have it.' He'd shrugged his shoulders dismissively as he turned away, not because the card was near to worthless—which it was—but in an act of simple generosity, like those of the farmers giving free food at their gates—slice of apple, segment of cheese, glass of fresh milk from the misty milking stations in the mountains, given freely. These were acts without formula. Like unspoken prayers.

Teresa tried to remember the words on that prayer card as their gaits quickened in expectation of their families. 'May today there be peace within . . . and allow your soul the freedom to sing, dance, praise and love.' That was it. In Spanish, then written below in English. Pure and simple.

Teresa grabbed at Dominic's hand again, stopping him. She nestled her cheek into his shoulder before looking up, and in sudden horror. Her chest panicked like a trapped bird. Her eyes were alight as on high-beam.

"Dom, life's scary, isn't it! But it's going to be so much fun from now on. The singing. Music. Dancing. Parties at weekends. All that love. I've now got myself an auntie back, new cousin of my own to spoil. The first thing I'm going to do is teach her how to climb trees. Everything just repeats itself, doesn't it, over and over. We mightn't ever leave home. We might end up like a couple of five year olds again." The thought seemed to amuse her greatly. Not Dominic.

"All right for you," Dominic whined back miserably, "if you're going to be five, then I have to be seven. Father Kevin says we're responsible by age seven. Why should I always have to be the one to carry the can?"

She playfully pushed him away, tittered at that thought as they edged on towards the two magnificent cathedral spires shining in gold out in front in the morning sun while imagining to herself a place where nothing could harm them. They felt good that their wills had prevailed. They'd blazed a trail. They'd found their way. At first, they'd doubted Fergus. Why wouldn't they! It seemed as if he was sending them off into the infinite reaches of The Milky Way.

Walking had pulsed them along with a definite rhythm like brief spaces of time, sparks of magic, and stepping into the lives of others.

Neither had asked the other if it was really worth it, even warranted, yet both knew now, along with Fergus, that life was not to run in too smooth a groove. Calm only called for floating. Resistance must be offered. If Fergus was her parole officer, then she'd certainly completed her probation. Preparatory to more. So she guessed.

Yes, Teresa thought, at last, a job well done. She had done her presentation. No cheating by taking short cuts. They had walked through a hundred stone portals and archways, through towns overshadowed by citadels, protected by fortified walls, seen houses with colorful shutters, intricate woven laces at inviting windows. Every town seemed molded into a singularly peaceful scene. She marveled at the thought that they'd just trod in the tread of St. Francis, stayed in places near where Ernest Hemingway stayed, and where statues of him abounded, traveled where Robert Louis Stevenson had traveled with his donkey, been where Chaucer's Wife of Bath stated she'd been in his Canterbury Tales, along with all the kings, saints, knights, men, women and children, even beggars(all without their Reeboks). She happily imagined things which had not happened yet as they moved forward onto journey's end, an ancient city with over one hundred climbing towers.

Printed in Great Britain
by Amazon